The Feminization Debate in Eighteenth-Century England

Literature, Commerce and Luxury

E.J. Clery

First published 2004 by
PALGRAVE MACMILLAN
Houndmills, Basingstoke, Hampshire RG21 6XS and
175 Fifth Avenue, New York, N. Y. 10010
Companies and representatives throughout the world

PALGRAVE MACMILLAN is the global academic imprint of the Palgrave
Macmillan division of St. Martin's Press, LLC and of Palgrave Macmillan Ltd.
Macmillan® is a registered trademark in the United States, United Kingdom
and other countries. Palgrave is a registered trademark in the European
Union and other countries.

ISBN 0–333–77731–X (HB)
ISBN 0–333–77732–8 (PB)

This book is printed on paper suitable for recycling and made from fully
managed and sustained forest sources.

A catalogue record for this book is available from the British Library.

Library of Congress Cataloging-in-Publication Data

Clery, E.J.
    The feminization debate in eighteenth-century England: literature,
commerce and luxury/by E.J. Clery.
        p. cm. – (Palgrave studies in the Enlightenment, romanticism and the
cultures of print)
Includes bibliographical references and index.
ISBN 0-333-77731-X – ISBN 0-333-77732-8 (pbk.)
    1. English literature–18th century–History and criticism. 2. Feminism and
literature–England–History–18th century. 3. Women and literature–England–
History–18th century. 4. English literature–Women authors–History and
criticism. 5. Great Britain–Commerce–History–18th century. 6. Feminism–
England–History–18th century. 7. Luxury–History–18th century.
8. Femininity in literature. 9. Sex role in literature. 10. Feminism in
literature. 11. Luxury in literature. 12. Women in literature. I. Title. II. Series.

PR448.F45C54 2004
820.9'3522'09033–dc22   2003070193

10   9   8   7   6   5   4   3   2   1
13 12 11 10 09 08 07 06 05 04

Printed and bound in Great Britain by
Antony Rowe Ltd, Chippenham and Eastbourne

For James, Benjamin and Joshua.

Contents

List of Illustrations   ix

Acknowledgements   x

Abbreviations   xi

Introduction   1

1. Sexual Alchemy in the Coffee-House   13

2. *The Athenian Mercury* and the Pindarick Lady   26
   'New Things'   26
   A Sexual Dialectic   26
   Elizabeth Singer Rowe and 'The Double Courtship'   32
   The Legacy of the *Athenian Mercury*   42
   The fate of John Dunton, pioneer feminizer   46

3. The South Sea Bubble and the Resurgence of Misogyny:
   Cato, Mandeville and Defoe   51
   The Progessivist Bubble Bursts   51
   The Role of the Passions   57
   False Feminists and Moral Crisis in Mandeville and Defoe   63

4. Elizabeth Carter in Pope's Garden: Literary Women of the
   1730s   74
   A Vignette   74
   A Female Author in the 1730s   75
   Pope and the Woman Writer   79
   Elizabeth Carter, the *Gentleman's Magazine* and the Challenge
   to Pope   85

5. *Clarissa* and the 'Total Revolution in Manners'   95
   Richardson's Historical Fictions   95
   The Opposition of the Sexes in *Clarissa*   99
   The Rake   104
   The 'Present Age'   107
   The Trial of Woman   113
   The Trial of Man   117
   The Apotheosis of Clarissa and the Redemption of Man   119
   Clarissa as a Progressivist Narrative   125

6. Out of the Closet: Richardson and the Cult of Literary Women   132
   The Closet as Laboratory of the Soul   132
   Elizabeth Carter, Catherine Talbot and the Richardson Effect   138
   Women's Writing at the Crossroads: 1750   148
   Sir Charles Grandison as Object of Desire   154
   Inventories of Literary Women   162

Coda: From Discourse to a Theory of Feminization in the *Essays* of David Hume   171

Notes   179

Bibliography   215

Index   227

List of Illustrations

1. *Interior of a London Coffee-House* (*c.* 1705). Reproduced
   courtesy of the British Museum. © The British Museum.   22
2. William Hogarth, *The South Sea Scheme* (1724). Reproduced
   courtesy of the British Museum. © The British Museum.   52
3. William Hogarth, *Morning, The Four Times of the Day* (1738).
   Reproduced courtesy of the British Museum. © The British
   Museum.   129

Acknowledgements

The idea for this book originated in the early 1990s with two invitations: one from Isobel Armstrong, to write an article for a special issue of *Women: A Cultural Review* on women and print culture, which started me thinking about gender, periodicals and coffee-houses; the other from Mark Cousins of the Architectural Association, to speak at a day conference on the topic of 'Home', which gave rise to some ideas about closets in Samuel Richardson.

I am also grateful to Markman Ellis, Richard Kroll, Josephine McDonagh and Sarah Prescott for sharing related work-in-progress; and to John Bender, John Birtwhistle, Peter De Bolla, Peter Garside, Charlotte Grant, Nigel Leask, Anne Mellor and Clifford Siskin for advice and encouragement. Elizabeth Clarke, Elizabeth Eger, Robert Jones, Josephine McDonagh, Robert Miles and Mary Peace have read chapters and made valuable suggestions. Lois Chaber and Carolyn Williams were extremely generous with their time and scholarly expertise in commenting on drafts dealing with Richardson's *Clarissa* and Alexander Pope. The organizers of the 'Enlightenment and Romanticism' reading group, Elizabeth Eger, Emma Francis and Anne Janowitz, gave me the opportunity to air some ideas on David Hume and receive stimulating feedback. Isobel Armstrong and John Barrell have given vital support to the project.

Completion of the book was made possible by the award of a Leverhulme Trust Fellowship, and the kind cooperation of colleagues at the Department of English Studies at Sheffield Hallam University.

Some material from chapter 1, 'Sexual Alchemy in the Coffee-House', first appeared in 'Women, Publicity and the Coffee-House Myth', *Women: A Cultural Review* 2: 2 (1991), 168-77.

Abbreviations

Books

BC   Sylvia Harcstark Myers, *The Bluestocking Circle: Women, Friendship, and the Life of the Mind in Eighteenth-Century England* (Oxford: Clarendon Press, 1990).

BF   Gary Kelly, gen. ed., *Bluestocking Feminism: Writings of the Bluestocking Circle, 1738-1785*, 6 vols (London: Pickering and Chatto, 1999).

C   Samuel Richardson, *Clarissa; or, The History of a Young Lady*, ed. Angus Ross (Harmondsworth: Penguin, 1985).

E&K   T.C. Duncan Eaves and Ben D. Kimpel, *Samuel Richardson: A Biography* (Oxford: Clarendon Press, 1971).

FB   Bernard Mandeville, *Fable of the Bees, or, Private Vices, Publick Benefits*, ed. F.B. Kaye, 2 vols. (1924; Indianapolis: Liberty Fund, 1988).

G   Samuel Richardson, *The History of Sir Charles Grandison*, ed. Jocelyn Harris, 3 vols. (London: Oxford University Press, 1972).

P   Samuel Richardson, *Pamela; or, Virtue Rewarded*, ed. Thomas Keymer (Oxford: Oxford University Press, 2001).

SL   *Selected Letters of Samuel Richardson*, ed. John Carroll (Oxford: Clarendon Press, 1964).

SRPCC   *Samuel Richardson's Published Commentary on 'Clarissa' 1747–65*, gen. ed. Florian Stuber, 3 vols. (London: Pickering and Chatto, 1998).

Periodicals

AM   *Athenian Mercury*
ECF   *Eighteenth-Century Fiction*
GM   *Gentleman's Magazine*
PMLA   *Proceedings of the Modern Language Association*

Introduction

The intellectual historian Albert Hirschman proposed that one of his aims was 'to renew the sense of wonder about the genesis of the "spirit of capitalism"'.[1] A similar aim lies behind the present study. The basic assertions about human nature that accompany the development of capitalist societies – the primacy of self-interest, acquisitiveness, the hedonistic desire to consume – were disputed right through the seventeenth and eighteenth centuries. The apologists for economic innovation were forced to find moral and political arguments to justify change.

The central strand of this dispute over the consequences of commerce in eighteenth-century England was fundamentally informed by the category of gender. It is my claim that it constituted a 'feminization debate'. This gendered debate on 'progress' was conducted in a multitude of genres. Evidence can be found not only in the journalism of the *Spectator* and *Cato's Letters*, the polemics of Bernard Mandeville and the essays of David Hume, but also in the prints of William Hogarth, the poetic satires of Alexander Pope and Jonathan Swift, and the novels of Daniel Defoe, Samuel Richardson, Henry Fielding and Tobias Smollett.

This book is about the way women came to be used as a measure of commercial growth and resulting historical changes. It is about the debate generated by the perception that the status of women in society was rising and that women were gaining an increasing influence over men and altering the manners and morals of the nation. This growing status and influence was variously condemned as cause and symptom of national decline, or celebrated as an index of increasing refinement or civility. The book is also about the way male disputants used women in the public eye – articulate, talented, educated women – to serve as emblems of this process of feminization; and the way literary women took advantage of the opportunities afforded by the feminization debate, or rejected them. The careers of the poet Elizabeth Singer Rowe and the poet, classical scholar and translator Elizabeth Carter will be discussed in detail.

The focal point of the study as a whole is Samuel Richardson, principally as the creator of *Clarissa*, one of the most significant and influential literary works of the century, and as the friend and rather officious patron of a number of literary women. I read *Clarissa* as an historical fiction in two senses: as a story unfolding in the particular conditions of the late 1720s and 1730s, at a time when the political culture of misogyny was at its height; and as a conscious reflection on the historical process itself, exploring the possibilities for a change in public discourse and private manners figured by a radical model of redemptive femininity. I argue further that in the 1750s Richardson pursued this project practically as well as imaginatively by enlisting literary women of his acquaintance to embody the new ideal and contribute to its imaginative apotheosis, *Sir Charles Grandison*.

In the 1980s two works of criticism employed the term 'feminization' to discuss the pioneering role of Richardson as a purveyor of femino-centric fictions, and gave it currency in eighteenth-century cultural studies. In *The Rape of Clarissa* (1982) Terry Eagleton used Richardson as an illustration of the way bourgeois writers promoted 'feminine' values in their bid for cultural hegemony, bringing about a broad 'feminization of discourse'.[2] Nancy Armstrong, in *Desire and Domestic Fiction: A Political History of the Novel* (1987), similarly saw Richardson's fictions, in particular *Pamela*, as contributions to the production of new forms of political power: 'the female was the figure, above all else, on whom depended the outcome of the struggle among competing ideologies'.[3]

Both Eagleton and Armstrong effectively demonstrate the way women's influence over men was conceived by Richardson as a component of modernity: a new form of cohesion, an attempt to rebuild the social body through innovative methods of symbolization, counteracting the fracturing force of the capitalist economy. In some respects the present study, by investigating precursors to Richardson, might be considered a prologue to these two works. But there are some points on which I part company with them. I will question two of Armstrong's most basic propositions: the claim that Richardson's feminine ideal is a *domestic* woman who derives from the conduct-book genre (although undoubtedly conduct-books promoted a specialization of the sexes that converges with his aims); and the use of Lockean contract theory as the key to Richardson's gender politics. In addition, both critics use 'feminization' as a neutral means of describing eighteenth-century cultural developments. I want to restore an idea of 'feminization' to its embattled eighteenth-century origins. Although the term 'feminization' is of recent coinage, Richardson was fully conscious of the way in which gender operated in political arguments, and he and other writers known today as 'literary' authors were part of a broad debate on commerce, luxury and the direction of history.[4]

There is abundant evidence to disprove Armstrong's assertion that while twentieth-century education 'teaches us to understand modern history in economic terms ... history itself was not understood in those terms until the beginning of the nineteenth century'.[5] Already in the 1690s, with the

beginnings of a literary public sphere, there are signs of an historical understanding of the relationship between economic and cultural change, and
this sharpens in the aftermath of the South Sea Bubble, the stock market
crash of 1720, because of the urgent need, on the part of apologists of
commerce and of the new economics, to rethink cyclical history as progressive history. But it is not until after the emergence of the Scottish historical
school in the 1750s that the economic interpretation of history is system-
atized. With regard to the debate on feminization, I would suggest that
there is a corresponding transition: the *discourse of feminization*, a rhetoric
that supports economic expansion and links it to the refinement of
manners, is superseded by an *enlightenment theory of feminization*, which
seeks to explain the relationship between economic and socio-cultural
change, and develops a 'scientific' model of history to support it.

The Origin of the Distinction of Ranks (1771) by John Millar, a student
of Adam Smith's, begins with a long chapter on 'the rank and condition of
women in different ages' as the foundation for its explication of the four-
stage history of economic and social development. Henry Home, Lord
Kames in his *Sketches of the History of Man* described the history of women
as 'a Capital branch' of his survey. Informed by these examples, William
Alexander, a Scottish physician, provides the clearest summary of the
theory of feminization, and the indexical thinking that characterized it, in
The History of Women, From the Earliest Antiquity to the Present Time (1779):

> As strength and courage are in savage life the only means of attaining
> to power and distinction, so weakness and timidity are the certain
> paths to slavery and oppression: on this account, we shall almost
> constantly find women among savages condemned to every species of
> servile, or rather, of slavish drudgery; and shall as constantly find them
> emerging from this state, in the same proportion as we find the men
> emerging from ignorance and brutality, and approaching to knowledge
> and refinement; the rank, therefore, and condition, in which we find
> women in any country, mark out to us with the greatest precision, the
> exact point in the scale of civil society, to which the people of such a
> country are arrived; and were their history entirely silent on every other
> subject, and only mentioned the manner in which they treated their
> women, we should, from thence, be enabled to form a tolerable
> judgment of the barbarity, or culture of their manners.[6]

This history was directed primarily at a female audience; 'composed',
according to the 'Advertisement' at the start, 'chiefly for the amusement and
instruction of the fair sex'. Alexander deplores the tendency alternately to
idealize and denigrate women, and sees education as the best means for bet-
tering their situation. Nevertheless, as the passage indicates, the improvement
of women's condition was seen not as a good in itself – let alone a right – but
rather as an infallible measure or index of the civilizing process in men.

Recognition of the importance of women in enlightenment thought is not new. In 1975 Katherine Clinton published an article on the 'Enlightenment origins of feminism', which surveyed arguments for reform of the condition of women, especially with regard to the institution of marriage, made by French, German and British philosophers as part of their concerted attack on oppressive custom.[7] Jane Rendall, in an extensive body of work which includes the monograph *The Origins of Modern Feminism* (1985) and the essay 'Virtue and commerce: women in the making of Adam Smith's political economy' (1987), has indicated the relevance of the civic humanist tradition to changing definitions of femininity and efforts to prescribe women's role in society, while giving equal or greater weight to the tradition of natural jurisprudence associated with Samuel Pufendorf and John Locke. A 1985 article by Sylvana Tomaselli observes the indexical role of women in enlightenment theories of history. Responding to currents which have since given rise to eco-feminism, she points to a 'forgotten tradition which linked women, not, as is all too swiftly done, to nature, but to culture and the process of historical development'.[8] In a more recent essay, 'The most public sphere of all: the family', Tomaselli discusses the eighteenth-century 'woman question' as a platform for dispute on the benefits or evils of civilization by Denis Diderot, Charles de Montesquieu and Jean-Jacques Rousseau, as well as the Scottish philosophers John Millar and Adam Smith.[9] Harriet Guest's *Small Change: Women, Learning, Patriotism, 1750–1810* (2000) charts the impact of the indexical theory uniting women and modernity on the writings and reception of a series of female authors, from the Bluestocking Elizabeth Carter to the feminist Mary Wollstonecraft, and identifies 'a series of small changes' that enabled 'their approximation to the public identities of political citizens'.[10]

The enlightenment theory of feminization was at its peak in the 1770s, coinciding with the towering headdresses that distinguished female fashion. I say something of the origins of the theory in the Coda on Hume's *Essays*, but the story of its rise and fall must be reserved for another volume. In this book I have chosen to investigate the relatively uncharted regions of the gendered debate on progress and decline in England, from the 1690s to the 1750s. It is important to recognize that the English debate on feminization was specific and unique. Obviously, it pre-dates the influence of the Scottish philosophers, but it is also exotically distant from the well-established discourse on the civilizing influence of women as it existed in France.[11] There are two main factors that served to differentiate the terms of its arguments. The first was the absence of anything like the salon culture that existed in Paris. The salon was a social institution that had developed in the mid-seventeenth century. It was a regular private gathering, typically organized and hosted by a female aristocrat with literary interests, at which mixed company engaged in polite conversation, the reading aloud of letters or sometimes manuscript work-in-progress, and intellectual debate. Most of the

French *philosophes* attended one salon or another, and the salons are commonly attributed with a major role in the genesis of the Enlightenment. Dena Goodman has outlined the reciprocal relationship between the salons and a progressive construction of history, both of them 'giving women a particular and central role in the formation of modern, civilized society, defined as peaceful, gentle, sociable and – eventually – enlightened'.[12] And yet it would seem that English progressivists were almost wholly ignorant of salons as a practice and the connection with arguments in favour of modernity in the first half of the eighteenth century. In chapter 2 I will indicate a few faint traces of French influence in the innovative periodicals of the 1690s, notably the strand of Neoplatonism in the *Athenian Mercury* and Pierre Motteux's *The Gentleman's Journal*; and in chapter 3 we see an approximation of a female-led French salon in Bernard Mandeville's papers from the *Female Tatler*. But these are rare exceptions. Instead, in the first two chapters I will show that it was a bourgeois and, paradoxically, all-male institution, the coffee-house, that first generated discussion in England of women's role as a civilizing force and initiated the idealization of the woman of letters as an emblem of civility.

The second factor peculiar to the English context, and one that helps to explain why for a time England was such barren ground for French ideas and practices, was the dominance of the civic humanist tradition. This mode of political thinking took the classical republic to be the most perfect form of government for the cultivation of public virtue among citizens, and made it the basis for criticizing present-day political corruption, the system of financial credit and the backstairs influence of the monied interest. J.G.A. Pocock, in *The Machiavellian Moment*, mapped the transmission of these ideas from the works of Niccolò Machiavelli in Renaissance Italy to James Harrington, writing in the era of the English Civil War, to Anthony Cooper, first Earl of Shaftesbury and the debates leading up to the Glorious Revolution and beyond to play a part in most areas of political and social controversy in the eighteenth century.[13] In chapters 3 and 4, I will look at the reanimation of civic humanist arguments in response first to the South Sea Bubble, and then to the emergence of the Whig oligarchy under the leadership of Robert Walpole, in the 1720s and 1730s.

As the prevailing language of political value, civic humanism set the terms to which apologists for modern innovation were forced to respond. Pocock and others have addressed the controversial question of how the republican paradigm gave rise in the course of the century to a 'commercial' humanism. John Barrell has arrestingly described how pro-commerce writers such as Daniel Defoe, Joseph Addison and Richard Steele implant 'within the matrix of civic humanism the embryo of a discourse which will eventually develop into a matricide, but which, until it does, will derive many advantages from its association with the virtues of its surrogate mother'.[14] In the course of the present study, I will in effect reverse the gendered metaphor, by attempting to show how a discourse of feminization came to challenge the masculinist paradigm that had shaped it fundamentally. To the question posed by civic humanism, 'Will material progress result in luxury, effeminacy and decline?', proponents of feminization return the heretical answer 'No'. But their arguments are derived from within the logic of civic humanism; they exist within the same discursive field. The belief that the growth of commerce will result in social and political benefits is shadowed and defined by the alternative possibility, sometimes implicit, sometimes articulated. Both perspectives share the rhetorical illustrations taken from classical history and mythology: Circe; Hercules; Lycurgus, the great legislator of Sparta; Cato Uticensis, incorruptible politician and bad husband; and Lucretia, whose rape and suicide instigated the moral regeneration of Rome.[15]

The language of civic humanism appears in many different contexts and guises in the eighteenth century. It was wielded by critics of the government, Christian campaigners for the reformation of manners, literary satirists and political economists, and strategically adapted to fight local battles. But it is possible to identify certain generic characteristics that had a determining effect on the feminization argument. To begin with, civic humanism was a gendered tradition: the public virtue it celebrated was a specifically masculine virtue, epitomized by the male warrior-citizen. Modernizers such as John Dunton of the *Athenian Mercury* and Samuel Richardson were to choose as their emblem the almost diametrically opposed figure of a woman of letters as the repository of value. Second, it was patrician: public virtue was predicated on the character of the owner of landed property, the legislator with a private income. The answering association of virtue with femininity helped to obscure the more threatening class antagonism implicit in the legitimation of the mobile property by the mid-century. But this association was not established without a considerable struggle against the entrenched public rhetoric of misogyny, which even such ardent progressivists as Mandeville and Defoe could not entirely subordinate in their own writing (as discussed in chapter 3). Third, civic humanism was an historical mode of thought, positing the growth of commerce and the consequent corruption of the social body as part of an inevitable, cyclical decline into effeminacy. Opponents were therefore required to formulate an alternative, linear, historical narrative, involving a gendered account of progress, a positive feminization, a triumphant movement towards increased civility and refinement.

Fourth, civic humanism was an ethic, as the prominence of the words 'virtue' and 'corruption' have suggested.[16] It had to be answered in moral terms, with an alternative version of 'virtue', and this is partly what sets English feminizers like Addison, Steele and Richardson apart from the French, who were able to conceptualize 'politeness', the refinement of the passions, as a good in itself. In chapters 5 and 6 I will argue for the importance of

Richardson's novels of the 1740s and early 1750s in presenting a new ideal of modern living, apparently cleansed of association with the passions of a market economy, and yet ideologically compatible with commercial society. Richardson's piety was heartfelt, but it was also a means of accommodating features of the market economy that were disallowed by the secular schema of the republican purist.

Fifth, civic humanism involves an economic explanation of the national culture. Poverty and asceticism, or at least a restriction of consumption to need, are the prerequisites of a virtuous, valorous citizenry. Private wealth and its accompanying excesses will inevitably result in cowardice and corruption. The progressivist rejoinder necessarily links feminization with the vindication of luxury.

John Sekora, the author of a classic study of the concept of luxury, has described it as probably 'the greatest single social issue and the greatest single commonplace' in eighteenth-century Britain.[17] The historian Paul Langford concurs:

> A history of luxury and attitudes to luxury would come very close to being a history of the eighteenth century. There is a sense in which politics in this period is about the distribution and representation of this luxury, religion about the attempt to control it, public polemic about generating and regulating it, and social policy about confining it to those who did not produce it.[18]

It is the civic humanist paradigm that sustains the prominence of luxury in the political and social debate of the century. The term has sometimes been rather narrowly defined by twentieth-century commentators as excessive consumption, an outgrowth of selfish passions which threatens to destabilize the *polis*. But in context, in the writings of civic humanist and enlightenment authors, it is apparent that luxury represents much more than this. It signifies change *per se*. Its excess is of an historical nature: the supersession of a social and political order, and the inability to contain forces of transformation that subvert the existing parameters of the state. It forms part of a 'problem in historical self-understanding'.[19] Almost invariably in the first half of the century, this change is understood as a decline. Luxury is also the point of conflict between economics and political morality. It encapsulates the confrontation of 'virtue' and 'corruption', and the success of blind unconscious economic passions in overtaking political will to determine the destiny of the state.

Most recent commentators, including Sekora, have been deaf to the rhetoric of gender in the literature on luxury and progress.[20] Pocock has made some notable asides on the subject, for instance concerning the female personifications of Fortune and Credit, but has never substantively addressed what he terms 'the female principle' as it appears in conjunction with economic innovation.[21] As regards Credit, the oversight has been corrected by Erin Mackie in *Market à la Mode: Fashion, Commodity, and Gender in 'The Tatler' and 'The Spectator'* (1997) and Catherine Ingrassia in *Authorship, Commerce and Gender in Early Eighteenth-Century England* (1998). But gender remains a neglected category in intellectual histories of the period, in spite of the obsessive interest shown by eighteenth-century writers themselves. Take, for instance, these anxious private jottings from the notebook of the civic humanist ideologue, the third Earl of Shaftesbury:

> Childish, womanish, bestial, brutal. – Words! Words! Or are they anything more: But how then not a child? How least like a woman? How far from the beast? How removed and at a distance from anything of this kind? How properly a *man*? ... ['Consider, then, by what you are distinguished on reason – from wild beasts – from cattle.' Epict. Disc. Bk. II, C. X, #2.] A man, and a woman; effeminate, soft, delicate, supine; impotent in pleasure, in anger, talk, pusillanimous, light, changeable, etc; but the contrary to this in each particular. – A man, and not a beast: ... A man, and not a child: ... the contraries. Manhood, manliness, humanity – manly, humane, masculine.[22]

The core civic humanist value of manliness, which represented the highest state of humanity, could be upheld only through a constant labour of differentiation with the non-human, the immature and, above all, the non-male. Yet this construct, precisely because it was dependent on the medium of words, was constantly subject to slippage. In particular, the boundary between manliness and effeminacy was a preoccupation. As Carolyn Williams has observed, 'early modern debates on gender usually occur within commonly accepted parameters. The most acrimonious disputants over the position of the line between manliness and effeminacy share the conviction that disaster will ensue if it is not firmly drawn'.[23]

What is meant by 'effeminate'? Present-day usage suggests the synonyms 'camp' or 'homosexual', but eighteenth-century categories of gender are a foreign language. This, I would argue, is insufficiently acknowledged in recent essays on sexual difference and the categories of gender by Randolph Trumbach. In his discussions of the significance attached to 'effeminacy', he places an exaggerated and anachronistic emphasis on sexual orientation and the existence of a 'sodomitical' subculture.[24] This cuts across the conventional links that joined 'effeminacy' with the debate on luxury, public spirit, military capability, women and the sumptuary laws. Although Michael McKeon, in an article on the emergence of gender difference in the period, concedes in a note that 'the apprehension of "effeminacy" in eighteenth-century England was a very general mode of social analysis that articulated a wide range of convictions, from the traditional ideology of civic humanism to the innovative ideology of sensibility', he gives too much weight in the main body of the argument to Trumbach's interpretation.[25]

Carolyn Williams' *Pope, Homer, and Manliness* (1993) is the most reliable guide through the semantic complexities surrounding masculinity in the early eighteenth century, due to the author's remarkable range of reference and incisive demonstration of the continuing importance of classical categories of gender identity.[26] Homosexuality in classical culture tended to be interpreted as manly rather than effeminate, while 'effeminacy' was understood to derive from excessive attachment to women.[27] Williams notes the 'pseudo-etymological rendering of the word as "devoted to women"' (OED):

> Thus 'effeminate' may describe a man who resembles women, or who desires women. It may mean both at once: the use of *effeminacy* to denote both deficient masculinity and excessive heterosexual activity fosters a tendency to connect these phenomena. Furthermore, this usage is itself encouraged by a preexisting belief that love impairs masculinity.[28]

Galenic theory warned against the weakness caused by excessive coitus with women. Even undue social contact with women could have an equivalent effect. Thomas Laqueur, discussing examples of effeminization in the literature of the sixteenth century, remarks that 'Bodies actually seem to slip from their sexual anchorage in the face of heterosexual sociability; being with women too much or being too devoted to them seems to lead to the blurring of what we would call sex'.[29] The same 'collapse of sex into gender' can be found in many eighteenth-century representations.[30]

Alternatively, effeminacy may bear no relation to sexual or social affinities with either sex, but relate to economic causes. In Pope's translation of Homer, the Phaeacians are effeminate because they are lazy and prosperous.[31] Elsewhere in the translation the commonplace vocabulary bundle 'Peace, Luxury, or Effeminacy' appears.[32] Pocock has usefully observed the (for us) unexpected gendering of the commercial subject in this period:

> Economic man as masculine conquering hero is a fantasy of nineteenth-century industrialisation (the *Communist Manifesto* is of course one classic example). His eighteenth-century predecessor was seen as on the whole a feminised, even an effeminate being, still wrestling with his own passions and hysterias and with interior and exterior forces let loose by his fantasies and appetites, and symbolised by such archetypically female goddesses of disorder as Fortune, Luxury, and most recently Credit herself.[33]

In the present study, I have drawn a distinction between 'effeminacy' and being 'feminized'. Here 'feminization' is reserved strictly for representations that approve or even advocate the acquisition of certain characteristics gen-dered 'feminine': sociability, civility, compassion, domesticity and love of family, the dynamic exercise of the passions and, above all, refinement, the mark of modernity. The 'feminized' man is a model of politeness, shaped by his contact with the female sex, full of respect and admiration for moral women, and ably fitted to undertake his heterosexual duties.

'Effeminacy' or 'effeminization', on the other hand, is employed as the sum of a complex of derogatory ideas also gendered 'feminine', including corruption, weakness, cowardice, luxury, immorality and the unbridled play of passions. The 'effeminate' man is not by definition homosexual, but may be hyper-sexual. He takes on the qualities of self-indulgence, wanton-ness, vanity and hysteria traditionally attributed to women by misogynist rhetoric. His manners towards women may be excessively gallant, while secretly he sneers at them, attempting to reduce them to his level. An 'effeminate' man is more likely to engage in immorality with women than with men, but the choice of object is not a deciding factor. What is crucial is the emphasis on his degraded nature, his unfitness to fulfil the appropri-ate manly civic role. 'Effeminacy' does not imply the existence of a 'third gender'. Instead, the term powerfully reinforces gender difference as a binary to think by, a system of moral/psychological categorization that overrides even the accidents of biology.

Though the term 'effeminacy' registers a transgression of the normal correlation of gender values and biological sex, the civic humanist dis-course that employs it does not go beyond the heterosexual order in the search of a vocabulary of disapprobation. It draws principally from the rich tradition of misogynist representations to evoke the negation of manly virtue. It follows that before the revaluation of feminized manliness could be achieved, and before feminization could be understood as an improvement, a radical rehabilitation of the category of 'woman' was required. Laqueur's *Making Sex: Body and Gender from the Greeks to Freud* (1990) provides valuable insights on this process. He posits a major point of transition in thinking about biological sex and gender difference in the eighteenth century, which, as I will attempt to show, is borne out by the evidence of the feminization debate. The one-sex model of sexuality, current from classical times to the Enlightenment, is founded on the idea that the male and female reproductive organs are homologous, the female being an internalized replica of the male, not extruded because of the rela-tive coldness of the female constitution. Laqueur's main thesis is that a one-sex model of sexual difference gave way to a two-sex model: 'Thus the old model, in which men and women were arrayed according to their degree of metaphysical perfection, their vital heat, along an axis whose telos was male, gave way by the late eighteenth century to a new model of radical dimorphism, of biological divergence.'[34] The assumption of two genders sharing a single sex gives place to dimorphism. It is only once 'woman' is reconceived as a separate and singular sex that she can become the repository of values to which men might aspire. As part of my interpretation of Richardson's novel *Clarissa* in chapter 5, I will propose that at mid-century we find a transitional stage in this supersession: the metaphysical hierarchy is reversed in advance of anatomical discoveries. There is a moral pressure among proponents of feminization like Richardson towards the system of 'two stable, incommensurable, opposite sexes', but this is not yet grounded by biological 'fact'.[35] In the one-sex model, as Laqueur observes, sexual nature is derived from the metaphysics of gender; logically enough, it was first challenged at the level of metaphysics.

In *Desire and Domestic Fiction*, Nancy Armstrong asked the important question 'why, at the inception of modern culture, [did] the literate classes in England suddenly develop an unprecedented taste for writing for, about, and by women'?[36] The achievements of feminist scholarship over the past few decades have gradually disproved the notion that educated and writing women were a rare and endangered species. I argue that the feminization debate was a means by which women, and in particular women of letters, were brought to public prominence in the early to mid-eighteenth century; a factor quite distinct from the history of sensibility or of domestic ideology, the most familiar contexts for discussion of the role of women in eighteenth-century culture. I concur with Lawrence Klein's scepticism about the 'domestic thesis', the notion of women's exclusion from the public sphere, and also agree on the need for an account of the 'legitimation of female publicity'.[37] But I believe the paradigm of 'politeness' he advocates, with its valorization of conversation between men and women taken from the French salons, is more relevant to the Britain of the late eighteenth century, as Klein himself partly grants.[38]

It remains to be asked, was the discourse of feminization a 'good thing' for women? To some extent the question is peripheral to the aims of this study: the investigation is centred not on what the debate about progress could do for women, but on what 'woman' could do for the feminization argument. But there are very evidently general and particular ways in which the discourse of feminization did not further the interests of women as a class. First, because it was a discourse primarily concerned with legitimating the capitalist economic order, it not only failed to address the real problems facing women in every rank of society – inadequate legal rights and the sexual double standard, lack of access to education, paid work and fair wages – but exacerbated them by imposing new restrictive definitions of idealized femininity. It contributes to the general tightening of the code of feminine propriety around the mid-century that has been observed by feminist historians.

Proponents of feminization were interested in exceptional examples of the female sex, women of genius like Elizabeth Singer Rowe, Elizabeth Carter and the historian Catharine Macaulay. The act of celebrating such women was equally a vindication of refinement and civility, in opposition to the pessimistic vision of civic humanism. There is no doubt that the emergence of the discourse of feminization in the 1690s, and then again more decisively in the 1740s, altered the climate of the republic of letters and made it more welcoming to female authors. For the handful of educated women with literary ambitions this sea change could not fail to be recognized as an opportunity. But there was a price to pay. The independent views of Carter and Macaulay, fundamentally at odds with capitalist ideology, were muffled by their reception as icons of modernity. Furthermore, should the moral standards expected of an icon be infringed in any way, as they were in the case of Macaulay, then a spectacular fall from grace was inevitable. In chapters 4 and 6 in particular I have focused in some detail on the personal repercussions of the feminization debate for those women who found themselves caught up in it.

The group of women writers most closely associated with the progressivist feminization argument were the Bluestockings – Carter, Catherine Talbot, Elizabeth Montagu and Hester Chapone in the 'first generation'; Hester Lynch Piozzi, Hannah More, Frances Burney and Anna Laetitia Barbauld in the second – along with other, more loosely associated authors like Sarah Scott, Frances Sheridan, Sarah Fielding, Frances Brooke, Clara Reeve, Anna Seward and Macaulay. Sylvia Harcstark Myers, author of the essential starting-point for any enquiry into their careers, *The Bluestocking Circle* (1990), suggested that they exhibited elements of a 'feminist consciousness' in spite of the social conservatism of most of them.[39] Gary Kelly has boldly declared the existence of 'Bluestocking Feminism', while Harriet Guest argues for a gradual and incremental relation between the Mary Wollstonecraft's language of citizens' rights and the tentative patriotism of her immediate precursors.[40]

I believe that the relationship between the feminism of Wollstonecraft and the feminization of the Bluestocking era is best described as dialectical. Wollstonecraft's sense of entitlement to a public platform was a consequence of the discourse of feminization, but she adopts elements of civic humanist rhetoric as a declaration of independence from it, beyond the immediate aim of attacking the political and economic establishment of Great Britain.[41] The 'republican' feminism of the 1790s broke decisively with the logic of feminization and its insidious linkage of the progress of commercial society and the progress of women. Women had been promoted as an emblem of improvement and to an extent it benefited them: most notably by countering misogyny in the literary public sphere. But it was also a trap, locking women into an association with economic innovation, including new and extreme forms of social injustice. The break with feminization gave women writers the freedom to forge new alliances, and freed feminism as well to develop in critical relation to the capitalist status quo.

1
Sexual Alchemy in the Coffee-House

Coffee was first introduced into Europe as a drug, reported to have extraordinary powers of transformation. In the early seventeenth century travellers to the Near East told of an aromatic drink made by infusing a powdered black berry, and related strange tales of its invigorating effects. Various legends involved the endorsement of *Kahveh* (meaning 'stimulating and invigorating') by the Prophet Mohammed. In one version he says of his exhilarated state, 'I felt able to unseat forty horsemen and to possess fifty women.'[1] Forbidden to touch alcohol, Muslims drank quantities of the hot black liquor. There were descriptions of coffee-houses in Arabia, Turkey and Egypt, where men sat and talked for much of the day; a travel book of 1609 explained, 'Their Coffa houses are more common than Ale-houses in England; but they use not so much to sit in the houses as on benches on both sides the streets ... if there be any news, it is talked of there.'[2] From the start, coffee drinking was understood to be primarily a homosocial experience. As such, it raised questions that were physiological and social: What was the nature of the product's effect on the male body? How might the institution of the coffee-house alter existing conventions of masculine behaviour? In addition, there was the association of coffee with news and public discussion, preserved intact in the establishments transplanted to the West. What effect might this new kind of public discourse have on the social body as a whole?

Dr William Harvey, discoverer of the circulation of blood, was among the first in England to obtain and sample the fabled bean. His student, Walter Rumsey, wrote *Experiments of Coffee* (1657)[3] in which he affirmed its value as a cure for drunkenness – one of the more moderate and well-founded claims made for it. Another pupil, Edward Pococke, regarded it as a panacea which guarded against consumption, ophthalmia, dropsy, gout scurvy and even smallpox.[4] There was an 'enormous pharmacological literature extending from at least 1622 to 1757' which dealt with coffee and other popular exotic imports – tea, chocolate and tobacco.[5] Each product was the subject of fierce debate, the claims of enthusiasts being countered by those of detractors, who often had a protectionist stake in traditional alternatives: ale, wine and herbal concoctions. The phenomenal expansion of Britain's global trading links and imperial interests in this period was experienced in the most intimate way through the ingestion of new substances by domestic consumers. The benefits of imperialism were tested on the body; economic and physical transformation combined.

The coffee-house experience arrived in England in 1650, when a Jewish immigrant from Turkey set up shop in Oxford. Here, says Anthony Wood in his *Annals*, coffee was drunk 'by some who delighted in noveltie'.[6] In 1652 a 'Turkey merchant' named Edwards set up his Greek servant, Pasqua Rosée, as the proprietor of a coffee-house in St. Michael's Alley, off Cornhill in the City of London. A handbill titled *The Vertue of the COFFEE Drink* was distributed, explaining at length the method of preparation, its numerous medical benefits and its usage in the Ottoman Empire: 'It is observed that in Turkey, where this is generally drunk, that they are not trobled with the Stone, Gout, Dropsie, or Scurvey, and that their Skins are exceeding cleer and white.'[7] Crowds were attracted to taste the strange beverage; neighbouring tavern-keepers petitioned the Lord Mayor, demanding that the business be closed on the grounds that the Greek was not a Freeman of the City. A supporter wrote a poem praising Rosée, who 'first did broach / This Necktar for the publick good'.[8] Rosée eventually left, but over the next 50 years other coffee-houses were established at an accelerating rate throughout England. It was in the capital, however, that the institution really took off and became a vital part of the fabric of urban life.

The coffee-house experience was almost from the start mediated by printed polemic, for or against, in handbills, newspaper advertisements, broadsides, engravings, pamphlets, treatises, plays and, eventually, periodicals. Throughout the 1650s and 1660s 'the drink called Coffee' continued to be sold as a wonder-drug, but gradually coffee-houses came to be sold with it as an innovative social space.[9] Advertisements mention the equally exotic tea and chocolate alongside coffee, but not alcoholic drinks; this novelty made them an ideal place to talk and do business.[10] There were special rules of conduct, discouraging swearing, gambling, rowdiness and sedition, and encouraging relaxed sociability and improving conversation. In spite of excise duty, coffee was cheap and, in contrast to taverns, customers were welcome to linger for an hour or two without buying more. Proprietors made a virtue of the mixed company attracted variously by low prices, sobriety and news, and seem to have established a policy of democratic seating.[11] Above all, the coffee-houses were a magnet for news and rumour:

> You that delight in Wit and Mirth,
> And long to hear such News,
> As comes from all Parts of the Earth,

> Dutch, Danes, and Tirks, and Jews,
> I'le send yee to a Rendezvous,
> Where it is smoaking new;
> Go hear it at a Coffee-house,
> It cannot be but true.[12]

In the late 1660s, the government of Charles II began to fear that the open political talk of the coffee-houses might be converted into active rebellion. Satirical pamphlets took note of their 'levelling character'.[13] The anonymous author of *A Character of Coffee and Coffee-Houses* (1661) remarked sarcastically, 'The great privilege of equality is only peculiar to the Golden Age, and to a coffee-house', and condemned the arrangement as 'a mere Chaos'.[14] In 1666 the matter was discussed in the King's Council, and in spite of counter-arguments that the sale of coffee brought in useful revenue and that any attempt at repression might be met with resistance, suspicions remained. In 1673 the government submitted to Parliament a proposal that coffee-houses not only encouraged treasonous talk, but also a loss of time among young gentlemen and tradesmen, which was damaging the economy.[15] In the same year a diatribe entitled *The Character of a Coffee-House* employed openly political language: 'each man seems a Leveller, and ranks and files himself as he lists, without regard to degree or order'.[16] Finally, in late December 1675, a Royal Proclamation for the Suppression of Coffee Houses was issued, only to be met with universal outrage and a staunch refusal to comply. The government beat a hasty retreat, issuing a second proclamation ten days later reversing the earlier order. As a face-saving exercise it was announced that contrite coffee-house proprietors would take an oath of allegiance and undertake to be on their guard against sedition in future.

It was the finest hour of the coffee-houses, subsequently celebrated as a victory for freedom of speech and individual liberty by Whig historians of the eighteenth and nineteenth centuries. It was also the moment when the coffee-house came closest to resembling the institution described in *The Structural Transformation of the Public Sphere: An Inquiry into a Category of Bourgeois Society* by the Marxist sociologist Jürgen Habermas. In Habermas's highly influential account, coffee-houses, like the salons in France and the *Tischgesellschaften* in Germany, provided a venue where private men could gather and discuss without regard to status: a new kind of public dissociated from the pre-existing sphere of public authority surrounding the state and court. Here, news of all kinds – cultural, intellectual and political – became generally accessible with the aid of the new medium of the news periodical and was opened to questioning and rational debate. This process ensured that the bourgeois public sphere, in contrast to the public sphere of the state apparatus, was in principle inclusive, although it might take intimate and apparently sectional forms, for 'all private people ... – in so

far as they were propertied and educated – as readers, listeners, and specta-
tors could avail themselves via the market of the objects that were subject
to discussion'.[17] It constituted a new form of bourgeois representation with
the potential to take a critical and even oppositional stance towards the
state. It is not my intention to dispute Habermas's identification of the
coffee-house with the emergence of specifically bourgeois forms of cohesion and discursive practice. On the contrary, my account will reinforce his
analysis of the fusion of public consciousness with private commercial
interest; a phenomenon occluded by critics who seek to rename the
'bourgeois public sphere' as the 'authentic public sphere' or the 'polite
public'.[18] However, one aspect of his thesis will be challenged: the idea that
coffee-houses as centres of criticism are 'literary at first, then also political'.[19] While literary criticism implies the involvement of women at some
level, the political is identified strictly with male interlocutors. Within the
framework of Habermas's argument this point is both incidental and – to
use one of his favourite terms – consequential. In his own exposition, a
strict sequence is rarely observed; instead, literary and political concerns are
frequently seen to overlap. On the other hand, the proposition represents a
masculinist teleology, to which feminist scholars have rightly responded. I
will return to the issue of the valorization of the all-male coffee-house
shortly.[20] Still, I would maintain that the notion of a transition from literary to political criticism is more in the nature of a speculative gambit,
based on rather patchy empirical evidence, than an essential doctrine.

The history of the coffee-house in fact suggests the reverse progression:
they were political at first, then literary. What began as a small-scale institution that posed a genuine political threat unexpectedly grew to become
the centre of a vastly expanded public culture of print, an instrument of
social consensus and stability, forming part of the long revolution of the
British bourgeoisie. The statistics are these: when the Royal Proclamation
was issued, coffee-houses in London numbered a mere 150[21] (as a measure
of comparison, Aytoun Ellis notes that when the first coffee-house was
established in Oxford in 1650 there were 350 taverns in the town); by the
end of the century, it has been calculated that there were 2,000 coffee-
houses in London,[22] rising to 3,000 ten years later.[23] If coffee-houses had
successfully been suppressed in 1675, they would have been a footnote in
the history of Restoration politics. It is only once they ceased to be a direct
threat to official public authority that their extraordinarily far-reaching role
began to take shape.

The influence was certainly not restricted to the trade in news. The nature
of coffee as a foreign import had connected coffee-houses from the start with
the emergence of Britain as a trading power. Coffee-house culture grew in
conjunction with the central mechanisms of capitalism, the institutions that
funded imperialist expansion. The epicentre was the Royal Exchange, built
in 1669 after the Great Fire and celebrated by Addison in *Spectator* No. 69 as

the institution which makes 'this Metropolis a kind of Emporium for the whole Earth'; dozens of coffee-houses were crowded into the square mile surrounding it, the greatest concentration in the City.[24] One of them, Jonathan's, became the regular meeting place of merchants and the new breed of stock-jobbers, speculators in public funds, who would eventually break away to found the Stock Exchange. Garraway's was another important venue for share-trading, auctions and gambling. From 1711 it housed the first fire insurance business; in 1720 it was the principal scene of the South Sea Bubble. The Virginia and the Jerusalem catered to the shipping trade for the Baltic and America. Lloyd's was opened in around 1688, specifically as a venue for marine insurance underwriters, and prepared 'ship's lists' as part of the service. Goldsmiths and the first bankers habitually met in coffee-houses to settle accounts in the innovative medium of paper money. The financial revolution of the 1690s evolved in this context.

There was a corresponding ideal of coffee-house man as *homo economicus*. Proponents spoke of enhanced productivity. The argument of a 1675 pamphlet *Coffee Houses Vindicated*[25] links altered physiology and business interests, *Asserting ... the Excellent Use and physical Virtues of that Liquor ... With the Grand Conveniency of such civil Places of Resort and ingenious Conversation.* Coffee-houses are not only cheaper than taverns; men of business can meet and trade here without 'continual sippings' being 'apt to fly into their brains and render them drowsy and indisposed'. Here, after 'dispatching their business', they 'go out more sprightly about their affairs, than before'. And as for recreation, 'where can young gentlemen, or shop-keepers, more innocently and advantageously spend an hour or two in the evening than at a coffee-house?' In sum, the 'well-regulated coffee-house' (as opposed to the 'sordid holes, that assume that name to cloke the practice of debauchery') is 'the sanctuary of health, the nursery of temperance, the delight of frugality, and academy of civility, the free-school of ingenuity'.[26]

Peter Stallybrass and Allon White, in *The Politics and Poetics of Transgression*, have made the strongest case for the coffee-house as a training ground in the Protestant work ethic. They investigate the process by which a self-consciously refined *bourgeois* public body distinguishes itself from the 'grotesque collective body' found in the theatre and the ale-house, the underside of the transformation Habermas examines from above. They draw attention to the list of rules which were posted on coffee-house walls: 'no swearing, no profane scripture, no cards, dice or gaming, no wagers over five shillings, no drinking of health'. As a space was cleared for rational discourse, it was simultaneously 'de-libidinized', cleared of the 'unruly demands of the body for pleasure and release'. A new form of public intercourse was promoted that was sober and productive. The epithet, 'this wakeful and civil drink', coined by a coffee enthusiast of the time, 'epitomizes the value of coffee as a new and unexpected agency in the prolonged struggle of capitalism to discipline its work-force'.[27]

The notion of the 'coffee-house politician' emerged as a caricature of the tension between public and private in the identity of the coffee-house clientele. It represents a quarrel over proper boundaries. The news commodity was a component in the growth of a monied interest; the activities of trade, insurance, banking and stock exchange fuelled the demand for 'insider' knowledge of public affairs. Private business created the pressure to breach the boundaries of the pre-existing public sphere of state business. The redefinition of the public necessitated by the intrusion of bourgeois traders was disruptive and volatile. Under the Stuart government, attacks tended to be fuelled by Tory and High Church ideology, focusing on the incompatibility of public knowledge and private economics. 'Coffee-house politicians' were represented as addictive news-readers who neglected their own business to meddle in affairs of state, understanding nothing, and to no effect. Satires also emphasized the diversity of coffee-house men, coming from all walks of life with greatly varying status; the message being that their disputes were bound to be fractured and ultimately meaningless.

The satire extended to the question of whether or not the anomalous breed of coffee-house politicians could properly be described as men. *The Women's Petition against Coffee* and *The Mens Answer to the Women's Petition against Coffee* were pamphlets published anonymously in 1674, on the brink of the government clampdown. Both are satirical attacks on 'the coffee revolution', which stage a crisis of male sexual identity by parodying the pharmacological discourse on coffee. The *Women's Petition* is not a protest at women's exclusion.[28] In fact, there is no reason to believe the pamphlet was written by women, or a woman, at all. The full title is: *The Women's Petition aainst Coffee. Representing to The Publick Consideration the Grand Inconveniences accruing to their Sex from the Excessive Use of that Drying, Enfeebling Liquor. Presented to the Right Honorable the Keeper of the Liberty of Venus*. The 'women' protest that

> the excessive use of that Newfangled, Abominable, Heathenish Liquor called COFFEE, which Riffling Nature of her Choicest *Treasures*, and Drying up the *Radical Moisture*, has so *Eunucht* our Husbands, and *Crippled* our more kind *Gallants*, that they are become as *Impotent*, as Age, and as unfruitful as those Desarts whence that unhappy Berry [i.e. the coffee-bean] is said to be brought. (1)

They go on to complain that coffee has altered not only men's physiology, but also their manners. In the coffee-houses, men will 'soon learn to excel us in Talkativeness: a Quality wherein our Sex has ever claimed prehemi-nence: For here like so many *Frogs* in a *puddle*, they sup muddy water, and murmer insignificant notes till half a dozen of them *out-babble* an equal number of us at a *Gossiping*' (4). Coffee-drinking men have strayed into the zone of the unsexed. If, as Aytoun Ellis states, the *Women's Petition* contributed to the temporary ban on coffee-houses in the following year, at that point the government's anxieties would have been demographic rather than political – in the latter regard the 'women' offer themselves as guarantors that the coffee-drinkers are 'too tame and too talkative to make any desperate Politicians' (5).

The *Mens Answer* is not a defence of coffee-houses, but rather another attack on them by other, less subtle, means.[29] The *soi-disant* coffee-house men protest their virility by slandering coffee-house women. They declare that their favourite resort, far from being an instrument of emasculation, is on the contrary almost a school for the amorous arts, 'there being scarce a Coffee-hut but affords a Tawdry Woman, a Wanton Daughter, or a Buxome Maide, to accommodate Customers' (3). Their womenfolk are recommended to take their own pleasures in the tavern. Any doubts about the physiological effects of coffee are allayed: 'Coffee collects and settles the Spirits, makes the erection more Vigorous, the Ejaculation more full, adds a spiritualescency to the Sperme, and renders it more firm and suitable to the Gusto of the womb' (4). Reproduction is always an economic issue, not only from the point of view of maintaining population levels (a pressing concern in a period of almost constant war), but also symbolically. The first pamphlet raises anxieties about virility. In doing so it transposes the more general question of whether a speculative outlay can be converted into profit, as the association of impotence with idle, impotent talk illustrates. The second pamphlet sustains the joking sexual displacement by taking it literally.

Coffee-houses raised the problem of a new-model man: an amalgamation of private passions (including the passion for acquisition) and public voice. In so far as the space of the coffee-house was envisaged as a crucible of transformation, and coffee itself conceived of as a metamorphosing drug, the men who participated in the experiment found the nature of their manhood called into question. In his novelty, coffee-house man departed from existing masculine roles, and triggered a renegotiation of gender values. The fact that coffee-houses had an all-male clientele merely intensified the focus on sexual difference.[30] To ask whether the exclusion of women from certain public spaces was constitutive of the public sphere or merely contingent, as some critics of Habermas have done, is to ask the wrong question. As we will see, women had a crucial symbolic, as well as economic, presence as workers in the coffee-house, while female readers and writers were a vital part of the dissemination of coffee-house culture in print.

The *Women's Petition* illustrates a struggle to reconceptualize the male body of the coffee-drinker. There was the threat that, falling outside the boundaries of homosocial behaviour, he would be classed as effeminate. The question became increasingly acute after 1688, when long-standing political and religious divisions were eclipsed by new conflicts over the movement for social reform, the effects of economic change and the wars in Europe. Denunciations of effeminacy in men and its correlative, masculine assertiveness in women, were rife during the reigns of William III and Queen Anne.[31] Symptomatically, sexual innuendo and outright libel attached to the monarchs themselves; in particular to William, who was freely characterized as a cross-dressing sodomite in street ballads. One of the most extraordinary examples of the rhetoric was Ned Ward's *The Humours of a Coffee-House*, a short-lived journal which appeared in the summer of 1707 and took the form of a soap opera in which a regular cast of diverse characters enter into dispute on topics of the day, with many satirical digs at coffee-house culture itself. In the penultimate issue, Ward, either attempting to increase sales or perhaps as a kamikaze flourish, includes a graphic description of sexual perversion. After a lively debate on the relative evils of whoring, swearing and lying versus stock-jobbing, wagering and news, Horoscope the Astrologist tells the story, derived from a secret eye-witness, of 'the *Monstrum Horrendum*', a man who 'assumes the Language, as well as the Shape, of a Woman'. With the assistance of two female prostitutes, he is ritually dressed in elaborate women's garb, consumes exotic liquor (in this case, tea, earlier branded with coffee a 'damn'd Mahometan and Heathenish' drink[32]) and then, in a play-acted assault, is bound, gagged and suspended by ropes, to be whipped 'till the Blood flows Plentifully, and Nature has every way discharg'd herself'.[33] Horoscope's auditors in the coffee-house are shaken; they cry in chorus: 'This is incredible!' And they evidently feel the relevance. In the final issue they enjoy a long poem warning against the 'Matrimonial Fetter' and recommending claret, tobacco and male company as an antidote to female dominance:

> The Hen-peck'd Fool, raises my Passion,
> He is a Scandal to the whole Creation:
> A Scorn to Angels, Man's Reverse,
> A Woman's Slave, A Dismal Curse;
> A Scavenger for Satan's A——.[34]

It is evident that satires associating coffee-houses with effeminacy were intended to quash any pretensions the clientele might have to presenting themselves as a rational and influential 'public'. At this time, while masculinist, civic humanist definitions of the public grew in authority (most notably as a result of the standing army debate of 1697–98), and coffee-houses became ever more closely tied to the spirit of socio-economic transformation involving an alternative inclusive and democratic definition of the public, the danger of provoking a sexual slur was redoubled. J.G.A. Pocock has suggested that the image of 'the man of commerce ... had to fight its way to political recognition in the teeth of the "patriot" ideal';[35]

the emphasis should be placed as much on 'man' as on 'commerce'. Discipline and rational discourse were insufficient. It was necessary to overcome the charge of emasculation by redefining the sexual orientation of the coffee-house public. Their reformist programme required a revised schema of sexual difference. Men were to be remasculinized by a new model of heterosexual interaction focused on the moral influence of women. This strategy required not only the elevation of the female object above misogynous constructions, but also the elevation of heterosexual desire itself to become an agent of moral change, as opposed to a motive for sensual gratification.[36]

The most obvious and immediate target for this ideological reworking of sexual difference was the coffee-house barmaid. She was to become the focus of intense interest and debate about the innovative character of coffee-house culture. The women who worked there would traditionally have been fair game for the lewd humour and advances of the customers (see the *Mens Answer*, cited above p. 19); now they were to be reconceived as the moral guardians of the establishment, angels in the coffee-house. And yet their role remained ambivalent, for it drew attention to the coffee-house as a place of commodity exchange and social labour, as opposed to a forum for the disinterested debating of political views. Further, it was to her that the men paid a penny when they left, tainting her with ideas of material gain.

Images from as early as 1668 (Figure 1) establish the iconographic importance of the female barkeeper, and prints up to the 1710s repeat the formula. In a company of men, a sole woman stands boxed in by a counter at one end of the room. Her stiffly vertical, even iconic figure, emphasized by a tall headdress of starched lace, contrasts with the relaxed, varied postures of the groups of men around the tables. Her formal isolation is counterpoised to the sociable interaction of the male customers. Sexual difference is theatricalized, not only by the physical barrier dividing male/female, work/consumption, confinement/liberty, but even by the arrangement of candles along the counter of the bar as if on a stage, their light projecting the silhouette of the woman on to the wall behind. She is presented as an inaccessible object, but at the same time, the spectacle of male sociability is caught within her gaze. The heterosexual sight-line cuts across the homosocial activity, which is constituted in relation to it. A structure of sexual difference underlies the democratic social scene. Bridging the distance between the men and the woman, the distance of institutionalized 'politeness', are those who belong to a third, liminal, gender category: the children, the 'coffee boys', whose exclusive task it seems to have been to pour the coffee, carry the cups to the tables and return them to the immobile female bar-keeper. Her iconic 'untouchability' was a crucial factor in the reformation of men.

Figure 1   *Interior of a London Coffee-House* (c. 1705).

The terms of the reform were laid out in the periodical the *Spectator* (1711–12, 1714), the most celebrated literary product of coffee-house culture. In No. 155 (Tuesday, 28 August 1711) a letter is printed from the female keeper of a coffee-house complaining of the 'improper Discourses' and insulting behaviour she is forced to put up with in her line of work, and begging Mr. Spectator to 'Say it is possible a Woman may be modest, and yet keep a publick House'. He willingly complies and represents to them the cruelty of taking liberties with women, 'naturally more helpless that the other sex', who are forced 'into a Way of Trade for their maintenance'.[37] By insisting that working women were to be treated with the same consideration and respect as genteel women, the *Spectator* legislates new standards of public demeanour and intercourse, implicitly distinguishing 'a Man of Honour and Sense' from, on the one hand, the dissipated nobleman, and on the other, the ill-bred plebeian. The clientele of the coffee-house was exclusively male yet it was asked to behave as though there were ladies present. The ladies themselves may have been absent in body, but their spirit had mysteriously descended to their more lowly sisters.

The coffee-house worker who authored the letter identifies herself as an 'Idol': 'half a dozen of [my Customers] loll at the Bar staring just in my Face, ready to interpret my Looks and Gestures, according to their own Imaginations'. The term was coined by Addison in *Spectator* No. 73 (Thursday, 24 May 1711), in an essay on the 'Passion for Praise', which causes women to set themselves up as objects of idolatry. Idols regularly appear 'in all publick Places and Assemblies, in order to seduce Men to their Worship'. But the emphasis is equally on the tendency of male 'Idolators' to attribute exorbitant powers to their female deity.

> Life and Death are in their Power: Joys of Heaven and Pains of Hell are at their disposal: Paradise is in their Arms, and Eternity in every Moment that you are present with them. Raptures, Transports and Extasies are the Rewards which they confer: Signs and Tears, Prayers and broken Hearts are the Offerings which are paid to them. Their Smiles make Men happy; their Frowns drive them to Despair.[38]

In No. 87 (Saturday, 9 June 1711) the term is first taken up in connection with coffee-house keepers. An elderly customer complains that 'six or seven' such 'Idols' are holding sway in establishments known to him, and causing havoc. The youth of each district spend the entire day in adoration, neglecting their studies or their jobs in the custom-house or law courts. The Idols themselves, distracted by such attention, make bad tea and coffee, and 'we who come to do Business, or talk Politicks, are utterly Poisoned'.[39] The letter elicits a condemnation of unproductive behaviour. But he gets no reply from Steele on this occasion. Instead, the old gentleman is answered by the motto at the head of the barmaid's letter nearly three months later, 'Hae nugae seria ducunt / In mala ...' ['These things which now seem frivolous and slight, / Will prove of serious consequence ...'].[40] What is at issue here is a change in public discourse: a shift away from both gallantry and misogynist raillery towards serious legislation of male/female interaction in public. Exaggerated idolatry, a kind of mocking courtliness, is to be replaced by true reverence for the vulnerable fair sex. The involvement of women in economic exchange should not lead to a confusion between the commodities they offer for sale and their own bodies. But in practice this 'elevated' indignation was hard to maintain. In No. 534 (Wednesday, 12 November 1712), Steele prints a letter from another coffee-house 'Idol' full of mock-gallant language, again suggesting the conflict of interests created by the fusing of the economic and the erotic.[41]

The problem was that the coffee-house Idol was also an icon, her own desirability symbolic of the desirability of new modes of social and economic exchange. It was requisite that men should worship at her shrine, confusing body with commodity, though ideally in a new-style gentlemanly fashion. The transmutation of the barkeeper was also a transmutation of coffee-house business in all its multiple facets: the circulation of news and exotic imports as commodities; the free exchange of rumour and political opinion; the conduct of commercial transactions on the premises. She is the presiding *genius loci*, but there is a residual ambivalence, a risk of regression: the 'Idol' may become merely an erotic focus and turn out to have feet of clay.

The female bar-keepers' moral significance can in part be gauged by the efforts of opponents of coffee-house culture to discredit her. Tom Brown, a satirist who typically opposed reform, moral or political, described in 1702 how

> Every Coffee-House is illuminated both without and within doors; without by a fine Glass Lanthorn and within by a Woman so *light* and *splendid*, you may see through her with the help of a Perspective. At the Bar the good man always places a charming Phillis or two, who invite you by their amorous Glances into their smoaky Territories, to the loss of your Sight.[42]

Ned Ward (already mentioned), who divided his time between tavern-keeping and anti-Whig journalism, gave details in *The London Spy* (1698) of a coffee-house that doubled as a brothel.[43]

The bar-keeper is a Circe: according to the direction of the polemic, she turns men into swine, or swine into gentlemen. She is akin to those other female figures of transformation who embody the anxieties of the nascent capitalist system of finance: the allegories of Trade and Public Credit invented by Defoe and Addison (both friends of the monied interest) to 'denote the idea that the credit mechanism has endowed society with an excessively hysterical nervous system',[44] while at the same time her attractions reconcile those fears. The ideological work that achieved this precarious resolution was begun in the 1690s, at the moment when the founding of the Bank of England made credit politics official, and the coffee-houses, basking in the favourable climate of the revolution settlement, branched out into a corresponding cultural politics.

2
The Athenian Mercury and the Pindarick Lady

New things

The greatest early innovator of the discourse of feminization was the printer and journalist John Dunton. In 1691 he founded the *Athenian Mercury*, the first literary periodical in Britain. It appeared, for the most part twice-weekly, until 1696 – one of the longest lived journals of the century.[1] Dunton came from a dissenting background and was an ardent supporter of King William.[2] The 1690 Act of Toleration and William's announced support for moral reformation cemented Dunton's identification with the new order. Before long he was publicly committing himself, ideologically and financially, to the experiment of the Glorious Revolution. After 1688, he launched a thriving new line in political biography, and made trials of political newsletters in the service of the Whigs (the short-lived *True Protestant Mercury* and *Coffee House Mercury*) and an account of his own 'Ramble Round the World' in instalments.[3] Towards the end of 1690, he had his big idea: a periodical paper that would go beyond simple news reporting. It would be an entirely new kind of interactive publication, which encouraged readers themselves to determine the content by submitting questions on any subject. These would then be answered by a panel of experts.[4] All contributions and replies would be anonymous.

This was a reconception of 'the new' within the genre of a news-sheet.[5] 'News' would no longer be restricted to a function of state policy and its consequences. Instead, novel information would permeate every aspect of life, 'Divine, Moral and Natural' (*AM*, I.1). The dialogic structure of the periodical was a mechanism for altering minds and manners. The periodical was *Athenian* in the sense derived from 'The Acts of the Apostles' in the New Testament: 'For all the Athenians, and strangers which were there, spent their time in nothing else, but either to tell or to hear of some new thing.' Dunton took as his motto lines from Robert Wild's poem '*In Nova Fert Animus*, &c. or a New Song to an Old Friend from an Old Poet, upon the Hopeful New Parliament' (1679):

26

We all are tainted with the Athenian Itch
News, and New Things, do the whole World bewitch –

In the universal taste for novelty lay the motive for change.

The periodical grew out of coffee-house culture and fed into it, with the aid of the Penny Post system founded in 1680. The initial base of operations was the coffee-house of James and Mary Smith, next door to Dunton's bookshop. In the first number, readers were instructed that answers would be given free of charge 'if they send their Questions by a Penny Post Letter to Mr. Smith at his Coffee-house in Stocks-Market in the Poultry'. Every Friday, the Athenians would meet here and sift through the mail, until 'finding the House too public, by the great number that flock'd thither, on purpose to hear, and see the Athenians', they moved elsewhere for greater anonymity.[6] Later a number of other coffee-houses – Turner's, Welsh's and the Rotterdam – also served as post offices.[7]

The economic interdependence of periodical and coffee-house was plainly understood. The *Mercury* depended on sales to coffee-houses, but before long, the editor was able to claim that coffee-houses might lose customers if they failed to subscribe to the journal. One of Dunton's novel practices was to collect separate numbers in groups of 30 to form a volume, and resell them in bound form, with a preface and index. On the 6 June 1691 (II: 4), a question was published asking 'of what Use or Interest will it be' to coffee-houses to carry the compilation? The answer states with confidence that customers are drawn to a coffee-house specifically by the desire to read the journal, that they will leave and go elsewhere if they fail to find it, and will take the trouble to seek out new places where it can be found. Furthermore, readers will return again and again to consult the bound volume with its index like a work of reference, as need arises.

As in the coffee-house, the *Mercury* maintained an 'open house' for questioners, with no enquiry into origins or condition. Anyone could participate in their dialogues, provided their queries were not obscene, malicious or atheistic. Critics of the *Mercury* were to object to the aimless and repetitive quality of the talk, as they did of coffee-house talk; that it was a kaleidoscope of fragmented perspectives, without social authority or consequence. The *Athenian Mercury* worked in various ways to mitigate the inherent hierarchy of the question-and-answer format. The anonymous respondents, who are described as unpaid and unambitious for fame (that is to say, disinterested gentlemen), do not claim infallibility, and questioners not satisfied with their replies are invited in the first issue to reapply. On a number of occasions, contributions were printed which disputed answers or attacked the attitude of the respondents. Although the editor had the power to select and prioritize questions according to their topic, he preserved a heterogeneous mix in each number, which typically ranged from issues of high principle to requests for practical tips to jokes ('Who is the Author of the last Question?', I.3.10) and mathematical puzzles, reflecting the social breadth and varied interests of the readership.[8]

One way in which the periodical's contents differed from coffee-house talk was in its apparent eschewal of political controversy, even after the lapse of the Licensing Act in 1695.[9] But, as in the case of *The Spectator*, the renunciation of politics was only apparent:[10] both were waging the Whig battle by other means. References to the government may have been few, but before long the entire enterprise was overtly dedicated to supporting the King's 'published desire for moral reformation'.[11] The *Athenian Mercury* shares a founding moment with the Societies for the Reformation of Manners.[12] Its specific, self-appointed role was the cultivation of the minds of readers the better to equip them to form an ethical public and encourage social consensus. The programme was wide-ranging, from matters of fact in science and technology to issues of doctrine in theology, and applied morality in economics and everyday life. Casuistical problems of manners and morals, love and marriage were especially prominent, with no evaluative distinction made about their public significance.[13] The coffee-house context is kept in view. In one remark it provides a tutelary model, as a place where 'the Youth will learn to be sober and drink Coffee, on purpose to make use of these Opportunities, which will make 'em Disputants, and fit Company for their Seniors.' (II: 4) The sense of civic purpose comes through strongly in the preface to Volume III.[14] In response to 'The Complaint we have met with from some Persons that we touch upon Subjects too high for the Publick View, and that 'tis not for such Questions as some we Answer, to lye for common Chatt and Entertainment on a Coffee-house Board', the editor asserts first, that the subjects are dictated by the questioners, 'But further, Why mayn't Discourses of this Nature be as proper for Coffee-houses as others? Since this is certain, that they may at least serve to hinder People from talking of what's worse.' In answer to the question 'Can you tell us what good was ever yet done by your *Athenian Mercury*?' (VIII: 1) the reply was given that apart from benefiting the Penny Post and pastry-cooks (presumably by providing wrapping), the periodical has 'ras'd a kind of Learned Ferment in the Nation, the Body of which was almost grown dead and vapid as to any taste of such things, by the hurries and distractions of the Last Reign' and made important contributions to 'that great and glorious Project, the Reformation of manners': 'if we had not broke the Ice, and crackt the Egg, none else had e're bin like to have done it.'

A sexual dialectic

Women quickly assumed a prominent position within the Athenian project. The title-page to the first collected volume of the *Mercury*, which ran from 17 March to 30 May 1691, speaks of 'Nice and Curious Questions

Proposed by the Ingenious'. In the second volume this was supplemented by 'the Ingenious *of Either Sex*' (original emphasis). The Athenians were unprepared for the strength of interest in 'feminine' topics of sexual and marital ethics, or the quantity of mail from female correspondents, but they embraced the opportunity and this arguably became the most radical part of the enterprise. Never before had women been offered an open platform for voicing their views and experiences. Dunton evidently felt the benefits worked both ways. As early as the 23 May 1691 (I: 18) he announced a fixed day each month for answering 'female Questions', to oblige 'the *fair Sex* ... as knowing they have a very *strong party* in the world'. This was not to ghettoize the female content; questions from women and about women continued to appear in other issues. Rather, it seems to have been a shrewd piece of niche marketing not necessarily aimed solely at women. Among the financial benefits to coffee-houses listed in the response from Dunton already mentioned is the idea that 'the Generous Lovers (who spend liberally) will throng the Coffee-houses every first Tuesday in the Month to read the Female Questions' (II: 4; 6 June 1691). As in the positioning of the coffee-house barmaid, heterosexual relations intersect the homosocial space of the coffee-house.

An important statement, almost amounting to a manifesto, appears in answer to the question from a male correspondent, 'Whether a tender Friendship between two Persons of a different Sex can be innocent?' at the head of the sheet for 28 April 1691 (II: 1). The response was almost certainly written by Dunton himself.[15]

I look upon the groundless suspitions so common in relation to matters of this nature, as base as they are wicked, and chiefly owing to the vice and lewdness of the Age, which makes some persons believe all the World as wicked as themselves. The Gentleman who proposes this question seems of a far different Character, and one who deserves that happiness which he mentions; for whose satisfaction, or theirs who desire it, we affirm, That such a Friendship is not on'y innocent, but commendable, and as advantagious as delightful. A strict Union of Souls, as has been formerly asserted, is the Essence of Friendship. Souls have no Sexes, nor while those only are concerned can any thing that's criminal intrude. 'Tis a Conversation truly Angelical, and has so many charms in't, that the Friendships between man and man deserve not to be compared with it. The very Souls of the fair Sex, as well as their Bodies, seem to have a softer turn that those of Men, while we reckon our selves Possessors of a more solid Judgment and stronger Reason, or rather may with more Justice pretend to greater Experience, and more advantages to improve our Minds; nor can any thing on Earth give a greater or purer Pleasure than communicating such knowledge to a capable Person, who if of another Sex, by the Charms of her Conversation inexpressibly sweetens the pleasant Labours, and by the advantage of a fine Mind and good Genius often starts such Notions as the Instructor himself would otherwise never have thought of. All the fear is lest the Friendship should in time degenerate, and the Body come in for a share with the Soul, as it did among Boccalins Poetesses and Vertuousi's, which if once it does, Farewel Friendship, and most of the Happiness arising from it.[16]

The response begins with the denunciation and overcoming of misogyny, which is the hallmark of feminizing polemic. It firmly settles the key question in debates on sexual difference: 'Souls have no Sexes'. But the delirious evocation of the pleasures of conversation with women goes beyond the instrumental requirements of question and answer. Equally the pathos of the final sentence. Here Dunton was sketching out the script of his own life as an exemplary feminized male. He was taking his first step on the tightrope named by him 'Platonick Love'.[16]

Dunton has been recognized for many innovations, but not for his introduction of platonic love into the supposedly masculine and bourgeois discourse of coffee-house culture.[17] It was one of his most startlingly eccentric acts, even among numerous others. By tradition, platonic love was the plaything of the aristocracy. Queen Henrietta Maria had formed the centre of a cult of platonic love at the court of Charles I.[18] Her courtier Abraham Cowley had written and published *The Mistress* (1647), an influential poetic treatment of ideal and physical love, while in exile with the English court in France. Dunton's decision to incorporate platonic love as part of the Williamite ideology he was forging from the base of the coffee-house was hardly predictable. Yet it connects suggestively with the origins of the doctrine in Renaissance Italy. Attempts by Italian classicists to assimilate the message of Plato's *Symposium* had involved the sublimation of its homoerotic content, first as a spiritual allegory of male friendship, then, via a disjunctive reinterpretation in Castiglione's *The Courtier* (1528), as a directive for the idealizing love of women by men who wished to refashion themselves.[19] The Song of Solomon was frequently cited as a comparable case of spiritual allegory in sensual dress; it too was to feature in the Athenian project, as we will see. The language of platonic love, then, first evolved as an instrument of self-fashioning, enabling male aristocrats to excel within the cultural and political arena of the court. It was this transformative potential that Dunton recognized and adapted. He too was to promote a new kind of feminized man, but with an earnest bourgeois dimension – a man subjected to the improving influence of women by a fusion of physical attraction and moral idealism. He was to be distinct from the 'effeminate' man, the aristocratic fop or libertine, drawn to women by narcissism or lust. The *Athenian Mercury* was not without genuine expertise on the score of platonic ideas and rhetoric. Samuel Wesley, a regular contributor, had begun his publishing career as an imitator and satirist of Cowley's lyrics. The philosopher John Norris, one of the Cambridge Platonists, was not an Athenian, as has sometimes been claimed, but he is referred to in the journal and Dunton was evidently familiar with his writings.[20]

Pierre Motteux, a Huguenot translator and journalist who contributed a poetic eulogy to Charles Gildon's *History of the Athenian Society*, followed Dunton's lead when he began the *Gentleman's Journal* (January 1692–November 1694), a monthly aimed at a country readership which actively courted the fair sex, in keeping with the genteel title.[21] He included in one of his early issues a poem entitled the 'The Platonic Lovers' framed by a pathetic true-life story, and the following month, an essay translated from Poulain de la Barre titled 'The Equality of the Sexes Asserted'.[22] A corollary of platonic gallantry was opposition to misogynist stereotypes and to behaviour among women that gave credence to them. Dunton launched a campaign against prostitution, or 'night-walking', in the pages of the *Mercury* in July 1691. This took the form of confessions wrung from prostitutes by 'a Gentleman' during 'six Night Rambles' (III: 3).[23] There was a vague idea of reclaiming lost souls, but the chief interest here appears to have been increased sales. Prurience was the reverse side of platonic love.

The *Mercury*'s excessive gallantry towards women aroused interest and also ridicule. One questioner asks 'Whether the Authors of this Athenian Mercury are not Batchelors, they speak so Obligingly of the Fair Sex?' (II.3; 3 June 1691). The somewhat incoherent response suggests the novelty of attempting an explanation; during the next century the reasoning would be smoothed into a glib reflex. The respondent explains that if not bachelors, they are 'Gentlemen', for 'all who pretend to that Name, as well as all civiliz'd Mankind, have ever treated Women with that respect and tenderness which their Beauty or at least their Sex deserve'. But he then, with incongruous effect, proposes that civility towards women is founded in nature: 'the fiercest Nations and most barbarous of Cannibals have acknowledg'd and practis'd this piece of good Breeding, but even the Beasts themselves teach it us'. Finally, he appeals to reason 'to authorize such a practice'. Women possess the means of future prosperity:

> We owe the Happiness of Society, the Defence of Nations, the best Riches of Kingdoms, which consists in the multitude of Inhabitants; nay, even the continuance of the World, which without them cou'd live at furthest no longer than the next Age, to that Sex whom we are so willing to oblige.

He signs off by declaring himself careless of 'the Censures we may possibly meet with for this piece of Justice'.

Censure came most virulently in the form of a parodic counter-*Mercury*; the *London Mercury* edited by Tom Brown (already mentioned here as an opponent of coffee-house culture), launched on 1 February 1692, and published for just four months.[24] The opening issue mocked the Athenians' assiduity with regard to female questioners, 'for whom they have a most profound Veneration ... from the Lady in her cock'd Commode, to the Oyster-wench in her lawful occupation at the Tavern-Door'. The second issue included two 'female' questions:

> A Certain Querist of the Fair Sex, for Quality a little Dirty (but that's nothing, they are all Ladies at Athens) having a terrible angry Corn between her Toes of the Left Foot, and a Wart or Mole on the inside of her Right Buttock, she begs to know of your Athenian Worships, which of these two small Tenements, thus placed as above said, you think to be best situated for Air and Prospect?

Kathryn Shevelow rightly observes that the attack is aimed at the Athenians' 'open-door' policy, and the mixture of high and low questions they welcomed, with many of the more practical and mundane questions posed by women.[25] But a second target is the elevated discourse on women ('they are all Ladies at Athens') and the ideal of platonic love as a spiritual and intellectual communion of the sexes. Brown's version of feminine concerns represents precisely the sort of fleshly misogyny that Dunton and his associates were concerned to stamp out. It is telling that Brown changed the name of the *London Mercury* to the *Lacedemonian Mercury* after four numbers. The opposition of Athens and Sparta (also known as Lacedemonia) was a civic humanist touchstone; luxurious, feminized Athens was unflatteringly contrasted with Sparta's strict cultivation of masculine virtue.[26]

Elizabeth Singer Rowe and 'The Double Courtship'

By this time the theory of 'Platonick Love', sketched out in the *Athenian Mercury*, was in the course of being played out in its pages as a living drama. The effect of the arrival of an unsolicited patriotic poem on William III at the battle of the Boyne, followed by a question, both from an obscure young woman living in Somerset, was nothing short of cataclysmic. Her question, published on Tuesday, 1 December 1691, evinced a passionate enthusiasm for the arts and an earnest desire to ally herself with the Athenian project.[27] She asked,

> Whether Songs on Moral, Religious or Divine Subjects, composed by Persons of Wit and Virtue, and set to both grave and pleasant Tunes, wou'd not the Charms of Poetry, and sweetness of Musick, make good impressions of Modesty and Sobriety on the Young and Noble, make them really in Love with Virtue and Goodness, and prepare their minds for the design'd Reformation?'

And added, with breathless anticipation, 'what are your Thoughts on the late Pastoral Poem, &c.?' (V: 1).

The response, from Dunton, or possibly Wesley (the in-house poetry specialist), shows the dawning of another great idea: to prepare the mind for reformation by making it 'really in Love with Virtue and Goodness'; in other words, to make virtue as seductive as vice. The effect on the discourse of the journal was immediate and profound. After nine months of prosaic casuistry, the Athenians themselves burst into song. The original poem, written by the questioner, was a panegyric dealing with William's 1690 victory over the forces of James II at the river Boyne near Dublin. It was not printed in the *Mercury*, though it later would be in her *Poems on Several Occasions* (1696), published at Dunton's instigation. Instead, the poem received its own panegyric in an ode entitled 'To the Author of the late Famous Pastoral Poem'.

> Yes, – by each Fountain, River, Stream and Grove,
> By all the pleasant haunts the Muses love,
> By them themselves, and great Apollo too,
> I'll swear I hardly love them more than you.
> Say, Dear unknown! what is't that charms me so?
> What secret Nectar through thy Lines does flow?
> What Deathless Beauties in thy Garden grow?
> Immortal Wit in Natures easiest Dress,
> A Paradise rais'd in a Wilderness.
> Tho' harsh thy Subject, haggard and unkind,
> And rough, as bitter blasts of Northern Wind,
> Thy Divine Spirits corrects each ruder Sound
> And breaths delicious Zephyrs all around.
> Thus can our Kindred, Art, and Painters Care
> Make even Storms look Beautiful and Fair.
>   But whilst I praise, I must accuse thee too,
> When thou hadst done so much, no more to do.
> When to the brink of Boyne thy Hero came
> There to break off the chase of him and Fame.
> Where had bin Albion now, had he thus stood,
> But floating in another Sea of Blood?
> To leave him when the Floods crept soft along,
> And Silver Boyne listened to hear thy Song,
> To hear the Naiads Sing what thou dost write,
> As when she rose to see thy Hero fight:
> See him all o're with springing Laurels spread,
> And all his Angel Guard around his Head.
> This wields his Flaming Sword, – the Rebels fly,
> And that the fatal Ball puts gently by,

Which Brittains MIGHTY GENIUS shook to see,
And trembled at the Danger more than He.
This! sweetest Bard, hadst thou proceeding Sung,
How had the Woods, how had the Valley's rung,
And Pollio's learned Muse, who sits above,
The Shepherds Admiration, and their Love,
Had deign'd thee Smiles, as all the World esteem,
Which dares not sure dislike what pleases him.

(ll. 1–37, V: 1)

The decision to print a poem about the poem stands as a curious act of appropriation. The fame of the 'Famous Pastoral' is purely second-hand, and one might suspect a hint of irony in the compliment. An earlier statement by the *Mercury* on literary ladies, while not dismissive, had not been wholly enthusiastic either; praise of Katherine Phillips ('Orinda') and Anna Maria van Schurman is offset by a reference to the Duchess of Newcastle, a 'Lady gone mad with Learning' (I: 18; 23 May 1691). But what is arguably most significant about the answer-poem is not the way it substitutes for the female-authored text, but its own status as a record of reader-response. It concerns the seduction of the male reader by the female poet, and therefore the slippage from words to woman. Beginning with an enraptured 'Yes' and suggestive hiatus, the first four lines identify the feminine excess that gives the object-poem its extraordinary affective power. The source lies in the 'Dear unknown', from whom the nectar flows that sweetens the 'harsh ... haggard and unkind' subject of war. What is at issue is the process of refinement at two levels: the feminine extraction of aesthetic and moral beauty from the masculine business of political violence; and the male reader's tutelage in this art, expressed and demonstrated in the subjective and pseudo-spontaneous form of an ode. The second part of the answer-poem appears, however, to withdraw from the posture of submission. The poetess is accused of leaving William stranded and impotent on the wrong side of the Boyne. But this is merely a pretext for continuing the game of literary innuendo. The male reader asks the female poet for more. She must cross the river and bring the story to a climax. The appeal for more was to be formalized in the periodical soon after, with the announcement of a monthly 'Poetical Mercury', devoted to questions and answers in verse. Over the next five years, the *Mercury* would publish more poetry than any other periodical of the century. In all, there were a total of 43 numbers containing versified questions or occasional poems.[28]

The author of the 'Famous Pastoral' was Elizabeth Singer, the seventeen-year-old daughter of a Presbyterian gentleman, who had been persecuted for his religion under Charles II and met his future wife when she charitably visited the inmates of the local prison.[29] Many years later, Elizabeth

Singer would marry and become Elizabeth Rowe, the name by which she is known to posterity. She would construct a new literary persona as a paragon of piety and self-denial, based on the strict suppression of her youthful exploits in the pages of the *Athenian Mercury*. Here I will be re-examining her early career as an exponent of 'Platonick Love' and idol of the coffee-house. Singer's contributions to the periodical were an important intervention in coffee-house culture. For Dunton and his associates her writings became the sexual correlative of their reformist agenda, powerfully libidinizing the drive to self-improvement and identification with 'the new'. Singer was the equivalent on a higher literary plane of the barmaid: an object of idealizing cathexis. But in no sense was she the mere creation of the Athenians, passively available for their constructions. She seems to have shared their aims, or at least was willing, knowingly and actively, to collude in them. King William at the Boyne, saviour of the nation; her choice of topic for an opening gambit was exact. She presents herself before the public as a 'coffee-house politician'.[30] She offers no apology as a woman taking a political stance, and the Athenians applaud her patriotism. Later, she would play the political card again. A poem on the biblical general Habbakkuk is unmasked at its conclusion as an allegory of William's triumph over France and the Jacobites ('A Pindarick Poem on Habbakuk', XI: 30; 21 October 1693); similarly a version of Ovid's story of 'The Fall of Phaeton'. The Athenians praise her in verse for her patriotic virtue and brilliant eloquence, equal to that of 'Orinda'. She feeds them a poetical question, employing her 'Loyal Quill' to ask the Athenians what foes could possibly threaten 'our unequall'd Hero'? They respond with gusto, offering another biblical allegory in the style of Milton (XIV: 3; 29 May 1694). There are no surprises in this political dialogue, apart from the fact of Singer's artful involvement in it. Political phrase-making is an integral part of the courtship.

In fact, it was not until October 1693, two years after the Pastoral, that the anonymous author came forward again and the affair proceeded in earnest. Together with the pindaric ode on Habakkuk, she sent 'The Rapture', a poem of religious yearning, and a poetical question asking advice on a matter of lovers' etiquette, a problem in the 'gallant' tradition tricked out in romance dress (a suitor is referred to as 'Orestes'). The three items effectively demonstrate the range of her writing in the 1690s: a mixture of high patriotism, sensuous piety and light coquetry. It was a combination that was both potent and unstable. It would play havoc with Dunton's personal feelings. Her contributions began to be printed with increasing frequency, in December 1693 (XII: 14), May 1694 (XIV: 3) and June 1694 (XIV: 5). By this stage she is toying with the idea of her growing celebrity, asking the Athenians, 'What if the Muses loudly sang my Fame, / The barren Mountains ecchoing with my Name?' before eliciting from them the appropriate response, that virtue is the only guarantee of immortality (XIV: 3). Singer, still anonymous, was now referred to in the *Mercury* as the 'Pindarick Lady'. The epithet marked her out as the successor of Cowley, who had published his groundbreaking odes in the style of Pindar in 1656 and begun a trend. It also celebrated her superior wit since its free metrical form required originality, and as Cowley had explained in his Preface, in this kind of poetry '[t]he Figures are unusual and bold even to Temeritie'.[31]

Dunton was in thrall. He dedicated the fifteenth volume (4 September–15 December 1694) of the *Mercury* to her.

> Madam,
> You have so often Oblig'd our Mercury, and the World, by your Ingenious Questions, that we think our selves bound both in Gratitude and Interest, to Dedicate this Volume to your self, though we fancy we neither are, nor ever shall be known to one another: A Testimony of our Respect, which wou'd cost us dear, shou'd we show the same to every one of our Querists. We won't disgrace your Words so much as to plead we offer you your Own, we can only say, we wish there were more such as yours here; most of which have such a peculiar delicacy of Stile, and Majesty of Verse, as will sufficiently distinguish 'em from all others, and the Gold will shine so much the Brighter for having so many heaps of Dross lying all about it.

The periodical was changing, partly as a result of the impact of Singer, partly because the Athenians themselves were becoming bored with the formula. Dunton was willing to print Singer's poems, even when they were not couched in question form. The casuistical structure was less absolute than formerly. At the same time, Singer was being elevated to the unprecedented position of star correspondent at the risk of insulting other contributors (presumably responsible for the 'heaps of Dross', in Dunton's unguarded words). It was a gradual metamorphosis in the direction of a journal in which poetry and sexual politics would take pride of place.

Meanwhile, Dunton was meditating new spin-offs. He had already attempted to set up an adjunct journal, the *Ladies Mercury* in 1693, but this lasted only a few issues, perhaps because it departed from the established coffee-house market.[32] He had also published a polemically feminist *Ladies Dictionary. Being a General Entertainer for the Fair-Sex. A Work never Attempted before in English* (1694).[33] In October 1694, with a view to compiling an edition of Singer's poetry, he placed an advertisement in the *Mercury* addressed to her: 'That Ingenious Pindarick Lady who formerly sent many Poetical Questions to the Athenian Society, is desir'd now to send all those Poems she formerly mention'd.– Directed to our Bookseller at the Raven in Jewen Street' (XV.10). The next month he placed another advertisement inviting the 'Pindarick Lady', among others, to contribute with replies to a project referred to as the *Female War* (XV: 20), which was to take the form of letters by a contingent of men attacking every possible point of weakness in female manners, together with equally outspoken defences from women.

Singer does not seem to have entered the war, but by January 1695 she had responded to Dunton's proposal to publish a book of her poems, without yet giving him any information about herself. He placed another call in the *Mercury*, announcing receipt of the Pindarick Lady's poems and asking for a return address (XVI: 7; 8 January 1695). What happened from this point is reconstructed with the help of various autobiographical statements by Dunton. He entered into a correspondence with Singer, discovered by her father only in August 1695.[34] He was nevertheless at pains to demonstrate its innocence, and on all possible occasions published a playful message from Singer to Elizabeth Dunton, enclosed with a letter to himself, sent in the knowledge that the wife would open it. Two years later, in September 1697, after the death of his wife, he travelled to Singer's home in Somerset and proposed marriage.[35] He was rejected, but this was not what rankled; or at least, not according to his account. Instead, he was haunted by his failure to maintain the ideal of platonic love and, in the fashion of the Ancient Mariner, felt the need to remind the reading public of this failure from time to time. By attempting to possess Elizabeth Singer's body it was as if he had somehow corrupted the feminizing mission she emblematized, although the ambivalence had been there from the start. He called this betrayal 'the Double Courtship'.[36]

This, however, lay in the future. In the summer and early autumn of 1695, a flood of Singer's poems were printed in the *Mercury*, as Dunton made use of the material which would later form the book. The number for 18 June is entirely devoted to her work. Other pieces appeared on 19 and 27 July, 11 August, 7 and 28 September. It was in the midst of this orgy of poetry that Dunton published his preface to the eighteenth volume of the *Mercury*, predicting it would be discontinued after the twentieth volume (which it was). He expresses pride:

> we shall have run a fair stage, and perhaps no publick paper, except the Gazette, can pretend to such a standing, for the design was lucky enough, and affected every one, the whole World being nothing else but one GYGANTIC ATHENIAN ...

but also bitterness:

> had our own abilities been suitable to the task, or the genius of the Age been a little wiser, we might instead of handling so many trifling and impertinent Love Questions, have done something that might have been really serviceable to the Age, but Sense and Reason would not sell, our Bookseller found more Fools than Wise, and Interest fixt the Calculation the wrong way ...

Several more poems by Singer were printed in December and January 1696.[37] After which, silence until more than a year later (XX: 9; 10 June 1697), when advertisements appear in the same issue for two long-cherished projects, 'Poems Written on several very Remarkable occasions, Written by Philomela, the most Ingenious Pindarick Lady. Price bound 2 s. Sold by the Booksellers of London and Westminster' and the *Female War*. Four days later, the *Athenian Mercury* ceased to exist, as if killed off in giving birth to these volumes. The *Mercury* had been the most successful journalistic extension of the coffee-house milieu to date, government newsletters aside. Its economic base was there, and the male clientele was presumed by the Athenians to be their core readership. Yet throughout its history the *Mercury* had addressed itself to female readers, encouraged female writers and projected the remodelling of male behaviour by challenging misogyny and celebrating the refining nature of contact with women. Singer's *Poems on Several Occasions* and the *Female War* should be seen as the culmination of the Athenian project.

The full title of the latter is *The Challenge, Sent by a Young Lady to Sir Thomas – &c. Or, The Female War. Wherein the Present Dresses and Humours, &c. Of the Fair Sex Are Vigorously attackt by MEN OF QUALITY, and as Bravely defended by Madam GODFREY, and other Ingenious Ladies, who set their Name to every Challenge*, with the rubric, *The Whole Encounter consists of Six Hundred LETTERS, Pro and Con, on all the Disputable Points relating to Women. AND IS The First Battle of this Nature that was ever fought in England* (London, 1697). In this volume, one of the most interesting and pertinent exchanges is on the subject of the 'she-wit'. The opening salvo by 'Sir Thomas' was likely to have been written by Dunton himself, given the appearance of his favourite reference to Boccalin. The letter begins by comparing she-wits to she-tigers or venomous reptiles. Their possession of wit reverses the proper subordination of women to men, authoritatively established by John Milton. But the main thrust is a scurrilous attack on literary women. Boccalin's story is retold of how 'virtuous Lady-Poetesses' were admitted to Parnassus by Apollo and applauded, until their misdemeanours were discovered and they were expelled by the god: 'because he had found by experience, that Womens best Poetry was in their Distaff and their Needle, and that their Exercises in common with the Virtuosi, was like Dogs Play, which generally ends in getting upon one another's Backs' (211). The reply, 'Being a Defence of Wit and Poetry in Women', is by 'Madam Godfrey', also quite likely to be Dunton, since the comparison of male with female behaviour was his favoured method of disputing misogyny. This letter is a clearly stated version of the argument, imported from the French salons, that contact with female wit had a refining action on men:

> Those who are refin'd and polish'd by their Conversation with the Fairer Sex, whose company you must own, exceeds the best Academys in these

matters, since for those of ye who run wild, and only herd with one another, how should you but retain your Native Fierceness, and yet certainly you might be tamed too, with our good management, unless you are worse than Elephants. (214–15)

'Madam Godfrey' claims that 'Sir Thomas' is threatened by the knowledge that women will excel in literature, if permitted; but softens the blow by assuring him that women attempt only the lower forms of poetry – love lyrics, farce and comedy, leaving the 'High and Mighty Epic' to men (217). Her sarcastic response to the accusation of immorality is to ask whether wit has had no such effect on men's morals.

Poems on Several Occasions, signed 'Philomela', is introduced polemically, as if it provided further ammunition for the women's side in the sex war. The preface, which is signed by Elizabeth Johnson, attacks the refusal to allow women sense, wit or learning. To do this is to reveal 'an open design to render us meer Slaves', a violation of 'the Liberties of Freeborn English Women': 'This makes the Meekest Worm amongst us all, ready to turn agen when we are thus trampled on; But alas! What can we do to Right ourselves? stingless and harmless as we are, we can only Kiss the Foot that hurts us'.[38] Philomela rises up as a champion of 'our Defenceless Sex', as Sappho, Aphra Behn, Anna Maria van Schurman and 'Orinda' had done, to silence the critics with her transcendent wit (vii). The terms for male reception are set by a dedicatory poem, in which the poet (possibly Dunton) at first expresses disbelief that the contents are the work of a woman, and compares them favourably to the productions of Edmund Waller, Abraham Cowley and John Dryden. But his masculine 'pride' is disabused by the discovery in the poems of a softness of sentiment beyond the powers of man, and a metamorphosis of the reader takes place.

> In vain, alas in vain our Fate we shun;
> We Read, and Sigh, and Love, and are undone:
> Circaean charms, and Female Arts we prove,
> Transported all to some New World of Love.
> Now our Ears tingle, and each thick-drawn-Breath
> Comes hard, as in the Agonys of Death:
> Back to the panting Heart the purple Rivers flow,
> Our Swimming Eyes, to see, our Feet unlearn to goe,
> In every trembling Nerve a short-liv'd Palsy reigns
> Strange Feavers boyl our Blood, yet shudder thro' our Veins,
> Tyrannous Charmer hold! our sence, our Souls restore!
> Monopolize not Love, nor make the World adore!
>
> (ll. 14–25, pp. xiii–xiv)

The theme of transformation, bodily and mental, so central to the emergence of coffee-house culture, reaches its apotheosis in this response to the coffee-house poetess, with its elaborate simulation of orgasm (or conceivably a caffeine overdose?). The open eroticism notwithstanding, the reader assures Philomela that her virtue will purify all earthly desires. He asks her to 'Prepare then for that Fame which you despise!' The eulogy ends with a picture of her as the literary guardian of King William.

It is possible that Singer herself was not involved in the preparation of the volume. A note from the printer explains that the author lives at too great a distance to correct the proofs and should not be held responsible for errors. Either author or editor arranged the collection to dramatize the tension between physical and spiritual desire as a dialogue. The first poem, 'Platonick Love', takes its cue from the first line of Cowley's sceptical 'Answer to the Platonicks', 'So angels love; so let them love for me'. Singer adapts the line to 'So Angels Love, and all the rest is dross', proposing a rival metaphysical union of minds, 'free and unconfin'd'. This is then countered by the next poem in the volume, 'Humane Love: By a Country Gentleman', which restores Cowley's words and revives the anti-platonic cause. The rest revolve around the dichotomy. The poems are of various kinds: short eulogies addressed to actual men and women; religious lyrics which wrestle with the desire to leave the world; paraphrases of sections of the Bible; poems in dialogue with the Athenians, which can be political, religious or gallant; pastoral poems dealing with the love woes of classically named youths and maidens; a small number of facetious love poems in the first person. The variety of modes, noted in the Preface, gives rise to a bewildering variety of authorial personae. Poems of a religious or a light-hearted nature are not grouped separately, but intermingled, keeping the reader in a constant fluctuation of mundane and pious sentiment. In a number of cases the confusion invades a single poem.

This is pre-eminently so of the 'Paraphrase on the Canticles', the most original and engaging poetic work she produced at this time. The Canticles, also known as the Song of Songs or the Song of Solomon, is a poetical book of the Old Testament in dialogue form, involving rhapsodic addresses between two lovers, with commentary by the 'daughters of Jerusalem'. The problematic sensuality of the narrative and imagery had been subdued by Christian commentators, who construed the relationship of the woman and her beloved as a figure of salvation. As already mentioned, the allegorical reading of the Song of Songs provided a model for the purification of Plato's *Symposium*. In her paraphrase, however, Singer uses the licence of the Bible text to assume the voice of a woman overcome by desire and careless of custom or reputation. She boldly heightens the disparity between the sensuous particularity of the language and its conventional allegorical function. To get the measure of her achievement, it is necessary only to contrast a passage from chapter 3 of the Song of Songs, in John Lloyd's wooden and orthodox paraphrase of 1682, which begins with a lament by the woman:

> 'Twas dark, the Stars withdrew their light ...
> When over-charg'd with Passions on my Bed,
>   And fraight with fear,
> I sought my Love, but he was fled.[39]

In Lloyd's version the lovers are categorically named as 'Christ' and 'Church'. In Singer's more ambiguous rendering they are 'Bridegroom' and 'Bride', leaving room for a profane reading:

> Twas in the deadness of a Gloomy Night,
> My Love, more pleasant than the wisht for Light,
> O're all my Bed I vainly sought; for there
> My Arms could Grasp no more than empty air:
> Griev'd with my Loss, through all the streets I rove,
> And every Ear with soft Complaints I move:
> Then to the Watch, Impatient, thus I Cry;
> When loe, a Glimpse of my approaching Lord,
> A Heaven of Joy did to my Soul afford:
> So the dark Souls confin'd to endless Night
> Would smile, and wellcome-in a beam of Light.
> I Claspt him, just as meeting Lovers wou'd,
> That had the stings of Absence understood
> I held him fast, and Centring in his Breast,
> My ravish'd Soul found her desired Rest.

> (ll. 1–14, p. 42)

Singer, in order to amplify the emotional experience of reunion, employs an almost blasphemous analogy with 'the dark Souls confin'd to endless Night' – hyperbole more in keeping with the language of gallantry. Then, in a second analogy calculated to destabilize the allegory, she points up the intensity of the embrace, equivalent to that of physical lovers who 'had the stings of Absence understood'. Singer not only appeals to the worldly experience of her readers, but also implies that she has felt and expressed such passion herself, so inviting speculation. In the Athenian context, furthermore, this specific scene, and another from chapter 5 in which the Bride runs into the street in search of her lover and again meets the night-watch (who on this occasion taunt and humiliate her), could not fail to evoke that other favourite cause of Dunton's, the investigation of fallen women or 'Night walkers'.

The legacy of the *Athenian Mercury*

What was the impact of the feminizing project of the *Athenian Mercury* and its adjunct publications? Much more work needs to be done to gather evidence of its reception. The early enthusiasm of Sir William Temple and his young relation Jonathan Swift is on record, and *The History of the Athenian Society* shows that a roster of the literati were prepared to put their names to poetic eulogies in 1692.[40] But what of the later years of the periodical, when platonic love and Elizabeth Singer came to the fore? It seems likely that it successfully generated a favourable climate for debate, both in and out of the coffee-houses, on the status of women and relations between the sexes. A number of significant feminist treatises and poems were published in the later 1690s and early 1700s.[41] But, most importantly, it established the case for the transformative influence of women on men, and of literary women on the newly emerging reading public. In 1696, *An Essay in Defence of the Female Sex* was published anonymously.[42] But the defence is in reality an attack on a variety of unreconstructed male characters: 'A Pedant, A Squire, A Beau, A Vertuous, A Poetaster, A City-Critick, &c.'. The frontispiece is an image of the Beau, an effeminate, degenerate man. A dedicatory poem, signed James Drake, refers to the beauty and wit of Orinda and Astraea (Aphra Behn) to which men must learn to 'proudly submit', and addresses the female author of the essay:

> Your Sex you with such Charming Grace defend,
> While that you vindicate, you Our Sex amend:
> We in your Glass may see each foul defect,
> And may not only see, but may correct.

The author then plainly states her central concern: 'The Question I shall at present handle is, whether the time an ingenious Gentleman spends in the Company of Women, may justly be said to be misemploy'd or not?' (6). After reviewing the male types, including the time-wasting, ineffectual 'Coffee-House Politician', she concludes with a summary of the effect of the polite qualities women elicit from men, civility and gallantry: 'Without 'em Honesty, Courage, or Wit, are like Rough Diamonds, or Gold in the Ore, they have their intrinsick Value, and Worth, before, but they are doubtful and obscure, till they are polish'd, refin'd, and receive Lustre, and Esteem from these' (135–6).

Mary Astell, often described as the first English feminist, had a link with the periodical. In the early 1690s she embarked on a correspondence with the Cambridge Platonist John Norris. His spiritualized version of Cartesian philosophy was to have a strong impact on her treatise, *A Serious Proposal to the Ladies, For the Advancement of their True and Greatest Interest* (1694), which most famously proposed a scheme for an all-female college, or

'Protestant Nunnery'. But the influence was not all one way. He persuaded her to allow him to publish their correspondence, which appeared in 1695 as *Letters Concerning the Love of God* 'Between the Author of the Proposal to the Ladies and Mr. John Norris'. Norris took some pride in his way with intellectual women, having already corresponded with Lady Damaris Masham, daughter of another Cambridge philosopher, Ralph Cudworth. In 1697 Daniel Defoe, launching his career as a writer with *An Essay on Projects*, declared himself a fervent supporter of women ('a woman of sense and manners is the finest and most delicate part of God's creation') and female education, making reference to Astell's *Proposal*.[43] Dunton, needless to say, was equally keen to recruit Astell to the Athenian cause. Her educational scheme was mentioned favourably in the periodical and the *Female War*. In his *Life and Errors* he refers to her as 'the divine Astell'; in the *Athenian Spy* she appears among the list of 'young Ladies that are Uningag'd', described as 'the young Gentlewoman that corresponded with Mr. Norris'.[44] In Charles Johnson's comedy *The Generous Husband: or, The Coffee House Politician* (1713) the abortive courtship of Florida, 'a Philosophress', by a tedious, news-addicted coffee-house man, may be a distant echo of this association.

By this time, the influence of the *Athenian Mercury* had been most powerfully demonstrated in the form of the *Tatler* and the *Spectator*, though it was never acknowledged by Steele or Addison and has rarely been explored by commentators. In marketing terms, the *Mercury* had shown the way a periodical based in the coffee-house could succeed by reaching out to female readers and correspondents, and making them central to its mission. Both the *Tatler* and the *Spectator* followed this formula religiously. The first number of the *Tatler* makes its appeal to two specified groups: 'politick Persons who are so publick-spirited as to neglect their own Affairs to look into Transactions of State' and need to be instructed 'what to think'; and 'the Fair Sex, in Honour of whom I have invented the Title of this Paper'.[45] The coffee-house politician and the tattling woman are even-handedly caricatured. Although the fiction is maintained that most of the essays are written by Steele's authorial persona Isaac Bickerstaff from within a number of named coffee-houses, the express intention is to breach their walls. In No. 10 (3 May 1709), Jenny Distaff assumes the editorial role and announces 'my Brother Isaac designs, for the Use of our Sex, to give the exact Characters of all the chief Politicians who frequent the Coffee-houses from St. James's to the Change [the Royal Exchange]' (I. 89). By this means women will be enabled to participate actively, if at a distance, in coffee-house deliberations. Bickerstaff had already invited 'any Gentleman or Lady' to send him 'by the Penny-Post, the Grief or Joy of their Soul' (No. 7, I. 63, 26 April 1709). Although essays had largely replaced the dialogic form of the *Mercury*, 200 letters were printed in the *Tatler* (some genuine, some written by Steele or other regular contributors). In No. 10 of the *Spectator*

(12 March 1711), Addison in the guise of 'Mr. Spectator' goes a step further than Bickerstaff in offering, as Dunton had done, materials for improving his readers, indiscriminately located in public or in the home. He will bring 'Philosophy out of Closets and Libraries, Schools and Colleges, to dwell in Clubs and Assemblies, at Tea-Tables, and in Coffee-Houses'. Among his target audience are 'the female World', who will be addressed not 'as they are Women' but 'as they are reasonable Creatures'.

Both Isaac Bickerstaff and Mr. Spectator follow the Athenians in advertising themselves as exemplary feminized males and exponents of feminization, though with a touch of irony foreign to Dunton's publications. In *Tatler* No. 10, Jenny, sitting in Bickerstaff's closet, examines a manuscript he is writing, 'A Treatise concerning *The Empire of Beauty*, and the Effects it has had in all Nations of the World, upon the publick and private Actions of Men'. He is himself, Jenny remarks,

> of a Complexion truly amorous; all his Thoughts and Actions carry in them a Tincture of that obliging Inclination; and this Turn has opened his Eyes to see, we are not the inconsiderable Creatures which unlucky Pretenders to our Favour would insinuate. He observes, that no Man begins to make any tolerable Figure till he sets out with the Hopes of pleasing some one of us. (I, 88)

In the *Spectator*, it is not until No. 130 (30 July 1711, by Addison) that a gypsy fortune-teller discovers by examining his palm that the remote Mr. Spectator is in fact a 'Woman's Man'. In No. 156 (29 August 1711) Steele defines the 'Woman's Man' as one who pleases women by imitating them; adopting informal dress, soft manners and insinuating conversation. The tone is lightly satirical, but shortly afterwards a letter is printed from a female reader, recommending that 'Men of Sense' should follow their example (No. 158, 31 August 1711, by Steele). For 'women are made for the Cements of Society, and came into the World to create Relations among Mankind' (II. 119); by making their conversation ornamental in the hope of pleasing women, men will learn how to spread their wisdom more effectively to the world at large. The observation stands reflexively as the motive for the obsessive interpellation of women by the *Spectator*, so striking to contemporaries. Jonathan Swift, a former associate of Steele and Addison, remarked (to his female correspondent), 'I will not meddle with the Spectator, let him fair-sex it to the world's end'.[46]

But the knowing, double-edged nature of Steele and Addison's gallantry, already noted, requires further investigation.[47] Rae Blanchard has placed Steele at the conservative end of the spectrum of opinion on women, after a thorough survey of all his publications alongside feminist polemics and conduct books of the time.[48] Kathryn Shevelow has argued that the *Tatler* and *Spectator* were engaged in promulgating 'an increasingly narrow and restrictive model of femininity' as part of their reformist agenda. She points to the uneasy encomium to the 'fair sex' in *Spectator* No. 4 (Monday, 5 March 1711) (by Steele), which (to coin a phrase) lifts and separates, while instructing women in male-centred 'duties':

> As [the Fair Sex] compose half the World, and by the just Complaisance and Gallantry of our Nation the more powerful Part of our People, I shall dedicate a considerable Share of these my Speculations to their Service, and shall lead the Young through all the becoming Duties of Virginity, Marriage, and Widowhood. When it is a Woman's Day, in my Works, I shall endeavour at a Stile and Air suitable to their Understanding. When I say this, I must be understood to mean, that I shall not lower but exalt the Subjects I treat upon. Discourse for their Entertainment, is not to be debased but refined...In a Word, I shall take it for the greatest Glory of my Work, if among reasonable Women this Paper may furnish Tea-Table Talk. (I, 21)

For Shevelow, the statement exemplifies

> a specialized discourse for women readers which focused on certain topics – those concerning 'Virginity, Marriage, and Widowhood,' women's places within the patriarchal order -expressed in a certain, 'exalted' manner, and suitable to a certain context – the 'Tea-Table,' formerly a private site of potentially malicious gossip, but now an area incorporated into the reformist periodical's sphere of influence.[49]

Where Dunton in the *Athenian Mercury* was eulogistic, Steele in the *Tatler* and the *Spectator* is highly prescriptive with regard to women. It is indicative that he deliberately sets out to correct one particular feature of female idolatry associated with Dunton. In *Tatler* Nos. 32 and 63 he discusses Madonella, a 'Platonne' and head of an 'Order of Platonick Ladies' (shades of Mary Astell), who ultimately falls prey to the artful intellectualism of a rake. In *Spectator* No. 400 (Monday, 9 June 1712), he explicitly warns women against the pleasures of 'Platonick Love', having seen 'the Waste of a Platonist lately swell to a Roundness which is inconsistent with that Philosophy' (III, 500). But it would be a mistake to see the legislation of female manners as an end in itself. This is a vital point. The topic of women is almost invariably put forward in the framework of their necessary influence on men and on society generally. Because this influence is acknowledged and celebrated as a sign of male politeness, it is vital to stabilize the exemplary woman. Steele (who had taken his first steps as a writer in the 1690s), witnessed the boom and bust scenario of Dunton's feminizing project, in which high idealism plummeted into illicit sensuality: the 'double courtship' of the Pindarick Lady was the most spectacular instance. Taking a more conservative line, Steele – with the occasional help of Addison and others – attempted to define a new kind of woman, whose highly public brand of domestic virtue would be proof against every test. But in 1713, when the *Spectator* drew to a close, the project was left incomplete and apparently defeated. There were no immediate heirs, and Dunton's own career was fast degenerating into farce.

The fate of John Dunton, pioneer feminizer

During the years in which the *Tatler* and the *Spectator* appeared, the career of Elizabeth Singer, the first coffee-house Idol, was on hold. In 1710 she married Thomas Rowe, a classics scholar and translator of Plutarch. Only after she was widowed in 1715 did she begin to publish again, with a new emphasis on piety (she had become a close friend of the religious poet Isaac Watts).[50] In the aftermath of the *Athenian Mercury*, Dunton had launched a number of 'projects' in a series of increasingly deranged permutations on its original themes, some of them putting Singer's aspirations to respectability at risk. *The Athenian Spy* (two editions, in 1704 and 1709) revived the project of platonic love and the memory of the 'Pindarick Lady'. It purported to consist of letters from 'ingenious ladies' to the Athenian Society providing instances of platonic love, together with a collection of 'love-secrets' for the benefit of lonely hearts. The Preface announces: 'the Athenian Society it self (with all its Gravity) has bin LOVE-SICK ... Philaret [Dunton] was Hanging himself for the Pindarick Lady. And not a Member of Athens but LOVES an Angel in Petticoats'.[51]

Around the time of Singer's marriage, Dunton appears to have been provoked into writing an extraordinary exposé in *Athenianism: or, The New Projects of Mr. John Dunton* (London, 1710). The first section is devoted to his erstwhile protégée: 'Project 1. *The Double Courtship, (according to the Mode of Plato, and Opportunity)* or Dunton's Character of Madam Singer, write when he was a Widower; in which is exemplify'd the Primitive Christian, or a nice Pattern of holy Living'. His writing revolves obsessively around ideas of platonic love and 'the new'.

> I thought no Project cou'd be so proper to lead the Way (to the Six Hundred that are to follow) as to attempt the Character of Madam Singer, (deservedly call'd, The Pindarick Lady) as 'tis only here (her Brain and Tongue is such a flowing Mint of Wit and Verse) we shall ever find Athenianism (or something New); and I the rather chuse to make Madam Singer's Character the Leading Project to all the rest, as I owe my chief Reason of Writing and Printing Six Hundred Projects to that Platonick Love (or innocent Pleasure) I found in corresponding with her for Six Years. (1–2)

He goes on to claim a correspondence amounting to 500 letters between the two of them (all his calculations involve multiples of a hundred at this time). He declares that if she protests about this published 'character' of her, he will publish the letters in spite of knowing her fear of publicity (23–6). But his threat is soon overtaken by a eulogy written in opposition to the 'Women-Haters'. He evokes a great tradition among literary men of platonic friendship with women (also described in the *Athenian Spy*), among them John Norris (who corresponded with Mary Astell) and all of the Athenians.

Through the 1710s Dunton's publishing output began to degenerate into bitter and incoherent pamphlets accusing the Whig government of ingratitude and neglect, one of which included a 'dying Farewell to Madam Elizabeth Singer' (he refused to use her married name).[52] He was now the thoroughly disreputable 'broken Bookseller' referred to in Pope's *Dunciad*. In advertisements included in publications of 1716 and 1717, Dunton was still announcing a revival of Athenianism.[53] It may have been this that provoked a threatening letter from one of the protectors of the widowed Rowe, worth quoting in full as a thorough obituary for his feminization enterprise.

To: Mr. John Dunton, to be left with Mr. William Lutwich, in West Harding Street, near Fetter Lane.

Sir   November 5, 1718
    I am glad to find you are not guilty of offering any such papers as I accused you of to sale. You accuse Mr. W—s unjustly; for, I protest to you, he is entirely ignorant of this affair. What I wrote is wholly a secret to yourself, and only for your own advantage.
    I have nothing in the world to say to you, Sir, neither in public nor private, provided Mrs. *Rowe*, nor Mrs. *Singer*, nor *Philomela*, is named any more by you; which I would ask as a piece of justice and honesty, or mere civility; for, though I am a man of the world, I am no bully nor rake; and, if you are not yourself the aggressor, I shall never treat you with the least ill-manners.
    The rest I have to say to you is merely to advise you, for your own profit, and with the same sincerity I would a friend. Such titles as 'Athenian Phoenix,' and 'Pindarick Lady,' are so senseless and impertinent, that it would spoil the credit of any Author that should use them: and for Plato's Notions, and Platonic Love, those terms have been so justly exposed by the Spectator, and are so very ridiculous and unfashionable, that nothing of those chimeras and whimsies would sell in the genteel part of the world. Pray look on the title of your Platonic Wedding again, and consider whether any person of common sense, or that knows the polite part of the world, would buy it; and it is they are

the greatest readers. Frolic and merry conceits are despised in this nice age.

The mentioning the 'Athenian Oracles' will do your Works an injury; for you know they are condemned to long oblivion. What I speak is not in the least to affront you; but if you have Essays or Letters that are valuable, call them Essays and Letters in short and plain language; and if you have any thing writ by men of sense, and on subjects of consequence, it may sell without your name to it; but pray leave out that, and all your female trumpery; for I am in too public a rank not to know the taste of the age; and I can assure you the mentioning of female correspondents and she-wits would ruin the sale of the best Authors we have.

This is no affront to Mrs. Rowe; for I know she has too just and modish a taste not to despise those characters.

What ill-natured reflections my value for Mrs. Rowe made me utter in my last, I have forgot; but really what I speak now will be for your advantage to regard; for the Marriage of Souls, and Treatises of Owls, and little correspondences and amusements in low-life with she-wits, will make a ridiculous figure, or not be at all regarded in this insolent busy world. This is only private advice: I have not the least design to wound your reputation. This is the last time you will hear of me. Never name Rowe in your Works, and there is peace between us for ever. Find other titles for your Wits, and I am satisfied; and really subjects of more gravity would suit your pen.

I have too much humanity to insult any man in distress, and did not mention your private circumstances with such a design. I would a thousand times sooner relieve a man in those perplexities than contribute to his distress; and wish with all my soul your expectations from the Public may not fail you.

You will hear no more from me, and I desire you would write no more to me without I give you new directions. There is no writing to a man that prints every thing.

Your Friend in earnest, J.W.[54]

Dunton, arbiter of the new, is declared obsolete. The success of the *Spectator* may have allowed him to cherish ideas of the continued relevance of the Athenian project and the feminizing coffee-house culture associated with it. But in the aftermath, and with the return of a Whig government in 1715, there was a changed literary climate. Pope and Swift, alienated from power, produced their bitterly satirical masterpieces in which misogyny features significantly. Defoe, formerly a journalist and pamphleteer like Dunton, pursued experiments in popular narrative incorporating the *Mercury*'s emphasis on everyday experience, but turning his back on the elevated rhetoric attached to its reformist aspirations. Nowhere in the 1720s or 1730s do we find the idealized and transformative image of the literary lady. The 'Marriage of Souls' and 'little correspondences and amusements in low-life with she-wits' are indeed a thing of the past. These were wilderness years for the woman writer who wrote for the public. Eliza Haywood and other producers of amatory fiction survived by catering to misogynist assumptions of female sexual weakness.[55] They were tough enough to withstand the vicious infighting which characterized the publishing world of the *Dunciad*. It is symptomatic that a serious scholar like Elizabeth Elstob, celebrated as a translator and grammarian of Anglo-Saxon in the early 1710s, should subsequently struggle to make ends meet as a country schoolteacher until rescued by the Bluestockings in the 1730s. The poet Elizabeth Thomas is another case. She achieved fame around the same time as Singer under the name of 'Corinna', but ended life ignominiously, having been pilloried as a sluttish dunce by her former friend Pope.

At the same time, a series of events was serving to stimulate civic humanist ideas: the national disaster of the South Sea Bubble in 1720 (a byword for economic corruption, in which Mary Astell and the family of Elizabeth Carter, among very many others, lost their fortunes), and the growing opposition to political corruption personified by Robert Walpole, during his long period as First Minister from 1721 to 1742. Within this order of things the inclusive public of the coffee-house became the limited public of patriotic property-holders, their identity firmly rooted in land, and civic virtue became a definitively male possession. Ironically, the founding text of the British neo-Machiavellian tradition, James Harrington's *Oceana* (1656), had first been introduced and discussed by the author in a coffee-house.[56] It would take some time before the modernizers rallied, but when they did, the cause of women would be more central than ever as a result of the civic humanist counter-definition.

The career of John Dunton, the consummate coffee-house man, illustrates in a striking fashion the rise and fall of the first wave of feminization. He died in penury and obscurity on 24 November 1732. The career of Rowe, the coffee-house Idol, is equally illuminating. She was unable to suppress completely the Pindarick Lady. When she died in 1737 Edmund Curll rushed out a second edition of *Poems on Several Occasions* to capitalize on the publicity provided by obituaries. As John Arbuthnot remarked, 'Curll is one of the new Terrors of Death'.[57] Her official *Works* were published two years later, and from this most of her earlier poems were excluded. A far tamer paraphrase of the *Canticles* was offered, as if to cancel out the first. Her brother-in-law Theophilus Rowe, in a hagiographic memoir, explained that though 'many of these poems are of the religious kind and all of them consistent with the strictest regard to the rules of virtue, yet some things in them gave her no little uneasiness in advanced life'.[58] By retreating into a stricter definition of exemplary femininity during the inhospitable years of anti-feminist backlash, she successfully preserved her reputation, like a frozen seed, to be germinated with the coming of the second wave of feminization.

Coffee-house culture was also frozen in time, its ideal image fixed forever in innumerable collected editions of the *Spectator*. The reality was a steady degeneration in the character of the coffee-house, marked by publication of the scandalous memoirs of two female coffee-house proprietors, Anne Rochford (*The Velvet Coffee-Woman*, 1728), and Moll King (*The Life and Character of Moll King*, ?1747).[59] In each of these the barkeeper features as a sexual adventurer and hostess to rakes and criminals. 'Literary' women were still prominent in determining the moral temperature of public life; for they exemplified its fallen nature. Other factors contributed to the decline. In 1729, coffee-house proprietors were discredited by a plan put forward to the government to create a monopoly for the publication of news. A proliferation of clubs shifted the topography of male sociability to private rooms in inns and taverns. Finally, while the trade in coffee remained relatively static, the interests of the British East India Company were backed by government policy which actively promoted tea, with the effect that consumption increased from 800,000 lb in 1710 to more than 1,000,000 in 1721 and 4,000,000 by 1757.[60] The tea-table, over which women commonly presided in their own homes, was poised to become the new site of influence in the land.[61]

In chapter 1, I suggested that the centrality of women in the early print culture connected with the coffee-house is difficult to assimilate to the Habermasian model. The attempt has been made by others to account for it as a secondary stage: first, the coffee-house exists as a homogeneous location for the production and consumption of print; then the 'bourgeois public sphere' comes to be reproduced as an *image* to be disseminated and consumed in other, generally domestic, spaces. In support of this assertion Jon Klancher quotes *The Bee* (1790–91) 'On the Advantages of Periodical Performances': 'A man, after the fatigues of the day are over, may thus sit down in his elbow chair, and together with his wife and family, be introduced, as it were, into a spacious coffee-house.'[62] But as we have seen, women were introduced 'as it were' into the coffee-house a century before, when the *Athenian Mercury* embraced them in its readership and its pages of correspondence. Their involvement was crucial to the redefinition of public man, the main ideological task of the coffee-house. They mediated the delicate attempt to balance private and public virtue. At the end of the reign of Queen Anne, this was a frustrated project. Polite Whiggism was on hold, awaiting conditions for a revival of the moral reform movement that would redeploy the energies of middle-class tradesmen and Dissenters.[63] Samuel Richardson succeeded to the problem of combining virtue and desire in a new-model female Idol.

3

The South Sea Bubble and the Resurgence of Misogyny: Cato, Mandeville and Defoe

The progressivist bubble bursts

Progress is commonly figured as a linear movement through time. But decline has from ancient times been represented not as a reversal, but as a recurrent event in the merry-go-round of history, a denial of even the possibility of genuine progress. William Hogarth depicted the South Sea Bubble, the great stock market crash of 1720, as a collision of lines and circles. His print, *The South Sea Scheme* (1721), is dominated by two circular emblems (figure 2). In the foreground, the naked figure of Honesty is broken on the wheel by Self-Interest. In the middle ground, crowds flock round a merry-go-round, where a prostitute, a clergyman, a female street-seller, an old crone (a brothel-keeper?) and a Jacobite with tam-o-shanter sit astride phallic horse-heads. The central pole is topped by the lubricious sign of the goat and a notice with the suggestive challenge 'Who'l Ride'. The speculative urge is damned by a combination of plain moral allegory and politico-sexual innuendo. Together the emblems signify the compulsive quality of the passion for acquisition and the repetitive nature of fate.

The circles are boxed in by receding lines. The massive neoclassical purity of the modern City of London, with its clean, straight lines and heroic scale expressive of fiscal integrity and noble prosperity, has been debased. On the right, the Monument, erected to symbolize regeneration following the Great Fire of 1666, is rededicated to the destruction wrought on the City by the 'South Sea'. Behind it can be seen the dome of Wren's cathedral. At the base of these structures swirl a crowd composed of dishevelled, bulbous and bestial forms, driven into a medley of discordant postures by vicious, selfish passions, while in the heavens a baroque gyration of clouds echoes the turbulence below.

As Ronald Paulson has noted, Hogarth's application of perspective is imperfect in this image: each building has a divergent vanishing point. But the effect fortuitously contributes to the polemic. It confirms the victory of

51

Figure 2   William Hogarth, *The South Sea Scheme* (1724).

circularity and 'the speculating principle of every man for himself', and the failure of linearity and the orderly application of general rules.[1] The lack of unified vanishing point suggests in turn the impossibility of a coherent vision of the future.

Hogarth's was just one of a flood of satirical prints generated by the South Sea Bubble; however, the rest were foreign imports, mainly from Holland, sometimes adapted by English engravers. His was 'the one original Bubble print by an English artist', the first surviving print of his career, and one which stands at the very beginning of the indigenous tradition of popular print-making.[2] The sexual politics of the Dutch prints tends to be formulaic: they almost all feature an alluring incarnation of the goddess Fortuna with her wheel. Although women may feature among the benighted crowd, the images essentially conflate the snares of financial greed and masculine desire, and subordinate them to the idea of cyclical recurrence, an irrational rise and fall.[3] The interplay of sexual categories in Hogarth's print is more complex and elusive, perhaps an indication of the continuing difficulty of pinning down the meaning of the Bubble for British observers (his satire was produced belatedly, as the initial moral outcry gave place to more precise charges of government and court corruption). He shows Fortune, not in her glory, but suspended by her hair and mutilated. The Devil has set up shop in the Guildhall (properly the abode of honest trade) and now cuts chunks of meat from the 'Golden Haunches' of Fortune to throw to the mob below. The illusion of her feminine allure is destroyed by the revelation of a more profound (and masculine) demonic agency.

Ultimately, Hogarth addresses the problems of innovation raised by the Bubble within an eschatological framework. The theology of 'last things' is one sort of answer to the dangers of mutability. The Devil dismembers Fortune with a scythe, an emblem of mortality, like the clock on the face of the building. The whipping of Honour by Villainy alludes to the flagellation of Christ. The text below emphasizes the dereliction of duty by religious leaders (prominent clerics were among the subscribers to South Sea stocks), illustrated by Catholic, Jewish and Protestant clerics playing at dice, while another minister presides over the martyrdom of Honesty. Two wolves, symbolizing evil, prowl at the foot of the Monument.

The religious iconography may literally cut across the secular satire associated with the wheel of Fortune, but it does not entirely efface other modes of explanation. The imagery is over-determined. Just as the lines of the buildings fail to meet at a single point, so a variety of theories of cause and effect are on offer. The merry-go-round eroticizes chance and disorder in the style of the French and Dutch prints, while also referring to the punishment wheel. To the left, there is a long queue of women waiting to buy raffle tickets for 'Husbands with Lottery Fortunes'; Hogarth places them in a parasitic relation to the speculative frenzy.[4] The cuckold's horns decorating the gable of the building they enter point to the inevitable connection of economic and sexual cupidity.

There are also elements of an alternative classical republican interpretation of events, which speaks of the decline of a sense of the public good into sordid egotism. This was a critique that was only just beginning to emerge at the end of 1720. It is partly expressed by the juxtaposition of classical buildings and grotesque actions, partly embodied by the statue of a Roman warrior who incongruously presides over the Devil's Shop. It is even hinted at by the wolves, which might also represent the founders of Rome, Romulus and Remus, surveying the scene of corruption, if not scavengers on the wreckage. The English Augustan age is declared over almost before it has begun. The predictions of the Roman historian Polybius have been fulfilled: the ideal republic must pass, along with monarchies, oligarchies and democracies; the various forms of polity will inevitably come and go. 'This is the Rotation of Governments and this is the Order of Nature, by which they are changed, transformed, and return to the same Point.'[5]

The South Sea Bubble has been described by J.G.A. Pocock as a 'psychic crisis'; a moment when the 'intelligibility of society' was thrown into question by a collapse of speculative hopes that affected thousands of investors and for a time threatened the stability of the political order.[6] Hogarth's kaleidoscopic assemblage of meanings is indicative of the wider struggle for coherence. In light of the facts, the faith in linear progress was unsustainable. The facts, very briefly, were these. In the spring of 1720 the transfer of part of the National Debt to the South Sea joint-stock company at highly favourable rates of interest sparked a frenzy of buying and selling stocks which intensified through the summer. By September the price of stock had dropped from £1,100 to £190, leaving ruin in its wake, with the Company Board accused of corruption and the Whig government implicated. George I was on a long visit to Hanover, and rumours circulated of an imminent Jacobite invasion.

The enterprise engaged in by the South Sea Company and the government had been a fabulous experiment, in part inspired by John Law's contemporary Mississippi Scheme, which had aimed to eliminate the French government's debts by involving private joint-stock companies. Following a similar route, the British projectors transformed long-standing creditors of the government into speculative investors, allowing them to dream of limitless profits. The contagion spread, drawing in sections of the population previously untouched by the money markets.

The Bubble has frequently been characterized by popular historians as an outbreak of collective madness. In recent academic accounts, faith in paper credit has been depicted as a form of imaginary investment; for it is 'unreal' property, a signifier without a signified, the buying and selling of it fuelled purely by desire and fantasy.[7] But the trade in stocks necessarily involved a philosophy of history, though of an exaggerated kind; the desire was specifically for betterment, a projection into an ameliorated future. Financial speculation had a foundation of sorts: belief in the possibility of limitless 'improvement'. For Pocock, this fantasy of the future is narrowly acquisitive and individualist.[8] P.G.M. Dickson, by contrast, views the South Sea Scheme as a daring initiative within the ongoing 'Financial Revolution' begun in England after 1688, to be understood in the context of a Europe-wide growth in state-sponsored speculation with the meliorist aim of restructuring public finance in wake of vast debts created by a long period of war (1689–1714). Investment in trading ventures or manufactures, Dickson claims, 'were schemes for economic betterment, which had a more solid basis in contemporary needs than has usually been acknowledged, but which were loosely controlled and unrealistically financed'.[9] Furthermore, when the price of South Sea stock rose from £128 in January 1720 to £1,000 in June, extraordinary opportunities were created for those few individuals with the steadiness of purpose to capitalize on it. Thomas Guy, for instance, sold out his £54,000 worth of holdings in small parcels from April to mid-June to net a sum of £234,000, some of which was channelled into creation of Guy's Hospital, 'the best monument the Bubble has left behind'.[10]

It was not therefore merely individual fortunes that were at stake. The response to the bursting of the Bubble is structured by this broadly progressivist impetus: 'Extreme optimism changed abruptly to extreme pessimism.'[11] Through the late summer and autumn of 1720 chance events were seized upon as signs of doom. The fall of South Sea stocks coincided with news of an outbreak of plague in the South of France. In 1721 it was succeeded by an epidemic of virulent smallpox that swept across Europe and numbered among its victims the Secretary of State James Craggs, one of the key figures in the ensuing financial scandal. Linear patterns of thought gave way to cyclical scenarios. The South Sea Bubble was interpreted religiously, as a resurgence of original sin, and through biblical analogy. Popular belief dictated that such a flagrant display of greed and materialism must be followed by divine punishment. The venerable politico-medical idiom was revived; 'Cato', in one of the first of long series of letters published in the *London Journal*, lamented the 'Epidemical Plague-Sores' on the 'Body Politick' (26 November 1720). Others employed the metaphor more optimistically: *The Weekly Journal: or British Gazeteer* of Saturday, 4 March 1721 sought to explain that 'The South Sea Affair ... is but the natural Effect of those Vices which have reign'd for so many Years; and as a sharp Distemper, by reclaiming Men from Intemporance, may prolong his Life, so it wou'd be well if this publick Calamity that lies so heavy on the Nation may prevent it's Ruin'.

In the political realm, the coincidental absence of the King spurred talk of an imminent Stuart restoration.[12] When Parliament finally reconvened in December 1720, Robert Walpole rallied the Whig government and attempted to restore public credit while postponing an inquiry into the causes of the Bubble and the responsibility of the Directors. This move provoked violent protest from a growing Opposition. Behind the demands for root-and-branch reform of the Whig–City nexus, was the Commonwealth ideal of the ancient constitution. In the rhetoric of the day this was mingled with the Machiavellian tenet that the only means of escaping the Polybian cycle lay in the mixed constitution as established by the legendary Spartan leader Lycurgus, a perfect balance of king, nobles and commoners. The call for an end to corruption and a renewal of first principles (*ridurre ai principii*) would be the theme of the journalism of the exiled Tory minister Viscount Bolingbroke on his return to England in 1725, as he whipped up opposition to Walpole. Attempts to restore an unprecedented disaster to moral meaningfulness were motivated by the troubling image of the wheel of Fortune, senselessly spinning.

Along with traditional systems of explication came intensified attacks on traditional targets of abuse: Jews, usurers (updated as stock-jobbers) and women. One notable aspect of the novelty or modernity of the South Sea affair had been the involvement of unusually large numbers of women as shareholders. Shares and bonds had not yet been legally or politically regularized: they were untaxed and freely saleable, and were a form of wealth that women could hold independently of their husbands or other male relations.[13] The Duchess of Marlborough and Madame Schulenberg, the Duchess of Kendal, the latter reputed to be the King's mistress, were large gainers from the Bubble.[14] Lady Mary Wortley Montagu was a loser, whose additional losses on behalf of a French admirer were spitefully alluded to years later by Pope in *The Dunciad* (II, 136). The irony needs to be acknowledged that for the majority of women, the novel pleasure of speculative investment would end with the unhappy experience of being fleeced and ruined.[15]

What is beyond doubt is that women featured out of all proportion to their real activity when it came to the backlash against the scheme. As Felicity Nussbaum has observed in her study of misogyny in Augustan writing: 'The myth of satires against women includes the myth that women create chaos, and the imposition of form (satire) on formlessness, provides meaning and rationality when the fear of meaninglessness and insanity arises.'[16] Hackneyed sexual slurs were an essential part of the healing 'familiarization' process enacted by the print media in graphic satires, street ballads and journalistic diatribes. The *Weekly Journal* of 28 May 1721 complained, with reference to Kendal and the Baroness von Kiemansegge, another royal favourite, 'We have been ruined by ... whores, nay, what is more vexatious, old ugly whores, such as could not find entertainment in the most hospitable hundreds of the Old Drury.'[17] A satirical epistle published the following year as *A Memorial of the Present*

State of the British Nation was equally clear that the blame for the nation's ills lay with the unwonted social and political power of women. After contrasting the 'Modesty, Reservedness, and Subjection' of the women of other countries with this 'Nation of Prostitutes', it concludes that 'A Prince who is resolv'd to live easy, and to suppress all Disturbance and Sedition, would impose a universal silence on all Females.'[18] During the crisis, what Pocock terms 'the rather prominent sexism found in Augustan social criticism' was converted into something far more virulent.[19]

At this time there was a reversion from the beginnings of a discrete version of sexual difference, emergent in the pro-feminization periodicals from the 1690s to the early 1710s, in which the attempt was made to establish women as a distinctively refined version of human nature, to be adored and imitated by men seeking improvement, towards the older one-sex model, in which women feature anatomically and temperamentally as introverted men.[20] Pope, in the *Epistle to a Lady* (1735), contends that 'Woman's at best a contradiction still':

> Heav'n, when it strives to polish all it can
> Its last best work, but forms a softer Man[.]
> (ll. 271–2)

This should not be considered as an example of witty sophistry, but rather as a literal belief that women are defective men; a belief shared by most writers of social commentary of the 1720s and 1730s. The use of the term 'polish' in Pope's aphorism is worth noting. As we have seen, it is constantly used within the discourse of feminization as an action carried out by women on men. Here it is applied to woman herself. The 'softness' of women serves not to elevate her above men, but to make her more dangerously impressionable by ruling passions. Crucially, in Pope's characterization, women must exhibit the same hedonistic appetites as men ('ev'ry Woman is at heart a Rake', l. 216). The histories of women were the ideal means of illustrating the vices of the age.

The role of the passions

In spite of the prevailing sense of shock at what John Dennis called '[t]his Conspiracy, so new and unheard of that it cannot be equall'd by any Nation in any Age',[21] it was not long before a few intrepid commentators attempted to break free of the circular paradigms and establish a new ground for progressive economic argument. These attempts involved in varying degrees the acceptance of economic innovation: the growth of commerce, the spread of credit and luxury, and the play of the passions (the latter termed by Pocock the 'psychology' of a 'trading nation').[22] In their address to a prepossessed audience, the writers engage in a delicate process of compromise and negotiation. One concession was adherence to the prevailing mood of misogyny. It is striking that even in the work of social critics as sympathetic to the condition of women as Mandeville and Defoe, who had been prominent in presenting feminist arguments in the heyday of Queen Anne, now abandoned the gendered rhetoric of improvement. Their respective cases in favour of economic modernization were made without the dubious benefit of womanhood as a figurehead. These apologists for trade and the acquisitive passions often chose to communicate their views through a female mouthpiece and women's histories, but there is no move to moralize economic progress by associating it with virtuous femininity. On the contrary, they shared with the most anti-progressivist thinkers a mode of representing women as the prime exponents of 'vicious' passions.

Cato's Letters were the first substantial response to the Bubble, a celebrated series of essays, signed 'Cato', which appeared the *London Journal* between 1720 and 1723, and were reprinted in book form many times.[23] The authors were John Trenchard, a Commonwealth man of long standing who had earned his spurs in the standing army debate of the 1690s, and Thomas Gordon, a young Scot on the make, who was later to succumb to Walpole's enticements. In the earliest letters from November 1720 there is little to distinguish Cato from the mass of voices calling for all stock-jobbers to be strung up. But already there is a rejection of the eschatological interpretation of the Bubble, an effort to create a distance from popular modes of thought. The notion that the plague in France is in any way connected with the financial crash is referred to and rejected; instead, as already mentioned, disease is limited to use as a political metaphor. It is fascinating to see the way the initial focus rapidly broadens, like ripples on the water, from stock-jobbers, to company directors, to hopes for intervention from Parliament (possibly disingenuous), followed by disillusionment on government screening of the culprits, to wide-ranging and often original reflection on the agency of the passions in the realms of politics, society, economics, as well as vigorous arguments for freedom of religion.

The Cato invoked as signatory was Cato Uticensis (95–46 BC), great-grandson of Cato the Censor, who became a republican figurehead for his opposition to Caesar. He had already featured as the eponymous hero of a famous drama by Addison (1713), making him a touchstone for English debate on politics and morality.[24] Tellingly, Addison overlooked his opposition to luxury (he called for harsher sumptuary laws to control women's dress), and sentimentalized his image with a courtship plot concerning his daughter. In more conventional representations he was admired for his unbending political principles and devotion to liberty, while his private morals were considered less admirable by some. He loaned his second wife to a friend, presumably on the Spartan model. Gordon may have had this notoriety in mind when he wrote a preface to the 1724 edition and praised his late friend and collaborator as a 'tender and obliging husband': 'He was partial to the fair sex, and had a great deal of gallantry in his temper.'[25] The Cato of the 1720s also departed from the example of his namesake in his remarkable eclecticism, the result of restless attempts to find a new means of imposing conceptual order on contemporary developments. One moment he is citing that most rigid of classical republican thinkers, Algernon Sidney, to condemn luxury and urge an agrarian law to limit wealth, or invoking Machiavelli on the need to recur to first principles;[26] the next he is marvelling at the magical ability of commerce, in a feminine guise, to bring about improvement.

> Nothing is more certain than that Trade cannot be forced; she is a coy and humorous Dame, who must be won by Flattery and Allurements, and always flies Force and Power; she is not confined to Nations, Sects, or Climates, but travels and wanders about the Earth till she fixes her Residence where she finds the best Welcome and kindest Reception; her Contexture is so nice and delicate, that she cannot breathe in a tyrannical Air; Will and Pleasure are so opposite to her Nature, that but touch her with the Sword and she dies: But if you give her gentle and kind Entertainment, she is a grateful and beneficent Mistress; she will turn Deserts into fruitful Fields, Villages into great Cities, Cottages into Palaces, Beggars into Princes, convert Cowards into Heroes, Blockheads into Philosophers; will change the Coverings of little Worms into the richest Brocades, the Fleeces of harmless Sheep into the Pride and Ornaments of Kings, and by a farther Metamorphosis will transmute them again into armed Hosts and haughty Fleets.[27]

This bravura passage, in the mode of Addison's portrait of the lady Publick Credit in the *Spectator*, is in itself capable of more than one reading. For Ronald Hamowy, the key would be the dichotomy of trade and tyranny, an anticipation of *laissez-faire* arguments, in the first half. Pocock focuses on the second half, which he sees as a grudging admission of the place of passion in a commercial society, an evocation of 'Circe's island' where 'the price to be paid is the admission that we are governed by our fantasies and passions'.[28] For the purposes of the present argument, what is most striking is the willingness to revive the gendered rhetoric of improvement, even if its deployment is slightly undercut by mock-wonder, and even if the experiment was not repeated elsewhere in the *Letters*.

Cato is not a univocal source of authority, but a manifestation of the tumultuous state of contemporary opinion. Over three years, in 138 installments, the two authors occupied a variety of positions. The text is open to divergent readings along one or other of its dual axes: civic humanist (virtue and corruption) or Lockean (liberty and tyranny). No one has attempted to argue that it 'falls squarely within the republican tradition'.[29]

Cato's main innovation within the civic tradition is an acceptance of the primacy of private passions. The passions must be analysed in order to rule and guide them towards the public good. Shelley Burtt has summarized the hybrid nature of this project: 'Cato's reworking of the notion of civic virtue stems from his effort to graft an egoistic psychology onto the republican tradition, to make a case that the virtuous citizen can and will thwart corruption and advance public liberty from quite selfish motives.'[30] Trade is not attacked and it is even declared a privilege of liberty to grow 'as rich as we can', provided that 'we hurt not the publick, nor one another'.[31] This is an important provision: ultimately, the play of the passions is to be orchestrated from above and provided with a safety net.

It seems likely that Mandeville was encouraged or provoked by the success of Cato to reissue in expanded form his own writings on the primacy of the passions in a commercial society. The poem *The Grumbling Hive: or, Knaves Turn'd Honest* first appeared in 1705, an Aesopean fable in the manner that Mandeville had explored in earlier publications.[32] In 1714 the poem was republished as *The Fable of the Bees: or, Private Vices, Public Benefits*, with the addition of a preface, introduction, an essay 'An Enquiry into the Origin of Moral Virtue' and twenty 'Remarks' or footnotes to the poem in 1714. On both occasions it went virtually unnoticed. It was reissued in 1723 with new material in the 'Remarks' and two new essays, on charity schools and on 'the nature of society'. The work found an audience only in the aftermath of the South Sea Bubble and, more specifically, in connection with *Cato's Letters*. Mandeville's work was catapulted into public consciousness and notoriety by being named with the *Letters* in a formal condemnation by the Grand Jury of Middlesex requesting that the publishers of both be prosecuted.

The publicity created by this 'Presentment' was so valuable that Mandeville incorporated the words of the Grand Jury in the 1724 edition along with his own 'Vindication', to ensure that they would continue to circulate. The complaint is essentially on religious grounds. The 'Goodness of the Almighty' in preserving Britain from the Marseilles plague of 1720 is now being put at risk by the 'flagrant Impieties' of works like the *Fable of the Bees* and *Cato's Letters*. Among other charges, they are accused of affirming an 'absolute Fate' rather than divine Providence, undermining religion and the clergy, and (with particular reference to Mandeville) recommending 'Luxury, Avarice, Pride, and all kind of Vices, as being necessary to *Publick Welfare*'.[33] The threat of divine punishment was joined in a second condemnation to the risk of political regression. A letter signed 'Theophilus Philo-Britannus' and addressed to an anonymous lord, also reprinted by Mandeville, raises the spectre of a Jacobite rebellion should the nation allow the Protestant religion to be undermined. The attack is primarily aimed at Cato, renamed 'Catiline' after the arch-conspirator, while the author of *Fable of the Bees* is represented as an 'Auxiliary' intent on tearing up 'the very Foundations of *Moral Virtue*, and establish *Vice* in her room' (*FB* I: 397).[34]

The grumbling of the hive had never been more clamorous than in the years following the South Sea Bubble. Mandeville originally published *The Grumbling Hive* at the time of a general election that returned a Whig majority, aimed at detractors who continued to hanker after the restoration of the Stuarts.[35] Two years earlier Mandeville had produced a Whig propaganda poem, *The Pamphleteers* (1703), defending the Revolution Settlement. Now, in the turmoil of the early 1720s, *The Grumbling Hive* became relevant in a different way, as a parody of ideas of a return to first principles, whether Christian asceticism or a Machiavellian *ridurre ai principii*. When Mandeville's bees grumble about the prevalence of vice and luxury in their prosperous, peaceful world, an angry Jove takes them at their word and turns them virtuous. Poverty, suffering, defensive wars and eventually social collapse are the result. The few survivors abandon their hive and take up new quarters in a hollow tree.

Mandeville's moral?

> Then leave Complaints: Fools only strive
> To make a Great an honest Hive.
> T'enjoy the World's Conveniencies,
> Be famed in War, yet live in Ease
> Without great Vices, is a vain
> Eutopia seated in the Brain.
> Fraud, Luxury, and Pride must live
> Whilst we the Benefits receive.

The fable and its addenda constitute a forceful defence of a modern commercial society, 'the World's Conveniencies', and a provocative substitute for the Court Whig political economy that was signally unforthcoming during the crisis.[36] But Mandeville is not a consistent progressivist or modernizer. He is a purveyor of hard 'truths'. The foundation of his theory of society is a static concept of human nature: man is 'a Compound of Various Passions' (*FB* I: 39); and it is a few of most regressive passions – pride, shame, self-love and the desire for domination – that accidentally drive society forward. For Mandeville, paradox is not simply a rhetorical habit but an indispensable instrument for interpreting the world. Politeness is the product of barbarism; it exists as a defence mechanism against the real threat of violence. Luxury and ease depend on a bedrock of hard labour. The lot of the manual worker must not be improved if society at large is to prosper. Hence Mandeville's criticism of the charity schools championed by the Societies for the Reformation of Manners.[37] It was his anti-ameliorist position on this popular cause that led to his name being joined to that of Cato, and provoked the fiercest attacks at the outset.[38] For Mandeville, the leap forward into happiness and enlightenment is simultaneously a step back into vice and inequity. Man in his savage state is never wholly left behind; he constantly peers out from behind the mask of civility.

A similar doubleness characterizes Mandeville's mode of argument. He is an advocate for the passions. He expands on the insights of the French sceptical tradition including Pierre Bayle (1647–1706) and the Duc de La Rochefoucauld (1613–80) to show how the base instinct of self-love, suitably directed, could work to the economic and social good of a whole society.[39] This was a utilitarian proposition in the loose sense; an 'ethics whose moral touchstone was results and not abstract principle' (*FB*, I, xlviii–xlix). But Mandeville chose to dress it in the language of rigourism, an extreme asceticism that censures almost all human actions and pleasures as the product of worldly appetites.[40] The effect, for many readers, was wildly irritating; some critics seem never to have got past the offensive subtitle with its conjunction of 'Private Vices, Publick Benefits'.[41] The device allowed Mandeville to defend the *Fable* as 'a Book of severe and exalted Morality' (*FB* I: 405), but in practice his use of moral vocabulary is strained to the point of absurdity. The word 'Vice' is stretched to show the ubiquity of self-interest and dishonesty in every walk of life. The word 'Luxury' is likewise stretched to include all commodities, however innocuous, not strictly needed to support life. In both cases, the elastic snaps and Mandeville is free to argue that 'Vice' and 'Luxury' are synonymous with society itself, and are thereby necessary evils.[42]

The 'Remarks' and essays added in the *Fable* are full of illustrations of the terse precepts of the *Grumbling Hive*; they maintain a dialogue with the resistant reader. It is notable that in the more extensive discussions especially, the actions of men and women are presented interchangeably to illustrate a single point. In 'An Enquiry into the Origin of Moral Virtue', placed before the 'Remarks', there is an attack on Steele's method of flattering his readers into good behaviour. Mandeville compares it to the tricks of women who 'teach Children to be mannerly' by praising their awkward first attempts at curtseying in the case of girls, or behaving politely in company in the case of boys (*FB* I: 52–4). Mandeville, as we have seen, has no intention of flattering. In 'Remark C' on the symbiosis of shame and honour, he begins with the perverse willingness of soldiers to risk death in order win good opinion and quickly moves on to female modesty and its origins in the avoidance of shame and social conditioning, rather than any innate propensity. It is likewise fear of being shamed that leads men to conceal their lust with good breeding, and at the other extreme, leads unmarried mothers to murder their offspring. When Mandeville writes that 'Shame and Education ... contain the seeds of all politeness' (*FB* I: 72), it is clear that politeness is by no means an unqualified good.

In 'Remark L' on luxury, Mandeville quickly dispatches the notion that luxury weakens a nation by encouraging the growth of effeminacy. While he admits that overindulgence is bad for the health, he mocks the central concerns of civic humanist discourse as a bugbear. Valuably for our purposes, he spells out the effect on an early eighteenth-century imagination of the term 'effeminacy':

> I remember, that when I have read of the Luxury of *Persia, AEgypt*, and other Countries where it has been a reigning Vice, and that were effeminated and enervated by it, it has sometimes put me in mind of the cramming and swilling of ordinary Tradesmen at a City Feast, and the beastliness their over-gorging themselves is often attended with; at other times it has made me think on the Distraction of dissolute Sailors, as I had seen them in Company of half a dozen lewd Women roaring along with Fiddles before them; and was I to have been carried into any of their great Cities, I would have expected to have found one third of the People Sick a Bed with Surfeits; another laid up with the Gout, or crippled by a more ignominious Distemper, and the rest, that could go without leading, walk along the Streets in Petticoats. (*FB* I: 117–18)

The effeminate man, therefore, was either incapacitated by excessive food or drink, or by a surfeit of women, with accompanying venereal disease, or in his dependency was *like* women, if not children (i.e. requiring leading-strings). But Mandeville conjures up these pictures only to dismiss them; experience has taught him that opulence is a danger neither to the social fabric nor to a nation's military strength. On the contrary, in addition to being a major stimulus for the economy, it is an essential precondition of civility.[43] His refusal to take the possibility of effeminization seriously at the same time forecloses the idea of feminization. The agency of women or the feminine, for better or for worse, is simply discounted. Instead of genuine *improvement*, astonishing achievements could be constructed on the back of unchanging passions, for '[a]s long as Men have the same Appetites, the same Vices will remain' (*FB* I: 118)

False feminists and moral crisis in Mandeville and Defoe

Mandeville's opposition to easy optimism was of long standing. It was first voiced in his contributions to the *Female Tatler*, a journal established in July 1710 to milk the success of the *Tatler*, for 'more ridiculous things are done every day than ten such papers can relate'.[44] From November 1709 to March 1710 he published 32 issues of the journal, all of them in the guise of one or other of the sisters 'Lucinda' and 'Artesia'. On the face of it, the '*Female Tatler*' is a tautology, for the title *The Tatler* was invented 'in Honour of' the 'Fair Sex' (No. 1, Tuesday, 12 April 1709).[45] One of the *Tatler*'s main claims to civility lay in the status of the editor Isaac Bickerstaff as a 'feminized' man, and in the prominent place he allotted to women as contributors and readers and as a topic for discussion.[46] But in the hands of Mandeville the paper became a robust dialogue rather than an imitation. He systematically disputed the reformist discourse of Steele with its combined emphasis on Christian personal virtue and the civic humanist conception of public virtue.[47] Both ideologies opposed vice and luxury, and called on the individual to suppress the passions; idealist prescriptions that already were anathema to Mandeville.

The antagonistic 'realism' of Mandeville's picture of the world is established in his first number, with Lucinda looking out of the window of her closet onto a London roofscape and seeing 'the Clouds of Smoak that were continually beat down by a thick mizzling Rain'.[48] She is soon joined by Colonel Worthy and three female friends who debate the morality of duelling, a favourite *Tatler* topic. Bickerstaff was first alerted to the question by a grief-stricken young lady whose lover has been wounded, and had proceeded to demolish the language of honour by ridicule.[49] In response Mandeville's Colonel argues that fear of violence is the only effective guarantee of good behaviour: 'The strict Observation of the point of Honour, said he, is a necessary Evil, and a large Nation can no more be call'd Polite without it, than it can be Rich and Flourishing without Pride or Luxury' (81). Typically, Bickerstaff is motivated to call for change by empathy with female softness; Colonel Worthy by contrast suggests that no woman would be safe from insult if duelling were to cease. One assumes altruism; the other egotism. The innate response to women is the test in each case. Battle-lines are drawn between the *Tatler*'s sentiment-driven reforming zeal, and Mandeville's bleak but good-humoured insistence on man as he is. In conclusion, Lucinda tartly observes that it is fortunate for women that they are not faced with the contradiction between the laws of honour, politics and interest and those of religion or patriotism.[50]

The redoubtable independence of mind displayed by Lucinda is characteristic of Mandeville's female personae. She, her sister Artesia, and another Lucinda from the *Virgin Unmask'd* (1709), written around the same time, are a band of hard-headed old maids. They are learned, keen to argue social issues and politics, down-to-earth to the point of ribaldry about the sexual urges of men and women, though they are chaste themselves and either have no ambition to be married, or a declared aversion to it. These features were undoubtedly intended to debunk the domestic feminine ideal as represented and promoted in the pages of the *Tatler* or *Spectator*. In certain respects Mandeville's spokeswomen are remarkably reminiscent of Mary Astell, whose treatises *A Serious Proposal to the Ladies* and *Some Reflections Upon Marriage* were still appearing in new editions and who pioneered a way of life: financially and socially independent of men; publicly outspoken on the key issues of the day; and prepared to write for money. But the sexual frankness and lack of religious sentiment are vital differentiating points. Mandeville's spinsters are, like Lord Hervey in Pope's *Epistle to*

Arbuthnot, 'amphibious things' somewhere between men and women. They are in no way qualified to be proper objects for the discourse of feminization, and neither are they suitable vehicles for sincere feminist argument.[51]

Lucinda's attempt to organize a 'Table of Fame for the Women' is a sad disappointment. In nos 68 and 70 of the *Female Tatler*, Mandeville gibed at the *Tatler*'s tables of fame, an all-male affair. In *Tatler* No. 84 a letter had been printed questioning the absence of Lucretia, and Bickerstaff offers to set up a 'little Tea Table' for the women. Now in the surroundings of Artesia's apartments a gathering of gentlemen and ladies demand of Lucinda that she makes good an earlier promise by the 'Society of Ladies' to arrange an alternative on a larger scale. Immediately, contention begins. The women who are present each propose heroines of their own stamp: the overbearing wife of an army officer suggests female warriors; a good homemaker wants famous matrons; a grief-stricken widow asks for loyal relicts; the long-suffering wife of a rake argues for models of forbearance; and an old maid insists that those who died in defence of their chastity best deserve to be celebrated.

Apart from the female military leaders, all of them classical and most legendary, the heroines all represent passive virtues. This point is made in No. 70, when 'a Gentleman of the Gown' (a cleric or lawyer) observes that although there are several ladies in the company who had 'been favour'd by the *Muses*' no woman had yet been nominated for learning in spite of their being 'no Branch of it in which Women have not excell'd as much as Men'. A few classical names are desultorily put forward and oddly, Pope Joan (who would feature 270 years later at the table in Caryl Churchill's play along similar lines, *Top Girls*).[52] But the conversation soon turns to other matters, the etymology of the name 'Eve' and the inflated reputation of Alexander the Great.[53] The number ends with a peculiar advertisement signed 'H.L.', a matchmaker and bawd, 'I not only make matches, but have always a breed of Young Girls, which as fast as they grow Ripe, I dispose of to the best Bidder'; presumably a satire, is its object the preceding high-flown discussion of women's excellencies?

In Mandeville's writings for the *Female Tatler* respect for women often tips over into degrading anecdote. An example in miniature is the moment when the widow speaks up for her chosen heroines only to be undermined by an 'unlucky Spark' who 'named the word *Ephesius*, and pretended to Cough'. The tale of the Ephesian widow who, while mourning over her husband's tomb, allows herself to be seduced by a soldier guarding the bodies of criminals nearby was a classic of misogynist literature. Mandeville's handling of the allusion can be compared to that of Steele in the *Spectator* (13 March 1711, No. 11), when it becomes part of a staged overcoming of misogyny, by provoking the counter-narrative of Inkle and Yarico. In the *Female Tatler*, more extended efforts to discountenance female pretensions to propriety and virtue appear elsewhere: Lucinda punishes the

scandalmongers Chloe and Celia by revealing that she knows lewd stories
about each of them (14 November 1709, No. 56); another time she relates
the history of Ephelia, a prude who is eventually discovered to have engaged
in a three-year affair with the gardener (10 March 1710, No, 102). Anti-
feminist mottoes appear at the head of some of the numbers in Latin and
therefore pointedly over the heads of most female readers: 'The outcome of
no vice is equal to the pride of women' attributed to St. Augustine (23
January 1710, No. 86, 164); 'Don't choose as a dinner partner a lady with a
command of rhetorical style, who can fire off well-formed arguments; let
her not know all of history, and not understand all she reads' from Juvenal's
notorious sixth satire on women (20 February 1710, No. 96, 198). The
discussion of the Women's Table of Fame descends further into squabbling
and tedious lists culled from Pierre Le Moyne's *The Gallery of Heroick Women*
(1652),[54] though there is a pleasant aside that if the same requirements of
valour and chastity were made of men, 'a very little Table would have serv'd
them' (1 February 1710, No. 88*, 176).

What appears in the contributions to the *Female Tatler* is a negative sort
of equality: the women are as bad as the men. And since a woman's claim
to virtue is her chastity, that is the principal target. Any hint of hypocrisy
must be castigated and the denial of desire exposed as a sham.
Nevertheless, a few affirmations of women's capabilities emerge, like
flowers on a dunghill. In No. 111 there is praise for improvements in
women's access to learning. Perhaps the most impressive argument in
favour of learned women is the picture of Lucinda and Artesia in action,
unapologetically debating an issue like the value of military service in a
commercial nation (their nephew Pompey is in danger of being sent abroad
as cannon fodder like his two older brothers). Although the quarrel is
handed over to two male seconds (Colonel Worthy and an '*Oxford
Gentleman*'), Artesia eventually wins the day by sending Pompey an anti-
war poem in doggerel, 'Grinning Honour'. Beyond the study and the
drawing-room, Mandeville, like Defoe, held up the commercial know-how
of the wives of Dutch merchants as something of an ideal: their practical
involvement in business meant that they could not be imposed on by their
husbands or treated merely as decorative amusements (31 March 1710,
No. 105, 238 and 31 March 1710, No, 111, 238).[55]

But the ultimately anti-progressivist nature of Mandeville's stance on the
condition of women, at a time when Astell's ideas were widely known, is
ironically revealed by the strongest statement of feminist principles in the
Female Tatler. A testy old gentleman provokes Artesia into an eloquent
defence of education for women, including knowledge of Latin and of the
choice to live as a spinster. In addition, she justifies the enterprise of the
Women's Table of Fame on the grounds that 'Women were as capable as
Men of that Sublimity of the Soul, and had at least equall'd if not excell'd
the greatest and most Heroick of the Cruel and Injurious Sex, that had used

so many Artifices to enslave them' (20 February 1710, No, 96, 202). The absurdity of Artesia's flight is indicated *ipso facto* by her hyperbole. Further clues to Mandeville's satirical intent are provided by the motto on women's rhetoric from Juvenal, already cited, by Artesia's defence of the 'polishing' agenda of the *Tatler*, and by her resistance to the gentleman's common-sense proposal that 'Solidity and Learning are no more becoming than Breeches' and disqualify women as wives (199).

The Virgin Unmask'd also contains outspoken arguments in favour of women and has frequently been described as feminist in tenor, but the same reservations apply. The very title announces the anti-idealist aim, and invites prurient interest that will not be wholly disappointed. Although a large part of the text is given over to a debate between Lucinda and her young niece Antonia on the greatness of Louis XIV, the focus is once again on the unruly passions of women. According to Lucinda, a middle-aged spinster, these passions, sexual, worldly and even sympathetic, expose women to exploitation by men. The thesis is illustrated for the benefit of Antonia by two lengthy, vividly told and shocking narratives relating the life histories of two women of their acquaintance. These stories are presented with the utmost seriousness and the history of Aurelia even includes a remarkably detailed analysis of the psychology of domestic violence. But Lucinda's objective, to force Antonia to recognize her sexual feelings in order to repress them, and to maintain a constant guard against all men to the point of abjuring marriage, invites scepticism from the reader through its very extremism.

In the Preface Mandeville explains with tongue in cheek that Lucinda's initial upbraiding of Antonia for her revealing costume is 'a Sophisticated Way of Arguing' to make the girl 'neglectful of her Charms'. In fact, the effect is one of outright hysteria as Lucinda rails at the exposure of her breasts: 'See how filthily and boldly they stand pouting out, and bid defiance to your stays.'[56] A similar shrillness is meant to detract from her accounts of the trials of morning sickness ('Poyson'd by Man'), pregnancy and childbirth. Although many women might concur with her assessment ('A Torture so exquisite, and so universal, that Art nor Cruelty, could ever imitate it') she is self-condemned by her opposition to nature (107–8, 109). When asked the origins of her dislike of marriage she replies 'Love and Reason', that is, self-love and the overcoming of appetite by reason. The first Mandeville could approve. Self-love is, as we have seen, one of the motors of a prosperous society. But the second is an aberration intended to put us on our guard against her plausible words.[57]

Like *The Fable of the Bees*, *The Virgin Unmask'd* found a new context and a heightened relevance in the 1720s. It was reissued in 1724, no doubt in order to capitalize on Mandeville's newfound notoriety. Although there was in fact little direct comment on the work of contemporaries, *Virgin Unmask'd* anticipated one rhetorical feature that attained prominence at this moment. This was the representation of feminist arguments within a text that otherwise insists upon the debased nature of women. The phenomenon has been identified by a recent critic in *A Modest Defence of Public Stews* (1724), attributed to Mandeville, which develops the idea of the social value of licensed prostitution put forward in *Fable of the Bees* (I: 95–100), and in George Lillo's *The London Merchant* (1731), an innovative domestic tragedy.[58] But the most notable example of the strategy can be found in Defoe's *The Fortunate Mistress: or, Roxana* also published in 1724.

At the heart of Defoe's novel, midway through the narrative, is a debate between Roxana and a Dutch merchant who wishes to marry her. She has by this stage distanced herself from the disaster at the outset, which found her an abandoned wife with five small children, and has emerged from two secret affairs with wealthy men the independent possessor of £20,000 worth of jewels, banknotes and credit. Now, in spite of her gratitude to the merchant who had helped to save her wealth as she transferred it from France to Holland, and perhaps even preserved her life, and in spite of the fact that she is willing to sleep with him, she rejects his proposal. She has no intention of handing over her fortune as convention and the marriage laws dictate, nor of vowing to honour and obey. In retelling the incident, she stresses to the reader that her main, indeed only, objection to marriage is losing control of her money. But she cannot admit this to the merchant and merely tells him that she has an aversion to marriage as a result of her first experience. He guesses the real reason and promises that he will not touch her estate and will leave it to her management.

Roxana is in a predicament: she does not want to admit that money was her motive and believes if she does agree on his terms, it would be a source of ill-will between them. She is forced to perform a feminist 'Turn', and 'talk upon a kind of an elevated Strain, which really was not in my Thoughts at first, at-all'.

> I told him, I had, perhaps, differing Notions of Matrimony, from what the receiv'd Custom had given us of it; that I thought a Woman was a free Agent, as well as a Man, and was born free, and cou'd she manage herself suitably, might enjoy that Liberty to as much purpose as the Men do …
>
> That the very Nature of the Marriage-Contract was, in short, nothing but giving up Liberty, Estate, Authority, and every-thing, to the Man, and the Woman was indeed, a meer Woman ever after, that is to say, a Slave.[59]

The merchant counters that men take on the burden of responsibility as their side of the bargain. She warms to her theme and insists that this is no recompense to women for the loss of their liberty and that it is better for them to 'entertain a Man, as a Man does a Mistress' than to cede control.

He argues for the overriding benefits of mutual love. She dismisses talk of love as a confidence trick, and recurs to her own bitter experience. He even goes so far as to offer to give up trade and hand over his fortune to her, but she has her eye on richer prizes and is obdurate. Although she soon finds she is pregnant by him, she rejects his urgent plea to legitimize their child and returns to London to set up shop as a high-class courtesan.

What this debate illustrates in part is the lapse of time and a change in historical vision. In the period of optimism from the 1690s to the early 1710s, Roxana's feminist language was used in earnest, widely circulated and seriously considered, by Defoe among others. In the fallen world of the 1720s, the world of the Bubble, newly attentive to the sway of the passions, it can only persist as debased coinage. The legitimacy her words are given by earlier suffering is cancelled by her acknowledged motives and her future actions. Greed drives her and she happily makes a symbolic sacrifice of her liberty by performing at private assemblies in the garb of a Turkish slave as 'Roxana'; a reversal of the trajectory of Montesquieu's *Persian Letters* (1721). There, the character named Roxana prefers to die rather than have her freewill smothered in the prison of the harem.[60] Defoe's Roxana submits to living entirely cut off from society, as she had done in France when mistress to a Prince, when she becomes the King's paramour for three years (223) and then remains in seclusion as the prize of an unprepossessing English nobleman, 'old wicked L—' (227, 241, 250).[61]

Although Roxana, now in her fifties, eventually extracts herself from the affair, her evil history is making of her a helpless, terrified victim of circumstances. Fate determines that a daughter, Susan, one of the abandoned children of her first marriage, has unknowingly been employed as a kitchen maid in her household. The servant Amy, Roxana's loyal shadow throughout her career, has been appointed the agent for belatedly and anonymously mending the fortunes of the children. In spite of all attempts to keep Susan in the dark about her mother's identity, she begins to chase after clues and make connections. Meanwhile, as part of the accelerating pace of repetition, the Dutch merchant reappears with a second proposal of marriage on similar terms. This time the opportunity is greeted by Roxana as a reassertion of autonomy, a chance to escape the weight of guilt closing in on her, to elude her past yet again.

But at the very moment when Roxana and her husband are poised to sail to Holland to a new life, Susan turns up on board ship as the friend and companion of the captain's wife. The plans are postponed and next Susan hears about the famous suit of Turkish clothes still in Roxana's possession, the exact same it would appear that her former employer once wore. Roxana flees and Susan follows her, desperate to be reunited with her mother. When Amy tries to circumvent the workings of providence by resolving to murder Susan and bury the secret, Roxana parts with her in anger. In the sketchy conclusion, although Amy and Susan ominously disappear, we are told that divine punishment finally catches up with Roxana after she has enjoyed a few more years 'Flourishing' and she is 'brought so low again, that my Repentance seem'd to be only the Consequence of my Misery, as my Misery was of my Crime' (379). Not even repentance can separate itself from the circular logic and permit the soul a leap towards salvation. The wheel of fortune is the governing structure, as it was in Hogarth's satire on the times discussed at the start of the chapter.

Only one critic, to my knowledge, has attempted to argue that Roxana was intended by Defoe as the admirable embodiment of the spirit of capitalism.[62] But Laura Brown has remarked that the moment when Roxana is at her most 'feminist', the scene discussed at length above, is also the moment when she comes 'closest to Defoe's ideal of mercantile success'.[63] In a reading strategy also followed by Laura Mandell, Brown goes on to suggest that the stigma of child murder finally demonizes the audacious she-merchant, in an effort by Defoe to purge commercial ideology of the more unsavoury aspects of the acquisitive drive. *Roxana*, through its 'misogynist turn', becomes an 'unwitting critique of mercantilist capitalist accumulation'.[64] But as I have tried to show, misogyny is implicit in the very presentation of the feminist argument; it is a calculating 'Turn' in its own right.[65] The meretricious nature of her feminism is matched by the flimsiness of her self-description as 'she-merchant'. Roxana trades in nothing, not even in her body: her first liaisons are the result of accident and her riches are initially derived from a mixture of luck and opportunism.

Later, Roxana does engage in rational profiteering, raking in interest from the money markets. She achieves this with the aid of an historical figure, Sir Robert Clayton (1629–1707; the events of the novel are situated, not without anomalies, in the reign of Charles II), one of the first powerbrokers of the monied interest, and a man condemned by Defoe elsewhere; he would have been a particularly potent symbol of corruption in the context of the South Sea Bubble.[66] Repeatedly, Roxana fails the test of economic sense and probity by a metonymic unwillingness to ally herself with an honest merchant in marriage. This perverse disregard for wholesome self-interest is represented as a kind of frenzy. She reflects, after her first refusal of the Dutch merchant:

> I am a Memorial to all that shall read my Story; a standing Monument of the Madness and Distraction which Pride and Infatuations from Hell runs us into; how ill our Passions guide us; and how dangerously we act, when we follow the Dictates of an ambitious Mind. (201)

Just a few pages later, she is presented with another generous and advantageous marriage proposal from a merchant. It is transmitted (somewhat ironically) by Sir Robert Clayton and comes with an extravagant encomium on the glories of trade and the value of merchants ('a true-bred Merchant is the best Gentleman in the Nation', 210) that expressed Defoe's heartfelt opinion. Again, she fends it off with feminist rhetoric ('seeing Liberty seem'd to be the Men's Property, I wou'd be a *Man-Woman*', 212). Although Roxana eventually accepts the third offer, it is not before she suffers a severe fit of madness, 'the Effect of a violent Fermentation in my blood' (279), when the simultaneous possibility arises of being reunited with her Prince in France and raised into the nobility. Probably the clearest indication that Roxana's brand of commerce is not to be considered on a par with that of the genuine merchant is her penitent, superstitious dread at the idea of combining her fortune with that of her second husband. She will marry him, but her tainted money – more infectious than any bodily fluid – must never be mingled with his, or she risks bringing down divine justice on his head (304–5).

The overt moral of *Roxana* is no advance on the deeply conservative message sent by Mandeville's 'Table of Fame', where Lucretia presides: 'a Woman ought rather to die, than to prostitute her Virtue and Honour, let the Temptation be what it will' (*R* 63). It has been remarked that, with regard to the poetics of sexual difference, *Roxana* is a blind alley in the history of the novel: it chronicles the acquisition of male characteristics by a woman rather than female characteristics by men.[67] But it could be said that Defoe never properly distinguishes the sexes at all: there is no attempt at an innate definition of what it is to be male or to be female. Masculinity is associated with a Utopia of liberty and agency. And although Defoe was generally liberal in his ideas regarding women, in *Roxana* he succumbed to the prevailing culture of moral panic. In keeping with misogynist convention, Roxana and Amy consistently manifest the worst side of humanity.

That there is insufficient distinction between the sexes is the real difficulty entertained by Mandeville, as later by Swift in his obscene poems. In *Virgin Unmask'd* Lucinda's insistence on the dangers of heterosexual desire masks the real message that men and women are all too similar in their passions. Obscenity is a spectacular diversion from the truth. Lucinda lectures her niece that all obscene parts of the body that expose the difference between men and women must be kept hidden, leading Antonia to joke that beards must therefore be covered. She is told that 'when the Difference that is between the two sexes, first begins to run in the Minds of Virgins, all Men are represented naked to their Imagination' (25); but what this really means is that a woman's sexuality is from the start as active and predatory as a man's is assumed to be.[68] Mandeville, a practising doctor, spells this out in anatomical detail in the *Modest Defence of Publick Stews*, where he describes the 'frequent erections' of the clitoris 'which are, doubtless, as provoking as those of the *Penis*, of which it is a perfect copy, tho' in Miniature'.[69]

Old maids and whores are the quintessential female types in a climate of misogyny. Mandeville and Defoe both circle obsessively round these anomalous, unstable categories, irresistibly attracted by their unintelligibility, their lack of a fixed juridical status.[70] They represent the polarities in the spectrum of femininity: with no man, or with too many men. In *Moll Flanders* and *Roxana* fornication plays havoc with legal definitions. Wives live as mistresses, mistresses masquerade as legitimate wives, there are multiple partners, marital and extramarital. In the *Modest Defence* Mandeville explains how every woman, of any type or condition, is at risk of succumbing to sexual temptation. Both Mandeville and Defoe, in his pamphlet *Some Considerations upon Street-Walkers* (1726), call for legislative intervention to forestall the universalization of prostitution. Women's susceptibility to the passions, their nature as chaotic versions of men, ultimately threatens the heterosexual matrix, the family unit and social order itself. But all of this can be understood, and a cure prescribed, within Mandeville's utilitarian schema. The disruptive supplement is the eunuch, who introduces the difference between sexed and sexless bodies. The only time that Mandeville's spokesman Cleomenes demurs at the justification of luxury is on the subject of opera *castrati*: no amount of pleasure can balance the 'destroying of Manhood' (*FB*, II, 104).[71]

In the 1720s the case for commerce and luxury as a beneficial force relates to the world of men alone. Mandeville had anticipated this development with his narrative of the happy capitalist 'Laborio' in the *Female Tatler*, a merchant who can find no pleasure greater than continuing to drudge in a counting-house well into his old age, while seeing the greater share of his profits converted into luxuries by his extravagant nephew: the symbiotic relation between gain and expenditure is the basis of a prosperous national economy.[72] In *Fable of the Bees* Part I, the civilizing process takes place through flattery and the threat of violence rather than through love and admiration of women. This part presents what has been called a 'conspiratorial' view of the connection between private vice and public benefits. It is through the agency of a great man, an expertly manipulative politician, that the people are led by their selfish desires to contribute to the public weal. Mandeville here leaves in place one of the key features of the Machiavellian paradigm: the omniscient legislator.[73]

In *Fable of the Bees* Part II (1729), there is a paradigm shift towards an evolutionary theory of the conversion of the passions into prosperity.[74] This volume takes the form of a series of dialogues between two gentlemen of leisure, the Mandevillian Cleomenes and Horatio, a disciple of Shaftesbury. The very name 'Cleomenes' is a taunt: Cleomenes was the legendary king who attempted to restore Sparta to its ancient purity by restricting private wealth. His eighteenth-century namesake is intent on explaining the naturalness and inevitability of the development towards affluence and material security. He dispenses with moral justification, and there is no hint of a comparable spiritual evolution. Although a 'Savage

Couple' is taken as the originary unit for society, the female partner adds nothing to the process and certainly no saving graces. It is symptomatic that before the end of the first dialogue a female interlocutor, Fulvia, exits the scene never to return, apparently driven out by the ironic method of Cleomenes.

Mandeville's refusal to join commerce to morality is matched by a lack of interest in deploying sexual difference as part of his argument in favour of luxury. Women and the feminine are not – cannot be – deployed for redemptive purposes, to counter republican rhetoric. The ideal woman is unimaginable. The revolution led by Richardson in the 1740s is fundamentally concerned with the institution of sexual difference; the tremendous labour of differentiating men from women on the basis of their inner selves and in turn opening up the possibility of a stable system of gendered identity formation and of influence between two distinctive sexes. Until this revolution takes place there can be no attempt to rehabilitate women as the emblems of a new moralized economic order.

4
Elizabeth Carter in Pope's Garden: Literary Women of the 1730s

A Vignette

Mary Wortley Montagu had been warned by Addison not to cultivate a friendship with Pope, whose 'appetite to satire' would inevitably lead him to play her 'some devilish trick'.[1] She ignored the advice, no doubt confident that she was capable of handling anything the poet could throw at her. Twenty years later Elizabeth Carter too, at the start of her literary career, was warned against Pope. Sir George Oxenden, a courtier and Member of Parliament friendly with her father, wrote to him that 'there is hardly an instance of a woman of letters entering into an intimacy or acquaintance with men of wit and parts, who were not thoroughly abused and maltreated by them, in print, after some time; and Mr. Pope has done it more than once'.[2] She became only distantly acquainted with the poet, but one day in July 1738, during a walk with friends in the meadows between Richmond and Twickenham, she found herself in his renowned garden. Carter explained in a letter that they had gained entry 'by the interest of his celebrated man John' and that 'of all the Things I have yet seen of this sort none ever suited my own Fancy so well'.[3]

Carter's trespass, with its shades of Beauty and the Beast, would have no fairy-tale ending; but in print it took on a life of its own.[4] The young Samuel Johnson, who had arrived in London from Litchfield in March of the previous year and started working for the *Gentleman's Magazine*, commemorated the occasion with a Latin epigram in the July issue. The next month the announcement 'Verses to Eliza' appeared on the front page, heralding no less than three Englished versions of Johnson's 'To Eliza plucking Laurel in Mr. Pope's Gardens', one by 'Alexis', another by the 'peasant poet' Stephen Duck and the third by Johnson himself under the name 'Urbanus'.[5] Johnson's translation ran as follows:

> As learn'd *Eliza*, sister of the Muse,
> Surveys with new contemplative delight
> *Pope*'s hallow'd glades, and never tiring views,
> Her conscious hand his laurel leaves invite.

> Cease, lovely thief! my tender limbs to wound,
> (Cry'd *Daphne* whisp'ring from the yielding tree;)
> Were *Pope* once void of wonted candour found,
> Just *Phoebus* would devote his plant to thee.

The theme of transgression and usurpation is even more starkly presented in Duck's version:

> Desirous of the laurel bough,
> She crops it to adorn her brow;
> Yet do not steal it, lovely maid,
> The wreath you wish shall grace your head;
> If *Pope* refuse it as your due,
> *Phoebus* himself shall give it you.

In the same issue 'Eliza' dealt with the charge of stealing Pope's laurels, and brushed away the homage lightly with an eight-line answer showily offered in Latin and English. It begins:

> In vain *Eliza*'s daring hand
> Usurp'd the laurel bough;
> Remov'd from *Pope*'s, the wreath must fade
> On ev'ry meaner brow.

This flurry of literary banter confirmed Carter's status as a rising star in the magazine at a time when the editor Edward Cave was also publishing her volume *Poems on Particular Occasions*, but at the risk of arousing Pope's ire. It is possible that Johnson was using 'Eliza' as bait in his own meditated challenge to Pope's ascendancy. He had recently published *London: A Poem*, an imitation of Juvenal to match Pope's contemporary series of imitations of Horace. In the event, Pope failed to rise to the provocation, and instead, impressed by Johnson's satire, generously attempted to arrange a royal pension. It is curious to note that Carter's slightly discomfiting symbolic brush with Pope was matched by a mishap that occurred around the same time to Catherine Talbot, another bookish young woman who would later become her closest friend. As Pope attempted to hand Talbot down the landing step from his garden into a boat, she lost her footing and fell into the Thames, pulling the diminutive poet with her and nearly drowning them both.[6] How appropriate had the poet of *The Rape of the Lock* and *Epistle to a Lady*, those exercises in abusive gallantry, met his end at the hands of a female author.

A female author in the 1730s

Writers of the 1730s continued to live and create in the shadow cast by the South Sea disaster.[7] Few were personally untouched by it. Both Pope and

Montagu lost substantial sums.[8] Catherine Talbot's father was carried off by the epidemic of smallpox that came in its wake and was interpreted as divine punishment by some moralists.[9] But in the case of Elizabeth Carter, the memory of the Bubble was preserved like a myth of origins. She was only three years old when the collapse of the stock market in 1720 blighted her family.[10] Her father, Nicholas Carter, was then a promising young clergyman, curate of the church of St George the Martyr at Deal in Kent; her mother, Margaret, was heiress to a modest fortune. Montagu Pennington, her nephew, related the consequences in his *Memoirs* of her life:

> When Mrs. Carter was about ten years of age, she had the misfortune to lose her mother. She died of a decline, partly, as is supposed, occasioned by vexation. She brought her husband a handsome fortune of several 1000 pounds, which they hoped to encrease, for a family, then likely to be large, by buying South Sea stock. They had not, however, the prudence to sell in time; and the bursting of that bubble in the memorable year 1720 swept the greatest part of it away. From this stroke she never recovered, and Dr. Carter himself was so much affected by it, that he never willingly mentioned it, nor chose to say how large a sum he had thus lost.[11]

Elizabeth was the eldest of five children from this marriage; later her father remarried and two more children were added. She was given the same education at home as her brothers, learning Greek, Latin and Hebrew as well as French; and went further, teaching herself Italian, Spanish, German and some Portuguese and Arabic. By the age of 16 she was showing such remarkable abilities as a scholar, linguist and poet that Nicholas Carter seems to have begun to hatch a highly unusual plan for her future. Unable to provide her with an adequate dowry, he determined to speculate on her literary assets. In effect, by encouraging her to submit poems and epigrams to the successful journal the *Gentleman's Magazine*, he 'floated' his prodigy in the London literary marketplace.

A later section of this chapter will discuss Elizabeth Carter's literary production and the association with the *Gentleman's Magazine* in more detail. In this section I want to dwell on the extraordinary nature of this sortie into authorship, and in the next to indicate the wider context of gender politics in the print culture of the 1730s, that makes it appear even more audacious. Nicholas Carter's motives for pushing Elizabeth into publication may have contained an element of self-interest. As Sylvia Myers has remarked, 'he was a clergyman with a small income and a large family, and seems to have been attempting to publicize himself and his daughter as a means of gaining preferment'.[12] Deal, a coastal village, consisted of three unpaved streets. He evidently had aspirations beyond it – Canterbury, the centre of the Anglican Church, was a mere 16 miles away – and was himself already an active contributor to the *Gentleman's Magazine*, which was founded in 1731.[13]

The established connection with the journal, and the good character of its proprietor Edward Cave, must have promised a relatively secure and respectable entry for Elizabeth into the literary scene. Its large circulation would entail wide exposure.[14] After her first poem, a riddle on fire, was published in November 1734, she began a routine of staying in London for part of each year from 1735 to 1739, producing a few poems for the *Gentleman's Magazine* and also engaging in translation work. She lodged in the home of her uncle, a tradesman, in Bishopsgate Street in the City, but also spent time with Cave and his family, meeting the literary men associated with the magazine, including Samuel Johnson. An increasing number of her poems appeared each year up to 1739 and attracted more and more interest from admiring respondents.

At the same time she took to translating recent high-profile publications: *Sir Isaac Newton's Philosophy Explain'd for the Use of the Ladies* by Francesco Algarotti and *An Examination of Mr Pope's Essay on Man* by Jean Paul de Crousaz were both produced in 1739 by arrangement with Cave. The Crousaz volume also will be discussed later in the chapter. *Il Newtonianismo per le dame* was originally written in 1733, when Algarotti was a guest of Voltaire and his learned mistress Emilie de Châtelet. The translation was significant in bringing to Britain a taste of the salon culture of France, in which educated women took a leading role. It is interesting to note that Mary Wortley Montagu, whose career at times forms a counterpoint to Carter's, carried a copy of her translation along with the original in her luggage when she left for Italy in July 1739, driven by an adulterous passion for Algarotti himself.[15] These translations should not be dismissed as hack-work. They were interventions in British intellectual and literary life through the indirect route of foreign commentary, and although Carter published anonymously, she was publicly praised for the Algarotti translation and her work on Crousaz was an open secret, for which she received compliments from her associates Samuel Johnson and Thomas Birch.[16]

Then suddenly in June 1739, when she was 22 and on the brink of achieving genuine literary celebrity, she retreated to Deal and for nearly 20 years scarcely ventured beyond Canterbury. The plans for advancement appear to have gone awry; the speculation had failed. Elizabeth devoted herself to housekeeping and educating the younger children; keeping her literary interests alive only through correspondence with bookish friends, notably Talbot, the ward of Thomas Secker, Bishop of Oxford. The two young women had first become acquainted in 1741 through Thomas Wright, a writer on mathematics and astronomy. Through the 1740s and early 1750s they maintained their friendship by letter, meeting infrequently, and it was with Talbot's encouragement that Elizabeth Carter found her way back to scholarship and literary fame in 1758, with the publication of her translation of the complete works of the Stoic philoso-pher Epictetus.

Most accounts of her life, in seeking to explain her withdrawal from London and a literary career in 1739, have emphasized her possible romantic entanglements. One of the most vocal admirers of her literary talents was Thomas Birch, a clergyman and busy man of letters, who at the time they met was preparing an English edition of Bayle's *General Dictionary*. Birch suggested the translation of Algarotti and may have helped her with it; they began meeting frequently in August 1738. He lavished praise on her in an article contributed to the *History of the Works of the Learned* published in June 1739:

> This Lady is a very extraordinary Phaenomenon in the Republick of Letters, and justly to be rank'd with the Cornelia's, Sulpicia's, and Hypatia's of the Ancients, and the Schurmans and Daciers of the Moderns. For to an uncommon Vivacity and Delicacy of Genius and an Accuracy of Judgment worthy of the maturest Years, she has added the Knowledge of the ancient and Modern Languages at an Age, when an equal Skill in any one of them would be a considerable Distinction in a Person of the other Sex.[17]

His partiality was noted by other men of letters. William Warburton remarked in a letter to Birch: 'The Phaenomenon of the Young Lady under twenty is indeed an extraordinary one. But you forgot to mention one particular that perhaps is of more importance to her than all her Greek & Latin[:] that is whether she be handsome.'[18] There have been suggestions that Elizabeth and her father feared scandal from Birch's blatant but inconclusive attentions.[19]

At around the same time she was also being courted by a 'Mr. G', about whom Nicholas Carter wrote to his daughter urging caution: 'Preserve the Character of an Inoffensive, & prudent Woman, & your other very extraord-inary qualifications will in Time, I doubt not, produce something desireable.'[20] It may be that Elizabeth felt unequal to the task of continually fending off unwanted or equivocal suitors; or perhaps her father, fearing long-term damage to her reputation and disappointed by the lack of results, decided the expense of sending her annually to London was no longer justified. Certainly his response was fundamentally cost-conscious when she turned down her last and most eligible proposal of marriage from a Mr Dalton in 1749. Writing to Elizabeth in London, where she was staying with her uncle for the first time in nine years, he concluded with more than a hint of annoyance that if she intended not to marry she should live 'retired, and not appear in ye World with an Expence, which is reasonable, upon ye Expectation of getting an Husband; But not otherwise'.[21]

There has been less attention to the escalating difficulty of her strictly lit-erary connections during the 1730s, which posed at least as great a threat to her reputation. It is vital to understand the nature of the literary scene in this decade in order to appreciate how intrepid it was for the Carters to attempt to use publication as a stepping stone to an advantageous match, or to bolstering Nicholas Carter's career prospects, or even the possibility of a position at Court for Elizabeth.[22] Reciprocally, the specific case of Elizabeth Carter will throw valuable light on the way socially engaged literature at this time endeavoured to overcome the protracted 'trauma' of England's financial collapse the decade before by rendering it intelligible. The poems and translations she produced in these years were implicated in this process of overcoming.

Pope and the woman writer

The first thing to note about the state of print culture at the moment of Carter's initiation is the absolute dominance of Pope. At the time her first poem was carried in the *Gentleman's Magazine* in the autumn of 1734, the journal was pirating Pope's most ambitious poem, *An Essay on Man*, in weekly instalments. *An Essay on Man* was the culmination of an extraordinary burst of activity which had produced other major works: *The Dunciad* (1728), *The Dunciad Variorum* (1729), *Epistle to Burlington* (1731), *Epistle to Bathurst* (1733). Pope's image as a writer had altered as a consequence of this phase: he was no longer the Pope of *The Rape of the Lock*, a light-hearted wit, nor the Pope of the translations from Homer, an industrious benefactor to British culture. Pope now stood as master of the venomous literary vendetta, a powerful ideologist in the 'Patriot' camp opposed to the Prime Minister, Sir Robert Walpole, and a scourge of women writers.

The last of these characters may seem of less general significance, and yet the three spheres of aggression were linked. Misogyny was not simply a peccadillo of Pope or other contemporary poets; it was a rhetorical tool, to be systematically applied within the field of political or aesthetic debate. The anti-Walpole sentiment of Pope and his allies formed part of an increasingly complex and articulate opposition to change and innovation, interpreted by them as a decline into social disorder and moral anarchy. Chapter 3 has explored the link between misogyny and financial disaster. As a target of satire, 'women become a metaphor for all that is threatening and offensive to the society at large'.[23]

The vision of effeminate decline extends to disapproval of the commercialization of print (in spite of the fact that Pope was perhaps the most skilful and successful operator in the changed climate) and to issues of taste. There was related opposition to the 'modern' in literature, and an intensified reliance on the 'ancient' as the touchstone of moral values. This was one source of the special sensitivity to the learned lady as a type. She was an Amazon of the library, transgressing on the some of the most cherished and defining ground of masculinity (knowledge of the classics and involvement in warfare being interchangeable as homosocial markers).[24] Beyond this special category, ordinary, semi-educated women were available as instances of regressive 'improvement'. Women were naturally on the side of the 'moderns' given the low standing of the sex in classical culture, their ignorance of Greek and Latin, and their supposed affinity with the capitalist world of luxury goods.

Occasionally, rival views of historical change became an underlying source of tension in Pope's dealings with female authors. This was so of Anne Finch, Countess of Winchelsea's depreciation of Sparta in her tragedy *Aristomenes* (1713) and her 'Invocation to the Southern Winds' (1717) with the lines 'Uncleanly *Sparta* taught contempt of death, / By making life not worth th'expence of breath': coded support for the process of feminization, voiced at the very moment when Pope was investing more heavily in the political ideal of Sparta.[25] By the 1730s Pope was fully converted to the idea of Britain's decline into corruption and luxury under the influence of his friend, the former Tory minister Viscount Bolingbroke (1678–1751), who returned to England from exile in 1725 and quickly set up the journal *The Craftsman* (1726–34) as the chief organ of anti-government opinion after the demise of *Cato's Letters*.[26] During the same period Pope's former comrade Mary Wortley Montagu was brought fully into the government camp by her friendship with Walpole's mistress, Maria Skerrett, and her favoured position at Court. These differences were ideological rather than personal, but the gender valences of the cultural debate meant that when women like Finch and Montagu were on the receiving end of an attack, the gendered rhetoric was especially pointed. However much polemical representations of grotesque or licentious women were designed to broadcast wider political and social meanings, these images could still be taken personally by female writers, even if they were not the named targets.

As early as 1714 Ann Finch had courteously and wittily taken Pope to task for his satire on women in *The Rape of the Lock*. She warns him to 'have a care / And shock the sex no more' and reminds him of the violent end of Orpheus, torn apart by bacchantes. She adds the reassurance:

> ... you our follies gently treat,
>   And spin so fine a thread,
> You need not fear his awkward fate,
>   The lock won't cost the head.

But she none the less advises him in future to address women with soothing admonitions to virtue, and acknowledgments of their native wit.

Instead Pope, while maintaining superficially cordial relations with the Countess, was engaged soon after with John Gay and Dr. Arbuthnot in writing the comic play *Three Hours After Marriage* (1717), which has been taken to satirize Finch in the character of Phoebe Clinket.[27] Whether or not she was the intended butt, the play elaborated on the stereotype of the ridiculous learned lady, which had its source in the comedies of Molière, and had already been aired in *The Female Wits* (1697), Susannah Centlivre's *The Basset-Table* (1705) and Charles Johnson's *The Generous Husband* (1711), among other British productions. The plot of *Three Hours After Marriage* actually centres on Fossile, an elderly antiquarian who marries a young woman and immediately finds that she seems to be involved in a variety of intricate affairs with other men. Eventually, she is discovered to be already married to a soldier who had been presumed dead.

Phoebe Clinket (her name derived from 'clink', to make jingling rhymes) is Fossile's niece. She makes a spectacular entrance in Act I with her maid 'bearing a Writing-Desk on her Back' followed by Phoebe 'Writing, her Head-dress stain'd with Ink, and Pens stuck in her Hair'.[28] The first Act is dominated by an episode in which her newly completed tragedy is given a small private performance. Mr. Plotwell pretends authorship for the sake of Phoebe's modesty, and the critic Sir Tremendous Longinus (John Dennis) gives his candid opinion. The occasion ends in a metaphorical bloodbath, with Sir Tremendous demanding endless cuts and alterations, to which Plotwell willingly agrees over Phoebe's anguished protests: 'Were the Play mine, you should gash my Flesh, mangle my Face, any thing sooner than scratch my Play ... Ah, hold, hold – I'm butcher'd, I'm massacred. For Mercy's Sake! murder, murder! ah! [faints ...]'. Fossile enters and, enraged by the uproar in his house, flings her papers into the fire. The other characters express wonder at her horrified reaction: has she lost her billet-doux, a fan or a pearl necklace (that is, something of genuine value to a young lady)? No, she has lost her 'Works', 'A Pindarick Ode! five Similes! & half an Epilogue!' The violent destruction of a female writer's papers or a female philosopher's laboratory was a recurrent motif in dramatic satire of learned ladies.[29] It was the act of exorcism that cleansed the narrative of her outrageous folly and aided the restoration of proper relations between the sexes.

Although *Three Hours After Marriage* was not particularly successful on the stage, it seems to have been effective in cultivating self-doubt and fear of publicity in intellectual young women. Catherine Talbot, then in her mid-twenties, wrote to a friend of her dread of being thought 'a Phoebe Clinkett', with reference to her lingering fame as a precocious child poet.[30] One particular line from the play was to have a long and malevolent afterlife. Phoebe's first appearance is prefaced by Fossile's remark: 'I took her into my House to regulate my Oeconomy; but instead of Puddings, she makes Pastorals; or when she should be raising Paste, is raising some Ghost in a new Tragedy.' This may have been the origin of the opposition between pudding-making and female learning which became almost proverbial by the mid-century.[31] Elizabeth Carter's elaborate anecdote in defence of her pudding-making skills in a letter to Talbot no doubt has its source in Phoebe Clinket, as does Samuel Johnson's celebrated remark about Carter's ability to 'make a pudding, as well as translate Epictetus'.[32] The association arises also in a letter from Elizabeth Robinson (later Montagu), aged 17, to a male mentor who recommended books to her. After remarking that 'there is a Mahometan Error crept even into the Christian Church that Women have no Souls, & it is thought very absurd for us to pretend to read or think like Reasonable Creatures', she explains that her solution is to pretend to acquaintances to have read only 'my Grandmothers receipts for Puddings & Cerecloths for Sprains'.[33] In Samuel Richardson's *Sir Charles Grandison* (1753–54) the bookish interests of the heroines Harriet and Charlotte are scrupulously balanced by reminders of their abilities as good housekeepers, in implicit dialogue with what might be called the Clinket syndrome, the idea that learning gives rise to dysfunctional femininity.[34]

As Elizabeth Carter took her first steps in publication, she had even more virulent instances of Pope's animus against women of letters to ponder. *The Dunciad* (first published 1728) declared war on a whole range of writers – those who wrote merely for profit, those who wrote for the government and those who had more directly offended Pope. But although amid this mob only four female authors are named, they are mentioned in especially vivid and damaging ways, with allusion to appearance, hygiene and sexual reputation.[35] Furthermore, it is no accident that the goddess Dulness, who initiates the action of the poem, is a female personification: 'With her uncontrollable fecundity, her feminine inconstancy, and her absolute power over the dunces, Dulness, Magna Mater to commercial writers, transgresses established boundaries and creates a powerful social incoherence that portends systemic disorder.'[36] The womb-like darkness of chaos she brings is a product of the misogynist imagination. Perhaps the most telling detail in the gender economy of the poem is the footnote to the lines in which the novelist Eliza Haywood is offered as prize to the winner of a pissing competition, while the runner-up will receive a china jordan (that is, chamber pot).[37] Pope in his note contrasts this ordering of goods with that of Homer in the games described in the *Iliad*, where a kettle is preferred over a female captive, and remarks on the protest made about this by Anne Dacier, the French translator of Homer.[38] Pope's own grotesque reversal of the hierarchy allows him to restate the low valuation of women in antiquity, while mocking two contemporary literary women.

Subsequently, a very public war of words had erupted between Pope and Lady Mary Wortley Montagu, former friends and collaborators. The cause was unclear (the story goes that she mocked his timid sexual advances), but the attacks became increasingly virulent on both sides. After a couple of preliminary digs from Pope, including one in the *Dunciad*, he suspected her of authoring *A Popp upon Pope*, a scurrilous pamphlet describing how the poet, while out walking, was set on by two literary enemies and given a thrashing on his 'naked Posteriors', an event he took the trouble to deny in a public advertisement.[39] In 1733 he launched a fresh attack in *Epistle to Bathurst* (ll. 62–5) deriding her husband's acquisitiveness in his coal-mining interests, and then again in *The First Satire of the Second Book of Horace Imitated*. The latter was Pope's most open strike yet at the Court and government, and here for the first time he used Montagu's poetic name 'Sappho', poisoning it as he had done in the *Dunciad* with Elizabeth Thomas's proud pseudonym 'Corinna', given her by Dryden.[40] She is charged with sexual promiscuity and, what was perhaps worse for a titled lady and *habituée* of the Court, authorship: her victims will be 'P-x'd by her love, or libell'd by her hate' (l. 84). Too truly Pope boasted in the same poem of his own satirical powers:

> Whoe'er offends, at some unlucky time
> Slides into verse, and hitches in a rhyme,
> Sacred to Ridicule his whole life long,
> And the sad burthen of some merry song.

> (ll. 76–80)

From this point 'Sappho' was the name usually attached to her in his diatribes, occasionally substituted by 'Lady Mary' and once by 'Fufidia'.[41] By invoking at the same time the original Sappho, the Greek poetess and Urfemale writer, Pope was able to sustain a broader campaign against women's trespasses into the realm of publication. When Montagu asked the Earl of Peterborough to intervene on her behalf with Pope, the latter feigned innocence, declaring that the lines would obviously be taken to refer to one of the most notorious female scribblers, 'Mrs Centlivre Mrs Haywood Mrs Manley & Mrs Been [*sic*, Behn]'.[42] In other words, the name was generic. The step from Sappho the denigrated contemporary to Sappho the emblem of illegitimate female authorship was easily taken, as an observation by Sir Charles Grandison in Richardson's novel makes clear: 'The title of *Wit* and *Poetess*, has been disgraced too often by Sappho's and Corinna's ancient and modern' to warrant any respectable young woman aspiring to write as 'the business of life'.[43]

Montagu, bravely or foolishly, attempted to give as good as she got. Instead of retreating from Pope's denomination, she embraced it by engaging in the same kind of libellous revenge as Eliza Haywood and Elizabeth Thomas had done.[44] Within three weeks of the appearance of *Horace Imitated*, she concocted and published on 8 March 1733 a poetic response in two separate versions, in collaboration with her ally Lord Hervey. Although issued anonymously, its authorship was widely known; Pope himself was in no doubt.[45] In *Verses Address'd to the Imitator of Horace* he was attacked for his low birth, his incompetence as a translator of Horace, his vicious misanthropic nature and his physical deformity and finally dismissed with a curse: 'with the Emblem of thy crooked Mind / Marked on thy Back, like *Cain*, by God's own Hand, / Wander like him, accursed through the Land'.[46] Pope's biographer Maynard Mack has observed, 'In this, Pope received the fiercest verbal thrashing of his life'.[47] But Montagu's biographer Isobel Grundy reflects that the weapon recoiled: 'In writing (or part-writing) this scorching assault, Lady Mary stepped outside the sheltered enclosure of high rank and gender chivalry. Its publication slammed the gates of the garden behind her, committing her to a wilderness inhabited by warring tribes of pamphleteers.'[48] A bevy of these pamphleteers entered the fray over the next few months, freely using or abusing the name of 'Sappho' or 'lady M—y'. In April the *Gentleman's Magazine* carried a short piece 'In Defence of Lady Mary Wortley' in which *Verses* is viewed as an appropriate retaliation for the indiscriminate 'Gall' of Pope and she is also linked to the infamous *Popp upon Pope*.[49]

Elizabeth Carter could not have been unaware of these developments, given the echo of the battle in the pages of the very journal to which her father contributed and to which perhaps she was already meditating a contribution. They must have operated as a strong disincentive, a terrible presage of the dangers of publicity for a female wit. Beginning with *Peri Bathous; or, The Art of Sinking in Poetry* (1728), a sly act of provocation designed to make the *Dunciad* appear a work of self-defence, Pope had been instrumental in turning the world of letters into a frightening maelstrom of libel and counter-libel, into which any writer, male or female, might hesitate to venture.[50] He had given due warning as early as the Preface to his 1717 *Works*:

> I believe, if any one, early is his life should contemplate the dangerous fate of authors, he would scarce be of their number on any consideration. The life of a Wit is a warfare upon earth; and the present spirit of the world is such, that to attempt to serve it (any way) one must have the constancy of a martyr, and a resolution to suffer for its sake.[51]

As Lawrence Lipking has added, 'Nor did he prove reluctant to add to that suffering.'[52] On this score, Catherine Talbot was to write passionately to a friend, that 'to sit down in Cold Blood & abuse an honest worthy Man because he has writ a dull Book ... This blackening all the World & Mauling so unmercifully all poor inconsiderable Authors is what I can forgive neither to Boileau nor Pope.'[53] With female authors, it went beyond mere professional mutilation to irreparable social damage; the reputations of Montagu, Haywood, Manley and the rest could never be fully recuperated, and are compromised, morally and personally, not merely as writers, to this day. Moira Ferguson has noted the gap in the production of feminist works between around 1710 and 1739, and that the achievements of Sarah Fyge

Field Egerton (died 1723) and Mary Astell (died 1731) were rapidly forgotten.[54] Given the temper of the times, oblivion was surely a blessing.

Elizabeth Carter, the *Gentleman's Magazine* and the challenge to Pope

Carter's 'A Riddle', published in the *Gentleman's Magazine* in November 1734, was cautiously unsigned. It is an accomplished exercise in a genre popular at the time. The convention of weaving a mystifying play of allusion to the answer (in this case 'fire') gave licence to a wilder strain of imagination than she allowed herself in most of her poetic output. Her identity was exposed in a verse response in June of the following year, 'To *Miss* CART-R, *Author of the Riddle in* Nov. 1734'. Beginning with the address 'Ingenious nymph!' the writer, who signs himself 'Sylvius', begs for more of her 'pleasing lays' in precisely the suggestive style of high gallantry ('wake our raptures with thy powerful muse') that greeted Elizabeth Singer in the pages of the *Athenian Mercury*.[55] Once her sex was known, her riddle itself could be eroticized on rereading. The subject of 'fire' irresistibly gives rise to *double entendre*. It is hidden and sought after by 'prying man'. And the final lines seem to take advantage of generic conventions to initiate a deliberate flirtation with the (male) reader:

> All men me court, and all alike me shun;
> I'm good to all, yet many have undone;
> Now flourish, now decay, now die, now live,
> Now pleasure, and now pain, by turns I give.
> Substance and form in me are but a name,
> For neither of the two I rightly claim;
> A spirit less, and yet such force enjoy,
> As all material beings shall destroy.
>
> (ll. 17–24)

Stereotypes of woman's nature are invoked: coquetry; capriciousness; lack of 'substance' or, as Pope would soon claim in *Epistle to a Lady*, character; the absence even of soul; destructiveness. The sexualized and anti-feminist effect of the portrait is not diminished by the presence on the same page of a poem 'Said to be written by the rev. Dr. Swift ... On his own Deafness', which ends with the lines 'Nay, what is incredible, alack! / I hardly hear woman's clack!'

The *Gentleman's Magazine* was considered by some contemporaries to be more moral than its competitors; modern scholars have characterized it as particularly favourable in its treatment of women, and on questions of relations between the sexes.[56] But a glance through its pages will reveal plenty of material in the 'libertine' mode, particularly in the early and mid-1730s. Like Dunton, Cave as editor liked to stage a debate. He encouraged female contributors, and was willing to include 'feminist' correctives to misogynist satire, as we will see in a moment. But the magazine was no safe haven for female self-expression. A poetess must risk her work jostling against the pirated compositions of Swift and Pope as well as those of their many imitators. Carter was acutely aware of the danger to her reputation posed by this randomness. Many years later she wrote to Talbot of having given Cave a 'hearty *twinkation*' for allowing her name to 'appear in bad company' on the page.[57]

Carter's response to her first brush with the public was a quickly produced verse reply 'To Sylvius' signed 'E C—R', insisting on her humble novice status and seeking safety in numbers by picking up his reference to 'sister muses' and deflecting praise onto 'Fidelia', an established contributor to the magazine. Interestingly, in light of Richard Samuel's future glorification of the Bluestockings in his painting *The Nine Living Muses*, here Carter already draws attention to the confusion that can arise, as it does in Sylvius' poem, when a female poet with her own muse (i.e. inspiration) is invoked as a muse for others ('How shall the blushing *muse* presume to write?'). She mentions an ambition to write on serious subjects – religious faith and the vicissitudes of human life – once her ideas are more mature. In the meantime, she published a free translation from the Greek of a love pastoral by Anacreon under cover of the pseudonym 'Camilla', which highlighted her abilities as a scholar if not as an original poet.[58]

Pope published his *Epistle to a Lady: Of the Characters of Women* (1735), and the *Gentleman's Magazine* printed an 'Epistle to Mr. Pope. By a LADY. Occasioned by his CHARACTERS OF WOMEN' (*GM* 6 (December 1736), 745). *Characters of Women* is a gallery of various types of defective femininity in the mode of the sixth satire of Juvenal. But within this diversity Pope emphasizes the sameness of women: unlike men, they are governed by two ruling passions, 'The Love of Pleasure, and the Love of Sway' (210), justifying the maxim that '"Most Women have no character at all"' (2). He also departs from Juvenal in framing the poem with references to a female ideal, the anonymous addressee his friend Martha Blount, an unmarried woman and a rare hybrid of masculine sense and feminine softness.[59]

Mary Wortley Montagu appears yet again as 'Sappho' ('Flavia' in the first version, which appeared in February), on this occasion charged with slovenliness, a time-honoured feature of caricatures of learned ladies which became a regular theme in Pope's references to her. Here, the study of Locke is held up as the ultimate incongruity with respect to women's native vanity;

> Rufa, whose eye quick-glancing o'er the Park,
> Attracts each light gay meteor of a Spark,

> Agrees as ill with Rufa studying Locke,
> As Sappho's diamonds with her dirty smock;
> Or Sappho at her toilet's greasy task,
> With Sappho fragrant at an ev'ning Mask:
> So morning Insects that in muck begun,
> Shine, buzz, and fly-blow in the setting-sun.

(ll. 21–8)

The apparent non-sequitur (what does studying Locke have to do with a dirty smock, and Sappho's diurnal resurrection from dung-hill to evening fragrance?) is explained by the logic of pollution: dirt is matter out of place, and the aberration of a woman in the library is equivalent to Sappho's ill-judged attempts to beautify herself and shine socially.[60]

The 'Lady' who replied with the 'Epistle to Pope' in the *Gentleman's Magazine* was Anne, Viscountess Irwin.[61] Her argument interestingly harnesses the language of Patriot opposition, of Bolingbroke and of Pope himself, with its focus on corruption and the influence of commerce, to the cause of women, anticipating the republican feminism of Mary Wollstonecraft. The restriction of women's minds is compared to the effect of the division of labour on the minds of professional men, with their areas of specialized knowledge and ignorance. 'Modern' women are compared unfavourably with the heroines of antiquity, who were trained to recognize truth, subdue the passions and value reason. Like Finch in her response to *The Rape of the Lock*, she tries to enlist Pope by flattery for the task of elevating the morals of women and making them capable of public spirit,

> To rescue woman from this *Gothic* state,
> New passions raise, their minds anew create:
> Then for the *Spartan* virtue we might hope;
> For who stands unconvinc'd by generous *Pope*?

No attempt is made to defend the female types pilloried in Pope's poem, and there is no sense of women's 'right' to education. Their elevation is to be instrumental; a means of breeding heroes.

In April 1737, Carter published her own indirect and far less deferential answer to Pope. Significantly, it was signed 'Eliza', a pen-name she would maintain until her retirement from the *Gentleman's Magazine* in 1739, chosen in defiance of Pope's blackening of 'Eliza' (Haywood) in *The Dunciad*, and heralding the arrival of a more confident and serious poetic persona. The poem was titled 'On the Death of Mrs. Rowe' and the high reputation of the precursor poet Elizabeth Singer Rowe is held up like a shield ('our sex's ornament and pride', 8) as Carter sallies forth to do battle with those who would slander all literary women as 'female wits', mere purveyors of 'Th' intriguing novel, and the wanton tale' (11–12).[62] The fulsome praise of Rowe's virtues may appear conventional, but the militant purpose underlying it can be registered when comparison is made with other tributes to Rowe that appeared in the magazine.[63] These invariably sought to subordinate her talents as a poet to her moral worth; true, the typical panegyrist will say, her voice has been silenced, but it is a small loss to set against her homecoming in heaven. Carter by contrast places great emphasis on the enduring power of her writings, their ability

> To charm the fancy, and emend the heart;
> From trifling follies to withdraw the mind,
> To relish pleasures of a nobler kind ...
> This still shall last...

> (ll.16–18, 21)

Carter boldly asserts the ability of a contemporary female writer not only to transcend the follies of modern times, but to teach others to resist them: the sex of those she will teach is not specified.

A new version of the poem, still called 'On the Death of Mrs Rowe' (1739), states the case even more strongly. Here, the issue of a denigrated and degraded tradition of 'Female wit' is brought forward and addressed in the opening lines:[64]

> Oft' did Intrigue it's guilty Arts unite,
> To blacken the Records of female Wit:
> The tuneful Song lost ev'ry modest Grace,
> And lawless Freedoms triumph'd in their Place:

> (ll. 5–8)

This could be taken as a straightforward indictment of Pope and other writers of misogynist satire, whose attacks on female intellectual endeavour were partly responsible for the low moral standard of literary production by women. At the same time, the personification of 'Intrigue' leaves agency ambiguous; writers like Eliza Haywood and Mary Delariviere Manley have had a hand in 'blackening the Records' themselves. By their publication of scandal chronicles and involvement in political smear campaigns, they have invited contempt. What emerges is the impression of a vicious circle of condemnation of women writers and Grub Street standards of writing by women. Rowe, now referred to as 'Philomela', her *Athenian Mercury* pen-name, is celebrated for her ability to break out of this trap.[65]

Again, Rowe's qualities of mind and soul are praised by Carter in terms that could equally be applied to a man. But the central topic of the piece, even more emphatically than before, is the proper nature of the poetic vocation itself: to elevate the reader's ideas, to teach morality and inspire faith. Carter is intent not only on making the point that a female poet was capable of achieving these aims, but also in laying claim, on Rowe's behalf and her own, to a new field of philosophical poetry most famously exemplified by Pope's *Essay on Man*. Claudia Thomas has observed a striking number of allusions to Pope's writing in what is a fairly short poem. Among them is his claim in *Epistle to Dr. Arbuthnot* to have 'moraliz'd his song' (341), and his addressing of the subject of 'th' Eternal Cause' (I, 130) in *Essay on Man*, affirmed by Carter's line that the Muse is rightly applied to 'celebrate the first Great CAUSE of Things' (12). Thomas finds the concluding lines of Carter's poem in close dialogue with the end of *Essay on Man*, creating a contrast that is 'almost comically pointed'.[66] In both works, the poets conclude by intruding themselves, their aspirations, and their desire for fame. Pope hails Henry St John, Viscount Bolingbroke, as his mentor; Carter, repeating Pope's terms, claims Rowe as her example. The one was a notorious deist and political opportunist (dangerously undercutting the moral intent of the poem, as Pope was aware when he altered the name 'St John' to 'Laelius' on first publication), the other a woman of saintly character. The implicit contrast continues in Carter's wish for fame only in so far as she adheres to Rowe's elevated model; while Pope hopes merely to have 'my little bark attendant sail' in the wake of his friend's very temporal and precarious reputation. Montagu had mocked these same sycophantic lines in an unpublished squib 'P[ope] to Bolingbroke' (*c.*1734–35), where the 'learned Doctor of the publick Stage' is addressed by 'Your poor Toad-eater' and assured that 'all is right in all we do' and that 'Using the Spight by the Creator given, / We only tread the Path that's mark'd by heaven'.[67]

For Thomas, these parallels are evidence of Carter's intention to articulate 'a new, feminine poetic tradition', 'a pious, feminine alternative to "masculine" deism', and she cites Harold Bloom's concept of a deliberate 'creative misreading' of a strong precursor poet in support of this.[68] What is missing from her interpretation are the elements of rivalry, aggression and absorption so prominent in Bloom's theory of influence. Carter aimed to join Pope on the high moral ground he had himself done so much to establish as poetry's proper sphere, to learn from his practice and improve on it spiritually if not aesthetically. The notion of piety as the property of a distinctive 'feminine tradition' would have been alien to her as the daughter of a clergyman. If she emphasized Rowe's sex it was because of the satirists' axiom that to be female was to be disqualified from serious literary work: an assumption borne out by the low 'female wits'. Carter's sex undoubtedly figured in the reception of her own work, but in ways she could not necessarily anticipate or control. 'Eliza' identified with 'Philomela' not least in her experience of the runaway nature of media fame.

Along with the persona 'Eliza', Carter took on at the age of 20 a project to challenge Pope, but indirectly, in the realm of ideas, rather than through verbal abuse. Her aim was the articulation of a personal brand of Christianized Stoicism, a direction she consistently followed right up to her most important work, the translation of Epictetus. The Stoic pursuit of *ataraxia* – peace of mind – is one solution to the problem of the uncertainties and unavoidable evils encountered in the world. Strict government of the passions enables an attitude of calm resignation. In Carter's view, however, the pagans ran the risk of a descent into passivity and the temptation of suicide. Resignation must be combined with active faith, a spiritual sense of duty and belief in a heavenly reward.

Carter and Pope were responding to the same state of affairs; a complex commercial society in which the unstable figure of fortune had an enhanced and very immediate relevance. Pope, like the Carter family, had been 'bit' in the South Sea Bubble.[69] And Pope's handicaps, his Roman Catholicism and physical ailments brought him closer than most men of the time to the perspective of an unendowed but intellectually precocious young woman engaged in the uphill struggle for social and economic survival. The difference between them hinges on the status of the passions. For Pope, in *Essay on Man* and other poems relating to the 'Opus Magnum', published around 1733 and 1734, the passions must be accepted not simply as a flaw in humanity, but as part of the providential plan which transforms apparent evil into good. With this broadened view comes a sense of detachment from the spectacle of immorality; contemporary critics would say that it leads Pope into fatalism and complacency about personal morality.

In the context of attempts to reformulate a progressivist view of history in the aftermath of economic collapse, what is most striking in the *Essay* is its vigorous ideological experimentation. We find there the same creative hybridizing of discourses as in *Cato's Letters* and Mandeville. The poem is presented in its opening lines as a peripatetic dialogue. A corresponding sense of movement and dialogism characterizes the method of its investigation into human nature, involving constant resort to paradox (bad produces good, strife produces harmony) and free combination of philosophical elements (rigour, scepticism, innate benevolence): 'Passions, like Elements, tho' born to fight, / Yet, mix'd and soften'd, in his work unite.' (II: 111–12).

Many a commentator has tried to pin down the meaning of the *Essay*, and certainly the poem and its paratext offer some fixed vantage points: in the prose 'Design' Pope speaks of 'steering betwixt the extremes of doctrines seemingly opposite' and there are several tributes to Order as the somewhat punitive absolution of discordant reality (I, 241–66, 281–94, III, 262, IV, 49–53). But attempts to argue that the *Essay* is a staunch defence of the landed interest or a verse translation of Bolingbroke's paternalistic civic humanism fail to account for contrary elements.[70] The dominant impression is of liquidity and turbulence, rise and fall, not of control, subordination or the imposition of form. The principle of perpetual motion is forcefully asserted by Pope:

> In lazy Apathy let Stoics boast
> Their Virtue fix'd; 'tis fix'd as in a frost,
> Contracting all, retiring to the breast;
> But strength of mind is Exercise, not Rest:
> The rising tempest puts in act the soul,
> Parts it may ravage, but preserves the whole.
> On life's vast ocean diversely we sail,
> Reason the card, but Passion is the gale;
> Nor God alone in the still calm we find,
> He mounts the storm, and walks upon the wind.
>
> (II: 101–10)

God himself is caught up in the agitation of his created world; the same might be said of the addressee, the glorious and fallen Bolingbroke, and also of the poet himself. The *Essay*, to a greater extent than the *Ethic Epistles*, with their more traditional censure of specific vices, shows the side of Pope that was prepared to gamble on the stock market and gloried in the combative nature of capitalist print culture, in his own successful commercial dealings and his ability to ride the storm of public controversy.[71]

The *Essay on Man* is further evidence of the special difficulty of matching ideology to political positions in the Walpole era. Pope was at this time a prominent spokesman of the Patriot Opposition, composed of Tories and disaffected Whigs. As we have seen, he elsewhere engaged in the classical tactic of representing the follies of women as an index of social decline. Yet in the *Essay* ideas derived from the ultra-Whig Bernard Mandeville and his master the French sceptic La Rochefoucauld are fundamental. In Epistle II self-love appears as the vital element in human nature, reason as a secondary force (ll. 53–92); social virtues spring from vicious passions (ll. 181–94). In Epistle III the apparent anarchy of a 'realm of Bees' or 'Ant's republic' is put forward as a model of smooth-running possessive individualism. But Epistle III is a *bricolage* in which the myth of the Golden Age jostles oddly with the philosophical fiction of the State of Nature in a version far different from that of *Fable of the Bees* (ll. 147–54), and a Hobbesian account of the origins of government cohabits with a Machiavellian call for a restoration of patriotic first principles (ll. 269–94). In Epistle IV Pope's sources are if anything yet more heterodox. Shaftesbury's theory of innate social affections makes a late appearance (ll. 39–44).[72] And in spite of two openly hostile references to Stoicism and the misappropriation of the Stoic convention of navigating stormy seas, there is even an embrace of self-denying virtue (ll. 77–92).[73] Pope struggles to find an appropriate ethical frame for the utilitarian vision pioneered by

Mandeville. The work would be completed in the economic theodicy of Adam Smith, which legitimized the unrestricted play of the free market under the sign of a providential 'invisible hand'.[74]

Contradictions between political allegiance and ideological statements similarly hold for the women writers of the time, though in the reverse direction. Mary Wortley Montagu was a Court Whig, an ally of Lord Hervey, one of the government's princiapl propagandists, and might have been expected to adopt a progressivist line. Yet throughout the 1720s and 1730s she wrote poetry in the libertine style of Pope and his associates, like them often mocking the follies and passions of women as a sign of the degenerate times, and the essays she published anonymously under the title *The Nonsense of Commonsense* are sometimes more austerely civic humanist in sentiment than those that appeared in the opposition journal *Commonsense*.[75] Elizabeth Carter was also allied with the Court Whigs by familial and professional ties; her father's patron Sir George Oxenden was himself the protégé of Walpole and the *Gentleman's Magazine* was Whig in tendency.[76] Yet Carter's poetry evinces a Stoic outlook, untouched by the new tendencies that Pope wrestled with. The irony is that Carter, alongside the other Bluestocking writers, would in future years come to emblematize the progressive tendency of the nation, while the ambivalent Pope would be portrayed as an enemy of modernity. The curious mismatch between ascetic femininity and apologies for the growth of commerce and luxury will be one of the central themes of my later chapters.

Carter's earliest philosophical poem was written on the occasion of her eighteenth birthday, '*In Diem Natalem*' (1735). It was never published in the *Gentleman's Magazine*, very likely because of its personal nature. Instead, it appeared in *Poems on Particular Occasions* and was the only piece from that collection republished in *Poems on Several Occasions* (1762). It was a declaration of faith and an act of self-dedication of enduring significance for Carter; its central idea is expressed with the simplicity of a hymn:

> Thro' all the shifting Scenes of varied Life,
> In Calms of Ease, or ruffling Storms of Grief,
> Thro' each Event of this inconstant State,
> Preserve my Temper equal and sedate.

> (ll. 35–8)[77]

The idea was reiterated in a translation of Horace Lib. II Ode 10, which teaches moderation – 'The same right temper, steady and sedate' – as the best method of navigating 'the storms of fate',[78] and in 'Horace Lib. I Ode 22. Imitated', which speaks of transcending changes of place and fortune by preserving 'a settled calm within' through the powers of the mind.[79] Her next substantial original poem, 'Fortune', was headed by a quotation in Latin from the Tenth Satire of Juvenal, rendered by a contemporary translator as: 'O Fortune, did Men act right, thou wouldst have no Divinity about thee; but we make thee a Goddess, and place thee in the skies', and in the gently satiric idiom of Edward Young, advises that the only way to overcome the fear of loss is to curtail desire.[80]

Carter's decision to carry out a translation of a critique of Pope's *Essay on Man* by the Swiss professor of philosophy Jean Paul de Crousaz was no doubt motivated by a number of factors. It seems likely that she was urged by Cave, Johnson, Birch and other friends, who must have regarded it as a sure-fire earner.[81] The *Essay* had first been published anonymously in 1733 and 1734, and won almost universal praise for its piety and philosophical profundity. It was only once the identities of Pope and his addressee Bolingbroke were known that a backlash slowly gathered force, centring on accusations of religious heterodoxy. Crousaz's attack, published in 1737, was the most erudite, prestigious and damaging of all. It may be that Carter was glad to contribute to the discomfiture of Pope, as a woman writer and potential target of his anti-feminist wit, or, as seems most likely, she had a keen interest in the issues raised by the poem and sought to participate vicariously in the debate surrounding it. There is a curious suggestion in Pennington's *Memoirs* of Carter that Nicholas Carter and Sir George Oxenden may have believed that her translation, which included a few editorial footnotes correcting Crousaz, might commend her to Pope's favour. But surely the reverse was probable: that once again she was risking his anger. Pope's arch-enemy, the publisher Edmund Curll, had rushed out *A Commentary Upon Mr. Pope's Four Ethic Epistles* (1738), containing sections from Crousaz's second treatise concerning *Essay on Man*. Once Carter had made the full text of the more important first treatise available in 1739, it became a vital resource for the anti-Pope camp. The government newspaper the *Daily Gazetteer* had a field day with the Carter translation and used it to launch a thoroughgoing ideological demolition of Pope.[82]

An Examination of Mr Pope's Essay on Man remains a controversial document even for Pope scholars today. For A.D. Nuttall, all commentators belong to one of two categories: the 'Crousazian' – those who note the logical and ideological contradictions present in the poem; and the 'Warburtian' – after Pope's chief contemporary apologist William Warburton, later Bishop of Gloucester, who insisted on the theological orthodoxy of the poem at the price of explaining away its connection with the deist Bolingbroke.[83] For Harry M. Solomon, Crousaz is at the root of a widespread misreading that denigrates the ideas while disregarding the significance of the poetic form.[84] Translation was an issue from the start: Crousaz did not know English and relied in the *Examen* on a poor prose rendering of the poem (Carter's footnotes point out some misconceptions deriving from this source) and in the supplementary *Commentaire* (1738; an English translation was published by Samuel Johnson in 1739), on a poetic version by Jean-Franc[,]ois du Resnel. He had no appreciation of irony or paradox. But his rhetorical strategy of repeatedly pointing to parallels with the philosophy of Gottfried Leibniz and Baruch Spinoza (both of whom he accuses of fatalism) while conceding that elsewhere Pope seems to adhere to orthodox Christian thinking had a devastating effect on the poet's standing. Crousaz represents him as a wilful, blundering *naif*, whose dazzling aesthetic gifts are not matched by intellectual ability. The real debate is among philosophers, Crousaz seems to be saying, and hapless Pope has been caught in the crossfire.

Pennington believed the effect of Carter's translation to have been decisive. It led some who had been blinded by the 'beauties' of the poem to look again. 'Perhaps too it had some effect on Mr. Pope's public character; for Dr. Carter says in a letter to his daughter in this year [1739], "Mr. Pope's reputation seems to be on the decline. It has had its run, and it is no wonder that (as is the condition of all sublunary things) it is out of breath".'[85] Pope published little subsequently, whatever the reasons. Five years later, as the poet lay on his deathbed, Catherine Talbot wrote to Carter, 'Poor Mr. Pope is in a very declining way' and a few months later, after his death, she laments the lack of any suitably elevated memorial poem; all that have appeared are 'paltry' panegyrics.[86] Carter made no comment.

5
Clarissa and the 'Total Revolution in Manners'

Richardson's historical fictions

In an appendix to *Sir Charles Grandison*, Samuel Richardson refers to his three novels in a way that suggests he saw them as a continuous historical chronicle.[1] The action of *Pamela* (1740), he says, takes place within thirty years of its publication, that is to say, after 1710; *Clarissa* (1747–48) within twenty years of its publication, therefore in the late 1720s or 1730s; and *Grandison* (1753–54) depicts 'scenes of life carried down nearly to the present time' (*G* III: 470). The brief remark opens up a vision of the works as a vast study of transformations in sexual politics through three generations. It also gives a new dimension to his description of the novels as 'histories'. This is generally taken to mean 'true to life'.[2] I want to propose that they should be understood as conscious registers of recent times and more specifically as works that anticipate the genre of 'general history' introduced by Voltaire and Hume, with its focus on the transformation of manners.[3] The novels trace the origins of the current crisis in thinking about social and economic change, responding to issues that were still in pressing need of resolution. I would argue that when Richardson decided to retain *The History of a Young Lady* as the subtitle to *Clarissa* as opposed to Aaron Hill's apt suggestion, *A Lady's Legacy*, it was because history, in the sense of recording and interpreting the past, was the essence of the work. In the title of his final novel, *The History of Sir Charles Grandison*, 'history' is given pride of place.

If we think of *Pamela* as a fable of reformation set in the early 1710s, the age of Addison and Steele, the historical dimension of Richardson's social mission is brought to the fore. The novel picks up where the essays of the *Tatler* and the *Spectator* left off, in developing a model woman as the agent of moral improvement. The specifically female virtue of the servant girl Pamela, a virtue activated in defence of her chastity, is so potent that it can overcome vast status difference. It makes a convert of the master who coveted her and leads him to marry her. Richardson radicalizes the model of female influence in a way that Steele would have found unthinkable, but that derives from another notable feature of the literary scene in the 1710s. Pamela is a writer. Like her contemporaries Mary Astell, Anne Finch and Elizabeth Elstob, she combines strict piety with wit and learning. Her letters and journal recount her trials and ultimately bring about her triumph, by turning her enemies into admiring readers. Richardson draws on these two elements of the cultural moment at the end of Queen Anne's reign – the ideal of female moral influence and the prominence of respectable female authors – and revives the spirit of optimism regarding the enhanced status of women in society and the progress of civility and refinement. Problematically, though, feminization in *Pamela* is tied to carnal desire, just as it had been in the representation of the 'Pindarick Lady' in the *Athenian Mercury*. Pamela herself is an unstable amalgam; a beautiful spirit whose body can be possessed and disparaged.

The tragic narrative of *Clarissa* runs for the course of a year during the 'dark ages' of historical pessimism and literary misogyny described in the previous two chapters.[4] Here, symptomatically, the rake is in the ascendant. He drives the plot and is given a voice, by turns seductive and repellent, impersonating the Restoration wit but also Mandeville, Bolingbroke and Pope, in correspondence with a fellow-rake. Clarissa, for all her high principles, is powerless to reform him. Again symptomatically, her correspondence is interrupted and infiltrated by the rake, Lovelace. She is of the same rank, but through his devices, she is alienated from her family, abducted, imprisoned and raped. As in *Pamela*, sexual difference takes precedence over class; here it warrants Lovelace's experiment, by which he attempts to prove that even a highborn lady of superlative accomplishments and great reputation is in the end, in Pope's words, merely 'a softer Man': that is, a creature of the passions, swayed by vanity, shame and lust. Clarissa transcends the trial in a way that neither Lovelace nor many contemporary readers expected. Instead of conceding the point and accepting his offer of marriage, she gradually sheds her alluring mortal frame and becomes pure soul, all mind. Dying from a mysterious wasting disease, the text of her history remains as a legacy to a fallen England, with which her virtues were incompatible. Feminization, the promise of reform through the example of female virtue, is violently detached from worldly expectations, including the promise of sexual pleasure. Richardson was renouncing what he now considered *Pamela*'s 'trite' aim of the 'perfecting a private Happiness, by the Reformation of a Libertine'.[5] The value of Clarissa lies solely in her textuality, her function as example, and in her demonstration of femininity as a rival system of values.

Sir Charles Grandison heralds the dawn of an age of enlightenment in relations between the sexes, the early 1750s, with a reformed cultural order that Richardson himself has been instrumental in shaping. It is worth noting that the characters in *Grandison* have read *Clarissa* (*G* I: 229). A new genus of 'good man' can now exist with Sir Charles as prototype, under the influence of virtuous women, cherishing and admiring them, and even sharing some of their feminine attributes. In spite of the title, its ideological work makes it the most female-centred of Richardson's works. The object is to imagine the 'good man' as an incentive and object of desire for good women. The sole area of dramatic tension in the novel concerns the anxieties of the two female paragons who both wish to marry him. This aside, the novel is chiefly concerned with determining the protocols of the new order, in letters and conversation. Two vital and controversial areas receive a great deal of attention but are finally left unresolved: the value of female education and the question of whether souls are sexed. The debates are open-ended. What matters is less a decision on these topics than the fact that the issue of the progress of women has been established as central to the moral welfare of the nation.

Richardson's femino-centrism has sometimes been taken as a withdrawal from the realm of political debate. The preceding chapters investigating the figure of woman in discussions of socio-economic change indicate that it shows, on the contrary, the extent of his engagement with current political discourses. The thread running through the whole of Richardson's work is the issue of reformation. This is not the narrow concern of a bourgeois puritan for personal salvation, but perhaps the most urgent question of the age.[6] The question of reformation is part of the general problem of change. Can the manners of the new commercial society be reconciled with morality? Opposition writers animated by civic humanist ideas flatly denied the possibility. Economic innovation, the expansion of the financial market and the growth of a consumer culture, were denounced as a decline into corruption, luxury and effeminacy. Even proponents of commerce, such as Mandeville and Defoe, could not see beyond the moral rhetoric that associated the acquisitive passions with the corrupting influence of women. When Richardson turned from printing to fiction-writing at the age of 50, he did so at a propitious moment. Walpole was in decline; the heat had gone out of the Patriot opposition.[7] It was the end of an era; a juncture when the future might be negotiated on revised terms. It is probably no accident that in 1739 the first substantial feminist polemic since 1710 appeared, *Women Not Inferior to Man* signed 'Sophia, A Person of Quality', which drew on Poulain de la Barre to argue against customary notions of the hierarchy of the sexes.[8] Richardson addressed the question of change by reversing the gendered bias of civic humanist pessimism: in place of effeminacy, feminization. The key to this revision was the imaginary creation of a virtuous woman.

Richardson began by imagining virtue in the form of a beautiful servant girl, her family fallen on hard times, who is isolated and tested by a libertine master unable to believe in the possibility of a virtuous woman. She marries him and her influence spreads through his household and beyond into neighbouring gentry families. This was the corner-stone of the programme of reform. Richardson continues to build on it through his next two novels, extending the sphere of female influence upwards through the ranks of society and outwards to incorporate ever more complex networks of kinship and private patronage, eventually embracing the lower nobility or gentry, untitled gentlemen, the clergy, merchants and upper tradesmen, until he leaves off with Sir Charles Grandison, poised on the brink of public life, urged by his friends to stand as a Member of Parliament. Richardson exalts the intimate, inward-turned private sphere in his narratives of female ascendancy. But they were written for the literary public sphere, to stimulate public debate and promote the reform of public morality.

Pamela is the new Cato. In place of the pagan legislator, the Christian exemplar. In place of a denunciation of luxury leading to sumptuary controls on women, the redirection of men's desires away from self-gratification and towards virtue in the shape of a beautiful woman. In place of the patrician method of reform, by which morality is restored by the fiat of lawgivers, regeneration from below by a female servant, through the medium of the passions. The instrumental place of the passions in Richardson's programme of reform is the sign of his acceptance of mod-ernity. Like Mandeville and Defoe, he assumes that change is the aggregate of individual impulses. In the 'Preface' to *Pamela* Richardson poses as editor of an authentic set of letters, and mounts an '*Appeal from his own Passions, which have been uncommonly moved in perusing these engaging Scenes) to the Passions of Every one who shall read them with the least Attention*'. In the novels, Richardson frequently deprecates greed and materialism, but the passions that exist in a commercial society are the materials with which he works. *Clarissa* appears in the world in 'the humble Guise of a *Novel* only by way of Accommodation to the Manners and Taste of an Age overwhelmed with a Torrent of Luxury, and abandoned to Sound and senselessness'.[9] What is crucial in this statement is the word 'Accommodation'. Richardson has no ideological argument with commercialization.

The difficulty with Pamela as legislator is that her moral authority is undermined by her earthly 'reward'. The ease with which she could revert to the misogynist stereotype was shown by Fielding's burlesque novella *Shamela*. Behind the mask of virtue, Pamela might be exposed as an acquis-itive whore on the make; as bad, if not worse, than her lascivious master. Although Richardson naturally resented criticism of this kind, it was of enormous value to him. There can never have been a novelist so zealous about the process of debating ideas raised by his novels with anyone who would play ball, from the teenaged girl next door to anonymous letter-writers. In this, he revives the spirit of the *Athenian Mercury* and the link between the question-and-answer method and the new.[10] The novelty of his project inevitably raised numerous questions of principle and conduct.

In attempting to answer such questions, he constantly revised his texts, before and after publication, and produced in addition a multitude of para-texts: letters, apologias, prefaces, postscripts, sometimes published and sometimes privately circulated. With *Clarissa* Richardson incorporated the criticism of Pamela by Fielding and others to produce a dialectically strengthened version of female virtue. The authority of Clarissa is supported by her incommensurable difference from the man who attempts to seduce her.

The opposition of the sexes in *Clarissa*

The word 'sex' appears 222 times in the first edition of *Pamela* (1740) and 215 times in *Sir Charles Grandison* (1753–54). There are no fewer that 456 appearances in the first edition of *Clarissa* (1747–48), rising to 545 in the third edition of 1751. Compare this with a mere seven mentions in Defoe's *Roxana* (1724), 46 in *Tom Jones* (1749), 29 in *Amelia* (1752), and ten in *Humphry Clinker* (1771), and one begins to get the measure of Richardson's epic labour of definition.[11] For by 'sex' is of course meant, nine times out of ten, the female sex. A speculative chronology of this phenomenon also becomes possible, beginning at the start of the 1740s, reaching a peak in the late 1740s, and steadying in the early 1750s.

In a letter to his friend Dr George Cheyne, Richardson wrote with reference to *Pamela*: 'As to the Difference between the sexes, I leave that Matter as I find it, because I think it necessary in my Plan to avoid all Notions not generally receiv'd or allowed.' He goes on to indicate that by 'the Difference between the sexes' he means the customary hierarchy of the sexes, and gives as an example of his observance of existing forms the scene in Part Two of *Pamela* where he allows Mr B. to exert his male prerogative by vetoing his wife's desire to nurse her children. He adds that it is, however, the 'only Debate' between them and that his own inclination is to 'do all the Honour I am capable of doing, to the fairer and *better Sex*, as I truly think it, *in the main*, as you say'.[12] In *Clarissa* he resolved to tackle the conventional 'Difference between the sexes' head on, with the express aim of reversing the hierarchy of the sexes and demonstrating the intrinsic moral superiority of women. Whereas in the first novel he avoided overt debate, the second is dominated by an extended debate between a man and a woman over rights and values. *Clarissa* does not simply demolish the basis of customary male authority, it dramatizes the process of destruction.

The foundation of male prerogative was the assumption that women are, in their physical being as in their moral being, imperfect versions of men. The existing hierarchy is crucially supported by similitude. In previous chapters I have shown the way socio-economic innovation was met by virulent reassertion of sexual hierarchy. The theory of the passions was deployed by social critics on the assumption that women will exhibit the same passions as men in a more debased form. Lovelace, as we will see, upholds this version of sexual difference of degree rather than kind, to the extent of assuming that reproduction is dependent on female as well as male orgasm. These are among the 'received notions' about the sexual order of things that Richardson sought to replace with a new differentiation of the sexes. He is among those who initiated the ideological assault on the one-sex model, a movement that achieved consensus by the end of the century, but he did so before the 'escape to a supposed biological substrate', a distinctive female anatomy, became available.[13] His challenge remains at the level of metaphysics.[14] It is a refusal of the masculine measure of women's physicality, without yet being able to posit dimorphism in its stead. Clarissa, as the reformed rake Belford comes to recognize, is 'all soul'. Her sex is no sex; it is pure gender, a nexus of cultural attributes. She epitomizes the revised definition of women as a spiritual avant-garde.

Clarissa has been mistaken for a creature of the conduct book.[15] It is true that she shares certain characteristics with the idealized femininity prescribed in works that sought to regulate the time of a new class of leisured women. We are told about her religious principles, her household economy, her charitable acts, her high notions of filial duty. But this kinship must not be allowed to obscure her revolutionary role. The specialization of the sexes she enacts involves a radical curtailment of the province of man. When Clarissa declares to Lovelace, 'My soul is above thee, man!' in one of the leaps into heroic diction that periodically disrupt the flow of the 'familiar letters', there is no doubt that 'man' is to be understood generically. Lovelace first resists the implicit reversal of hierarchy: 'Let me worship an angel, said I, no woman.' Then he struggles to assimilate her elevated nature to the old model by proposing that she has a masculine soul trapped in a feeble woman's body (L201, 646–7 cf. 1037). But femininity can no longer be classified as a colony of the masculine. Richardson saw the necessity of establishing the radical otherness of women, freed of invidious analogy. This is her redemptive capability. Instead of being dragged down by love of a woman, a man might be saved.

What is this new woman made of? There are few hints about the heroine's formation in the novel, nor an adequate explanation of how a family that produced her brother and sister, the loathsome James and Arabella, also gave rise to a Clarissa. In a letter to Frances Grainger, Richardson speaks of the early foundations of her goodness: the care of her nurse, Mrs Norton, 'whose chief attention', curiously enough, 'was to the Beauties of the *Iliad*', and also frequent visits and correspondence with the pious Dr Lewen and other clerics.[16] Claims can be made for her debt to contemporary currents of Christian mysticism and the related tradition of Neoplatonism.[17] There is a connection here with the feminist discourse of platonic love in the 1690s.[18] On the other hand, it must be conceded that Clarissa's difference is partly an effect of iteration, the repetition of the idea that 'the Cause of Women is generally the Cause of Virtue'.[19] It was a theme of Richardson's own correspondence from the period, and in the letter just quoted he turns it into a jingle:

> 'The cause of Virtue and the Sex is one:
> If Women give it up, the World's undone.'

But above all Clarissa's exemplary nature evolves through its opposition to those who would deny the identity of virtue and the sex, and under the pressure to 'give it up'. Anna Howe memorably avers, 'ADVERSITY is your SHINING-TIME' (L178, 579). Clarissa's nature is the product of debate, and therefore remains volatile and problematic within the world of the novel.

Sexual difference is implicit in the epistolary form of the novel itself. Where *Pamela* was essentially monologic, the greater part of *Clarissa* is composed of two sets of correspondence, between women (Clarissa and Anna Howe) and between men (Lovelace and fellow-rake Jack Belford), displaying the divergence of their assumptions, interests, experience and even their language, as they tirelessly discuss and debate the same set of events. The rare letters that cross the sexual divide are generally disastrous. As Anna Howe remarks, it is 'a dangerous thing for two single persons of different sexes to enter into familiarity and correspondence with each other' (L229, 748). At the start of the novel we learn that Clarissa is persisting in a correspondence with Lovelace that was at first encouraged then vetoed by her family. She does so with the good intention of mitigating his resentment against her relations, but it is this correspondence that leads to her undoing. In order to ensure Lovelace's receipt of a message hidden under a loose brick in the wall, Clarissa meets him at the door of her father's garden. Against her will, she is drawn outside in the wake of her letters into his power. Some time later when Clarissa escapes, Lovelace is able, as a result, to intercept a letter from Anna. He uses it to infiltrate their dialogue, impersonating their feminine discourse and sending false signals to each in order to lure Clarissa back into his clutches. As his plots reach their climax, he rereads passages from Anna's correspondence to fortify his animus against women.

In the letters, the 'innate' characters of the two sexes are constantly asserted, denied and revised, and there is animated exchange on cases that blur the boundaries. Ian Watt states that the novel demonstrates 'a more complete and comprehensive separation between the male and female roles than had previously existed',[20] but the separation is not secure; it is a flux of charge and counter-charge, appropriation and rejection. Take, for instance, Clarissa's denial that generosity is 'a *manly* virtue ... I have ever yet observed that it is not to be met with in that sex one time in ten that it is to be found in ours' (L5, 55). Sexual epithets are traded as weapons in the sex war. Men are described by women as insolent, mischievous, hardhearted, 'incroaching', bold, devilish, flattering.[21] However, they have greater stores of ammunition. Women are judged by men to be unsteady, wavering, changeable, imaginative, sly, deluding, artful, plotting, 'eye-judging … undistinguishing … self-flattering … too confiding' (L229, 747), inconsiderate, helpless, curious, credulous. They can be well or ill at pleasure; they lack courage; they exhibit 'sweet cowardice' (L103, 412), 'horrid romantic perverseness', 'frowardness' (L74, 291); they 'love to trade in surprises' (L49, 215), 'love busy scenes' (L242, 820), and delight in 'seeing fine clothes' (L69, 281).[22]

At one end of the battleground, Clarissa and Anna Howe vigilantly inspect the boundaries of the female encampment. Anna Howe is critical of 'managing' housewives: 'I do not think a *man-woman* a pretty character at all' (L132, 475–6). On a more sombre note, Clarissa harbours a suspicion derived from the enemy camp, a hypothetical Trojan Horse:

> Those passions in our sex, which we take no pains to subdue, may have one and the same source with those infinitely blacker passions which we used so often to condemn in the violent and headstrong of the other sex; and which may be heightened in them only by custom, and their freer education. Let us both, my dear, ponder well this thought; look into ourselves, and fear. (L165, 550)

It is vital for them to banish such intimations of equivalence and to maintain the difference of men from women in tastes, passions, mind, manners and morals. Clarissa and Anna cling to the creed of sexual solidarity. Female friendship is exalted as the highest form of human bond.[23] They dream of living together as single women, for marriage, according to all the evidence at their disposal, is a prospect to be dreaded. They believe that trust, sincerity and genuine sympathy are possible only between those of the same sex. Femininity is another country with its own allegiances. The rigid code of propriety that applies only to ladies is at times a life-threatening constraint, but it is also a badge of honour. Clarissa and Anna, along with their female relations, fiercely assert the idea that women owe a debt to their sex to represent it well.[24]

The ideal of female solidarity is constantly betrayed in this *History of a Young Lady*. Even in her own home Clarissa suffers persecution from her sister and cowardly abandonment by her mother and aunt. Her treatment at the hands of the London prostitutes should have been the deathblow of any notion of natural sympathy among women. Instead, Clarissa emerges from these experiences with her faith undamaged, and even strengthened. Her first reaction is now to flinch at any contact with men and in her will she states that her corpse is not to be touched by a person of the other sex. This is because the category of woman is abstracted from biological sex; it is virtue, a metaphysical quality, which defines it. Aberrations are distressing, but they are explicable as evidence of a masculine incursion and cannot ultimately challenge the concept of the female. The same view of an absolute gendered morality that transcends biological sex had been put forward by 'Sophia' in *Woman Not Inferior to Man*: based on the fact that 'humanity and integrity' are 'the characteristics of our sex ... when a *Man* is possest of our virtues he shou'd be call'd *effeminate* by way of the highest praise of his good nature and justice; and a *Woman* who shou'd depart from our sex by espousing the injustic and cruelty of the *Men's* nature, shou'd be call'd a *Man*'.[25] By this token Arabella 'has been thought to be masculine in her air, and in her spirit. She has then, perhaps, a soul of the *other* sex in a body of *ours*' (L78, 309–10). Similarly, Clarissa doubts the prostitutes can be women, and Mrs Sinclair's 'masculine air' appears to confirm it (L256, 882).[26] The coincidence between these examples and Lovelace's awe at Clarissa's 'masculine' soul is only apparent. They are concerned with keeping vice out of the definition of woman; his words are concerned with accounting for improbable perfections in a woman, and retaining man as her measure in all things.[27]

At the other end of the battleground are the men convinced that women are on the whole inferior specimens of human nature, prey to the worst impulses of physical being, and rightly subordinated. In good society this conviction is generally masked by politeness; among lovers, it is concealed by gallantry. Richardson, in order to make the battle lines clearer, exposes misogyny in all its nakedness. He begins with the crude conviction of female inferiority firmly rooted in Clarissa's family: in her father with his slighting treatment of her morally superior mother, in her indulgent but doltish uncles, and in her brother with his bad temper and willingness to resort to physical force against women.[28] It is epitomized by the 'low and familiar expression' complacently opined by James Harlowe the younger, 'That a man who has sons brings up chickens for his own table ... whereas daughters are chickens brought up for the tables of other men'. This is patriarchy in all its self-interested shabbiness; prudential misogyny. Clarissa can easily shrug it off, asking her brother, 'if the sons to make it hold were to have their necks wrung off' (L13, 77). It is simply the atmosphere in which the propertied classes exist. Lord M, who would like nothing better than to have Clarissa at his table, remarks to his nephew and heir Lovelace, 'May this marriage be crowned with a great many fine boys (I desire no girls) to build up again a family so antient' (L233, 787). Although she is pushed to the point of desperation by her reduction to the status of a dynastic bargaining chip, she feels equal to this battle. She later learns that if she had stood her ground, her father would ultimately have backed down.

The rake

Misogyny as a philosophy and an ethic is personified in the more complex and insidious figure of the rake: a man who 'loves' women, behaves with gallantry towards them and believes himself a master of their psychology, but only as a means of demonstrating women's fundamental depravity. In *Pamela* the rake is assimilated; in *Sir Charles Grandison* he will be contemptuously marginalized. But in *Clarissa* the rake is engaged head-on in mortal combat, and eventually destroyed. The letter-form lends itself brilliantly to exposure of the hatred of the sex that lies beneath the mask of politeness. I will argue, against the tide of recent critical judgement, that Richardson's failure to carry all of his audience with him in condemnation of Lovelace should be taken, not as a defect of his art, but as a sign of the difficulty and novelty of his project. He was trying to make contemporaries see the misogyny of the libertine as an evil that must be crushed in the same way as atheism, rather than a venial error that can be put aside at any moment in favour of conventional married life. It is important to recognize that Richardson's version of a rake drastically narrows the prototype found in Restoration drama. Lovelace is not a free-thinker, he does not drink or carouse or blaspheme or use bawdy language.[29] Richardson was intransigent on these points when friends given a preview of the novel urged him to signal Lovelace's badness in these more easily recognizable ways.[30] The author's agenda is asserted when the character declares '[a]ll my vice is women', and explains that he abjures profaneness and obscenity precisely in order to ingratiate himself with women (L370, 1146). All the interest of the narrative is centred on women. Womanizing is the beginning and end of Lovelace's transgressions.

The motives of Lovelace are governed by a structure of repetition. His attitude to the female sex is laid out clearly – even programmatically – in his first letter to Belford. The origin of his libertinism was the experience of being jilted by his first love, a blow to his pride that stimulated an insatiable desire for revenge on women in general. He revisits the pattern of seduction and abandonment on any woman he can get in his power. Now this compulsion has been exacerbated by the collapse of plans for marriage with Clarissa (L31, 143–7). His first love chose a titled suitor over him. Clarissa is being pressured by her family to accept the proposal of Solmes, a grasping, charmless landowner in the vicinity, over his. Her brother has a quarrel with Lovelace dating from their university days, and when he returned to the Harlowe household from a visit to the North and discovered him in the role of suitor, revived it with a duel. Lovelace allowed him to live for Clarissa's sake, and though the unpunished insults of her family 'un-*man* me' (146), his resentment of Clarissa's apparent indifference to him as she attempts to placate her family, is far greater. She is a 'charming frost-piece', seemingly 'inpenetrable' (145). The primal wound to his self-love has been reopened more painfully than ever before. If by *'matrimonial* or *equal* intimacies' he is able to prove her 'less than an angel': 'What a triumph! – What a triumph over the whole sex!' (31, 147).

The eruption of Lovelace's voice into the narrative, more than halfway through the first volume, is accompanied by a volley of quotations from the love poetry and tragic drama of the Restoration era, ostensibly designed to trumpet his love for Clarissa, but in fact demonstrating its artificial, hypothetical nature. He has been compared with the 'tyrant-lover' type of the Restoration stage, torn by the rival passions of love and the will to power.[31] But this overlap also reveals important differences. Right from the start, claims that he is compelled to act by ungovernable emotion are undercut by the repetitive, mechanical drive to expose the base nature of 'virtuous' women. Lovelace's tyrannizing over Clarissa is more theoretical than passionate. Desire is intermittent; it is the spirit of epistemological enquiry that persists. The seriousness and persistence of the endeavour also marks his difference from the rake of Restoration comedy. His enterprise is not sexually motivated but obsessively concerned with determining the status of the female sex: the equivalence or non-equivalence of men and women; the degree of influence of one sex on the other; the moral ratio of the sexes. At one point he gives as his excuse for tormenting Clarissa that 'the wife of a libertine ought to be pure, spotless, uncontaminated' (L253, 870). But elsewhere he acknowledges that the pleasure is in the enquiry itself – 'charming *roundabouts*, to come the *nearest way home*' – since the end is predetermined, 'to find an angel in imagination dwindled down to a woman in fact' (L271, 920).

In the Preface to the first edition, Richardson states that one of the two 'principal views of the publication' is to warn young women against 'the too commonly received notion, *that a reformed rake makes the best husband'* (the other being to caution parents against forced marriages) (36). In *A Modest Defence of Publick Stews* (1724) Mandeville had argued in favour of this very point as an instance of the potential usefulness of state-run brothels (37). He held that women realized it was in their own interest to marry a man with a realistic view of the sex, with the implication that any more idealized view was bound to disappointment. After 1735, any discussion of relations between women and rakes had to include Pope's *Epistle to a Lady*, and Richardson repeatedly alludes to the poem. It is first invoked ('Woman's at best a Contradiction still') by Lovelace when he describes how, by raising a false alarm, he tricked Clarissa into his carriage and into his preconceptions of female behaviour: 'flying from friends she was resolved not to abandon to the man she was determined not to go off with? -The sex! the sex, all over! – charming contradiction!' (L99, 400).

Pope's explanation in the poem of why 'ev'ry Woman is at heart a Rake' wittily takes up the maxim about women preferring rakes and turns it into paradox. He plays on the term 'at heart' which means 'in essence'. Instead of women taking rakes to their hearts, they become rakes themselves. He proceeds to explain. Men have a variety of passions, but nature has granted all women a love of pleasure as their ruling passion. This makes the entire sex the equivalent of one class of man, the rake.[32] Women's bias is supported by education; they are taught 'but to please' and pleasure is therefore all their business from the earliest age. At the same time they experience man's oppression, an originary 'curse' of Eve, and this makes them determined to tyrannize in return as far as they can, to safeguard their pleasures. The 'Love of Sway' is their secondary ruling passion, and beauty allows them to conquer in youth. But as this fades so does their power, and their relentless pursuit of diversion becomes increasingly desperate and pathetic. It is their fate to be 'Alive, ridiculous, and dead, forgot!' Society merely supplements the biological determinism of this picture. While men have options, the only alternative for the rare woman of sense is to secede from society altogether, and earn a plaudit from the poet.

Richardson misreads Pope's lesson in the natural history of women, perhaps strategically. He returns the arresting metaphor 'ev'ry Woman is at heart a Rake' to prosaic analogy, a resemblance between women and rakes that explains women's attraction to rakes. And he allots the insight not to a detached moralist, but to the rake himself, complicating its status as a truth-claim and making it instead a facet of devious self-interest. Having captured Clarissa, Lovelace sees no need to disguise his dissolute tastes, 'what occasion has a man to be an hypocrite, who has hitherto found his views upon the sex better answered for his being known to be a rake?' (L104, 415; cf. L702, 703). He goes on to anatomize the equivalence of rakes and modest women, with a direct and daring appropriation of Pope,

> One argument let me plead in proof of my assertion: that even we rakes love modesty in a woman; while the modest women, as they are accounted, that is to say, the slyest, love and generally prefer an impudent man. Whence can this be, but from a likeness in nature? And this made the poet say, that every woman is a rake in her heart. It concerns them by their *actions* to prove the contrary, if they can. (L115, 441)

This challenge to women to prove the epigram wrong by their actions becomes the driving force of the plot. The purity of women is an article of faith. Lovelace says he wants to believe in Clarissa, but his previous disillusionments lead him to test her again and again. Clarissa's cousin Colonel Morden, himself no puritan, is able to explain to her the motivation of a rake in a letter of urgent warning: 'He has great contempt for your sex: he believes no woman chaste, because he is a profligate: every woman who favours him confirms him in his wicked incredulity' (L173, 563).[33] The rake projects his desires onto women, and narcissistically interprets their submission as a sign of their identity with him, their secret tasting of his pleasure.

Pope's allegation that women are power-hungry is also answered. On the contrary, says Lovelace, 'the sex love rakes ... because they [the rake] know how to direct their uncertain wills, and manage them', and he cites in support another poet, 'gentle Waller': *'Women are born to be controlled'* (L207, 670). Later he puts a similarly masochistic spin on Pope's reference to the curse of oppression felt by women: 'That sex is made to bear pain. It is a curse that the first of it entailed upon all her succeeding daughters, when she brought the curse upon us all. And they love those best, whether man or child, who give them most ...' (L335, 1069). The sub-clause, 'whether man or child', is appropriate, since the whole thrust of Lovelace's thesis is to suggest that rakes are the creation of women; they are willed into being by the inner rottenness of the sex. This is the story of Lovelace's own origin as a rake.

An official citation of Pope's dictum comes when Clarissa has escaped Lovelace after the rape and is dying alone in rented rooms near Covent Garden. Lovelace meanwhile attends a ball in the neighbourhood of the Howes, and Anna sends her friend an appalled account of his suave manner and the admiring reception he is given by young women who know of his recent exploits. Anna is accosted by a 'grave gentleman' (analogue of Pope himself?) who remarks

> that the poet's observation was too true, that the generality of ladies
> were *rakes in their hearts*, or they could not be so much taken in with a
> man who had so notorious a character.
> I told him the reflection both of the poet and the applier was much
> too general, and made with more ill-nature than good manners. (L367,
> 1137)

This is a kind of postscript, a meta-narrative moment, which moves outside the central drama and directly interpellates the reader, especially the female reader who might allow herself to be seduced by Lovelace or condone his behaviour in the interests of a 'happy' ending. The sentiment identifying women and rakes is returned to the mouth of the detached moralist, though with a gloss Pope would not have recognized. Anna's rebuke is somewhat lame; but then, the whole of the preceding novel is a passionate refutation of the view of women that the 'rake' remark is taken to imply.

The 'present age'

Lovelace's view of human nature and of women is specifically shaped by the culture of the 1720s and 1730s. For Richardson, sexual difference is not simply a theoretical question, but also an historical question, and *Clarissa* is a systematic refutation of the cynical and misogynist assumptions of the literature of the previous generation, through the defeat of Lovelace. Richardson's knowledge of this culture through his work as a printer was intimate. When he first set up a printing business in 1721, he was quickly drawn into the ferment of opposition politics created by the South Sea Bubble débâcle. He published works by prominent enemies of the government: an edition of the writings of Francis Atterbury, Bishop of Rochester, following his trial for conspiracy and subsequent banishment; and the journal the *True Briton*, which included attacks on the South Sea Company, government bribery and corruption, and Hanoverian foreign policy and was the work of a renegade Whig, Philip, Duke of Wharton, who later turned Jacobite and died penniless in exile in 1731.[34] In 1722 Richardson appears on a list sent to the Secretary of State of printers known to be 'High Flyers': extreme Tories. Richardson was lucky to escape prosecution for his involvement with the *True Briton*. The publisher of the journal, Thomas Payne, was arrested and charged with sedition, and Richardson stood surety for him.[35] In the 1720s Richardson used his vote to support Tory candidates in local and parliamentary elections.[36]

It was natural for a man of strong moral views to take an opposition stance in this epoch. Yet in *Clarissa*, Richardson shows that he has seen the way the critique of the monied interest and of the Walpole government gives rise to a corrosive scepticism about man's moral nature as bad as the spiritual bankruptcy it condemns. After Clarissa's first escape from Lovelace, she takes refuge in a boarding-house in Hampstead run by a Mrs Moore. Lovelace soon tracks her down and sets about winning the landlady, a well-meaning but gullible woman, to his cause, by subliminal economic interest. Instead of outright bribery, he rents every spare room in the house for a month. Although he is not permitted by Mrs Moore to lodge there, out of deference to Clarissa, he is allowed to board, giving him opportunities to insinuate himself further. Writing to Belford, he compares himself to a South Sea Company director in the year 1720, who draws 'proud senators' into complicity with 'a scheme big with national ruin' by making presents of stock, when a fixed sum of double the value would have alerted their suspicions. 'Have I not said that human nature is a rogue?' he crows, 'And do not I know it?' (L241, 816).

Clarissa's second escape, after the rape, brings on another merry fit of cod-philosophizing as a block against conscience, once again in the mode of a satirist of the Bubble. Lovelace adopts the iconography of Hogarth's print *The South Sea Scheme* (1721), described in chapter 3 (see above p. 51). Again, the libertine is found to be equivalent to a purveyor of stocks. He is a '*laced-hat orator*' drawing pretty girls onto his merry-go-round with its 'flying coaches and flying horses' with his cry '*Who rides next! Who rides next!*' In a levelling allegory of Clarissa's misadventures, he pictures her as a 'pretty little miss' at the fair, who 'slily pops' onto his 'one-go-up, the other-go-down picture-of-the-world vehicle ... when *none of her friends are near her'*. If after a few ups and downs 'her pretty head turns giddy, and she throws herself out of the coach when at its elevation, and so dashes out her pretty little brains, who can help it!' After all, it is the proprietor's *'professed trade* ... to set the pretty little creatures a-flying' (L294, 970–1). Although she is 'a very *good* little miss', the mishap is of no more nor less consequence than the downfall of any other unlucky girl. This 'picture-of-the-world vehicle', a variant of the wheel of fortune, was a standard feature of popular engravings satirizing the repetitive, irrational human behaviour exhibited by the great financial scandals. A Dutch print reflecting on the Law scandal in 1720 (see above p. 54) is titled *The Actions and Designs of the World go round as if in a Mill*.[37] The picture of the world it presents is one of automatic impulses outside the control of reason or morality. Stock-jobbers are compelled to cheat, and acquisitive buyers to be cheated. Rakes are compelled to take pretty girls for a ride, and vain girls to be dishonoured.

Lovelace is fluent in the low opposition discourse of the period, and also in the high. In another set-piece of extravagant fancy, having reluctantly obtained a marriage licence while plotting a rape, he tells Belford of his scheme for annual marriages (L254, 872–4). Laying claim to the elevated principles of civic humanism, he compares himself as a lawgiver to Lycurgus, who returned Sparta to its ancient virtues by radical reform. At a stroke, Lovelace's reform would eliminate rapes, adultery, fornication and polygamy, while murders and duelling would be drastically reduced by the removal of jealousy. Unwanted offspring would become *'children of the public*, and provided for like the children of the ancient Spartans; who were (as ours would in this case be) a nation of heroes'. Physicians would have to enlist as auxiliary parsons to deal with the demand for weddings, for the good of 'the public'.[38] With typical disingenuousness Lovelace insists that the ladies would be the chief beneficiaries 'for dearly do I love the sweet rogues'. He is tempted to avail himself of one of the rotten boroughs controlled by Lord M. and himself become a Member of Parliament and pursue his plan of reform in earnest, for 'a total alteration for the better in the *morals* and *way of life* in both sexes must, in a very few years, be the consequence of such a salutary law'. He concludes, 'Let me add, that *annual Parliaments*, and *annual marriages*, are the projects next my heart.' Annual parliamentary elections were one of the chief demands of the anti-Walpole opposition, as it would hamper the ministerial system of patronage and 'corruption'. Lovelace's mention of it has been taken up in all seriousness as an indication of Patriot allegiance.[39] But since in the course of the novel he shows no interest in any subject beyond the promotion of his career in sexual conquest, it is more plausibly the clever finishing touch to his brief masquerade as a 'Patriot King'.

Elsewhere we see him take up the mask momentarily again, as 'like Addison's Cato' he gives 'laws to his little senate' of brother-rakes (L371, 1147). This is an ironic reference to Pope's prologue to Addison's tragedy *Cato* (1713), which asks the audience 'While Cato gives his little senate laws, / What bosom beats not in his Country's cause?', calling for the display of patriotic sentiment. But there was another side to Cato more appropriate to a band of libertines, and one Pope spelled out in an epilogue to Rowe's *Jane Shore* published the following year (1714):

> Plu-Plutarch, what's his name, that writes his life?
> Tells us, that Cato dearly lov'd his wife:
> Yet if a friend, a night or so, should need her,
> He'd recommend her as a special breeder.

> (ll. 31–4)

The stutter, 'Plu-Plutarch', is owing to the fact that the lines were to be spoken by an unlearned woman, an actress. The Augustan satirists passed with ease from exhortations to public virtue to satire of private vice, as found in Cato's defective marital arrangements. The systematic relationship between the elevation of the political public sphere and the abasement of the private and the feminine in classical republican discourse has been discussed at length in earlier chapters.

Richardson, as has often been remarked, had limited schooling and was an outsider when it came to the classics; this gave him a fellow-feeling with women, excluded from classical culture by their sex. In addition, although he was enfranchised as a property-holder, he was essentially a 'private' man, relatively detached from party politics and current affairs, centred instead on the workplace, a home full of women (four daughters as well as a wife), and a circle of friends and correspondents. But this order of priorities by no means signalled 'retirement', the classical antithesis of public engagement. On the contrary, Richardson's conception of the private becomes increasingly militant as his writing career progresses. In a direct challenge to the public ethos, he begins to promote the belief that the source of moral reform is the private sphere, and that the impetus is to come from women. The first part of *Pamela* was reticent on these points; it could be mistaken for an improving fable directed solely at the 'little people', servants and booby squires. This seems to have been the assumption behind the somewhat condescending approval of the novel by Pope and his friend and chief apologist, William Warburton.[40] They were soon to be disabused. No one could have anticipated the extent to which this seemingly modest scribbling artisan was prepared to attack the literary establishment in the cause of female virtue.

Already in Part II of *Pamela* Richardson has his heroine refer to Swift's *Letter to a Young Lady* (1727) as an illustration of that '*unmanly* Contempt with which a certain celebrated Genius treats our Sex in general'.[41] The attack was sustained in *Clarissa* with a comprehensive reworking of *The Lady's Dressing Room*, to be discussed in the next chapter (see below p. 135). In a letter to Lady Bradshaigh in 1752, Richardson criticizes Swift for ill-treatment of the women in his life and for his 'endeavours to debase the human, and to raise above it the brutal nature'.[42] With regard to Pope, no sooner had Richardson humbly requested from him corrections to *Pamela* (via Warburton), than he was treasonably muttering with George Cheyne and Aaron Hill about the poet's shortcomings as a social critic and a moralist.[43] Pope died in 1744, but Warburton remained guardian of his reputation. Relations deteriorated with the publication of *Clarissa*. Warburton attempted to act as patron by producing a learned preface in which he placed Richardson in the context of a developing French anti-romance tradition. Richardson printed it at the head of the second instalment of the first edition, but perhaps resented the slur on his originality and dropped it in the second edition the following year. Warburton revenged himself by reprinting the rejected preface as a note in his edition of Pope in 1751, but ending with praise of Fielding and no mention of Richardson. In 1753 Richardson got wind of the fact that Warburton was aggrieved because 'I had in a new Edition of Clarissa, reflected upon his Friend Mr. Pope by some Passages not in the first'; a charge he strongly denied.[44] Certainly, he had added no reflections on Pope. As we have seen, the first edition was already full of them; Warburton had not read carefully enough the first time.[45] However, in 1759 Richardson wrote to Edward Young happily reporting Warburton's praise of Young's *Conjectures on Original Composition*.[46] This was a work addressed 'To the Author of Sir Charles Grandison' and framed to enhance the authority of Richardson's untutored mode of writing and moral programme. The enthusiasm of Warburton is curious, given the conclusion that accuses Pope and, still more, Swift of 'tyranny in wit' and places them both far below Joseph Addison, Richardson's precursor, as agents of reform.[47] Perhaps the arch-controversialist had recognized defeat and was prepared to surrender arms.

Richardson's opposition to the civic humanist ethic and the literary giants of the Walpole era was a reasonably clear-cut battle of ideas. Bernard Mandeville, with his theory of the selfish passions as the driving force in society, was a more insidious foe, because Richardson shared his class perspective, individualist assumptions and emphasis on the private sphere. Although we cannot be sure that Richardson was familiar with Mandeville's works, he evidently found the well-known doctrine that social interaction was governed by unacknowledged currents of pride, shame and self-love of inestimable value in his plans for *Clarissa*. Eve Tavor has put forward a reading of the novel that exposes the Mandevillian underpinning of the conflict in the Harlowe household and the stand-off between

Lovelace and Clarissa with startling clarity.[48] Provided, that is, one can accept the proposition that Clarissa is as amoral as her enemies and that her apparently high-minded dispute with her family is in fact animated by 'passions of lust and shame': physical revulsion in response to Solmes and attraction to Lovelace; and obstinate pride, in the form of 'shame-based modesty', which helps to stymie her dealings with Lovelace. According to Tavor, it is only after the rape, when she has lost every worldly hope, that Clarissa can acknowledge these guilty secrets, conquer her passions and achieve the genuine Christian virtue required by Richardson's 'dogmatic' answer to 'scepticism and infidelity'.[49] Such a reading, of course, precludes the notion of Clarissa as a workable example for the female sex, or of her story as a model for a change in social values.

As we have established, it is crucial to Richardson's purpose that Clarissa should be understood from the start as the upholder of the 'Cause of Virtue', a set of values diametrically opposed to the scepticism of Lovelace. However, there are at least two points of ambivalence that might make it possible to describe his conduct of the narrative as Mandevillian. The first relates to the oft-noted idea of Lovelace as Richardson's *alter ego*. Even if one restricts the identification to Lovelace's narrative function as tormentor (rather than trying to suggest, for instance, that by creating Lovelace, Richardson was giving rein to libertine fantasies), it still lends a peculiar resonance to the one direct reference to Mandeville's tenets.[50] Just as Richardson justified Clarissa's sufferings as an indispensable part of his lesson, so Lovelace declares that she must be sacrificed to his desires in order to provide a cautionary tale for 'pretty fools of the sex':

> Do we not then see that an honest prowling fellow is a necessary evil on many accounts? Do we not see that it is highly requisite that a sweet girl should be now and then drawn aside by him? – And the more eminent the lady, in the graces of person, mind, and fortune, is not the example likely to be the more efficacious?
>
> If these *postula* be granted me, who I pray, can equal my charmer in all these? Who therefore so fit for an example to the rest of the sex? – At worst, I am entirely within my worthy friend Mandeville's rule, *That private vices are public benefits*. (L246, 847)

Does a Clarissa, then, require a Lovelace to make an example of her? Are libertines, like the state brothels proposed by Mandeville, necessary to the public good? I believe Richardson would waive these questions with an historical argument: shock tactics were required to jolt out of their preconceptions readers whose worldly values were formed in the era of public corruption. In this provisional and non-Mandevillian manner, yes, Lovelace's private vices may give rise to public benefits, as poison may affect a cure. Richardson's remarks in a letter to Frances Grainger are relevant here: 'If the present age can be awakened and amended, the next perhaps will not, duly weighing all Circumstances, think Clarissa too delicate or too good for Imitation.'[51] In contrast to Lovelace's compulsive repetitions, Richardson posits a single sacrifice as the precondition of moral progress. In the next generation, a Harriet Byron can live unviolated and thrive.

A second and more convincing case could be made by considering *Clarissa* not as an illustration of Mandeville's ideas, but as a performance of them. In the 'Enquiry into the Origin of Moral Virtue' prefixed to *Fable of the Bees*, Mandeville describes how, through the ages, lawgivers and moralists have laboured to create a cohesive society by presenting an elevated conception of human nature and attempting to persuade the people they govern to conquer their appetites and attempt to emulate the ideal.[52] It is arguable that Richardson by his creation of a female paragon takes up the 'bewitching Engine' of politic flattery to appeal to the pride of women and produce an improvement in manners. Mandeville himself is ambivalent about the practice. On the one hand, as a teller of unappetizing truths, he despises those who, like Richard Steele, resort to attractive 'lies'; and the picture of society he gives in the *Fable* involves a self-regulating economy of vicious appetites. On the other, the final words of Part 1 revert to the notion of a legislative puppeteer: 'Private Vices by the dextrous management of a skilful Politician may be turned into Publick Benefits' (I: 369). It would seem that Mandeville could not wholly free himself from the civic humanist figure of the originary great politician, and it is clear that Richardson and his admirers also saw the application. When Richardson made a contribution to the *Rambler* in 1751 he was introduced by Samuel Johnson as an author 'who has enlarged the knowledge of human nature, and taught the passions to move at the command of virtue'.[53]

If it was Richardson's intention to flatter into good behaviour, then his aim was evidently partial.[54] As women are elevated in *Clarissa*, so men are denigrated. Women may be drawn to virtue through pride, but it appears that men must undergo moral reform through a more complex procedure of heterosociality and sublimation. They must temper and redirect their passions in the company of good women and learn to reverence female virtue as a model for their own behaviour, without hope of a carnal reward. It is the heroine's stubborn refusal to flatter and placate Lovelace that partially stimulates his brutal treatment of her.

The trial of woman

After the abduction, Lovelace's first plan, confided in letters to Belford, is to marry Clarissa in the teeth of Harlowe opposition. That would be sufficient revenge. He does not expect Clarissa herself to present a problem once she is in his power. He is puzzled when she continues freely to criticize his behaviour and proves impervious to his well-tried methods of seduction. The love of praise is key to his definition of women ('How greedily do the whole sex swallow praise!' (L105, 418)) and he asks plaintively, 'What can be done with a woman who is above flattery, and despises all praise but that which flows from the approbation of her own heart?' (L108, 423). The plan for the trial of Clarissa, and through her, of the female sex, is hatched. A full exposition of Lovelace's motives is presented in Letter 17 in Volume III (first edition; L110, 426–31). Plans for marriage are postponed indefinitely; the aim is to determine whether Clarissa really loves him, in spite of her moral objections, and whether her resistance is inspired by affectation or pride, rather than by genuine virtue. He will continue working away on her, submitting her to a series of crises, on the basis that 'a woman's heart may be at one time *adamant*, at another *wax* – as I have often experienced' (430). His immediate justification is that his wife must demonstrate superlative purity. But it would be an absurd simplification to say that what will be determined is whether or not he will marry her. What hangs in the balance is woman. Clarissa's success will be the triumph of the sex; her failure will be the proof of its innate corruption.[55]

As already noted, Lovelace upholds the one-sex model, and fully expects that Clarissa's capitulation will reaffirm it. In his next letter, he compares himself to Tiresias, the seer of Greek myth, who, as the result of metamorphosis, experienced love as a man and as a woman. He claims that as a 'bashful man' he knows what women really think, through identification with their modesty.[56] What he means is that he knows what they really *feel*. In Ovid's rendering, Tiresias was asked whether men or women had the greater pleasure in love-making and decided for women. He was punished with blindness by Juno for his answer; a sign of the anti-feminist tenor of the judgement. 'Though differing perhaps in nuance, orgasm is orgasm in the one-flesh body, Ovid's story seems to say.'[57] And Lovelace too is saying, women feel the same, want the same as I do; only more so, because of their greater animality: 'the immodest ones outdo the worst of us by a bar's length, both in thinking and acting' (L115, 440–1).

When Lovelace speaks of women's '*identicalness*' (L199, 638), he means their monotonous similarity to each other. But elsewhere he remarks on their similarity to men. Anna Howe 'had she been a man, would have sworn and cursed, and committed rapes, and played the devil, as far as I knew (and I have no doubt of it, Jack)', but had been kept within bounds by female education (L236, 801). Satirizing Anna's declarations of attachment to Clarissa, he avers that female friendship is but a poor imitation of male friendship: 'Apes! mere apes of us!' (L252, 862).[58] Education, an artificial gloss, is all that ultimately differentiates women from men in passions and weaknesses. Lovelace repeatedly speculates that Clarissa's virtue is a triumph of education over nature (e.g. L191, 609; L216, 695).[59]

It is because they are the perfect illustration of his thesis that the prostitutes play such a vital part in the testing of Clarissa.[60] Sally Martin and Polly Horton were from respectable families and received a 'good modern education' (Postscript, 1491 cf. L277, 940, L333, 1061); Mrs Sinclair was well born and well educated, as were Lovelace's other two instruments, 'Lady' Bab Wallis and Johanetta Golding, who successfully impersonate his aristocratic relations (L255, 875). Sally spontaneously quotes lines from Dryden at first sight of Lovelace's new quarry (L154, 522). The younger whores, Sally, Polly and Johanetta, have all been debauched by Lovelace. They are Clarissa's wicked doubles. They represent one possible afterlife for her, once the trial is completed. Who will define the sex? As Judith Wilt has observed, 'Sinclair and Clarissa. The names alone suggest the mandala.'[61] But the role of the prostitutes is by no means solely that of didactic representation. They too have a stake in the downfall of Clarissa and the demonstration that all women are alike. It will support the belief that they themselves could not have escaped their fate, their biological destiny. Their desire to see Clarissa brought down to their level is even stronger and more compulsive than Lovelace's, a predatory urge that resembles vampirism: 'You owe us such a Lady' (L154, 522 cf. 729). When Lovelace falters at the crisis of the trial, they nettle him into resolution. Wilt's proposal that ultimately they turn him into their 'machine' and perform the rape themselves perhaps gives too much credence to Lovelace's own increasingly plaintive and self-exonerating presentation of events as they fail to take the course he intended. The whores' knowledge of the sex is merely the echo of the rake's. Nevertheless they are attributed with imaginings more sadistic than any Lovelace will own:

> they all pretend to remember what *once* they were; and vouch for the inclinations and hypocrisy of the whole sex; and wish for nothing so ardently as that I will leave the perverse lady to their management while I am gone to Berkshire; undertaking absolutely for her humility and passiveness on my return; and continually boasting of the many perverse creatures whom they have obliged to draw in their traces. (L277, 940)

The trial plot of *Clarissa* is importantly unlike that of the preceding genres of rape or seduction, Restoration tragedy or amatory fiction. In these the female fall is without theoretical tension; it is a mere collapse into predetermined fallen nature. The case of Nicholas Rowe's *The Fair Penitent* (1703), a popular drama throughout the eighteenth century, is discussed by Belton in the novel. The heroine Calista, who falls prey to Lothario ('another wicked ungenerous varlet as thou knowest who'), is a 'desiring luscious wench, and her penitence is nothing else but rage, insolence, and scorn'. The author has failed to observe the fundamental difference of men and women manifested in 'the finer passions of the sex, which if naturally

drawn will distinguish themselves from the masculine passions by a softness that will even shine through rage and despair' (L412: 1205–6).
Richardson corrects this mistake in his own fiction; proceeding by reference
to precursors through a characteristic method of absorption and supersession. He invests the rape of Clarissa with a gravity that recalls the mythic
example of Lucretia and her role in determining the moral destiny of
Rome:[62]

> Is not *this* the hour of her trial – and in *her*–, of the trial of the virtue of
> her whole sex, so long premeditated, so long threatened? – Whether her
> frost is frost indeed? Whether her virtue is principle? Whether if *once
> subdued, she will not be always subdued*? And will she not want the very
> crown of her glory, the proof of her till now all-surpassing excellence, if
> I stop short of the ultimate trial? (L256, 879)

It is a problem for the novel and its reception that Richardson with his
moral project has as much invested in the outcome of Clarissa's trial as
Lovelace does. The issue of Richardson's identification with Lovelace has
already been mentioned. Without question the impersonation of a young
aristocratic rake by an elderly puritanical master-printer is one of the most
miraculous imaginative feats in the history of English literature. There is no
reason to doubt Richardson's insistence that he created the character in
order to damn him. The stress he laid on the value of representing wicked-
ness can be seen in the volume of *Moral and Instructive Sentiments* culled
from his novels, in which the largest section from *Clarissa* is of 'Reflections
on Women ... Designed principally to incite Caution, and inspire Prudence, &c.
by letting them know what Libertines and free Speakers say and think of the
Sex'.[63] At the same time there is an undeniable identity of purpose, and of
language, when Richardson insists in his function as 'editor' on the necessity of the trial of Clarissa that leads to her death: 'her Trials are multiplied
to give her so many Opportunities to shine thro' the various Stages of those
Trials.'[64] The first edition of the novel was published in three instalments.
In the intermissions, during which Richardson undertook revisions of the
remaining parts, he refused to heed those who, like Belford or Anna Howe
in the narrative, pleaded for a happy ending to Clarissa's story. To Lady
Bradshaigh, the most ardent advocate for a last-minute reconciliation of
Clarissa and Lovelace, he reiterated the need to destroy his creation, in
spite of his love for her. The determination to test Clarissa to the limits
creates certain absurdities, notably when he turns the screw of her isolation
in the final scenes. The endless delays and excuses depriving her of aid and
consolation even from her most ardent supporters are the most contrived
part of the plot.[65] Clarissa must be 'got above all human dependence'
(L438, 1268). Torture by degrees is an integral part of what Aaron Hill
described in a letter to Richardson as 'this amiably killing Progress'.[66]

The trial of man

The trial of woman unexpectedly and inadvertently turns out to be a trial of man. The clash between the rival hermeneutics of Clarissa and Lovelace is dialectical. Both are self-divided by inner debate, but Clarissa gathers strength and consistency in the course of the trial and Lovelace, the would-be detached experimentalist, is irrevocably torn by contradiction. No sooner does he get her in his power and plan his trial of her than he is overcome by a sincere desire to marry her.

> Was the devil in me! – I no more intended all this ecstatic nonsense than I thought the same moment of flying in the air! – All power is with this charming creature! – It is I, not she, at this rate, that must fail in the arduous trial. (L138, 493)

He analyses the effect at a later and more desperate stage. Lovelace has almost despaired of softening Clarissa by love vows, gestures of sympathy or sly caresses, and is reluctantly contemplating the use of force ('There is no triumph in *force*! No conquest over the will!') and the possibility that she may indeed disprove his assumptions: 'her LOVE OF VIRTUE seems to be *principle*, native, or if *not* native, so deeply rooted that its fibres have struck into her heart, and, as she grew up, so blended and twisted themselves with the strings of life that I doubt there is no separating of the one, without cutting the others asunder' (L202, 657). He feels himself internalizing Clarissa's nature – 'this lady, the moment I come into her presence, half assimilates me to her own virtue' – an effect he personifies as the presence within him of the 'lurking varletess CONSCIENCE' (658). As the contours of his purpose begin to lose their definition, he speaks increasingly of the need for artificial aids to strengthen it. There is goading from below ('BELOW indeed!', 658), the quarters inhabited by the prostitutes, and from above, the letters from Anna Howe purloined from Clarissa's room and transcribed. The rape of the letter fuels Lovelace's misogyny, allowing him to attribute the resistance of Clarissa to a female conspiracy. He keeps the transcriptions by him, to apply like sal volatile whenever his resolve weakens (L198, 633),

Lovelace's plotting continues its ebb and flow. Just before staging what he believes will be the final and determining assault on Clarissa's virtue, an 'opportunistic' rape carried out after a fire alarm, he smugly parodies the notion of the female sex's influence on a man's moral character; his love of women means that if they had required more virtue, he would have been ready to supply it (L224, 721). But the fire scene does not go according to plan. Lovelace announces at the start of his account to Belford, written immediately after the event, 'Now is my reformation secured' (L225, 723). Clarissa starts from her room, in a state of undress as intended, and is carried back to her bed, but she succeeds in repelling his advances by a mixture of commands and piteous pleading. As a consequence Lovelace has retreated like 'a woman's fool ... What a triumph has her sex obtained in my thoughts by this trial, and this resistance!' (L225, 727) By the time of the next instalment from Lovelace, three hours later, at 8 am, there has been a relapse: 'A little silly soul, what troubles does she make to herself by her over-niceness' (L266, 728–9). In the reception of *Clarissa*, a controversy blew up in response to this scene, when a number of readers criticized the 'warmth' of its descriptions, and Richardson published an *Answer to the Letter of a Very Reverend and Worthy Gentleman* (1749) defending it. Richardson sees it as his duty to impersonate libertine discourse, while distancing his work from amatory fiction by pointing to the way the scene is contextualized as a warning to women. His friend Jane Collier in a private letter makes the point he could not, in politeness, make to his reverend critic: that the scene was a test of the responses of the male reader. '[T]he Reason of a Man's blaming it as being too highly painted must be from his dwelling more strongly on the Person of the lovely Sufferer, than on her Innocence and Distress.'[67] The reader must cross-examine himself on the degree to which he too is a Lovelace.

The internal drama continues to escalate with Clarissa's first escape and Lovelace's determination to lure her back and make good his previous failure of nerve. On tracking her down in a boarding house in Hampstead, he becomes aware of the uncanny effect of her gaze, an *'eye-beam'* that appears to search the soul, as if Clarissa in spite of her youth and innocence has anticipated the plot (L 243, 824, 827; cf. L244, 836). These pangs culminate in a letter written to Belford at the dead of midnight, exactly 48 hours before the rape. It begins in his best rakish mode with the reference to Mandeville already cited ('if this sweet creature must *fall* ... for the benefit of all the pretty fools of the sex, she *must*'), but abruptly swerves into a mood of penitence and dread: 'Why was such a woman as this thrown in my way, whose very fall will be her glory, and perhaps not only my shame, but my destruction' (L246, 848). The letter becomes a palimpsest, as Lovelace wafers over it a slip of paper to explain that conscience, 'a thief, an imposter, as well as a tormentor', had stolen his pen, but that he has now murdered the '[p]oor impertinent opposer' and she lies 'weltering in her blood' (848).[68]

The semi-parodic echoes of *Macbeth* are sustained as the hour approaches. On the brink of committing the rape Lovelace asks himself, 'Why should this enervating pity unsteel my foolish heart?' (L256, 879). He is spurred on by the fallen women, a crew of Lady Macbeths. Dorothy van Ghent in a 1953 essay that was regarded as definitive in its day, made the now notorious remark that in abstract terms the 'central event of the novel' is 'a singularly thin and unrewarding piece of action – the deflowering of a young lady – and one which scarcely seems to deserve the universal uproar it provokes'.[69] Later responses to van Ghent have ranged from involuntary flinching and outrage to compassion for a female critic operating in the pre-feminist dark ages.[70] But the reader needs to hang on to precisely that sense of disproportion (again a theme borrowed from *Macbeth*); the disparity is constantly discussed by Lovelace and the prostitutes, but also by Clarissa's well-wishers within the novel and even by some of Richardson's most sympathetic correspondents. The universal uproar was unprecedented and unequalled. Richardson managed to turn a rape into an eighteenth-century equivalent of regicide.

The rape is an admission of defeat by Lovelace. The use of force, and in particular the use of a drug to sedate his victim, invalidates the original terms of the trial of female nature. Instead, what he is now looking for is Clarissa's complicity after the fact: her capitulation to marriage, waiving the demand for Lovelace's reformation. He believes that 'when her pride of being corporeally inviolate is brought down ... she can tell no tales', 'that modesty ... will lock up her speech' (L256, 879). It is self-evident that the goal of the rape was not sexual pleasure; but neither is it undertaken with the conventional aim of devaluing a woman as property in the eyes of other men. There is already a major concession to the feminizing principle in that the rape is intended to prove a point to women; it is an acknowledgement of their moral autonomy and at the same time an attempt to remind them of their true nature. In her temporary derangement, caused by the after-effect of the drug, Clarissa produces fragments of writing, some of which seem to show her conversion to Lovelace's philosophy. She berates herself for her pride and in an allegory of a lady who nurses up a lion or bear cub and makes it her pet, but is torn to pieces when it 'resumed its nature', she seems to concede that Mandevillian point that politeness is hypocrisy: 'who was most to blame, I pray? The brute, or the lady? The lady, surely! – For what *she* did, was *out* of nature, *out* of character at least: what *it* did, was *in* its own nature' (L261, 891). But as her head begins to clear it becomes evident that Lovelace's plan has backfired entirely: Clarissa is more adamant than ever in her refusal to marry him or even to see him, and eventually shows that she is more than willing to publicize her fall. Although she dismisses the idea of allying herself with a noble family on the grounds that she is 'a creature whom thou hast levelled with the dirt of the street, and classed with the vilest of her sex' (L267, 912), the heroic idiom once again signals the fact that she has risen above him. Lovelace can never again hope to 'get her out of her altitudes' (L264, 907).

The apotheosis of Clarissa and the redemption of man

To read *Clarissa* as an intervention in the feminization debate is to read it in the beam of a searchlight. It exposes a powerful logic, but also appears to flatten out some aspects of the narrative, though it brings others into unaccustomed clarity. It is an engaged interpretation, a reading of the novel as Richardson said he wanted it to be read (a different thing, perhaps, from his more unruly impulses as a creator of fiction), for the morals as much as for the story. Certain ambiguities are minimized. There is no suspense in the Lovelace-Clarissa relationship whatsoever, not a moment's possibility that Lovelace could or should marry her.[71] Lovelace appears entirely without charm, unrecognizable as the heroic artificer celebrated by William B. Warner in his well-known Nietzschean study of the book.[72] He is the incarnation of the benighted past, to be swept away with little regret. All interest is contained in Clarissa, the nuances of her response to the twists and turns of adversity, and her ultimate triumph. And for readers of the time who recognized how much was riding on this progress, nothing less than the moral tenor of the future, it was an infinitely fascinating and moving spectacle.

If Clarissa has a weakness, it is her tendency to superstition. In the middle part of the book she is periodically struck down by the recollection of her father's curse, relayed to her by Arabella. Richardson's acquaintance, the young Hester Mulso, wrote to him formally and at length to argue that the credence the heroine lends to Mr Harlowe's barbaric oath is unworthy of her, and Anna Howe briefly says as much in the novel.[73] After the rape, although Clarissa is undaunted in her dealings with Lovelace, she develops a morbid fear of the proprietor of the house.[74] Mrs Sinclair hardly speaks or even features until the time of Clarissa's second arrival at Dover Street, but she becomes a totemic figure in the moment when Clarissa, drugged and fainting, begs to be released from the 'hated house'. Rushing into the room 'in a great ferment', she accuses Clarissa of slander, in a tragi-comic simulation of propriety, and begins to metamorphose:

> The old dragon straddled up to her, with her arms kemboed again – her eyebrows erect, like the bristles upon a hog's back and, scowling over her shortened nose, more than half-hid her ferret eyes. Her mouth was distorted. She pouted out her blubber-lips, as if to bellow up wind and sputter into her horse-nostrils; and her chin was curdled, and more than usually prominent with passion. (L256, 883)

Mrs Sinclair, always a cipher, becomes now (in Lovelace's retelling, accounting for Clarissa's horrified reaction) a half-mythic, half-bestial emblem of woman's sinfulness, the absolute alienation from virtue. Although Clarissa, in her account written to Anna much later, does not describe Sinclair at any length, she speaks of her as the chief among the 'female figures flitting ... before my sight' in her 'visionary remembrance' of the crime; 'these confused ideas might be owing to the terror I had conceived of the worse than masculine violence she had been permitted to assume to me, for expressing my abhorrence of her house' (L314, 1011).

Mrs Sinclair and her cohort seem to violate not only sexual difference, but also the boundaries of the human. Subsequently, Lovelace relates how as Clarissa slowly recoups her powers of resistance, Mrs Sinclair has only to appear on the scene, huffing and puffing '*Hoh! Madam*' with her 'kemboed' arms, for her to retreat in terror (L276, 935 cf. 894, 898, 926, 929).

Meanwhile, Lovelace dithers and dallies. Unwilling to let Clarissa go, unable to persuade her to marry, called to the bedside of his ailing uncle but afraid to leave Clarissa to the women of the house, he allows himself to be convinced by the whores that the problem derives from his failure to rape Clarissa properly, without the aid of a narcotic. '*Had* she been sensible, she *must* have been sensible (L279, 943); if conscious, she will unquestionably be sensualized. Or if she emerges as nobly a second time, he will reform forthwith (945). And so the trial is on again, and Lovelace stages a farce whereby Clarissa is to be lured out of her room by the hubbub of her maidservant Dorcas being accused of conspiring in her escape. The women will be assembled to judge her for bribing Dorcas, and Lovelace will use a display of righteous anger to molest her or extract promises. Clarissa enters the scene and steals the show: with her noble calm ('she seemed to tread air, and to be all soul'), she silences her enemies and then contemptuously upbraids them for their plotting. This is a victory not over Lovelace, but over her fear of Mrs Sinclair: 'Thou woman ... once my terror! always my dislike! but now my detestation!' (L281, 949). Lovelace describes a 'history of the Lady and the Penknife' in which he is terrified into inaction by her resolve to plunge a penknife into her heart if he approaches. In Clarissa's letter to Anna the scene is summed up by the editor: 'Of her triumph over all the creatures of the house assembled to terrify her; and perhaps to commit fresh outrages upon her' (L315, 1012). The most crucial circumstance is the reinstatement of the singular, invulnerable female ideal, beyond the influence of man. This is also the moment at which she publicly abandons the pretence that she and Lovelace are married, which he had insisted on at the start of their habitation at Mrs Sinclair's; it is the start of her publicizing of her case and the abandonment of false shame. The following day Lovelace leaves for Berkshire, never to see her again; she escapes and finds obscure lodgings near Covent Garden, from which she reestablishes her network of correspondence.

Clarissa's refusal to marry, in defiance of the strongest urgings of Lovelace and, in due course, his family and her friends and relations, can be usefully contrasted with the refusal of Defoe's Roxana. Both declare their attachment to liberty, but in the case of Roxana this is a mask for greed, while in Clarissa it is the mark of disinterestedness: in place of rank and riches she chooses 'to expose her disgrace to the whole world; to forgo the reconciliation with her friends which her heart was so set upon; and to hazard a thousand evils to which her youth and her sex may too probably expose an indigent and friendless beauty' (L294, 969). Each has lain with her suitor: Roxana becomes pregnant and her refusal to legitimize the child is a damning consequence of her callous self-interest; Clarissa falls ill and dies, and the question of whether or not she was pregnant is left open-ended. Pregnancy arising from rape was by long tradition held to be a sign of the woman's complicity and pleasure. As late as 1756, a handbook for magistrates repeated the maxim that 'a woman can not conceive unless she doth consent', though it also throws doubt on the philosophy underlying it.[75] According to the one-sex model of sexual difference, reproduction was as dependent on female orgasm as on male orgasm. The philosophy is implicit in the brusque letters from her uncles questioning Clarissa on this score, and perhaps also Lovelace's hope that 'all her grievous distresses shall end in a man-child', and his earlier flippant remarks on Miss Betterton, who dies in childbirth after his 'rape' of her.[76] It is the last turn in the trial of woman; the last chance to demonstrate the 'triumph of nature over principle' (L371, 1147); the last, faint hint of her carnal nature. Clarissa's own mysteriousness on the subject ('a cruel question ... which a little, a very little time, will better answer than I can: for I am not either a hardened or shameless creature', L403, 1193 cf. 1197) is indicative of the vacuum left by the rejection of the one-sex model. It would not be possible to justify Richardson's assertion of the spiritual opposition of the sexes on anatomical grounds until early in the nineteenth century. The imputation could not yet be dismissed as irrelevant. But there is a premonitory resentment of the question as a second violation of modesty. There is no body that it would be ideologically appropriate for Clarissa to inhabit.

When Lovelace is called upon to explain his actions to his uncle Lord M. and his female relations, he reverts to precisely the strategy he had used at the start of his conflict with Clarissa, at the moment when she declared her soul was above him (see above p. 100). Correcting his initial summary – 'she has done more honour to the sex in her fall ... than ever any other could in her standing' – he moves her beyond sex: 'In short, ladies, in a word, my lord, Miss Clarissa Harlowe is an angel' (L324, 1037; cf. L511, 1429). To a large extent the other commentators in the novel concur, but Clarissa's transfiguration during her dying phase is not entirely straightforward. For a time she takes on the mantle of Christ.[77] Anna Howe calls her 'my earthly saviour' (L329, 1045). Immediately we learn that at the instigation of the prostitutes, Clarissa has been arrested for non-payment of board and lodgings and thrown into a miserable debtors' prison. The protracted scenes in which Sally and Polly visit to taunt and cajole her recall the mocking of Christ (L333 1053–8 and 1060–2). But this intensity is not sustained. Bland sexual superlatives take over from the period of Belford's protective intervention – 'most injured of her sex', 'loveliest of her sex', 'most deserving of her sex' – and Clarissa is filtered; it is a process of distancing in which she colludes by proffering extracts from scripture in place of her own words. Belford is, like Lovelace, a rake, though in a course of reformation; like Lovelace he seeks an explanation for the superiority of Clarissa that transcends the conventional interplay of the sexes: 'couldst thou have thy senses so much absorbed in the WOMAN in her charming person as to be blind to the ANGEL that shines out in such full glory in her mind? ... I am sure it would be impossible for me, were she to be as beautiful and as crimsoned over with health as I have seen her, to have the least thought of sex when I heard her talk' (L446, 1299). The reader is reminded from time to time of Clarissa's physicality: she suffers from a 'violent stomach-ache', and when in prison for debt, Sally points out that her linen is 'a little *soily*' (L276, 932; L333, 1060). Belford's epitaph for her is a more accurate summary of her posthumous value: 'not only an ornament to her sex, but to human nature (481, 1363).[78] Although Lovelace appears unregenerate even after her death, her exemplary influence is already extending beyond woman to affect the reformation of man.

Richardson's friend Aaron Hill called the influence of *Clarissa* the equivalent of Circe's enchantment in reverse; this writing turn beasts into men.[79] Belford – for so long the recipient of Lovelace's letters and letters by Clarissa enclosed with them – undergoes a transformation from dispassionate bystander to sympathetic advocate to active Samaritan to instrument of her will, conserver of her memory, speaker of her words. His first intervention on her behalf, a letter written to Lovelace after he has announced his intention to stage the trial at Mrs Sinclair's brothel, strives to argue for fair play on the grounds of friendship, without renouncing the rake's creed or having recourse to the notion of virtue (L143, 500–3 cf. L419, 1226). By the end, under the direct influence of Clarissa, he has formed a new plan of life that involves making himself fit to be a good woman's husband (L531, 1474). When he attempts to rescue her from debtors' prison, Clarissa addresses him as 'MAN': her initial rejection of his aid is symbolic (L334, 1066 and L336, 1070). The subsequent regeneration has a general bearing for the male sex. His behaviour soon after at the deathbed of his fellow-rake Belton is a measure of his progress in feminization. He reassures Belton that his tears 'are no signs of an *unmanly*, but contrarily of a humane nature', and reassuringly cites Juvenal as an authority, '*Tears are the prerogative of manhood*' (L419, 1225); a correction of Lovelace's insouciant comment on Clarissa's grief: 'I believe the anatomists allow *that women have more watery heads than men*' (L276, 932). The peculiarities of women's language had been a subject of ridicule in the correspondence between Lovelace and Belford. Now the latter begins a revaluation, and adopts the feminine phrase '*battered* to death' to register his disapproval of Lovelace's characteristic ill-treatment of his servants; 'all female words, though we are not sure of their derivation, have very significant meanings'. He expresses his newfound sensibility through the term, '*flurries*'.[80] More earnestly, he takes as his task the recollection and circulation of Clarissa's words that will lead to his formal appointment as the editor of her story.

Belford's formal renunciation of the rake's creed comes after he has witnessed in turn the peaceful death of Clarissa and the agonized death throes of Mrs Sinclair. Writing to Lovelace, he reprises the central thesis of the novel, that 'the false and inconsiderate notion ... *that a reformed rake makes the best husband*' must be rejected and that women must discountenance Pope's dictum that they are 'rakes in their *hearts*' by 'rejecting the address of every man whose character will not stand the test of that virtue which is the glory of a woman: and indeed, I may say, of a man too. Why should it not?' But the route to reformation is a difficult one: 'little do innocents think what a total revolution of manners, what a change of fixed habits, nay, what a conquest of a *bad nature*, is required to make a man a good husband, a worthy father, and true friend, from *principle*; especially when it is considered that it is not in a man's own power to reform when he will' (L499, 1393).[81] He takes Lovelace's inability to sustain and act upon his intense feelings of remorse as the illustration of that difficulty.

Incapable of genuine reform, Lovelace ends by plotting his own death. Belford gives him the notion with his remark, provoked by the news of Clarissa's imprisonment for debt, that spreading about his desire to marry her will be 'a means to make mankind, who know not what I know of the matter, herd a little longer with thee, and forbear to hunt thee to thy fellow-savages in the Libyan wilds and deserts' (L333, 1051). Lovelace always favoured hunting metaphors in his narration of the trial of Clarissa; he subscribes to the idea of a state of nature according to Hobbes or Mandeville, which erupts into view when the artificial fabric of politeness is torn. Now it gives rise to his self-portrait as a 'poor, single, harmless prowler; at least *comparatively* harmless' compared to 'our Christian princes', yet 'every mouth is opened, every hand is lifted up against me' (L515, 1437). He is determined to make 'his Fate according to his mind' (as a citation from Horace puts it) (L530, 1473). Clarissa, in the letters delivered after her death, begged that she should not be avenged by her brother or her cousin Morden, a military man. Lovelace goes abroad after Clarissa's death, but instead of avoiding a duel, arranges for Colonel Morden to hunt him down. He is fatally wounded, and the account sent by his second, a French manservant, emphasizes the loneliness of his death, but also a final act of grace, his dying words, 'distinctly pronounced', 'LET THIS EXPIATE!' After Lovelace's unceasing flow of words throughout the novel, the reticence is striking. But what is most important is the way these words join him in community with Clarissa at the last, by a distant recollection of her desire for the 'happy moments' of death 'which shall expiate for all!' (L201, 651). He was, after all, the most vital chronicler of Clarissa and her voice in his blow-by-blow transmissions from the front line, and he is the closest witness to her active virtue. In his final letter to Belford he reiterates the challenge to the female reader: 'this lady has asserted the worthiness of her sex, and most gloriously has she exalted it with me now. Yet, surely, as I have said and written an hundred times, there cannot be such another woman' (L535, 1481).

Clarissa as a progressivist narrative

Although her first wish was 'of sliding through life to the end of it unnoted' (L1, 40), by the end of the story Clarissa has no fear of becoming a public spectacle, unlike previous literary victims of libertinism such as Calista in *The Fair Penitent*. Lovelace had complacently told himself that 'Women often, for their own sakes, will keep the *last secret*' (L244, 837). But Clarissa is 'glad if I may be warning, since I cannot be an example' (L306, 985). She is urged by Mrs Howe and her own relations to bring a legal case against Lovelace, courting publicity as a warning and protection to other women. She refuses, but only because of ill health and the doubtful evidence. Instead, she ensures memorialization of her story by making Belford executor of her will on condition that he writes up the case: a result that will be more enduring than a court case. Lines from the first of Clarissa's meditations from scripture contain the earliest hint of her intention: 'Oh that my words were now written! Oh that they were printed in a book! that they were graven with an iron pen and lead in the book for ever!' (L364, 1125). A little more than two weeks later, Clarissa writes to Belford explaining that although Anna Howe and her mother have requested her to prepare an account of her experience to justify her conduct, ill health and the pain of reflecting on the events make it impossible to comply. She asks him instead for a specimen of Lovelace's letters, which she has been assured do justice to her character, in the hope that a compilation from them may serve instead (L387, 1173). The following day she asks him formally to be 'protector of my memory' (L389, 1176 cf. L507, 1418). Just over a month later, she is dead.

When Anna Howe sees her friend lying in the coffin her predominant concern, beyond immediate grief, is with the perpetuation of Clarissa's life as narrative: 'This cannot, surely, be all of my CLARISSA's story!' (L502, 1403). Anna becomes a collaborator in the publication of the memorial book. Lovelace remarks that she 'threatens to have the case published to the whole world' (L515, 1437). Anna and Belford strive to prevent Clarissa's story being told as the hackneyed tale of a coquette broken by a libertine, with the circular moral that woman will be undone by her own defective nature. They must circumvent the kind of simplistic misogyny expressed by Mowbray as he surveys the wreckage, a hollow echo of Lovelace's initial standpoint: 'I wish the poor fellow had never known her ... And what is there in one woman more than another, for matter of that?' (L480, 1359). In response to this danger they must put together a linear, progressive history that turns tragedy into triumph. It will be based on an 'afflictive model of progress', 'the sense of living in times of religious trouble, accompanied by the dream of a far better future brought about by redoubled human effort working in concert with the divine plan'.[82]

Anna receives Belford's correspondences with Lovelace and Morden and additional material written by Clarissa, and is invited by him to provide a testament to her friend as a postscript summing up her extraordinary qualities. There is pathos in the placing of Clarissa's prehistory at the end. After the incessant drama and passion, Anna's relation of Clarissa's chosen way of life offers a point of stillness. Clarissa measured out her days in a regular pattern of writing, household management, needlework, drawing and music, domestic sociability, charity and reading, with a maximum of six hours' sleep, and by this means lived more years at 16 than others had lived at 26. Her excessively methodical dispensation of hours has been called mercantilist: she draws up accounts, regarding the loss of time due to a particular duty as a debt to be repaid, and keeping a fund of four hours each day in reserve.[83]

In the concluding section of the novel the heroine is firmly established as an emblem of moral progress. But the extent to which she also embodies a progressive socio-economic outlook has been a long-standing topic of critical debate. Clarissa's market method of self-employment, her knowledge of accounting in household management, and elsewhere, as in the case of Pamela, the many instances of her strict financial rectitude, all exemplify the virtues of a commercial society.[84] She adopts her method because 'it teaches me to be covetous of time; the only thing of which we can be *allowably* covetous; since we live but once in this world; and when gone, are gone from it for ever' (L529, 1472). This remark could be understood as a rebuke to capitalist acquisitiveness, but most immediately it is a criticism of the feudal drive towards the consolidation of land exhibited by Solmes and her own family, and the related evil of dynasticism: 'in my opinion, the world is but one great family; originally it was so; what then is this narrow selfishness that reigns in us, but relationship remembered against relationship forgot?' (L8, 62) This challenge to traditional property rights is actualized in Clarissa's case by the legacy of a small estate from her grandfather; a bequest motivated by sentiment in defiance of patrilineal expectations. Although she cedes possession to her father, the fact of the inheritance is a constant source of irritation to her brother, the archproponent of patrilineal inheritance. It relates to the gradual reform of property law in this period through the employment of principles of equity, partly in response to the demands of the commercial classes, and Clarissa's handling of the estate is equally forward-looking. As Margaret Anne Doody has observed, Clarissa before the abduction is a worker, an improver, who manages the dairy along lines of 'elegant simplicity and convenience' (L2, 41).[85]

But to interpret the narrative of *Clarissa* as a whole in terms of class conflict is to run headlong into anachronism and abstraction.[86] The surest measure of Richardson's socio-economic progressivism can be found in his treatment of the question of luxury. This is subtle, and through the first half of the novel, might be described as teasing. Again and again he signals what might be the makings of a polarity between the ascetic Clarissa and her unscrupulous opponents, but then fails to develop it into a critique of luxury. Arabella, with her misplaced vanity and slovenly lie-a-bed habits, is an obvious candidate as moral contrast, but Richardson prefers to examine the workings of her spiteful envy. The elder Harlowes are self-satisfied children of fortune: Clarissa's father made rich by a lucky marriage; Uncle John by the fortunate discovery of mines on his property; and above all there is Uncle Anthony, the nabob, whose East India Company wealth, noted in the description of characters at the beginning of the first edition, is an invitation to unite themes of moral and economic corruption. Again the invitation is declined. Solmes, Clarissa's suitor, is a grasping, antisocial miser, but we are not permitted to understand him as one half of the luxury equation; he has no prodigal heir as an economic counterweight, like Cotta and his son in Pope's *Epistle to Bathurst*. Finally, and most curiously of all, there is the refusal to associate Lovelace with luxury. Although Clarissa's father remarks at the start that he has 'the air of a spendthrift' and he is reputed to have contracted debts abroad, this report is immediately countered by the testimony of a discharged bailiff of Lord M. that he is attentive to his economic affairs, has high credit and has 'spared nothing for solid and lasting improvements upon his estate' (L2, 46 and L4, 50). The divergence of the character of Lovelace from the freethinking libertines of the Restoration period has been mentioned; just as foreign to him are the rakes who are made emblematic of luxury in the 'realist' moral progresses of Hogarth and Mary Davys.[87]

In the second half of the novel, Richardson adopts a new tactic, understated but unmistakable, of bringing luxury into *alliance* with Clarissa and the cause of virtue. Margaret Anne Doody, who in the essay 'The Man-made World of Clarissa Harlowe and Robert Lovelace' provides the best introduction to the relationship between the novel and commercial culture, has tellingly observed two instances of this, though without making reference to the luxury debate.[88] After Clarissa has been at Dover Street for a month, subjected to Lovelace's '*amorous seesaw*' (L108, 424), Anna proposes that she might take refuge with an acquaintance of hers, 'one Mrs Townshend, who is a great dealer in Indian silks, Brussels and French laces, cambrics, linen, and other valuable goods; which she has a way of coming at, duty-free; and has a great vend for them, and for other curiosities which she imports, in the private families of the gentry round us'. This independent businesswoman is a purveyor of luxuries on a grand scale, and the fact that she is 'upon a very good foot of understanding' with the virtuous Anna is a counter-thrust to that ancient subdivision of the luxury debate that brings together misogynist rhetoric and sumptuary laws.

She was introduced into the Howe household at the mother's behest in order to furnish the daughter with a wedding trousseau fit for a princess 'at a moderate expense'. Although Anna hesitates to patronize a contraband trader (and is in no hurry to get married), she has listened with pleasure to her entertaining accounts of business trips abroad (L196, 621–2).[89] Her home and principal warehouse is at Deptford, a dock close to London, where Clarissa could stay concealed until her cousin Colonel Morden arrives in England. Mrs Townshend also has two brothers, each the master of a ship, who would be willing to help protect her. Intriguingly, she shares a name with the prominent Whig politician Charles, Viscount Townshend (1674–1738), brother-in-law of Walpole, who helped the government weather the South Sea Bubble and later Jacobite scares, but retired from politics and spent the 1730s improving his estates with new farming methods so earning the nickname 'Turnip' Townshend; the model of an aristocrat animated by the passion for commercial progress.

Clarissa, in a reply written the same day, begs Anna to pursue the scheme with Mrs Townshend. It remains her best hope, indeed her only hope, of eluding Lovelace. Unfortunately, it coincides with Lovelace's infiltration of the correspondence, and he finds ways to scupper it. Mrs Townshend duly undertakes to rescue Clarissa but arrives at Mrs Moore's boarding house the day after the rape has taken place, to be told that the young lady had departed voluntarily with Lovelace and his relations (L316, 1015). Anna had cherished hopes of engineering class struggle of a literal kind; Mrs Townshend leading her seafaring brothers and their crews into battle with Lovelace and leaving him with '*broken bones, at least*, for all his vileness!' (L252.1, 860).[90] In spite of this missed opportunity, the reliance on Mrs Townshend with her '*manlike spirit*' (a rare affirmative usage) and 'knowledge of the world' establishes the credit of the luxury trade in the moral economy of the novel.

The alliance with Mrs Townshend is the prelude to a second instance of great emblematic significance. When Clarissa flees from Lovelace and Sinclair for the second time she makes her way, not to the semi-rural suburbs, but to the heart of the modern West End of London, Covent Garden, and takes lodgings over a glove shop owned by Mr John Smith. Hogarth's *Morning* from the series of engravings *The Four Times of the Day* (1738; figure 3) shows Covent Garden piazza against the backdrop of St Paul's church, a stone's throw from the glove shop in King Street, at around the time when Clarissa is set. Hogarth presents the scene in the spirit of the age. As in the engraving of the *South Sea Scheme* (figure 2, p. 52) a noble civic edifice, in this case the Palladian façade designed by Inigo Jones, is partly obscured by a degraded place of public entertainment, here Tom King's Coffee House, the property of the infamous Moll King who took over the establishment after her husband's death in 1737 and was among those responsible for giving coffee-houses a bad name.[91] And as in the earlier print, the neoclassical setting is compromised by a turbulent mass of humanity, a group in the doorway of King's fighting, the cluster in the foreground love-making or struggling to keep warm in front of a meagre fire, on the left the main business of the place, the selling and

Figure 3   William Hogarth, *Morning, The Four Times of the Day* (1738).

buying of produce. But the focus for social criticism in this image is the comical, dried-up spinster on her way to early morning service, finely dressed but incarnating the frigidity of the weather, fan raised to lips pursed in disapproval as she views a libertine fondling the bosom of his girl, and indifferent to the shivering of the boy in livery who carries her prayer book. It is a satire of moral hypocrisy of the kind Mandeville favoured, and Hogarth shares his interest in the old maid as a denier of sensuous human nature and a perversion of female nature. Against this backdrop of teeming, disreputable life Clarissa passes her final two months. It is not impossible that Richardson was familiar with Hogarth's print and, as was his way, set out to correct it. Clarissa, a spinster of genuine piety, sympathetic humanity and ascetic tastes, is also a patron of morning prayers and twice attends the 6 am service at St Paul's, hoping that the early hour will be a protection against Lovelace's spies. It is at the rear exit of the church, in Bedford Street, that she is arrested for debt.

Once released from prison she returns to Smith's, although her residence there is no longer a secret to Lovelace and his accomplices. A letter to Anna had described her situation there. Smith is a 'dealer in stockings, ribands, snuff and perfumes' (L320, 1022). He and his wife, who keeps shop, are plain, prudent people whose companionate marriage Clarissa takes as an indication of good-heartedness. She lives in two rooms on the first floor and on the second floor is another lodger, Mrs Lovick, a worthy, pious widow. The moral significance of the topography of Mrs Sinclair's house, with the prostitutes situated below, Clarissa above, and Lovelace shuttling between the two, has often been discussed. The layout of Smith's is equally and relatedly meaningful. The fallen women have been replaced by honest shopkeepers; the sale of sex by an innocent trade in petty luxury items. Like Mrs Townshend, the Smiths cater to the consuming desires of people of fashion, but in contrast, their commodities are above board and John Smith, Clarissa stresses, is 'a glove-*maker* as well as *seller*', for the process of production is an additional sign of integrity.[92] Clarissa actually joins the trade, selling her own lace and fine dresses to private buyers, with the help of Mrs Lovick, in order to pay for her board, doctor's fees and a coffin.

Lovelace's visit to the shop on an occasion when Clarissa, forewarned, is absent, leads him to provide an exact description of the place.

> I went behind the counter and sat down under an arched kind of canopy of carved work, which these proud traders, emulating the royal niche-fillers, often give themselves, while a joint-stool perhaps serves those by whom they get their bread; such is the dignity of trade in this mercantile nation! (L416, 1213)

As in the coffee-house, this is a space where the female vendor's presence is formalized and dignified by her seated position behind a counter. Lovelace, for a jape, usurps Mrs Smith's place and mocks the arrangement. He ridicules the Smiths and when he gets their journeyman, Joseph, in a head grip and threatens to cut some of his teeth out to to fill the gap in his own servant's mouth, it looks as though the class battle thwarted in the Townshend episode will take place after all. But he turns off the conflict by some slapstick play with customers and exits in his chair amid a gathering crowd.

It is above this shop, with its 'powder, patches, wash-balls, stockings, garters, snuffs, and pin-cushions', that Clarissa chooses to die (L416, 1215). As Doody remarks, 'Richardson could have made Clarissa end her days in the house of some artisan or trader dealing in more "worthy" goods – if not printer or bookseller, then the shop of a tailor or greengrocer. But Smiths' shop is an extra, an exhibition of what human beings make and use beyond mere necessities.'[93] Lovelace treats it as a low comic backdrop for an interval in his personal drama. Clarissa treats the inhabitants of the house with respect and they play an integral part in her death rites, as surrogates for her own family. Her calm, pious manner of dying sanctifies this temple of merchandise. Reciprocally, it is this ordinary storehouse of the comforts, conveniences and ornaments of modern living in a commercial nation that provides Clarissa with a sanctuary in which to prepare herself for the next world. There is evidently no paradox intended. Richardson treats the trading classes with the matter-of-fact appreciation of an insider, as Defoe had done. But the consequences of this treatment, both spiritual by association and quotidian, are considerable; by such means he detaches luxury from a degenerative or cyclical theory of history. Although, as will become apparent in the next chapter, Richardson was critical of conspicuous consumption and pleasure-seeking when it compromised the feminine ideal, commercial prosperity is linked to the reformation of manners.

6
Out of the Closet: Richardson and the Cult of Literary Women

The closet as laboratory of the soul

When Anna Howe describes the daily routine of Clarissa before her abduction, she notes that the three extra hours gained in the morning by early rising were devoted, not to household duties, but to 'closet-work ... epistolary amusements' (1470). In explanation, Anna records Clarissa's views on women's natural affinity for writing: 'it was always a matter of surprise to her, that the sex are generally so averse as they are to writing; since the pen, next to the needle, of all employments is the most proper and best adapted to their geniuses; and this as well for improvement as amusement' (1467). 'Who sees not,' she quotes Clarissa as saying, 'that those women who take delight in writing excel the men in all the graces of the familiar style?'

For all the accompanying insistence on the heroine's domestic excellence, it is Clarissa the writer we see in the novel, rather than the domestic goddess. We seldom find her plying the needle, but she is never long separated from her pen. In the most famous and influential part of *Pamela*, we see not an angel in the house but a writing woman, relieved of her domestic duties by imprisonment. *Clarissa* follows the same scenario. This chapter will show the impact of Richardson's scribbling heroines on the fortunes of a network of literary women, and how it eventually helped to bring about a reappraisal of women's writing as a source of national pride. He prepared the way for the adoption of virtuous femininity as a figurehead for the progress of Britain as a commercial society; though this association was not without its logistical problems. The paradox that joins a cult of ascetic, virginal, ink-spilling women to the justification of the growth of luxury is largely owing to Richardson for its origins. It would be a fundamental feature of social and political debate for the next thirty years.

This book began with the coffee-house, identified by Habermas as one of the founding institutions of the bourgeois public sphere. It will end with the closet, which I would argue is the social space most importantly connecting the private 'intimate' sphere and the literary public sphere at the mid-century.[1] The counterpoint is worth pursuing. The coffee-house is a space for the self-transformation of men. The closet is a space for the self-transformation of women. The coffee-house is tied by innumerable links to commerce and trade. The closet mimics monastic seclusion from the world, though it is enabling of written communication and argument. There is a crucial way in which the closet improves on the coffee-house as the matrix of the modern, that is to say, as a means of producing a modern moral subject: it genders the modern subject female, as a stamp of disinterestedness. By her rigidly maintained virtue, for which space of the closet serves as sign, she is able to validate the modern society that seeks to celebrate her. In the coffee-house the idealized image of woman propagated in periodicals like the *Athenian Mercury* or the *Spectator* was compromised by the flesh-and-blood proximity of working women (see chapter 1 pp. 21–5). The latter were an unavoidable metonym for the alluring closeness of the money markets and luxury trades: a closeness that was geographical as well as functional, since most coffee-houses were located in the City. In Richardson's novels the ideal woman is relocated to the core of the household. She is not involved in any of the activities of material consumption. Instead, she is engaged in reading and writing, the spiritualized production and consumption of letters.[2] By ornamenting the world of commerce and luxury without tasting its vices or sharing its passions, she helps to sanction it.[3]

The closet was not an empty receptacle in 1740. Richardson had to reclaim it and redefine its function. The reconceptualization of the closet as a physical space and a site of moral values in *Pamela* is a central part of its conscious distance from the amatory fiction of 1720s. Richardson adopts the household topography of seduction, the 'locked doors, passages, back stairs, walls, and keys', found in the sordid tales of Eliza Haywood.[4] In Haywood's *Idalia, or the Unfortunate Mistress* (1723) the rapist Don Ferdinand enters the bedroom of his victim via a closet 'which had a passage into another Room'.[5] It is this familiar scenario, the violation of the privacy of the closet followed by the violation of the heroine's body, which Richardson deliberately employs at the start of his novel.[6] But the outcomes are radically different. Haywood's heroines pay lip service to terms like 'honour' and 'virtue', but they are betrayed by bodies that soften and yield, making them complicit in their own undoing. Although apparently high-minded, they are involuntarily lustful. Pamela by contrast goes into unalluring fits; the body freezes in spasms; there can be no question of her feeling or delivering pleasure. A pre-emptive Lucretia, she successfully drives off the male predator. The deterrent effect is formalized by the rendering of the event in Pamela's own blunt idiom, so different from the luxuriant third-person descriptions of Haywood. The performance draws a negative superlative from Mrs Jervis, the sole first-hand observer: 'I never saw any body so frightful in my life!' (64). We are witnessing, with Mrs Jervis, the miraculous revival of John Dunton's realm of the new: a new woman, with a new kind of body and a new elevation of mind. No longer will the anatomy of the drowsy heroine act as an echo chamber for masculine desire. Pamela's body has a mind of its own; a distinctive and autonomous female mind. It is cultivated in the closet, through reading and writing.

Pamela will be betrayed by 'closet-work' one further time; when Mr B hides once again in a closet, eavesdropping on Pamela's pert rejection of his gifts: '*Closet* for that!' There is a neat circularity; his repetition of the device brings him unwelcome evidence of the ease with which she dismisses his assault and the promise of future favours. From now on, the closet will become the exclusive resource of the heroine, a stronghold of virtuous resolve, rather than a point of weakness in her defences. Pamela is abducted and confined at B's Lincolnshire estate, but she obtains permission to have a closet in her bedroom reserved for her own use, 'with a Key to lock up my Things' (112). The move from Bedfordshire to Lincolnshire marks a change in conception of the closet, from the scene of sexual licence to sanctuary.[7] In the room she secretes supplies of pens, ink, paper, wax and wafers, her weapons against the master's siege. Richardson would redeploy the formula in his second novel. Even through a long succession of imprisonments, Clarissa is rarely deprived of a closet and key.

It is within the confines of the closet that Richardson's heroines write their letters, keeping up a running commentary on their persecutions. Even when there is no way of sending the letters, or making sure they arrive, they continue writing. What is important is that they sustain this personal account, this projection of self as subject into a plot in which they are intended by others to play the part of object. And eventually this writing doubles back and seizes hold of events: the complete story in letters is assembled, the heroine is vindicated, corrupt authority is forced to capitulate. *Pamela* and *Clarissa* are histories of closet rebellions, and the victory of reflective subjectivity over convention backed by violence. Compare these militantly literate heroines with those of Fielding: Joseph Andrew's beloved Fanny who could 'neither write nor read';[8] Sophia in *Tom Jones* who reads as a sentimental indulgence;[9] the transcendental worth of Amelia, the heroine of his final novel, is first shown by her heroic forbearance at the damage to her nose caused by a carriage accident. The omniscient narrator makes the independent voice of female virtue unnecessary. When women speak it is to become comic travesties, and 'learned ladies' like Mrs Slipslop and Mrs Fitzherbert women are objects of satire in the tradition of Molière's *Les Précieuses Ridicules*.[10]

The closet was a 'characteristic feature of the Georgian house', a 'small private apartment usually adjoining the bedroom', the feminine counterpart within the household of the masculine library or study.[11] It was a place of contemplative isolation, a place for activities of the mind, its seclusion distinguished from that of the bedroom or the dressing-room by the absence of distracting bodily associations. Ian Watt in *The Rise of the Novel* remarks, 'it was much more characteristically the *locus* of woman's liberty and even licence than its French equivalent, the boudoir, for it was used, not to conceal gallants but to lock them out'.[12] The closet was in effect a counter-boudoir. In Richardson, the closet is dialogically constituted not only by the amatory fiction of women, but also by that venerable target of misogynist satire, the lady's dressing-room.[13] Ovid in *Remedia Amoris* recommended that a love-sick suitor should secretly penetrate the privacy of his beloved in order to cure him of his delusions. In the Sixth Satire of Juvenal, the infiltration of the dressing-room becomes a guerrilla tactic in the open warfare between men and women: 'A woman standing before her dressing table is engaged in exploring her sexual and psychic independence as she creates a separate, private, and self-glorified identity. A man's surreptitious entrance into the forbidden territory subverts her independence in the name of destroying vice.'[14] Poets who adapted the tradition in the late seventeenth and early eighteenth centuries, Richard Ames, Robert Gould and, above all, Jonathan Swift, delighted in exposing the nauseating filth and ugliness of the female body beneath the artful public image.

Today Swift's 'A Lady's Dressing Room' (1730), with its climactic revelation of the overflowing chamber pot and the pervasive smell of shit, is generally interpreted as an attack on ideal femininity and a rationalist attempt to liberate both men and women from the ideology of romantic love.[15] But this was a subtlety lost on many contemporary readers. In two response-poems by female authors it is taken as a straightforward attack on women, while Swift's former friend Lord Orrery interpreted it as the product of general misanthropy.[16] In *Clarissa* Richardson explicitly rewrites the scene depicted by Swift when he shows the nightmarish death of Mrs Sinclair amid a dishevelled company of whores. A footnote makes the comparison and finds that 'this description [is] not only more natural but more decent painting, as well as better justified by the design' (1388). But the deflection of the device from an idealised woman to a group of fallen women inevitably dulls the point; it becomes lurid expressionism rather than demystification. Richardson finds a far more effective response with his redeployment of the closet. This is a region that even in the worst of circumstances will always provide a showcase for the beauties of the female mind. In *Clarissa* the prostitutes, under Lovelace's instructions, furnish a light closet with a selection of pious and literary standard works in order to lure Clarissa into agreeing to lodge at Mrs. Sinclair's.[17] They do their work too well. With a barricade of Tillotson's *Sermons* and Inett's *Devotions*, *Telemachus* in French and English and the plays of Shakespeare, Clarissa's spirit is fortified against all attacks.

Watt calls the closet a 'forcing-house of the feminine sensibility', but it is far more than that. It is a workshop of the mind, a laboratory of the soul. A woman is isolated in the closet as if in a glass bell; but she conducts the experiment herself, on herself, for the benefit of the world. In *Clarissa* and throughout *Grandison* the rhetorical question 'Do women have a soul?' is repeatedly raised as a pretext for expounding the doctrine that women are pre-eminently soulful.[18] The proof is found in their letters and in their fortitude, both the products of closet-work. In the late seventeenth century, the two strands of philosophy animating the feminism found in the *Athenian Mercury* and the works of Mary Astell, Neoplatonism and Cartesianism, both make a link between the immortal soul and powers of reflection and reasoning. Improvement of the mind is a Christian duty. This conviction came into constant collision through the eighteenth century with customary advice to women to limit themselves to household duties and obedience to father or husband, and warranted outbursts against 'Mahometan' treatment of the female sex. In around 1737, the young Elizabeth Robinson (later Montagu) wrote to her intellectual mentor, William Friend, 'there is a Mahometan Error crept even into the Christian Church that Women have no Souls, & it is thought very absurd for us to pretend to read or think like Reasonable Creatures'.[19]

In 1748, the year the final part of *Clarissa* was published, Thomas Seward (1708–90, whose daughter Anna, born in 1742, would figure as a second-generation Bluestocking) published 'The Female Right to Literature'. He dramatizes the charge of 'Mahometanism' in this progress poem addressed to Athenia, 'a young Lady from Florence'. The history of women presents a fall from a natural state of freedom into the different forms of debasement and slavery imposed by the Islamic East and the Roman Catholic West. Britain arises as the new champion of Liberty, but even there 'does Custom bind / in chains of Ignorance the female mind', and male pedants fear a learned wife. The poet demands

> can'st thou think
> That virtues, which exalt the soul, can sink
> The outward charms? must knowledge give offence?
> And are the graces all at war with sense?

and concludes that Athenia herself is the perfect exemplar of the union of knowledge, virtue, and beauty.[20]

At the midpoint of *Clarissa* there is an allegorical confrontation between Lovelace and the heroine that illustrates the connection between the closet, literacy and the soul. After her escape from Mrs. Sinclair's, he tracks her down to a boarding-house in Hampstead, and, disguised as a gouty old lawyer, is shown round her quarters as a prospective lodger. Clarissa has retired to the closet. Lovelace grills the landlady Mrs. Moore about the mysterious, solitary young lady: '[H]ow does she employ herself?' 'Writing continually, sir.' 'Then stumping towards the closet, over the door of which hung a picture – What picture is that? – Oh! I see: A St Cecilia!' St Cecilia took a vow of celibacy prior to her marriage to a Roman aristocrat. (Lovelace will shortly claim that Clarissa has unreasonably done the same, due to a breach with her family, in his attempt to win over Mrs. Moore and her friends to his cause.) St Cecilia converted her bridegroom to Christianity on their wedding night.[21] The disguised Lovelace requests a look at the closet.

> Then my charmer opened the door, and blazed upon me, as it were in a flood of light, like what one might imagine would strike a man who, born blind, had by some propitious power been blessed with his sight, all at once, in a meridian sun.
> Upon my soul, I never was so strangely affected before. (*C*: 772)

Continual writing within the confines of the closet has translated itself into a spiritual emanation. Lovelace's conversion experience, like all his crises of conscience, is short-lived. He is quickly recognized by Clarissa and tears off his costume, standing before her 'like the devil in Milton'. Her transfiguration, however, is permanent. Lovelace and his associates start complaining of the 'eye-beams', effusions of her soul that scour their inner emptiness.

Richardson's advocacy of time spent in the closet and the activity of letter writing was not confined to his fiction; he urged the young women of his acquaintance to take this route to self-improvement. He wrote to Sarah Wescomb on 15 September 1746, encouraging her to overcome her diffidence as a writer:

> Retired, the modest lady, happy in herself, happy in the Choice of the dear Correspondent of her own Sex (for ours are too generally Designers); uninterrupted; her Closet her Paradise; her Company, herself, and ideally, the beloved Absent: there she can distinguish Her Self: By this means she can vindicate her Claim to Sense and Meaning. And shall a modest Lady refuse to write?[22]

In the same terms he writes to Susanna Highmore on 2 August 1748, referring to the 'beauties of contemplation which she enjoys in her Clarissa-closet (as she is pleased to call it) with pen, pencil, and books!'[23] Always with Richardson, the pleasures of seclusion are joined to the duties of communication; the more intensive the closeting, the more effective the influence of the self on the other by means of writing. Writing to Sarah Wescomb again: 'The Pen is, almost the *only Means* a very modest and diffident Lady (who in Company will not attempt to glare) has to show herself, and that she has a *Mind*.'[24]

The letters from which the novels are constructed exhibit an amazing ability to undermine the reality of physical confinement. Writing materials pass into the locked chamber and letters pass out in a way that is scarcely credible, if not supernatural. Letters routinely transgress the boundary of inside and outside, public and private, within the narrative itself; and at a meta-narrative level, the published letter (the novels being entirely constructed of letters) is the private made public, closeted ruminations revealed to the gaze of a reading public. What we have is a private sense of self with a constant tendency to pass through its containing walls and permeate external spaces. It is as if the more absolute the confinement, the more extensive the subsequent leakage.

Richardson's heroines come out of the closet to conquer the world. Pamela achieves a worldly ascendancy by marriage to the master who planned to seduce her. What brings about this miracle is her letters, the text woven out of her isolation, the written evidence of her flawless interiority. By reading her collected letters the master is forced to recognize her as his moral superior and resolves to make her private writings the textbook of his future conduct. The house where she was held against her will, and where her only refuge was the closet to which she held the key, is now all her own; she concludes, 'my prison has become my palace'.

In *Clarissa*, we see the inverse proportion of spatial enclosure and the powers of the externalizing private mind at its most radical extreme. We witness Clarissa, free of Lovelace but in terminal decline, planning for death with meticulous care; ordering the coffin in advance, arranging for it to be decorated with symbols and inscriptions: her final letter, a message from the other side; from the inside. Clarissa's entry into her most cramped quarters yet coincides with her maximum influence over the minds of others, and her reappropriation of the household space, her father's house, from which she had been excluded. Ultimate containment gives rise to omnipresence. The fact that she is no longer alive is a side issue; what matters is the survival of Clarissa's perfect humanity as example, memorialized in her closet correspondence, to be internalized by her readers.

Elizabeth Carter, Catherine Talbot and the Richardson effect

The early correspondence of Elizabeth Carter and Catherine Talbot gives a view in miniature of the impact of the new feminizing current in literature on two talented female authors. It also shows that Richardson's model of the learned lady as exemplar was not immediately embraced by all those who formed its natural constituency.

We left Elizabeth Carter in chapter 4 in her father's home in Deal following her abrupt retirement from the London literary scene at the age of 22. She had abandoned her London career partly to escape her own growing fame, but also because of the threat of being drawn into the controversies and public vendettas that raged in the world of letters. But fame and controversy pursued her to Kent. On 1 December 1739, Elizabeth Carter wrote urgently to her former employer Edward Cave, the editor of the *Gentleman's Magazine*. A work had just appeared titled *Woman not Inferior to Man* that described her as one who combined the 'several excellencies' of Sappho, Cornelia, van Schurman and Dacier; 'an *Eliza* not more to be envied, for the towering superioirity of her genius and judgment, than honour'd for the use she makes of them'.[25] The work was published under the pseudonym 'Sophia', and made reference to the eulogistic review by Thomas Birch of her translation of Algarotti's *Sir Isaac Newton's Philosophy Explain'd for the Use of the Ladies* in the *Works of the Learned*.[26] Carter asked Cave if he know the identity of 'Sophia'. She is not explicit about her purpose, but it may be that she suspected a link with Birch and wanted to stem the flow of embarrassing publicity. This appearance as an exemplar in the context of a virulent anti-misogynist polemic was undoubtedly unwelcome, and confirmed her in her decision to abandon publishing.

A year later, Carter made the acquaintance of Catherine Talbot, a well-educated young woman four years her junior whose father, like Carter's, had been a clergyman, though with higher connections.[27] The Reverend Edward Talbot was the son of the Bishop of Salisbury; he had died of small-pox in December 1720 before Catherine was born and his widow and her baby went to live with a friend, Catherine Benson. In 1725 Benson became the wife of Thomas Secker, an energetic and learned cleric who had been close to Edward Talbot and would end his distinguished career as Archbishop of Canterbury. The four-year-old Catherine joined the Secker household along with her mother, and was raised as a surrogate daughter by the childless couple. She was passionately interested in literature and history, and Secker encouraged and supervised her studies.[28] Some of Catherine's poems and letters circulated in manuscript and won praise, but she was acutely conscious from an early age of the dangers of being recognized as exceptional. She became used to keen scrutiny of her conduct within a social world that joined the elite of the Church of England with people of fashion.

In 1739 Talbot was invited to contribute to a volume entitled *Athenian Letters* put together by two Cambridge undergradutes, the eldest son of Lord Hardwicke, Philip Yorke (who married (Talbot's friend Jemima Campbell the following year), and his brother Charles. It was devised as an academic exercise by Thomas Birch, the adviser and admirer of Elizabeth Carter, who wrote some of the letters and edited the complete work.[29] *Athenian Letters* is presented as a translation of ancient manuscripts discovered in 1688. It is the equivalent of Montesquieu's *Persian Letters* backdated to the period of the Peleponnesian War in the fifth century BC; a correspondence between Cleander, a representative of the King of Persia based in Athens, and friends and politicians at home. It lacks Montesquieu's wit however, and chiefly aims to instruct a readership without classical languages in Greek history, culture and religion. Although Talbot knew neither Latin nor Greek, two of the four letters she wrote, from Cleander to Osmanes and from Smerdis to Cleander, are heavy with classical lore. The others, however, are a curious departure. She creates the persona of Sappho, a namesake of the poetess, who writes on two occasions to Cleander to rebuke him bitterly for publishing her praises in verse, and then to warn him that his involvement in a plot against the Athenian state has been discovered and that, disgusted by his treachery towards her and her country, she has resolved to become a priestess of Minerva. No replies from Cleander are included, and these are the only letters penned by a female character; a note from the 'translator' of the *Letters* remarks that their purport is 'extremely obscure'. The translator's note also remarks rather waspishly that there is no evidence of anything but respectful appreciation of women in Cleander's letters, and that Sappho must have been motivated by an overactive sense of honour. Her letters appear as a non-sequitur. They express a feminine horror of publicity that coincided with Talbot's own sentiments.

Athenian Letters was initially published anonymously in a limited edition of just twelve copies.[30] But even this was not limited enough for Talbot. Although she continued to write essays, poems and miscellaneous pieces sporadically throughout her life, she was willing to publish only one item, an essay for the *Rambler*. After her death in 1770 Carter quickly edited and published her writings in two works, *Reflections on the Seven Days of the Week* (1770), which went through ten editions in 18 years, and *Essays on Various Subjects* (1772). It was Talbot, however, who had encouraged Carter back into publishing, by spurring her to complete a translation of the complete works of the Stoic philosopher Epictetus that would secure her livelihood.

But through the 1740s, as their epistolary friendship developed (they were not to meet again until 1747), they viewed events in the contemporary literary world in a leisurely way from the sidelines. In June 1742 Talbot recommends *Joseph Andrews*. Carter replies in August that she has not yet read Fielding's novel and plans to read 'the last volumes of Pamela, which I have yet had no sort of inclination to'. By January 1743 she has read *Joseph Andrews* and approves of it. In October 1744 Carter found Edward Young's *Night Thoughts* 'too gloomy a picture of life'. In January the following year it occurs to Talbot that there is a need for 'useful sentiments' conveyed in 'an amusing lively way' for working people, and she suggests the 'author of Pamela' would be ideally suited to the task. In September 1745 they are exercised by the question of whether or not to subscribe to Mr Fancourt's innovation, a circulating library – Carter is cautious and Talbot admits that she has given verbal approval though she concurs with Carter's view of the 'wild scheme'. Such topics give way to the Jacobite rebellion until the autumn of 1746 when a mild dispute over the merits of Homer allows Carter to get the upper hand again by denying she had read Pope's translation. In October Carter finds herself at a loss: 'Have people utterly left off writing books? I have not heard of a new one this century, excepting one on the wonders of Tar-water.' In February 1747 Talbot enthuses about Colley Cibber. Carter encloses a work of her own with her reply, an 'Ode to Wisdom'.[31]

Then on 28 December 1747, Talbot writes to say that she has discovered the 'Ode' in print, and not just in print, but in the pages of the publishing sensation of the year:

> Oh but your owl! how was I charmed, and how we were all charmed, when t'other day in reading Clarissa, out it flew most unexpectedly, and outdid the nightingale. I was going to write to you directly and ask ten thousand questions. How came it there? Are you so happy as to be acquainted with these Richardsons? I am sure they must be excellent people, and most delightful acquaintance. There can be no doubt, can there, that you love Clarissa?[32]

Carter did not know the Richardsons and had not given permission for the poem to be printed. The first two volumes of *Clarissa* were published on 1 December and already by the 12th she had written to complain of the piracy to Edward Cave, who had advised her to have a corrected version of the 'Ode' published in the *Gentleman's Magazine*. This she did – the first contribution she had made to the journal since 1739 – and she also wrote to Richardson directly. By the time Carter replied to Talbot on 20 January she had received a disarming letter of apology and explanation from Richardson. He had been sent the poem by a relation who had seen it on a visit to Wiltshire, greatly admired it and wished to incorporate it in the novel, but had tried in vain to discover the author. Since copies seemed to be freely circulating he decided to proceed with publication. He had not been 'govern'd by any low or selfish Views' to profit by the poem, but rather had paid for it to be set to music and engraved. He offered to atone in any way he could and sent the two volumes to enable her to see how the ode had been introduced into the story.[33]

Clarissa transcribes the ode in a letter written to Anna Howe at 11 o'clock at night after a day of painful conflict with her family over her refusal to marry Solmes.

> I have been forced to try to compose my angry passions at my harpsi-chord; having first shut close my doors and windows, that I might not be heard below. As I was closing the shutters of the windows, the distant whooting of the bird of Minerva as from the often-visited woodhouse gave the subject in that charming ODE TO WISDOM, which does honour to our sex, as it was written by one of it. (L54, 231)

Richardson uses the poem, as Clarissa does, to punctuate the stormy scenes that have prevailed since the opening letter with an interval of calm. It is a privileged moment of interiority, the closing of the shutters making the privacy of the closet yet more private, at a time when 'the violent passions are now, most probably, asleep all around me' (L55, 234). The poem develops this mood and defines subjectivity in neoplatonic terms. It is an address to the owl as the agent of Athena, then to the goddess herself that initiates the association of Clarissa with spiritual as opposed to empirical knowledge. Worldly forms and worldly attachments melt away in the darkness of the night as the subject is redirected towards 'ev'ry form of beauty bright, / That captivates the *mental* sight / With pleasure and surprise' (ll. 22–4). The ode is the creed of a closeted learned lady, to set against Lovelace's rake's creed. In place of the 'envied glitt'ring toys' of '*avarice, vanity*, and *pride*', she seeks 'Each moral beauty of the heart, / By studious thought refined' (ll. 35, 34, 38–9). The final three stanzas, which Clarissa takes as her lesson and has set to music, effect a transition from pagan mythology to Christian faith, but retains the female gender of Wisdom, 'eternal source / Of intellect light!', the soul's guide 'Through life's perplexing road'. The poem ends:

> Beneath her clear discerning eye
> The Visionary shadows fly
>   Of folly's painted show.
> She sees through ev'ry fair disguise,
> That all, but VIRTUE's solid joys,
>   Is vanity and woe.

> (ll. 91–6)

As Harriet Guest has pointed out, Richardson's presentation of the poem, privileging the last three stanzas, obscures the way Wisdom earlier in the poem links private virtues with a concept of public spirit defined in civic humanist terms.[34] Stanza XII describe how the 'wild, licentious youth' of Athens exchange passion for virtue under her influence, and stanza XIII asserts Wisdom's equal relevance to men engaged in public and patriotic endeavour or women in domestic retirement:

> *Thy* breath inspires the POET's song,
> The PATRIOT's free, unbiased tongue,
>   The HERO's gen'rous strife;
> *Thine* are RETIREMENT's silent joys,
> And all the sweet engaging ties
>   Of still, domestic life.

> (ll. 73–8)

The continuity of masculine and feminine spheres is a tenet Carter would uphold in letters and, more indirectly, in her preface to *Epictetus*. In terms of Richardson's project in *Clarissa*, where the redemption of 'wild, licentious' men can be achieved only through the medium of retired and virtuous women, an operation that requires absolute differentiation of the sexes, Carter is distinctly off-message. In the second edition of the novel, he dispensed with all but the final stanzas, but restored the remainder in the third edition, and in *Sir Charles Grandison*, as we will see, he again introduces her dissenting voice.

The most radical aspect of Richardson's appropriation of Carter's intellectual property is the way it serves as a 'call' to the woman writer to come forward into the realm of moral and social debate. When he committed an act of piracy, which Carter rightly condemned as 'very ungenerous' and Richardson would himself condemn when it was committed against him soon after, he presumably had no idea that he had netted one of the best-respected authoresses of the 1730s. It was a tremendous stroke of luck, and the prelude to his strenuous cultivation of a circle of learned young women in the wake of *Clarissa*. Previously, he had had to make do with the daughters of friends and neighbours as protégées. While he remained the author of *Pamela* he was a humble printer with a knack for conveying moral lessons to literate workers and their families. By moving *Clarissa* up the social scale, he opened up a whole new order of possibilities for personal contact. And by making Clarissa and Anna Howe studious, articulate, critical, perpetually scribbling young women from genteel families, he made a direct appeal to their counterparts in real life. Catherine Talbot's start of recognition in her letter to Carter, 'Will you give me leave to say that some things in Miss Howe's letters put me in mind of you?', must have been repeated up and down the land.[35] And quite a number were now, like Talbot, eager to make his acquaintance. At around this time, Samuel Johnson also began to develop a coterie of writing women whom he encouraged to publish, notably Charlotte Lennox.[36] But there was nothing in their relationship like the moral zealotry with which Susannah Highmore, Sarah Fielding, the Collier sisters, Hester Mulso, Catherine Talbot, Frances Sheridan and, from an older generation, Sarah Chapone, Mary Delany and Lady Bradshaigh, clustered around the luminary at North End (his 'country' address in Fulham), who had asserted the cause of virtuous women as a manifesto for social regeneration.

*

Richardson's courteous reply forced Carter to withdraw her objections to his use of the poem, but she remained wary. Although she wrote to thank him for a gift of the final volumes of the novel and praised the 'very judicious Conclusion', there was no further contact for more than four years.[37] Carter had an independent spirit, she was a mature woman of 30 and already a seasoned author, and she suspected Richardson of the sort of flattery that had disgusted her during her first excursion into print.[38] She would prove the most grumpy and recalcitrant of disciples.

Already she had indicated a preference for *Joseph Andrews* over *Pamela*, and after the publication of *Tom Jones* her judgement in favour of Fielding hardened in the face of Talbot's Richardsonian disapproval. She writes to Talbot on 20 June 1749:

> I am sorry to find you so outrageous about poor Tom Jones; he is no doubt an imperfect, but not a detestable character, with all that honesty, goodnature, and generosity of temper. Tho' nobody can admire Clarissa more than I do; yet with all our partiality, I am afraid, it must be confessed, that Fielding's book is the most natural representation of what passes in the world, and of the bizarreries which arise from the mixture of good and bad which makes up the composition of most folks. Richardson has no doubt a very good hand at painting extravagance in his vicious characters. To be sure, poor man, he had read in a book, or heard some one say, there was such a thing in the world as wickedness, but being totally ignorant in what manner the said wickedness operates upon the human heart, and what checks and restraints it meets with to prevent its ever being perfectly uniform and consistent in any one character, he has drawn such a monster, as I hope never existed in mortal shape, for to the honor of human nature, and the gracious author of it, be it spoken, Clarissa is an infintely more imitable character, than Lovelace, or the Harlowe's.[39]

Carter refuses to acknowledge the strategic purpose of Richardson's polarization of moral character, and the new conception of the novel as a means of social engineering, that would be definitively stated in the fourth issue of Johnson's journal *The Rambler* published the following year. Instead, she maintains that the value of fiction lies in its accurate reflection of things as they are. The playful note of sarcasm in her handling of Richardson is characteristic. Not long before Talbot had been capable of appreciating the naturalism of the descriptions of low life in *Roderick Random* (1748).[40] Smollett's accounts of the career of a prostitute and of Roderick's indiscriminate sexual adventures were more lurid than anything found in *Tom Jones*. But for a while, the difference of opinion of Talbot and Carter on Richardson's moral mission drives a wedge between them. Talbot internalizes the feminine ideal in a way that accentuates her tendency to self-criticism: the main symptom is chronic anxiety about wasting time. Carter attempts to set herself apart from it, elaborating on her favourite self-image as a creature running wild in the Kent countryside (she was a fanatical walker) and evidently delighted with Talbot's description of her as an 'ancient savage Briton', opposed to civility and French fashion.[41]

On 20 March 1750 Johnson began writing and publishing his twice-weekly periodical *The Rambler* and at around the same time Talbot and her mother called on Richardson to see a 'portrait' of Clarissa. The visit initiated a friendship and soon she was part of the ad hoc consultative committee for the new novel. These two events together, the advent of a didactic periodical by Johnson, an old friend of Carter's, and the new collaborative friendship with Richardson, as well as recent publications by Mrs Cockburn and Charlotte Lennox, aroused in Talbot a renewed enthusiasm for participating actively in the literary public sphere. The sense of new horizons is palpable in her correspondence with Carter. She views each issue of *The Rambler* with an eagerly critical eye, praising but also concerned about Johnson's use of 'hard words' and his ponderous style. Within a week of its first appearance she has written an essay herself, which Johnson accepted and which became the second of only four issues he did not write himself. The piece, published as No. 30 (Saturday, 30 June 1750), is a humorous discourse in the persona of 'Sunday', presenting the life history of the Sabbath, deprecating any association with fashionable manners and prescribing the best use of the day. At Talbot's instigation Carter also sent a contribution, published as *Rambler* 44 (Saturday, 18 August 1750), a dream vision in which the dreamer is snatched away from the gloomy asceticism of Superstition by true Religion who recommends enjoyment of the beauty and pleasures of this world. Talbot had suggested that she recommend enjoyment less strongly. She may have recognized a veiled protest by Carter against the sacrificial conclusion of *Clarissa*, and perhaps even an argument against her own habit of repining. The precepts of Religion are a warning against the 'closet' route to virtue:

> 'Return from the contracted Views of Solitude, to the proper Duties of a relative and dependent Being. Religion is not confined to Cells and Closets, nor restrained to sullen Retirement: these are the gloomy Doctrines of Superstition, by which she endeavours to break those Chains of Benevolence and social Affection, that link the Welfare of every Particular with that of the Whole. Remember, that the greatest Honour you can pay to the Author of your Being, is by such a chearful Behaviour, as discovers a Mind satisfied with his Dispensations.'[42]

It has been the custom to describe the Bluestocking circle as a mutually supportive sisterhood. But the Carter-Talbot correspondence between December 1750 and March 1751 reveals a rift between the two that highlights the continuing difficulties of female authorship, even in the more propitious conditions of this time. On 17 December 1750 Talbot sends a letter from London bubbling over with literary gossip and plans. She has had two visits with Richardson, and asks Carter to send her ideas for the character of 'good and agreeable man', the subject of the new novel. She enquires after Miss Mulso having read some of her correspondence with Richardson. She airs her fears about the future of the *Rambler*, mentions the publisher Cave's view that there should be more contributors, and presses Carter urgently to write another essay, providing a long list of possible topics with an emphasis on the critique of fashionable life. Carter responds with alacrity on the 28 December, praises Hester Mulso whom she had met in Canterbury and answers the request for the qualities of an ideal man by referring to Richardson in the usual teasing manner: 'As to my hero, I do not think it is possible for me to think or say any thing which Mr Richardson, who thinks of more things and says more about them than any body, has not thought of before me', but she specifies 'absolute superiority to false glory and false shame' as a requisite feature.[43]

Carter enclosed with her letter a rather crudely ironic essay for the *Rambler* recommending in copious detail the 'Improvements' of 'modish Life' that ensure a round of 'perpetual Dissipation'. The piece begins with a request to Mr Rambler with perhaps a tinge of personal bitterness, given Carter's immurement in Kent and Talbot's social whirl in London:

> SIR,
> As very many well-disposed Persons, by the unavoidable Necessity of their Affairs, are so unfortunate as to be totally buried in the Country, where they labour under the most deplorable Ignorance of what is transacting among the polite Part of Mankind, I cannot help thinking but that, as a public Writer, you should take the Case of these truly-compassionable Objects under your Consideration.[44]

Carter herself calls it in the accompanying letter a 'nonsensical thing' but she was surely not prepared for Talbot's dismissive response on the 19 January, in which she judges it 'very pretty', but explains that it has gone 'into my considering drawer, from whence nothing ever comes out again under half a year'. She passes on the Bishop of Norwich's comment that Carter ought to write something to enliven the *Rambler*, but says she has not mentioned the essay 'because I didn't know whether you should care I should'. After this slight it is unsurprisingly nearly a month before Carter writes again, 'indolence and the headache' having prevented her from taking up 'a pen in your service, or rather in my own, for I know no good you are likely to get by it; and it would probably have been as well if my said pen had laid quietly in its standish, or, to give it a more perfect quietus, had been conveyed to that same drawer of yours, where departed dullness slumbers in peace'. She added, somewhat spitefully, 'I am told the Rambler will be continued no longer than to compleat the year'.[45]

Talbot writes a relatively quick and abjectly apologetic reply on 29 February: 'What shall I say, dear Miss Carter, about my considering drawer? I am downright ashamed of it, and most heartily beg, not your's, but Mr Johnson's and all his readers' pardon, for suffering so many idlenesses to delay my returning you a piece deserving a much better fate.'[46] But Carter's pride is still hurt, and she follows up within days with an affected dismissal of her own work as 'not worth a second reading' and a critical mauling of another paper contributed to the *Rambler* by none other than Talbot's pet, Samuel Richardson (No. 97, 19 February 1751). This was an innocuous piece, idealizing female manners and methods of courtship in the days of the *Spectator*, in comparison with the 'idle amusements ... and wicked rackets' of the women of today. Female readers are advised to observe filial duty and cultivate modesty if they wish to win the love of a worthy man. Carter, determined to pick a fight, asserts that it must be founded on the supposition 'that Providence designed one half of the human species for idiots and slaves. One whould think the man was, in this respect, a Mahometan.'[47] Her anger is exaggerated, but she does identify an element in the essay that would be expanded upon in Rousseau's *Emile* and contemporary British conduct books, and then subjected to a comprehensive critique by Mary Wollstonecraft in *Vindication of the Rights of Woman* (1792) using language identical to that of Carter.[48] That is, that girls should be trained to use modesty as an artifice for attracting and manipulating the desires of men, and that pleasing the opposite sex should be their principal business in life, regardless of their own immortal souls. Carter throws back at Richardson the charge of 'Mahometanism' that he had connected with the rakes in *Clarissa*.[49]

The tension between Carter and Talbot continues in the latter's next communication dated 16 March 1751:

> first for the *Mahometan* Mr Richardson. Fie upon you! indeed I see no harm in that poor paper, and must own myself particularly fond of it. He does not pretend to give a scheme (not an entire scheme) of female education, only to say how when well educated they should behave in opposition to the racketing life of the Ranelagh-educated misses of these our days. Do read it over a little candidly. How can you ever imagine that the author of Clarissa has not an idea high enough of what women may be, and ought to be? Have you seen the new edition? There are most incomparable additions to it.[50]

Carter climbs down, but only to the extent of admitting that she may have been prejudiced against the essay 'by the opinions of those who read it before me, and from some of his own notions which I had lately seen on another subject', with the implication that she is among a critical mass who regard Richardson's influence with suspicion.[51] When Talbot next writes, on 10 May 1751, it is with her normal concern for Carter's wellbeing and admiration for her talents.

The correspondence reveals personal barriers to active involvement in the moral crusade led by Johnson and Richardson. Although initially enthusiastic, Talbot quickly reverts to a censoring attitude in her dealings with her friend. The onset of Carter's 'indolence' is also symptomatic: it speaks of the strain and exhaustion of possessing a vocation for the life of a scholar and author against the grain of social expectations and approval, and might perhaps also be interpreted as a psychosomatic resistance to the new pressures imposed by Richardson's feminine ideal.

Women's writing at the crossroads: 1750

While the dispute between Carter and Talbot was being resolved, a general battle for the soul of women's writing was in progress. In December 1750 Richardson took note of the virtually simultaneous appearance of three memoirs all by women of loose morality, 'a Set of Wretches, wishing to perpetuate their Infamy'.[52] The first of these, Laetitia Pilkington's *Memoirs* (1748–54), was by a friend of Colley Cibber with whom Richardson was also well acquainted. Born in Dublin in around 1706, a poet and once part of the circle of Swift and Dr Delany, she was divorced for adultery in 1738 and thereafter lived a life of poverty, desperate literary projects and disrepute in London and Ireland. During typical crises in 1743 and 1745 Richardson, on the strength of his own acquaintance with Dr Delany, aided her financially and practically. She achieved profitable notoriety in her native city before her early death in 1750. The second was *An Apology* (1748–49) by Teresia Constantia Phillips, also known as Mrs Muilman, a courtesan whose career included early ruin (accredited to the Earl of Chesterfield), a bigamous marriage, a long series of lovers, court cases and imprisonment for debt. The third was 'The Memoirs of a Lady of Quality' by Lady Vane, included as an inset first-person narrative in Tobias Smollett's *The Adventures of Peregrine Pickle*. Since the novel would not be published until early the next year, Richardson must have received advanced notice within the printing fraternity.[53] John Cleland's pornographic novel *Memoirs of a Woman of Pleasure; or, Fanny Hill* appeared at the same moment, 1748–49, but Richardson, fortunately for his delicate nerves, does not seem to have been aware of it. The documentary effusions by a troop of anti-Clarissas, coming so soon after the publication of Clarissa's own memorial book, sufficiently dismayed him. It was as if his fictional prostitutes Sally and Polly, with their 'good modern education', had taken up the pen to justify their misspent lives. But these works were also dangerously close to an uncharitable interpretation of *Clarissa*, as itself a scandalous memoir.

In Richardson's view, expressed to correspondents, such women might deserve sympathy, they might be regretful, but by advertising their survivor's tales of female frailty, hedonism and the pursuit of financial security by any means they reinforced misogynist stereotypes and threatened the effectiveness of the feminine ideal he sought to propagate. The phenomenon was observed by others. Richard Graves wrote *The Heroines: or, Modern Memoirs* (1751), a poetic satire which appeared in *General Advertiser* on 16 March, and also *London Magazine* and *Universal Magazine*:

> Without a blush behold each nymph advance,
> The luscious heroine of her own romance;
> Each Harlot triumphs in her Loss of Fame,
> And boldly prints – & publishes her Shame.[54]

In 1748 an 'Oxford Scholar' produced an avowedly catchpenny title, *The Parallel; or, Pilkington and Phillips Compared*. He found Phillips' memoirs in particular

> a very just Representation of the present Age: and if nothing of the like kind … should survive these admirable Adventures, will afford indisputable Proofs that Pleasure was the reigning Taste; that Profusion passed for Magnificence; that Show and Equipage gained Admittance every where; that Money was the one thing necessary, and that all Ways of coming at it were esteemed lawful amongst those who lived in a continual State of Dissipation … In short, it will shew what Sort of Folks we were, and thereby serve as an admirable Key to the History, Politicks, and Learning of the *British* Nation during the eighteenth century.[55]

Richardson equally saw the trend as an historical issue, a threatened repetition of previous troughs in the standing of women writers that carried through to a general depreciation of sex. These modern 'heroines' stand 'to make the Behn's, the Manley's, and the Heywood's, look white'.[56]

The crisis seems to have heightened his sense of the need to nurture the writing talent of virtuous women as a retaliatory force. In the autumn of 1750 he had drawn up a list of 36 'superior women' he knew, in a letter to Frances Grainger, one of several young ladies with whom he corresponded, 'to disprove the contention of men who consider women an inferior breed'.[57] Among them was Sarah Chapone, who had written a courteous but firmly corrective response to the latest instalment from Constantia Phillips, *Remarks on Mrs. Muilman's Letter to the Right Honourable The Earl of Chesterfield*. Richardson read it in manuscript and it may have been at his press that it was printed in the summer of 1750.[58] His remark on the 'Set of Wretches' is addressed to her and he goes on to say, 'From the same injured, disgraced, profaned Sex, let us be favoured with the Antidote to these Women's Poison!'[59] To further encourage her, he sent Lady Vane's not yet published memoirs, 'that Part of a bad Book which contains the very bad Story of a wicked woman. I could be glad to see it animadverted upon by so admirable a Pen. Ladies, as I have said, should antidote the Poison shed by the vile of their Sex.'[60] However, unlike Phillips, Lady Vane was not remotely penitent; Chapone hesitated and Richardson agreed the work was too immoral for a respectable woman to address.[61]

It is a coincidence almost too neat to be true that Lady Vane was the daughter of one of the South Sea Company directors, born Frances Anne Hawes in 1713 or 1715, depending on the source;[62] in either case, shortly before the birth of Elizabeth Carter, whose family was ruined in the Bubble. The opposed versions of female authorship were equally divided by their contrasting relationship to financial corruption. At an early age Frances contracted a runaway marriage with the younger son of the Duke of Hamilton, only to be widowed two years later. A mere ten months passed before her family persuaded her, a more malleable subject than Clarissa, to accept a ludicrous but wealthy suitor as her second husband. In her memoirs, written with considerable comic aplomb and possibly revised by Smollett, she recounts how and why she spent the early years of this marriage either eloping from or returning to the apparently insufferable Lord Vane, continually racketing around England and France, Flanders and Holland in attempts to elude him, entertaining a bevy of titled lovers in the intervals between more or less half-hearted efforts at conjugal duty. Her account rushes to embrace the misogynist assumptions of the day: restricted by her notoriety to male company when in England, she castigates the 'weakness, pride, and vanity of our sex'; her portrait of the man who first seduced her into adultery makes him out to be the double of Lovelace, 'absolutely master of those insinuating qualifications which few women of passion and sensibility can resist ... well acquainted with the human heart, conscious of his own power and capacity', but even in retrospect she avows her overpowering love for him.[63] The claims of propriety are rejected as mere slavery. Throughout, her actions are excused as the inevitable consequence of her credo, triumphantly marked out by italics:

> *Interest and ambition have no share in my composition; love which is pleasure, or pleasure which is love, makes up the whole. A heart so disposed cannot be devoid of other good qualities; it must be subject to the impressions of humanity and benevolence, and an enemy to nothing but itself.*[64]

Behind every scandalous memoir by a woman lies a murky web of political manoeuvring by men. Phillips' *Apology* was said to have been edited by Paul Whitehead, a satirical poet in the manner of Pope, 'whose services were remunerated "in kind"'.[65] Mysteriously, Whitehead, who had a long track record with the opposition party, published a poem 'Honour' (1747) celebrating the Earl of Chesterfield for his resignation from the government at the same time that he was supposedly conspiring with Phillips to blackmail him.[66] Vane's memoirs were purportedly written with the aid of John Shebbeare, a doctor turned political writer and professional misanthrope, who authored the novel *The Marriage Act* (1754) and dedicated it to the Duke of Bedford, who had opposed the government's Marriage Act passed the previous year. Smollett, too, was a vehement critic of the government. Back in the 1730s Lady Vane had been part of the social circle of Maria Skerrett, mistress and then second wife of Robert Walpole. Vane's dizzy brand of corruption might be seen as an outgrowth of the deeper corruption of Walpole's reign. Yet her adventures were read with urbane good humour by patrician Whigs like Horace Walpole and Lady Mary Wortley Montagu, one the resentful stepson of Skerrett, the other a close friend.[67]

Mary Wortley Montagu has been described as an 'anti-model' for the Bluestocking writers.[68] In the 1720s and 1730s, while the discourse of feminization languished, she had been a literary and political insider, a collaborator of the Augustan satirists. Now at the start of the 1750s, as she whiled away the time in her Italian exile with parcels of new books sent from London, it was she who was observing from the sidelines, and virtuous maiden ladies like Elizabeth Carter and Catherine Talbot who were being drawn into the cultural mainstream. Her remarks on the discreditable counter-current in women's writing are defiantly libertine: 'I think Lady Vane's memoirs contain more Truth and less malice than any I ever read in my life.' She was not in a position to throw stones, of course, having also eloped with a forbidden suitor at an early age and then left her husband to live disreputably in Italy. But there is a sense of deliberate ideological opposition to the new morality spearheaded by Richardson in a further observation that Lady Vane's 'History, rightly consider'd, would be more instructive to young Women than any Sermon I know'.[69] The terminology may be conventional, but it had been widely applied to Richardson's work, and elsewhere in her letters Montagu recorded her complex reaction to *Clarissa* (and later, *Sir Charles Grandison*), combining visceral class antagonism with poignant personal recollection.

> This Richardson is a strange Fellow. I heartily despise him and eagerly read him, nay, sob over his works in a most scandalous manner. The two first Tomes of Clarissa touch'd me as very resembling to my Maiden Days. I find in the pictures of Sir Thomas Grandison and his Lady what I have heard of my Mother and seen of my Father.[70]

The basic scenarios of the novels – the pressing into a mercenary match of a young lady whose idealism leads to an unwilling abduction; the horror of family life with a tyrannical rake for a father – these touched Lady Mary to the core. But the edifice of moral reflection supported by these narratives, and the bourgeois idiom in which they were communicated, she found repulsively discordant, an affront to her own values and assumptions.

In 1750, Elizabeth Montagu, aged 30 and distantly related to Lady Mary by marriage, wrote to her sister, 'I recommend to your perusal "The Adventures of Peregrine Pickle"'.[71] She is blithely unaware that the response to Lady Vane's memoirs had become a touchstone of female moral sensibility in certain quarters, and indeed, there was little in her background or habits to mark her out as a future intimate of Carter and Talbot and prospective 'Queen of the Bluestockings'.[72] As a young woman from a genteel but relatively impoverished family her tastes had been formed in the company of her friend Margaret, Duchess of Portland. Lady Margaret was the daughter of the Earl of Oxford and granddaughter of the Tory minister Robert Harley, patron of Matthew Prior, Swift and Pope. She and Elizabeth Robinson met as girls when the latter visited relations in Cambridge, close to the family seat of the Earl at Wimpole Hall.[73] Elizabeth's early letters to Lady Margaret consist of humorously related anecdotes and family gossip and at times betray a keen interest in social scandal.[74] There is a distinct lack of moral earnestness and no great evidence of scholarly interests. After Lady Margaret's marriage to the Duke of Portland in 1734 she resided either at Whitehall in London or at their country house, Bulstrode Manor, and from 1738 Elizabeth began staying with them there for extended periods. Although she joined the Duchess in her eccentric pastime of reading sermons, evening readings of the letters of Pope and Swift were a more typical manifestation of the literary culture of the household. At Bulstrode she was introduced to Edward Young, a friend of the Portlands, with whom she declared herself in a letter 'in platonick Love'.[75] In 1740 he was chiefly known to the world of letters as the author of the satirical poem *Universal Passion* (1725–28), which included animadversions on women. Elizabeth's sister Sarah disapproved of the acquaintance on these grounds but Elizabeth defended him, insisting that he 'honors the best of [women] extreamly & seems delighted with those who act & think reasonably'.[76] She was herself capable of satirical remarks on the slovenly appearance of some learned young ladies she knew in Canterbury (no doubt also acquaintances of Carter).[77] The Duchess's older female friends, Mary Pendarves (later Delany) and Anne Donellan, encouraged her to extend her reading into translations of the classics, and would eventually provide a link to the Richardson circle. Her chief pleasure at this time, however, was the leisurely round of aristocratic sociability, and she ensured permanent access to it with her marriage to the wealthy and well-connected Edward Montagu, a man thirty years her senior, in August 1742.

In 1750, while Montagu was setting up as a London hostess in her newly decorated Chinese Room, Richardson was engaged in rigorous training of the most promising of his recruits to the campaign to publicize female virtue, Hester Mulso, aged 23. He met her through Susanna Highmore, whose father, the artist Joseph Highmore, had painted a series of scenes from Pamela. In July 1750 Richardson and Mulso began a correspondence and she made visits to North End with her brothers. The acquaintance soon warmed into a friendship combining banter and mutual admiration. Among their favorite topics for dispute was parental authority: Mulso held that the tyrannical behaviour of Mr Harlowe absolved Clarissa from strict filial duty and that her sense of guilt at disobeying her parents was exaggerated and unworthy of a rational being. Richardson invited her to an epistolary duel.[78] On 12 October and 10 November 1750 and again on 3 January 1751 Mulso sent three long 'Letters on Filial Obediance', eventually published in her *Posthumous Works* (1807). Richardson sent even longer letters in reply, but they have been lost. The correspondence was read by the Richardson circle, including Bishop Secker and the Speaker of the House of Commons, Arthur Onslow, and Mulso's style and close reasoning were much admired. As her brother John remarked, they thought 'Mr. R- hard pressed, & Heck has gained great Honour'.[79] Elizabeth Carter, having heard of the quarrel, automatically took Mulso's part.[80]

Although Richardson accused Mulso of tenaciousness, he was sufficiently persuaded by her arguments to soften Clarissa's response to her father's curse in the third edition of *Clarissa* (1751).[81] But his ulterior motive for engaging in the debate becomes apparent in a letter to Lady Bradshaigh, accounting for the inordinate length of his replies: 'When I love my correspondents, I write treatises, Madam, rather than letters. What care I for that, if I can but whet, but stimulate ladies, to shew what they are able to do, and how fit they are to be intellectual, as well as domestic, companions to men of the best sense!'[82] The remark is further to a general defence of women's learning. Lady Bradshaigh had adopted an anti-feminist quip by the minor French writer Guez de Balzac, remarking: '"I could more willingly tolerate a woman with a beard, than one that pretends to learning. In earnest, had I authority in the civil government, I would condemn all those women to the distaff, that undertook to write books, that transform their souls by a masculine disguise, and break the rank they hold in the world."'[83] Richardson insists in reply:

> The pen is almost as pretty an implement in a woman's fingers, as a needle...were I to chuse the attitude that I would have one of the dearest of my lady-correspondents drawn in, it should be with a pen in her hand, in the act of writing, and I know to whom. Madame Sevigne, Madame Dacier, the Marchioness of Lambert, three of that writer's countrywomen, wrote more to the purpose a great deal than Balzac.[84]

Richardson playfully aestheticizes the female writer with her 'pretty' pen and places her in the context of personal correspondence, yet she forms part of a continuum with published female authors: 'the woman who writes a book, breaks not thereby the rank she holds in the world'.[85] Mulso's literary abilities were to be fostered by private debate as preparation for more public interventions.[86] The value he placed on the dialectical method in his own epistolary contentions is well expressed by Lovelace in a letter to Bedford: 'I love opposition. As gold is tried by fire and virtue by temptation; so is sterling wit by opposition' (519). Richardson called Mulso his 'little spitfire'; she was his secret weapon.[87] And ultimately she did not disappoint his hopes. Her *Letters on the Improvement of the Mind* (1773), a manual for the creation of future generations of Clarissas, went through innumerable editions well into the nineteenth century.

Sir Charles Grandison as object of desire

Richardson's third and final novel is the product of this period of crisis over the public display of female interiority. It was devised as a way of involving his high-minded female friends in the business of publication. They were to be active participants in his latest project to reform the manners of the nation. The focus of the novel was to be a 'good man', to complement the portrait of the ideal woman in *Clarissa*. But the objective is more complex than at first appears. Sir Charles Grandison was invented, less as a model for male readers than as an incentive for women. In keeping with Richardson's belief in the crucial regenerative agency of women, it was necessary to show them the extent of their powers, to demonstrate the kind of hero that could be produced under the regime of feminization in order to dissuade them from settling for a rake. He had been greatly troubled by the way the decent Mr Hickman, always at the service of his mocking fiancée Anna Howe, suffered by comparison with Lovelace in the eyes of readers.

Richardson began canvassing every woman he knew for hints for the creation of an ideal man. It was a delicate business, susceptible to a certain amount of nervous badinage. In one sense he was asking them to reveal their innermost desires; an especially sensitive request in view of the fact that the majority of them were either confirmed old maids or young ladies whose unusual intellectualism put them in danger of remaining unmarried. In another sense he was engaging them in a social intervention with potentially important consequences. The success of *Clarissa* had gained Richardson an international stage for his ideas. No wonder that the majority were reticent. He was asking his female correspondents to *perform* the process of feminization as an act of imagination; to literally *make* the man they would have as mate.[88]

On 20 July 1750 Richardson wrote to Anne Donnellan regarding a young lady she had recently introduced to him. Isabella Sutton, daughter of the Countess of Sunderland, was one of those diffident young women whom Richardson was constantly urging to express themselves in writing.

The young ladies will the more readily become my correspondents, you think, Madam, were I to draw the fine man. But the young ladies must help to *make* such a one. It is more in the power of young ladies than they seem to imagine, to make fine men.[89]

Here and in letters from around the same time to Lady Bradshaigh and Hester Mulso, Richardson revolves the question of whether a Hickman can be made more attractive than a Lovelace to ladies. He grows heated at the suggestion that female readers cannot tolerate a man of flawless virtue and chastity. 'Must he be a moderate rake?' he asks Lady Bradshaigh.[90]

Catherine Talbot became so closely involved with the writing and revision of *Sir Charles Grandison* that she might have claimed co-authorship. Her guardian Thomas Secker was appointed Dean of St Paul's Cathedral in 1750, and from this date the family divided their time between Oxford, where he continued his duties as Bishop, and the City of London. Richardson's town address at Salisbury Court was close to the Deanery, and he began paying her visits during which they discussed the progress of the novel. Talbot's letter to Carter in December 1750, asking her for the characteristics of a good man, has already been mentioned.[91] By December of the following year Talbot is reporting to Carter on Richardson's work-in-progress, which she is permitted to read by instalments. There is a suspenseful wait for the appearance of the good man himself. The novel begins with Harriet Byron, a witty, beautiful and virtuous young woman, sending accounts of a stay in London with friends to relations at home. Harriet, like Clarissa, is assailed by proposals from a range of unwanted suitors: a libertine, a sniggering fool, a sickly nonentity, a shy bumpkin. Thus Harriet is faced with the same problem as Richardson's female collaborators: what kind of man can match the desires of such a woman? Sir Charles appears out of nowhere, as the answer to her prayers. She has been abducted from a masquerade by the dissolute Sir Hargrave Pollexfen, and her spangly fancy-dress costume heightens the magical quality of the rescue. Sir Charles, having briskly overpowered his wicked double without the use of a sword, carries Harriet with the greatest care and respect to his country house and delivers her into the protection of his two admirable sisters, before discreetly retiring to finish his interrupted business. This mode of introduction had its full effect on Talbot: 'And now what shall I say of Sir Charles – My long sought & never to be found, Ideal. –The World of Angels is made up of Sir Charles's'.[92]

The world of *Sir Charles Grandison* is a world of angels; or rather, a world where an angel can comfortably unfurl its wings and be confident of having an influence. Margaret Doody has astutely contrasted the moral climate of Richardson's previous novel: 'In *Clarissa* the world is not sympathetic to virtue, and virtue is not triumphant in it.'[93] Although the heroine dies with all the signs of martyrdom, she makes only one convert from among the surrounding characters. The reverse is the case in *Grandison*, where virtue flourishes like Japanese knotweed and sinners are converted with industrial efficiency. Sir Charles's benevolence is matched by his wealth and status. His social authority has important consequences for the female characters, and for female readers. *Clarissa* had dramatized the ultimate vulnerability of even a highborn, independently wealthy and strong-minded woman. Doody observes, 'The Grandisonian ethos means that the women can also attain a wider freedom, as neither conscience nor desire is antagonistic to the social life. Because he assures us of the goodness of human nature and of social life, the other characters are free to live and move and develop within this optimistic moral setting.'[94] She proposes that the contrast in perspective of the two works derives from their respective affiliation to tragedy or social comedy.

The novels undoubtedly differ in terms of the formal management of narrative, but their disparity goes beyond generic conventions. It is also the result of a shift in historical setting. Richardson was precise about the chronology of *Grandison*; more so than in the previous novels. The action of the novel begins a year or so after the Jacobite Rebellion of 1745.[95] Fielding had intertwined the history of the '45 Rebellion with his *History of Tom Jones, A Foundling* (1749). The hero's ineffectual part in the shambolic military response to the Jacobite progress from Scotland into England, his parodic resemblance to the landless Young Pretender, contribute to the general picture of an emasculated nation struggling to rise to the Stuart challenge. Richardson's hero is significantly absent from the country during this period of trial. His history belongs to the victorious aftermath, when he comes into his inheritance. The Hanoverian regime was now secured and with it, the Whig oligarchy and the whole complex of political and commercial interests it held in place. This was the era of the Pelham administration (1744–54), headed by Henry Pelham and his brother the Duke of Newcastle, sometimes known as the 'Broad Bottom' government because of the coalition with members of the opposition, notably the Earl of Chesterfield. The Pelhams were successors to Walpole and they maintained Walpole's methods and priorities without providing the same irresistible target for attack. The unpopular War of the Austrian Succession was drawing to a close and would end in 1748 with a peace mildly favourable to Britain and its trading empire. The focus of the government was on the reduction of the national debt and the minutiae of economic improvement: transport reform affecting roads, rivers and harbours; encouragement of enclosures and drainage. Sir Charles is the embodiment of a new confidence in the possibility of aligning morality with wealth. The spirit of improvement can be seen to animate the realms of manners and economics alike. There is a vision of the compatibility, or even symbiosis, of virtue and profit. Even more decisively than in *Pamela*, worldly prosperity is made the manifest reward of virtue. And virtue in turn legitimates wealth by good works. From the moment of his first appearance, Sir Charles is busied in resolving the difficulties of family, friends, neighbours and strangers, employing his social influence and money as an active force for good in the world.[96]

As we have seen, Sir Charles was born out of discussion and debate, and it is as a nexus of issues concerning the definition of masculinity that he is best understood. He is chaste, an attribute that many at the time found ludicrous in a man, but that Richardson insisted upon.[97] To compensate and create an alternative measure of the hero's animal spirits, Richardson was forced to evoke a whole galaxy of female desire. It was not sufficient to show the ill-repressed yearnings of Harriet and of Sir Charles's young ward, Emily. The action must extend beyond British shores to Italy, a place Richardson had never visited and knew little of, but where reputedly the amorous passions were more unbridled, in order to introduce female characters who could legitimately go mad or threaten to commit murder for love of the English baronet. The famous 'double love' that serves as a plot for the novel – Sir Charles's predicament in being loved by two equally excellent ladies, Clementina della Porretta and Harriet Byron, and returning their love with gratitude in one case and more straightforward admiration in the other – does little to externalize his own feelings, but rather reinforces the idea of his intense desirability through the evidence of the women's feelings.

Sir Charles does not duel, and again this discloses vistas of ideological contention over the nature of honour and manliness, developed at some length in his verbal disputes with an assortment of rakes and con men. The suppression of duelling had long been an objective in campaigns for the reformation of manners.[98] The Reverend Jeremy Collier's denunciation, *Of Duelling*, dates back to 1698. Typically, Mandeville had argued in favour of duelling, against the tide of optimistic progressivism. He saw it as a means of regulating and restricting the natural human tendency to aggression.[99] *Clarissa* begins and ends with a duel; the practice signals the uncivilized state of the male sex in the period of the novel. In vain the heroine argues that it is 'much more *manly* to *despise*' an unwarranted insult 'than to *resent*' (L55, 237). But her hopes are fulfilled by Sir Charles in the next generation. His will to embrace a new mode of masculine behaviour derives from his parentage, a mismatch between a rake and a woman of the most elevated virtue, just such a marriage as that of Lovelace and Clarissa would have been. His father had instilled in him 'high notions of honour' and arranged for him to be trained in swordsmanship from the age of twelve, an exercise at which he excelled. His mother had meanwhile been propagating countervailing 'notions of moral rectitude, and the first principles of Christianity'. She taught him to regard his skill with a sword as purely defensive and instructed him in words that echo those of Clarissa 'that it was much more noble to forgive an injury than to resent it'. He avers that his father 'had great qualities. But my Mother was my oracle'. And when Sir Thomas is nearly killed in a duel and Lady Grandison dies of a decline resulting from the shock, his aversion to the 'vile practice of duelling' is completed, though he later takes the trouble to inform himself of the shabby history of the practice in ancient and modern times (I, 260–5).

Sir Charles has pride, and admits it as his chief fault: 'I *have* vanity, madam; I have pride, and some consequential failings, which I cannot always get above' (III, 124). This pride is inseparable from filial piety, a determination to exonerate his father in spite of the plentiful evidence presented elsewhere that he was a selfish, profligate, hardened sinner, who treated his wife and daughters with great cruelty. Although on Sir Charles's accession to the estate many of his benevolent actions are an implicit condemnation of Sir Thomas he refuses to criticize openly, insisting that 'all my father's steps in which I could tread, I did; and have chosen rather to build upon, than demolish, his foundations' (III, 124). In practice, this results in the curiously frivolous trait of dressing fashionably and choosing an equipage that is 'gay' rather than 'plain'. The foundations that could be built on with a clear conscience are evidently narrow indeed. But in principle, this pride, a patrilineal defect, is of the utmost importance; it enables Richardson to exorcise the colourless Hickman. Writing of his hero to Hester Mulso he remarked, 'He should have all the human passions to struggle with; and those he cannot conquer he shall endeavour to make subservient to the cause of virtue.'[100] It is an undoubted flaw in the plan of the novel that he is given insufficient opportunity to display that inner struggle, but the existence of Sir Charles's passionate nature in theory is what gives value to his dedication to virtue. And since here, as much as in *Clarissa*, the cause of virtue is the cause of women, it also gives significance to his reverence for the fair sex.

An emblematic scene comes when Sir Charles has proposed marriage to Harriet and is visiting her in her family's home. Harriet reports to Grandison's sister that, on entering the room and finding all the seats taken, Sir Charles

> threw himself at the feet of my aunt and me, making the floor his seat.
> I don't know how it was; but I though I never saw him look to more advantage. His attitude and behaviour had such a Lover-like appearance. (III, 92)

Harriet and her swain become a tableau of Hercules at the feet of Omphale. The warrior puts aside his weapon and allows himself to be feminized, acknowledging the sovereignty of woman. The episode was a favourite subject in Renaissance and Baroque painting; Rousseau was to make it a figure of the dangers of modern civility in *Emile*. Sir Charles is already voluntarily disarmed by his anti-duelling stance, but here it is the disparity between his accustomed pride and this delightful gesture of subservience that heightens Harriet's already exorbitant valuation of him. Irresistibly the idea of the rake, the forbidden object of female desire, comes forward: 'did you think of your brother, Lady G. when you once said, that the man who would commend himself to the general favour of us young women, should be a Rake in his address, and a Saint in his heart?' Harriet searches for a better word than 'rake' to sum up 'agreeable freedom', but fails to find one.

Lady Bradshaigh, who had argued for the hero to be a 'moderate rake', was triumphant when she read this phrase.[101] Richardson's concession is typical of the novel as a whole which, in spite of its imposing bulk, aims rather to stimulate debate about the respective roles of men and women in a reformed society than to provide definitive answers. A central part of this project is the play of ideas, detached from physical threat, in the narrative itself. Epistolary form is not prominent dramatically in this novel. Letters are no longer weapons or vehicles of manipulation. Rather, it has been suggested that they function here, as in the Bluestocking circle (and indeed the Richardson circle), 'selectively used as part of a social currency, enhancing the worth of those who send and those who receive them'.[102] They are also employed extensively for the purpose of narrative flashback, and the access to earlier letters reciprocally given to Harriet and Grandison is the foundation of their courtship. With the diminution of the gulf between the course of events and the writer's own desires found in the earlier novels, the letters become less reflective, more documentary: 'narrative letter-writing' is the prevailing mode, consisting of 'minute and characteristic descriptions and conversations' (I, 60). *Clarissa*, as has already been noted, is framed by two duels by men over a woman, which draw real blood. *Grandison*, by contrast, is framed by two heated but civilized debates between men and women at social gatherings, recorded at length by Harriet and Charlotte respectively.[103]

The first of the debates takes place at a dinner party attended by, among others, Mr Walden, 'an Oxford scholar', an aggressive man-woman, Miss Barneveldt, and the aforementioned rake, Sir Hargrave. It finds Richardson still determined to pick a fight with long-dead Augustans. Harriet and Mr Walden revive the argument of the ancients versus the moderns, with Harriet arguing that the lack of classical languages is not a bar to the search for truth. Mr Walden brings in Swift's *Battle of the Books* in his defence and sneers at Addison (I, 53, 56).[104] Harriet claims Milton as a 'modern' (I, 56). Harriet's cousin Mr Reeves eventually steps in as moderator and, with useful citations from Bishop Burnet and Locke, closes the discussion in the familiar mode of Richardson himself in his correspondence, urging women to pursue learning, though not at the expense of more 'useful' accomplishments.

The episode is otherwise notable for its depiction of Miss Barneveldt. Harriet tells us that the one reason 'she every-where gives, for being satisfied with being a woman ... is, *that she cannot be married to a WOMAN*' (I, 43), a witticism that the outraged Mary Wortley Montagu instantly recognized as her own, protesting in her commonplace book that a 'light thing said in Gay Company should not be call'd upon for a serious Defence, especially when it injures no body'.[105] This, of course, is precisely what Richardson could not agree. In *Clarissa* misogyny kills, however lightly expressed. Montagu is punished with the same treatment meted out to Arabella Harlowe and Mrs Sinclair: partial masculinization as the evidence of alienation from the feminine ideal. The difference is that while in the previous work these 'mannish' women are a genuine threat, here Miss Barneveldt is permitted only one libertine squeeze of the heroine's hand before disappearing from the novel forever.

The second of the debates is more consequential and problematic. It takes place at breakfast-time in the home of Harriet's aunt and uncle Selby, on the day following her wedding to Sir Charles. The sharp-witted Charlotte Grandison, who has been repeatedly provoked by the complacent, good-natured misogyny of Mr Selby, proposes to 'enter the lists' with him and battle over the topic of '[m]an's usurpation, and woman's natural independency' (III, 242). All the other men are permitted to take his side, apart from Sir Charles who must remain neutral. But although Charlotte relates that she easily demolishes all their arguments she does not give the content of this stage in the war of the sexes. The topic is passed on to Mrs Shirley, Harriet's dignified grandmother, as moderator, and her speech is recorded in its entirety. Anna Laetitia Barbauld in her edition of Richardson's correspondence gives Elizabeth Carter as its author. She begins with what appears to be a direct criticism of Richardson's insistence on the opposition of the sexes, discussed in chapter 5, 'women are generally too much considered as a species apart'. While acknowledging that providence has generally allotted the sexes their different spheres, she asks 'why are we to be perpetually considering the *Sex* of the person we are talking to?' (III, 243)

This line of thinking is irreconcilable with the discourse of feminization – if women are not considered to be fundamentally different from men, they cannot represent an alternative, aspirational set of values for them – but interestingly it leads to an alternative way of connecting the improved state of women with the progress of commerce. The specialized knowledge of women arising from their duties, and qualifying them for rational conversation, is compared to the specialized knowledge of professional men like merchants and army officers. In this way a common cause is made between women in general and middle-class men, whose views are determined by the division of labour, in opposition to the 'pedant', a man whose imagined superiority is based on classical learning and status as a gentleman. This hint is taken up by another female interlocutor in the debate, Lady W., who gives as illustration a satire by 'an East-India officer' on the obscure language of a learned pedant that she happens to have in her pocket-book. The comparison between the jargon of a cloth dealer and the exclusive vocabulary of the classical scholar demote the latter from elevated master-discourse to just one among a Babel of vocational idioms in a complex modern society.

Sir Charles now intervenes on the value of knowledge of classical languages, and seems to take issue (in the politest possible manner) with both Harriet's downgrading of them in the earlier debate and with Mrs Shirley's position. He reinstates innate distinctions between the sexes and goes so far as to argue that there is an 'inequality of Souls' (meaning an inferiority of mind in women) produced by the different purposes of the sexes in this world, though not in the next (III, 250). He pays lip service to the notion of feminization: 'a degree of knowledge' in women 'will improve a man of sense, sweeten his manners, and render him a much more sociable, a much more amiable creature' (III, 250). What is the reader meant to make of this discord between two highly respected characters, Mrs Shirley and Sir Charles? Or the departure from the exalted view of woman found in *Clarissa*? Does it indicate a limitation in Sir Charles's thinking?[106] It must be noted that he is here in the persona of the 'moderate libertine', gallant and critical by turns, and his remarks should be taken in the context of playful debate, not as an unchallengeable dictum.[107] They are intended to provoke his sister Charlotte, and they do provoke her to pointed refutations: she allots herself the last word. The episode recalls Richardson's own mock-battle with Hester Mulso, mentioned in the previous section, in which he assumed the role of defender of patriarchy in order to further the aim of 'stimulat[ing] ladies, to shew what they are able to do, and how fit they are to be intellectual ... companions to men of the best sense!'[108]

The most telling remarks in the episode are made parenthetically. Sir Charles is pictured at the start, 'Wrapping his arms about himself, with inimitable humour – 'O my Charlotte, said he, how I love my Country! ENGLAND is the *only* spot in the world, in which this argument *can* be properly debated!' (III, 242). It is not the content of the debate but the civilized heterosocial activity of debating the relative merits of the sexes itself that signifies; it confirms the enlightened state of the nation. Charlotte finds this intervention 'very sly', as well she might: it effectively reifies her as a product of English liberality, even as she struggles to articulate her rebellion against social custom.[109] This is even more the case in the asides on Mrs Shirley, modelled after Elizabeth Carter. She is directly described as an exception to Grandison's general rule, surpassing 'all the men I ever knew, in wisdom' (III, 247). Once again, as with the inclusion without permission of the 'Ode on Wisdom' in *Clarissa*, Carter is made an exemplar in spite of herself and in the most flattering way. She is also alluded to indirectly in answer to Charlotte's barbed request to her brother to elucidate what kind of learning would be compatible with a woman's duties 'that we may not mistake – and so become eccentric, as I may say, burst our orb, and do more mischief than ever we could do good?' Sir Charles replies,

> *Could* I point out the boundaries, Charlotte, it might not to *some* spirits be so proper: The limit might be treated as the one prohibited tree in the garden. But let me say, That genius, whether in man or woman, will push itself into light. If it has a laudable tendency, let it, as a ray of the Divinity, be encouraged, as well in the one Sex as in the other: I would not, by any means, have it limited. (III, 251)

This call for genius, female as well as male, to 'push itself into light' and the sense that contemporary England is the centre of progressive thinking about women were evidently what the exceptional, learned women of Richardson's acquaintance took away from the novel, in spite of minor irritations produced by some of the episodes. It is not in reality Grandison who prescribes a role for women, but women who have created him, as an agent of their moral and intellectual influence on the nation. After an early view of the novel, Catherine Talbot was open about the narcissistic enchantment cast by the hero:

> Oh! Miss Carter, did you ever call Pigmalion a fool, for making an image and falling in love with it – and do you know that you and I are two Pigmalionesses? Did not Mr. Richardson ask us for some traits of his good man's character! And did not we give him some? And has not he gone and put these and his own charming ideas into a book, and formed a Sir Charles Grandison? And though all the rising generation should copy after them, what good will that do poor us, who must sigh and pine till they are educated.[110]

Even Carter was won over and similarly declared her love in a letter to Richardson once she had seen a preview copy, adding that she would 'have a very bad opinion of every lady who is not in love with him too'.[111] The enthusiasm of Jane Austen and George Eliot for *Sir Charles Grandison* has always been considered something of a mystery. Perhaps they were intrigued by a perception of the novel as a self-addressed love-letter sent by an earlier generation of literary women, as they hesitated, poised on the threshold between domestic retirement and public intervention, dizzy with the opportunity Richardson held out to them to 'become eccentric, I may say, burst our orb'.

Inventories of literary women

The 1750s saw a surge of publications describing the lives of female authors, celebrating their achievements and recirculating their work. The first of these was *Memoirs of Several Ladies of Great Britain, Who have been Celebrated for their Writings, or Skill in the Learned Languages, Arts and Sciences* (1752). It was the work of George Ballard (1706–55), a working man who had trained as a stay-maker, but who taught himself Anglo-Saxon at night and became a clerk at Magdalen College, Oxford after receiving financial help from Lord Chedworth. His interest lay in antiquities and he published and corresponded on the subject in a modest way. Ballard was inspired to write the *Memoirs* by his acquaintance with Elizabeth Elstob, a pioneer of Anglo-Saxon scholarship who had lived for many years in obscurity and financial hardship, running a village school, until Ballard sought her out in 1735 and encouraged her to renew her old interests. Many years earlier she had prepared notes for a series of biographies of learned ladies and this provided the basis of Ballard's work. The aim seems to have been to improve the climate for learned women such as Elstob, by publicizing the literary achievements of women in the past, and showing the compatibility of intellectual pursuits and strict virtue in a series of exemplary lives.[112]

Memoirs of Several Ladies of Great Britain begins in the fourteenth century with 'Juliana, Anchoret of Norwich' and ends with Constantia Grierson who died in 1732. Katherine Philips, Mary, Lady Chudleigh, and Mary Astell are included; the less reputable Aphra Behn and Delariviere Manley are not. The clue to this censorship lies in the polemical aim of the work and its intended audience. It is dedicated to two socially elevated women who would become central figures in the Bluestocking circle: Catherine Talbot and Mary Delany. There were 411 subscribers (the list does not indicate how many copies were taken by each), including a high proportion of clergymen, minor nobility and Oxford dons. Among the familiar names were Thomas Secker, Bishop of Oxford, the Duchess of Portland (who employed Elstob as governess from 1738, and was a close friend of Delany and Elizabeth Montagu), Sir George Lyttelton (also friend to Delany and Elizabeth Montagu), Henry Chapone (future husband of Hester Mulso), William Blackstone, Edward Gibbon, Bonnell Thornton (who would shortly afterwards edit an anthology of women's poetry) and Samuel Richardson.

Sylvia Myers has emphasized the extent to which those connected with publication of the *Memoirs* formed a mutually supportive network. But it should also be viewed as a public declaration, even a manifesto. This interpretation is supported by the bold lettering of the title-page, announcing the discussion of 'Several Ladies of Great Britain'. The patriotic intent is spelled out in the preface: 'it is pretty certain, that England hath produced more women famous for literary accomplishments, than any other nation in Europe'.[113] Literary women are represented as a national resource. The list of subscribers identifies a potential reading public for women writers, a promise of a 'critical mass' in favour of a republic of letters that includes women.

The following year *The Lives of the Poets of Great Britain and Ireland to the Time of Dean Swift* appeared in five volumes, including accounts of several women authors. It was probably the product of a number of writers, among them Robert Shiels (Samuel Johnson's amanuensis), and was padded out with borrowings from other compilations, but the name on the title-page is that of Theophilus Cibber (1703–58), the disreputable son of Richardson's friend, the playwright and poet laureate Colley Cibber. Theophilus was an actor, self-publicist and chronic debtor, best known for a court action brought against William Sloper in 1738 for 'criminal conversation' with Mrs. Cibber.[114] He claimed £5,000 damages for loss of earnings from Susannah Cibber's successful career on stage, and was awarded £10, on the grounds that he had connived in the adultery. The following year he claimed £10,000 from Sloper for detaining his wife, and received £500.[115]

Evidently Cibber was capable of setting a high value on women; perhaps that is reflected in the generally favourable treatment of them in his *Lives of the Poets*. There are twelve female poets included, scattered through the five volumes, beginning with Katherine Philips (1631–64) and ending (chronologically) with Laetitia Pilkington (1712–50). The unapologetic inclusion of Aphra Behn, Delariviere Manley and Pilkington points to a different agenda from that of Ballard. The *Memoirs* had suggested the marketability of female literary biography, but its accompanying moral message was still something of a novelty and was downplayed in the *Lives* in favour of the accustomed resort to mild satire and the recycling of scandal. The life of Philips borrows from Ballard, but takes a less than reverent line on Philips' display of aggrieved modesty on learning of a clandestine edition of her poetry ('we are not to suppose Mrs. P. so much a saint').[116] The life of Behn includes a rollicking account of her gallantries in Antwerp. The occasional indecency of her writing is excused: 'let those who are ready to blame her, consider that her's was a sad alternative to write or starve; the taste of the times was corrupt; and it is a true observation, that they who live to please must please to live'. Her own love life passed off as 'human frailty'.[117] Pilkington's divorce for adultery gives rise only to strictures on the necessity of concealing superior learning from a husband.

Cibber's lack of interest in upholding standards of female propriety is shared by George Colman and Bonnell Thornton, the editors of an anthology, *Poems by Eminent Ladies* (1755), who borrow indiscriminately from Cibber and Ballard for the head notes to their selections, but also bring the inventory up to the present. The editorial discourse is a curious hybrid. There is talk in the preface of the female genius that 'often glows with equal warmth' to that of men, 'and perhaps with more delicacy'.[118] Ballard's nationalist sentiment is echoed; the ladies are 'not only an honour to their sex, but to their native-country'. On the other hand, the Antwerp anecdote concerning Behn is re-used from Cibber, and the immodest Pilkington and Mary Wortley Montagu appear.

In the same year another dubious champion of the female sex appeared in the form of Thomas Amory (1691?–1788), an eccentric recluse and fervent Unitarian. *Memoirs containing the Lives of Several Ladies of Great Britain* is a miscellany designed to include 'notes on antiquities, curiosities, travels, meetings and opinions'. Twelve volumes were promised, one was produced, and there only one memoir is formally presented (of Mrs. Marinda Benlow), although it includes many digressions into other lives. The broken pledges irresistibly bring to mind the late John Dunton of *Athenian* fame. Amory claims to have met all the ladies he discusses on his travels around the country, and have gathered the information at first hand. He dismisses Ballard's account of Mrs. Grierson as 'not worth a rush': 'I was intimately acquainted with Mrs. Grierson, and having passed a hundred afternoons with her in literary conversations in her own parlour, therefore it is in my power to give a very particular and exact account of this extraordinary woman.' He adds, 'In the Appendix you shall have it' (it was never published).[119] The same concerns spilled over into a semi-autobiographical novel, *The Life of John Buncle, Esq.* (vol. I, 1756; vol. II, 1766). The remarks on this work in the *Dictionary of the National Biography* admirably sum up Amory's pet obsessions: 'He marries seven wives in the two volumes of Buncle, generally after a day's acquaintance, and buries them as rapidly. They are all of superlative beauty, virtue, and genius, and, in particular, sound unitarians ... Much of his love-making and religious discussion takes place in the north of England, and there is some interest in his references to the beauty of the lake scenery.'

Only a brief reading of Amory is necessary to reach the conclusion that he was mad. Yet *John Buncle* was a moderately successful work (reprinted in 1770 and 1825), and in the prefatory remarks to his *Memoirs* Amory adds to a growing chorus of praise for the female sex which begins in the early 1750s: 'women of sense and breeding' are 'the noblest part of human creation'; 'the ladies are a glory to Great Britain, and an honour to womankind, for their fine understandings, their valuable learning, their strong judgements, and their good lives'.[120] It was part of the emergence of a new consensus, a revised paradigm of social order.

The new symbolic pre-eminence of women was most resoundingly signalled at this time by John Duncombe (1729–86) in his poem *The Feminiad* (1754). Duncombe was a clergyman and a member of Samuel Richardson's North End circle, who in 1761 was to marry Susanna Highmore, an author herself, daughter of the artist Joseph Highmore and his wife Susanna, who also wrote.[121] Like Elizabeth Carter's father, another Kentish vicar, he was a prolific contributor to the *Gentleman's Magazine*, which, as we have seen in chapter 4, actively promoted female writers.[122] *The Feminiad* was written in 1751 and circulated for some time in manuscript. It arose from the crisis in the reputation of women's writing discussed earlier in this chapter, and was ardently concerned to sort the wheat from the chaff: exemplary female authors are distinguished from those who fail to combine wit and virtue, including the topical triad Phillips, Pilkington and Vane. Once published, it was extremely popular, appearing in a second edition in 1757, in volume IV of Dodsley's *Miscellany* in 1755, and then in numerous anthologies from the 1760s through to the 1780s.[123]

Like Thomas Seward's 'Female Right to Literature', this is a progress poem, here given the additional authority of an epic title. It begins with an injunction from the muse to the male poet to overcome the prejudices of the past:

> Rise, rise, bold swain; and to the list'ning grove
> Resound the praises of the sex you love;
> Tell how, adorn'd with every charm, they shine,
> In mind and person equally divine,
> Till man, no more to female merit blind,
> *Admire* the person, but *adore* the mind.
>
> (ll. 9–14)

Richardson is presented as an exemplar of the enlightened view of women and praised for his patronage of female self-expression. 'Prejudice' then voices the traditional misogynist opinion of women as at best merely sensual and ornamental creatures, designed for the pleasure of man. The poet protests that this philosophy is unworthy of the 'freeborn sons of *Britain's* polish'd isle', and only fit for an eastern seraglio: 'Our *British* nymphs with happier omens rove, / At Freedom's call, thro' Wisdom's sacred grove' (49–50).

The poet asserts the compatibility of modesty and literary talent, study and 'domestic excellence', and invokes the Richardsonian choice between time invested in closet employments or frittered away on fashionable diversions, 'visits, cards and noise' (94, 97). He proceeds to sing the praises of the paragons who have achieved the ideal balance. They include Elizabeth Singer Rowe, Viscountess Irwin for her defence of women against Pope in the *Gentleman's Magazine* ('By her disarm'd, ye witlings! now give o'er / Your empty sneers, and shock the sex no more', 182), and, with great fulsomeness, Elizabeth Carter.

The poem concludes with the argument that their continuing fame will reflect glory on 'every polish'd, wise and virtuous age' and demonstrate the insignificance of short-lived beauty compared to more enduring qualities. The fame of female writers is regarded not only as a just reward for their achievements, but also as an important indication of a 'polish'd' society, anticipating accounts of the progress of women in the historical writings of John Millar or Lord Kames. Although the imagery of the *Feminiad* is pastoral and the allusions Homeric, it is this rhetoric of 'polish' and 'improvement' that distinguishes the appreciation of women's writing as an argument in favour of modernization. It reveals a powerful desire, at this specific juncture in the mid-eighteenth century, to publicize women, to bring their works and their lives centrally into the public realm, as a sign of the nation's enlightenment.

A tension running through Duncombe's poem, as in Richardson's correspondence, is the preference of some of these eminent women for privacy and obscurity, and the countervailing necessity of presenting them to the public for the good of society at large. Amory had been insistent on the reclusiveness of his paragons, and equally insistent on the need to advertise their virtues. Duncombe, in his short and rather elliptical 'Advertisement' to *The Feminiad*, explains that some of the writers praised under cover of pseudonyms are part of a 'Circle of private Friends' including the author, and are unknown to the wider world,

> their Performances being yet in Manuscript. Should the public Curiosity be hereby rais'd, and could the Diffidence of the fair Authors be so far remov'd as to gratify it, *one* great End of the present Publication would be answer'd.

The poem must therefore be seen in part as an 'outing' of female genius: the inhibitions of literary women in their closets, hoarding up their manuscripts for private consumption, are to be conquered at the insistence of a newly alerted reading public. As an example of this, Duncombe's father, also a well-connected man of letters, had in 1749 been urging Elizabeth Carter to undertake translations of Horace's *Odes* for a collection to be edited with his son, among 'several schemes for her advantage'.[124] The assumption of the first politicized feminist scholars, beginning in the 1970s, that female aspirations to authorship had been universally discouraged, repressed or despised is gradually being revised in response to this kind of evidence. In mid-eighteenth-century England there was a growing clamour for women writers to come forward, however unwillingly, and make their merits known.

The dearth of publications by women presented a problem. There was an unfortunate disparity between the standard female education and the wish that female genius should shed its lustre on the nation. It is instructive to see the alacrity with which the reviewers seized on the rare public offerings of the Bluestocking writers, the group of women who gradually became associated with Elizabeth Carter and Catherine Talbot, and then found a new nucleus in the brilliant society hostess Elizabeth Montagu. In 1758 Samuel Richardson printed Carter's translation of the works of Epictetus, begun in 1749. It arrived with a fanfare of 1,031 subscribers, headed by the Prince of Wales, and was greeted with acclaim.[125] In 1762 her *Poems on Several Occasions* (based on the 1738 *Poems on Particular Occasions*) was also warmly received.[126] She published nothing further in her lifetime apart from seven new items in a third edition of *Poems* in 1776. Elizabeth Montagu had the grace to feel some embarrassment at being publicly hailed for her genius before managing to produce a single work. Although she contributed two dialogues anonymously to George Lyttelton's *Dialogues of the Dead* (1760), it was not until 1769 that *An Essay on the Writings and Genius of Shakespear* appeared and justified her preexisting pedestal. There was a hiatus in the promotion of a feminized literary culture as the champions of the female sex looked in vain for adequate objects of appreciation. Although a school of female novelists appeared in the wake of Richardson, including Frances Sheridan, Sarah Fielding and Sarah Scott, most novels were not sufficiently ambitious to warrant iconic status for the author. Catharine Macaulay was the answer to the feminizers' prayers. The amazing hyperbole, the rapturous applause, that greeted the appearance of each successive volume of her *History of England* through the 1760s to 1770s is best explained by Macaulay's apparent fulfilment of the expectations created by proponents of the link between progress and women, those John the Baptists active from the 1750s.[127]

The reception accorded these works would have confirmed for all with an interest in letters that they were living in a Grandisonian era, where female virtue was revered and female genius materially rewarded. No matter that the content of Carter's translation of *Epictetus* and Macaulay's *History* were at odds with the ideological burden of the discourse of feminization: the fame of literary women had become a cultural imperative that obscured such inconveniences. In the case of Macaulay, the contradiction was stark. She was an ultra-Whig in politics, a republican ideologue, and in her writings she employs the language of civic humanism, of public virtue, the martial spirit, luxury and corruption.[128] Yet although she did not embrace the ethos of feminization, she consented to be embraced by it.[129]

The relationship of Carter's *Epictetus* to the feminizing impetus involved more in the way of conscious accommodation. In an earlier chapter I looked at the way she dealt with the themes of fortune and loss inspired by her own family's catastrophic experience of the South Sea Bubble, a national disaster still vivid in public discourse. In her poems for the *Gentleman's Magazine* in the 1730s she experimented with a stance uniting Stoic indifference and Christian faith. Epictetus urged his followers to subdue the passions of avarice as well as grief and desire, and to avoid self-indulgence and effeminacy.[130] These sentiments made him a favourite philosopher of the civic humanist thinker the Earl of Shaftesbury.[131] Interestingly, Mary Wortley Montagu in 1710 had completed a translation of Epictetus's *Encheiridion* from Latin which she sent for approval to Bishop Burnet with the complaint that women are generally 'permitted no Books but such as tend to the weakening and Effeminateing [*sic*] of the Mind', while conceding that learning in women should never be flaunted.[132]

For Carter, the task of translating from Greek to English the complete remains of one of the major figures of Stoicism led her to reexamine the relevance of the philosophy in the changed conditions of the 1750s.

Although the project was begun as a private gift for Catherine Talbot to comfort her after the death of Mrs Secker, from the start Carter was concerned with questions of literary style and reception. Her first impulse was to render the prose in polished, ornamented, 'feminized' English, to make it more accessible to modern tastes. But this course was strongly opposed by Thomas Secker, who acted as mentor. He urged her to adopt instead a 'plain, home, awakening' and implicitly more virile style, which he felt would be more in keeping with the spirit of Epictetus and more arresting for an English audience. Carter, after some resistance, relented.[133]

A further reason for presenting the ideas of the philosopher in plain English was to distance and historicize them. Talbot relayed to Carter the challenge from Secker that 'unless you can prove to him that Epictetus wore a laced coat, he will not allow you to dress him in one'. This tactic was to prove valuable once the project had been reconceived as a publication, and Carter, Talbot and Secker were considering how the translation should be put before the public. In 1755 Talbot and Secker began to raise alarms at the dangerous influence the translation might have if opinions such as the sanction of suicide were not placed in a Christian perspective by a substantial introduction and notes. Carter, understandably put out, wondered whether it was worth publishing at all, and protested that such a moral work would surely 'be read by none but very good Christians'. But Talbot envisaged a far more extensive, fashionable and morally vulnerable readership, motivated variously by idle curiosity, feminine partiality, vocational interest and scepticism, the besetting sin of the modern age: 'Fine gentlemen will read it because it is new; fine ladies because it is yours; critics because it is a translation out of Greek; and Shaftsburian Heathens because Epictetus was an honour to Heathenism, and an idolator of the beauty of virtue.' Carter was now driven even further on the defensive (commenting with exasperation, 'it is surely a dangerous experiment to administer poison to try the force of an antidote'), but again she submitted in the end.[134]

The result is a textual apparatus that tends to criticize Epictetus for what he did not say, rather than explicating his philosophy in positive terms. At best Carter applauds the convergence between Stoic and Christian ideas. The vigorous asceticism that is at the heart of Epictetus' teaching and was most highly valued by Carter herself, is lost in this negotiation. In the anxiety to demolish heathen 'pride' (the self-reliance that sets the individual above worldly misfortune, without the aid of religious faith), Christian complacency is set up in its place. The Introduction makes the civic humanist point that Stoicism was 'useful to the Public', but fails it on the score of 'real inward Improvement', the private-turned-public system of values characteristic of a modern, mercantile society.[135] Stoic ideas remain at a distance, marked out by 'home' style and editorial precautions, and as by modern-day assumptions about the inevitability of the passions are relatively untroubled by them. To be sure, all of Epictetus is there, for the first time in English, available to be read. But the formulation of Stoic virtue that is the matter of the text comes to serve as a signifier for Carter's own inner worth, to act as guarantee of her disinterestedness, in the same way republican virtue functioned to support Macaulay's mythic status.[136] The translator's Introduction provided the cue for reception and facilitated the celebration of the work as a triumph for modern scholarship and the reification of Carter herself as a national treasure.[137]

Self-formation along Stoic lines was wholly at odds with the contemporary culture of commerce and luxury, and ironically the success of the translation of *Epictetus* allowed Carter to attain a new form of selfhood more in keeping with it. The subscription brought Carter a fortune of nearly £1,000. This released her from her retirement in Deal, and she henceforth spent several months each winter in lodgings in Piccadilly (in the fashionable West End rather than the City, her previous London address). In 1762 she bought a house in Deal where she installed her aged father, but was able to live independently.[138] Carter was taken up by Montagu and her friend Lord Bath, and travelled in style with them in England and the Continent. Financial good fortune pursued her, and in the coming years she benefited from a series of legacies and an annuity settled on her by Mrs Montagu.[139] An inheritance from her uncle in 1763 led her to venture £1,500 in South Sea annuities; the shadow of the South Sea Bubble was apparently exorcised.[140] Born into family ruin, her early career aborted by the misogynist climate of letters, she eventually succeeded on the strength of her talents to modest affluence, a life of leisured sociability and a place among a new literary establishment that reigned into the 1790s, but at some cost to her critical liberty of mind.

Coda: From Discourse to a Theory of Feminization in the *Essays* of David Hume

At the time Elizabeth Carter's translation of Epictetus appeared in 1758, the political climate in England had moved on from the prosperous stasis of the Pelham administration. The Seven Years' War with France began in 1756, and after a disastrous start and the replacement of the Duke of Newcastle by William Pitt as head of the government, a few victories in Europe and the colonies were reported. The patriotic tendency of the discourse of feminization was quickly mobilized in the reception of *Epictetus*. The *Monthly Review* commented, 'France can now no longer boast her *Dacier*, but must be compelled to own that our women excel theirs in Sense and Genius, as far as they surpass them in Modesty and Beauty'; George, Lord Lyttelton, observed in a letter to Mrs Montagu: 'I have lately read over again our friend Miss Carter's preface to Epictetus, and admire it more and more. I am also much struck with the poem prefixed to it by another female hand [Hester Mulso]. The English ladies will appear as much superior to the French in wit and in learning, as the men in arms.'[1]

But there were also those who blamed Britain's poor initial showing on the effeminization of the nation at the hands of corrupt politicians, a standing army and the growth of luxury, and civic humanist rhetoric became current again. Pitt himself was an adept who, when first returned as an MP for Old Sarum in 1735, had joined the ranks of the Patriot opposition, and he reused the old tactics in his critique of the Newcastle government, stimulating a wave of popular protest that eventually brought him to power. It was in this context that the Reverend John Brown's *An Estimate of the Manners and Principles of the Times* (1757), a blistering attack on the 'Manners of our Times', went through seven editions in a year. The argument, simply stated, was that England was degenerating into a *'vain, luxurious* and *selfish* EFFEMINACY'. The charge of 'effeminacy' is the principal weapon in Brown's arsenal; nowhere in eighteenth-century writings on the economy is the threat posed by luxury to gender identity more explicitly or exhaustively rehearsed. Lest the reader mistakenly assume that he speaks in merely abstract or figurative terms of the threat to masculine virility, he takes pains to bring the argument down to the level of real men and women:

> It may probably be asked, Why the ruling Manners of our Women have not been particularly delineated? The Reason is, because they are essentially the same with those of the Men, and are therefore included in this Estimate. The Sexes have now little other apparent Distinction, beyond that of Person and Dress: Their peculiar and characteristic Manners are confounded and lost: The one Sex having advanced into *Boldness*, as the other have sunk into *Effeminacy*.[2]

Brown went back to the first principles of classical republicanism, applying them in their crudest form to the modern state. Trade and wealth are the root of all evil, undermining morality and religion, and weakening the nation's military capacity. Montesquieu is frequently cited as an authority: the maxim 'Commerce polishes Manners, but corrupts Manners' is quoted from *The Spirit of the Laws* XX.i. But Brown himself is concerned only with corruption, not with polish. While he does not go so far as to propose the suppression of commerce, he nevertheless concludes that the only hope of salvation lies in the emergence of wise and virtuous leader who, like Lycurgus in Sparta, could accomplish a miraculous reversal of decline.

The *Estimate* is the comic flourish that concludes the feminization debate in so far as it is restricted to England. Brown was never regarded as a serious contender in the argument over modernity and morality. The *Monthly Review* sniffed, 'When the Estimate appeared, it was applauded by the multitude, and it raised a smile from the judicious.'[3] William Cowper remarked that it 'rose like a paper kite and charmed the town'; James Ralph described it as a 'tinsel performance'.[4] But the debate was far from over by the late 1750s. On the contrary, the discussion of economic 'improvement' as a gendered concept broadens in scope, decisively informed by ideas from France, notably those of Montesquieu and Rousseau, and invested with new energy by the collective efforts of the newly emerging Scottish historical school. Simultaneously the works of participants in the earlier English debate – such as Mandeville and Richardson – were being disseminated and discussed on the Continent.

As an indication of the way in which the new cosmopolitanism of the feminization debate enabled fresh lines of argument to develop in the moral legitimation of commerce and luxury, I will finish by looking in some detail at three essays by David Hume (1711–76), 'Of Essay-Writing', 'Of the Rise and Progress of the Arts and Sciences' and 'Of Luxury'. Hume's career epitomizes the international cross-currents: in his youth an eager student of English polite letters, he spend a crucial period of intellectual development in France (1734–37), and returned to Edinburgh to become one of the central figures of the Scottish Enlightenment.

The essays by Hume under discussion are exactly contemporary with Samuel Richardson's novels, and they share with Richardson a concern with the progressive social influence of women that, I have maintained in chapter 5, was avant-garde in the Britain of the 1740s. Hume was writing 'Of Essay-Writing' and 'Of the Rise and Progress of the Arts and Sciences' at the same moment as *Pamela* was being created, and their publication was contemporary with the cult of *Pamela*. 'Of Luxury' was first published in a separate volume titled *Political Discourses* that came out in 1752, in the interval between *Clarissa* (1747–48) and *Sir Charles Grandison* (1753–54). The impact of the writings of Richardson and of Hume was felt in Paris at the same moment. Diderot has been described as greeting every returned visitor to London with the words 'Have you met Richardson? Have you met Hume?' They were at one in their concern with the reformation of manners. And yet, almost without exception, commentators have overlooked the prominent place Hume allots to women and feminine influence in certain sections of the *Essays*.[5]

In Hume's advertisement to the first volume of *Essays, Moral and Political*, he named the *Spectator* and the *Craftsman* as his models. These were two of the most successful examples of the periodical essay form, but their agendas could not have been more contrary. The *Spectator* implicitly supported the beginnings of the Whig oligarchy; the *Craftsman*, two decades later, violently opposed it. The *Spectator* supported reform and modernization; the *Craftsman* described the contemporary scene as one of corruption and decline. At a basic level what Hume means by proposing to combine the two is that he intends to talk about both manners and morals (the *Spectator*'s main preserve) and the world of politics (the *Craftsman*'s).[6] But at the same time the refusal to acknowledge a substantive difference is the mark of the outsider. He intends to rise above the politically partisan analysis of society and view the world objectively and dispassionately. This outsider status was Hume's great strength when it came to presenting original ideas about economic and cultural change.

'Of Essay Writing', which appeared in the second volume of the 1742 *Essays*, proposes a revival of the project of Addison and Steele, a marriage of the library and the tea table, scholarship and sociability, in the name of politeness.[7] Hume talks of women as agents of civility, just as Addison and Steele had done. But as in the case of Richardson, it needs to be appreciated what a remarkable thing it was to attempt to revive this discourse of feminization at the start of the 1740s. The optimism of the *Spectator* was a thing of the distant past. For twenty years classical republicanism had been the dominant political discourse, with its profound suspicion of the new. The rhetoric of misogyny was part of it, since the accusation that the nation was becoming weak and effeminate carried over into satire of women and their faults.

Hume seems oblivious to all this, as well he might be, since he was in France from 1734 to 1737, and prior to that, mainly in Edinburgh, trying half-heartedly to train as a lawyer and then as a merchant. He was insulated from the pessimistic, misogynist culture that prevailed in England through the 1730s, during this period of Patriot opposition to the Walpole government. Instead, while in France, he was exposed to an entirely contrary influence. Although much of his time there was spent shut up in the country intensively writing his *Treatise of Human Nature* with only a nearby monastery as a social resource, he also made brief stays in Paris and Rheims and he seems to have absorbed French cultural attitudes like a sponge; attitudes that bore some resemblance to those of the *Spectator* that he had imbibed in his youth. After only a few weeks he was writing to friends like a seasoned expatriate. He insists that the French have more 'real Politeness' than the English, more 'softness of Temper, and a sincere Inclination to oblige and be serviceable'. He refers to his own constant socializing among the 'People of Fashion' in Rheims, with 'Parties of Diversion' almost every day.[8]

This is the experience and the language that characterizes 'Of Essay-Writing'. The project of the *Spectator* to bring together pleasure with intellectual and moral seriousness is to be revived via France, with its thriving salon culture centred on women. Hume refers his readers to the example of 'a neighbouring Nation', where women are 'Sovereigns' of the '*learned* World, as well as the *conversible*'; or rather, the distinction between the two is obscured by the higher category of politeness: 'no polite Writer pretends to venture upon the Public, without the Approbation of some celebrated Judges of that Sex'.[9] This homology between the authority of women and the cultural superiority of France has been identified by Dena Goodman as fundamental to the French Enlightenment, which was 'grounded in a female-centred mixed-gender sociability [the *salon*] that gendered French culture, the Enlightenment and civilization itself as feminine'.[10] She cites Voltaire's introduction to his tragedy *Zaire*, published in 1736 at the time Hume was at La Flèche:

> Of all the nations France is the one which has most experienced society. The continual commerce between the two sexes, so lively and so polite, has introduced a politeness quite unknown elsewhere. Society depends on women.[11]

A statement of this kind in England would have been inconceivable. The previous year Pope's *Epistle to a Lady: Of the Characters of Women* had stated with equal conviction that '"Most Women have no character at all"'.

In 'The Rise and Progress of the Arts and Sciences' (1742) Hume is writing in dialogue with the Opposition writers of the 1730s, with their correlation of the corruption of government under Walpole and the decay of the arts and polite learning. Pope is once again an obvious point of reference, specifically *The Dunciad*, and it is likely that he also had the *Craftsman* in mind.[12] Hume's essay could be considered groundwork for the much better known

'Of Refinement in the Arts'. It opens with exaggerated tentativeness about methodology: whether advances in learning can be discussed in terms of causes at all (an interesting tactic, because this was typically a theme for sweeping, partisan statements). The argument proceeds in a loose-knit, discursive way. It is only about halfway through (after the relatively obvious causes of the development of learning, security and exchange with neighbouring nations, have been disposed of) that he warms to the subject.

Hume introduces the category of the 'civilized monarchy' as the form of government most propitious to the 'arts of luxury' and the 'liberal arts', and it soon becomes apparent that he is describing modern France (124). He is precise about the way political conditions operate on the intellect: in a republic, men of talent must make themselves useful to the people, and this favours science; in a monarchy, they must 'look up' and make themselves agreeable, and this leads to 'refined taste' (126). He allots a central place to the 'arts of conversation' and 'politeness of manners' (126-7), and the absence of these attributes reflects poorly on the less sophisticated European nations (England, and the republics of Switzerland and Holland), as well as the classical world (127-30). The battle of ancients and moderns was rerun in many of the essays, complete with its gendered associations.[13]

Gallantry is then introduced as a further cause of refinement. At first it is presented as a secondary cause: it is the 'natural produce of courts and monarchies' (131). But he then corrects this: gallantry is '*natural* in the highest degree', 'Nature has implanted in all living creatures an affection between the sexes'. The art and education available in courts 'only turn the mind more towards it' (131). They refine it, but it is already innate. Agreeable behaviour towards women is therefore a primary cause of the rise of the arts.

Hume goes on to explore the 'generosity' of gallantry; a social dimension that complements its naturalness (132-3). Nature has given man superiority over women, but gallantry mitigates the hierarchy of nature. There is a parallel implied with the role of law in the earlier part of the essay, which moderates the harsh disparity between ruler and subject.

Hume wants to associate gallantry with 'wisdom and prudence' and detach it from its more bodily associations (134-5). But there is a problem of terminology. The word 'gallantry' was a French import, which had taken on the dual meanings of politeness towards women and sexual intrigue in the late seventeenth century. The latter emphasis was particularly strong in English parlance – Byron would later quip, 'What men call gallantry, and gods adultery / Is much more common when the climate's sultry (*Don Juan*, I, ll. 503-4)'. Richardson would never have employed gallantry in a positive sense. For most Englishmen it was synonymous with libertinism. Hume attempts to purify 'gallantry', insisting that it should be understood with all the attributes of politeness: 'Were we to rob the feast [of gallantry] of all its garniture of reason, discourse, sympathy, friendship, and gaiety, what remains would scarcely be worth acceptance, in the judgment of the truly elegant and luxurious' (134). It is perhaps to underline the novelty of the view that he uses the word 'luxurious' (which originally meant 'lecherous') as an affirmation.

'What better school for manners,' Hume asks,

> than the company of virtuous women; where the mutual endeavour to please must insensibly polish the mind, where the example of the female softness and modesty must communicate itself to their admirers, and where the delicacy of that sex puts every one on his guard, lest he give offence by any breach of decency?' (134)

But he must have been aware that this virtue was no requirement of Parisian salon culture, where the salonnières frequently carried on multiple affairs with their protégés. Adultery was very much a part of the feast. Hume was later to comment, after frequenting all the major salons in the 1760s, 'Scarce a double Entendre ever to be heard; scarce a free Joke. What lies below this Veil is not commonly supposed to be so pure.'[14] He was being coy, since it appears that he himself had an affair with one of them, the Comtesse de Boufflers.

This is the point at which Hume parts company with the discourse of feminization as it existed in France. The signs of his dissatisfaction or discomfort are also apparent in 'Essay-Writing': in his recommendation at the end to would-be salonnières among his readers to correct the warmth of their taste in literature, that is, the sensuality (537); and in his aside in 'Refinement in the Arts' on the 'effeminacy' of the French theatre (122). This is equally the point at which his aims seem to converge, though quite independently, with those of Richardson. Both of them saw the need for a virtuous woman to bear the weight of symbolizing the process of refinement. Only a chaste woman was sufficiently stable to vindicate the growth of luxury or the morality of progress, in opposition to the charge of effeminacy as levelled by civic humanist ideologues. A female libertine, however intellectually brilliant, would always risk becoming a misogynist stereotype, part of a vision of decadence and decline.

Ten years later Hume published *Political Discourses* (1752) in which the essay 'Of Luxury' (retitled 'Of Refinement in the Arts' in 1760). It marks a transition from the discourse of feminization employed in the two earlier essays, to the beginnings of an enlightenment *theory* of feminization. The discourse of feminization, is a means of placing positive value on cultural change, the refinement of manners: it concerns the superstructure or symptoms of the modern. The theory of feminization is a systematic response to the classical republican gendering of historical decline; it is a gendered account of progress. The thesis of classical republicanism is economically determinist: poverty is necessary to virtue; wealth, commodification and consumerism lead to corruption and military weakness.[15] The notion that the poverty of a nation might ensure its military and moral strength might seem a bizarre survival in eighteenth-century Britain, but it continued to require an answer through the first half of the century; and then Rousseau updated it for the second half. Progressivists beginning with Hume counter this notion with a newly 'scientific' account of why virtue is not simply compatible with commercial prosperity, but a necessary accompaniment to it. Femino-centrism is a component in this account. It becomes an axiom that the growing importance of women in society is integral to historical improvement, simultaneously symptom and cause. Women become vital to the explication and justification of capitalism. The theory culminates in the 1770s with Lord Kames *Sketches of the History of Man* (1774), the histories of women by the French Antoine-Leonard Thomas and Scottish William Alexander,[16] and especially John Millar's *Origin of the Distinction of Ranks*, the most complete formulation of the four-stage theory of the way society progresses in relation to the changing modes of subsistence, a quarter of which is devoted to the progress of women.[17]

What has happened to alter Hume's thinking between 1742 and 1752 is above all Montesquieu's *De L'Esprit des lois* (1748): the 'first systematic treatise on politics',[18] the foundation of the social sciences, and a huge contemporary success (22 French editions in the author's lifetime). Soon after it was published Montesquieu and Hume began a correspondence. Flatteringly for Hume, still relatively unknown, Montesquieu initiated it by sending a letter expressing admiration of the essay 'Of National Characters' from Hume's *Essays Moral and Political* (1748). Hume replied with a long and appreciative critique of *Esprit des lois*, which Montesquieu found 'full of light and good sense'.[19] Part of the impact of Montesquieu was to encourage Hume to focus on what the former argued were the base conditions of historical change: geography, climate and economic conditions. In the *Political Discourses* of 1752, seven out of the twelve essays were devoted to economics.

Jerome Christensen, in comparing 'Of Essay-Writing' and 'Of Commerce' which was also from the 1752 collection, proposes that 'what Hume calls "woman" in the earlier essay he calls "commodity" here'.[20] This is a suggestive remark, but it would be more accurate to apply it to 'Of Luxury' and say that what he once called 'woman' he now calls 'luxury'. The association had of course always been there, but now the identities of woman and of luxury are fused as metaphor.

Hume's first concern in 'Of Luxury' is to establish a new kind of distinction between 'innocent' and 'immoral' luxury. The need for a virtuous woman that had made itself felt in 'Of Refinement in the Arts' has carried over to the imagining of virtuous luxury: the first aim of the essay is to prove 'that the ages of refinement are both the happiest and most virtuous' (269). 'Industry' and 'refinements in the mechanical arts' have replaced the court in this analysis as the necessary precondition for refinements in the liberal arts: there is a turn from the cultural and political to the economic (270). Admittedly, the account of the advance of the refined arts and its offshoots is familiar from the discourse of feminization: it brings sociability, the communication of knowledge, the art of living, clubs and societies, and polite commerce between the sexes. 'Both sexes meet in an easy and sociable manner; and the tempers of men, as well as their behaviour, refine apace' (271). But this is now just one factor among many leading to change, and its relative downgrading is also indicated in the following paragraph where Hume uses the word 'gallantry' in connection with 'libertine love'. 'Gallantry' is now a minor sin rather than a causal factor.

The argument for feminization is no longer primarily about salon culture, the refined arts, or the effect of individual men and women on each other, as in the 1742 essays. It is about commercialization and its consequences for the nation. The gender categories have become internal to the case for economic change. This is most apparent when the classical republican link between refinement and the decline of the martial spirit is directly addressed. Hume avoids the word 'effeminacy' at first, but it is evident that he is articulating a new-model masculine identity for the modern era, combining refinement and productivity. He states flatly, 'The arts have no such effect in enervating either the mind or body' and goes on to explain, 'industry, their inseparable attendant, adds new force to both' (274). This is a rewording of Montesquieu's remark in *Persian Letters*, No. 106: 'When people say that the arts of civilization make men effeminate, they cannot at any rate be referring to the men who practise them, for they are never idle, and of all the vices idleness is the one which does most to diminish a man's courage.'[21] In the companion essay 'Of Commerce', Hume discusses at greater length how the growth of the luxury market can become a source of strength to the nation, by providing, from the ranks of artisans, a pool of manpower for the army. But he does not rely on logistical arguments alone; he insists, as Mandeville had done (in 'Remark L' of *Fable of the Bees*), that there was nothing in the spirit of modern luxurious nations that prevented effective warfare, using England and France as examples.

In the final section of the essay 'Of Luxury' Hume defends a newly established notion of 'innocent luxury', guarding it against the moralists of the civic tradition on the one hand, and on the other, exorcising the spirit of Mandeville, who had provocatively accepted that all luxury is vicious, although it produces public benefits.[22] In this way Hume, atheist though he was, helps to lay the ground for the economic theodicy of Adam Smith: a providential theory of capitalism. I have argued in the course of this study that the overcoming of misogyny was a vital part of the moralizing of commerce. Although Hume and Richardson were divided on many issues, they both recognized that the moral recuperation and elevation of women within public discourse was an urgent task, if a vision of progress was to become a possibility.

Notes

Introduction

1 Albert O. Hirschman, *The Passions and the Interests: Political Arguments for Capitalism before its Triumph* (Princeton, 1984) 9.
2 Terry Eagleton, *The Rape of Clarissa: Writing, Sexuality, and Class Struggle in Samuel Richardson* (Oxford, 1982) 13.
3 Nancy Armstrong, *Desire and Domestic Fiction: A Political History of the Novel* (New York and Oxford, 1987) 5.
4 My usage is also distinct from the pragmatic application of 'feminization' to describe the growing public prominence of women, notably in literary production. See, for instance, Gary Kelly, *Women, Writing, and Revolution* (Oxford, 1993) v. It is closer to Laura Brown's description of the 'feminization of ideology', the polemical association of the 'female figure' with 'commodification and trade', but I will want to distinguish between *effeminization*, the negative version of this nexus, which Brown principally addresses, and arguments in favour of progressive *feminization* (see below p. 00); *Ends of Empire: Women and Ideology in Early Eighteenth-Century English Literature* (Ithaca and London, 1993) 3.
5 Armstrong, *Desire and Domestic Fiction*, 9.
6 William Alexander, *The History of Women, From the Earliest Antiquity to the Present Time* (London, 1779) I, 107.
7 Katherine B. Clinton, 'Femme et philosophe: enlightenment origins of feminism', *Eighteenth-Century Studies* 8: 3 (Spring, 1975) 283–99.
8 Sylvana Tomaselli, 'The enlightenment debate on women', *History Workshop Journal*, 20 (1985) 101–24; 101.
9 In Elizabeth Eger et al., eds, *Women, Writing and the Public Sphere, 1700–1830* (Cambridge, 2001) 239–56.
10 Harriet Guest, *Small Change: Women, Learning, Patriotism, 1750–1810* (Chicago and London, 2000) 14.
11 On the first flowering of the discourse of feminization in France, see Carolyn C. Lougee, *Le Paradis des Femmes: Women, Salons, and Social Stratification in Seventeenth-Century France* (Princeton, 1976); Ian MacLean, *Woman Triumphant: Feminism in French Literature 1610–1652* (Oxford, 1977); and for later developments, Joan B. Landes, *Women and the Public Sphere in the Age of the French Revolution* (Ithaca and London, 1988); Madelyn Gutwirth, *The Twilight of the Goddesses: Women and Representation in the French Revolutionary Era* (New Brunswick, 1992); and Dena Goodman, *The Republic of Letters: A Cultural History of the French Enlightenment* (Ithaca and London, 1994).
12 Goodman, *Republic of Letters*, 8.
13 In addition to J.G.A. Pocock, *The Machiavellian Moment: Florentine Political Thought and the Atlantic Republican Tradition* (Princeton, 1975), see, for instance, J.G.A. Pocock, *Virtue, Commerce, and History* (Cambridge, 1985) especially 48–50; essays by John Robertson and Pocock in Istvan Hort and Michael Ignatieff, eds, *Wealth and Virtue: The Shaping of Political Economy in the Scottish Enlightenment* (Cambridge, 1983); and Shelley Burtt, *Virtue Transformed: Political Arguments in England 1688–1740* (Cambridge, 1992), who argues for

the development in the early eighteenth century of 'a privately oriented conception of civic virtue', 35.

14 John Barrell, *The Political Theory of Painting from Reynolds to Hazlitt* (New Haven and London, 1986) 10. Barrell here makes reference to Stephen Copley's positing of a 'bourgeois' humanism in *Literature and the Social Order in Eighteenth-Century England* (London, 1984) 3–7.

15 Lycurgus, Cato and Lucretia have in common their connection with efforts to cleanse the body politic of tyranny, corruption or effeminacy. Further reference to these narratives will be made elsewhere in this text, but special mention should be made here to Ian Donaldson's valuable study *The Rapes of Lucretia: A Myth and its Transformations* (Oxford, 1982), which emphasises the dual private and public dimensions of the Lucretia story. After her rape by Sextus Tarquinius and subsequent suicide, her kinsman Lucius Junius Brutus swore vengeance on the Tarquins who reigned as tyrants in Rome, and led a popular uprising against them which resulted in the reinstatement of the Roman republic. Donaldson suggests that the two acts of the drama, the sexual and the political, are separated in certain eighteenth-century renditions, notably *Clarissa*; in chapter 5, I shall argue to the contrary.

16 On the vocabulary of civic humanism, see Pocock, *Machiavellian Moment*, ix.

17 John Sekora, *Luxury: The Concept in Western Thought, Eden to Smollet* (Baltimore and London, 1977) 75. The more recent *The Idea of Luxury: A Conceptual and Historical Investigation* by Christopher J. Berry (Cambridge, 1994) contains a rather less incisive account of classical and eighteenth-century ideas. For a brief overview, see Maxine Berg and Elizabeth Eger, 'The rise and fall of the luxury debates', in Maxine Berg and Elizabeth Eger, eds, *Luxury in the Eighteenth Century: Debates, Desires and Delectable Goods* (Basingstoke, 2003) 7–27.

18 Paul Langford, *A Polite and Commercial People: England 1727–1783* (Oxford, 1989) 3–4.

19 Pocock, *Machiavellian Moment*, vii–viii.

20 The essays in Mary Peace and Vincent Quinn, eds, *Luxurious Sexualities*, *Textual Practice* 11: 3 (1997) and in Berg and Eger, eds, *Luxury in the Eighteenth Century*, suggest a momentum towards re-evaluation.

21 Pocock, *Virtue, Commerce, and History*, 114; see also 99–100, 235, and in *Machiavellian Moment*, 37, 41, 96.

22 *The Life, Unpublished Letters, and Philosophical Regimen of Anthony, Earl of Shaftesbury*, ed. Benjamin Rand (London, 1900) 216–17, cit. Gutwirth, *Twilight of the Goddesses*, 4.

23 Carolyn D. Williams, *Pope, Homer, and Manliness: Some Aspects of Eighteenth-Century Learning* (London and New York, 1993) 9.

24 For a summary of his thesis, which has been put forward in several articles, see Ronald Trumbach, *Sex and the Gender Revolution*, Vol. 1, *Heterosexuality and the Third Gender in Enlightenment London* (Chicago and London, 1998) 3–18. For discussions of the limited validity of his characterization of 'effeminate' man, see Philip Carter, *Men and the Emergence of Polite Society, Britain 166–1800* (Harlow, 2001) especially 144–7; and the essays by the same author, 'An effeminate or efficient nation? Masculinity and 18th-century social commentary', *Textual Practice*, 11:3 (1997) 429–44; and 'Men about town: representations of foppery and masculinity in early eighteenth-century urban society', in Hannah Barker and Elaine Chalus, eds, *Gender in Eighteenth-Century England: Roles Representations and Responsibilities* (London and New York, 1997) 31–57.

25 Michael McKeon, 'Historicizing patriarchy: the emergence of gender difference in England, 1660–1760', *Eighteenth-Century Studies*, 28: 3 (1995) 295–322; 320.

26 See also Carter, *Men*, chapter 4; and G.J. Barker-Benfield, *The Culture of Sensibility: Sex and Society in Eighteenth-Century Britain* (Chicago and London, 1992) chapter 3, both of which range more generally through the century. Anthony Fletcher's *Gender, Sex and Subordination in England 1500–1800* (New Haven and London, 1995) chapter 5, covers three centuries, but with no purchase on the socio-political connotations of 'effeminacy' deriving from the classical era. On effeminacy and francophobia, see Michèle Cohen, *Fashioning Masculinity: National Identity and Language in the Eighteenth Century* (London and New York, 1996) which includes a brief but valuable introduction to the concept and a review of recent work on it, 4–10.

27 Williams, *Pope*, 102, 103.

28 Ibid., 36–7. She notes that in *The Iliad* Paris's effeminacy is based on his affinity with women, 97–9.

29 Thomas Laqueur, *Making Sex: Body and Gender from the Greeks to Freud* (Cambridge, Mass. and London, 1990) 124.

30 Ibid., 123.

31 Williams, *Pope*, 111–14, cf. 47 on the Cyprians in Pope's *Homer*.

32 Ibid., 115, referring to Pope, *Iliad*, XII, 455.; cf. xii, 381–5.

33 *Virtue, Commerce, and History*, 114.

34 Laqueur, *Making Sex*, 5–6.

35 Ibid., 6. Erin Mackie has suggested that already, at the start of the century, Addison and Steele were preparing the way for this ideological transition; *Market à la Mode: Fashion, Commodity, and Gender in 'The Tatler' and 'The Spectator'* (Baltimore and London, 1997) 164–202.

36 Armstrong, *Desire and Domestic Fiction*, 7.

37 Lawrence E. Klein, 'Gender, conversation and the public sphere in the early eighteenth-century England', in Judith Still and Michael Worton, eds, *Textuality and Sexuality: Reading Theories and Practices* (Manchester and New York, 1993) 100–15; 104. For other work challenging the idea of separate spheres, see Amanda Vickery, 'Golden age to separate spheres? A review of the categories and chronology of English women's history', *The Historical Journal* 36: 2 (1993) 383–414; Lawrence E. Klein, 'Gender and the public/private distinction in the eighteenth century: some questions about evidence and analytical procedure', *Eighteenth-Century Studies* 29: 1 (1995) 97–109; Dario Castiglione and Lesley Sharpe, eds, *Shifting the Boundaries: Transformation of the Languages of Public and Private in the Eighteenth Century* (Exeter, 1995); Paula Backsheider, ed., *The Intersections of the Public and Private Spheres in Early Modern England* (London, 1996); Anne K. Mellor, *Mothers of the Novel: Women's Political Writing in England, 1780–1830* (Bloomington, 2000).

38 'The Parisian salon does not seem to have been imitated in London until after 1750 (though it is unclear whether that impression reflects historical actuality or simply our historical ignorance), and even then salons functioned differently in the two capitals'; Klein, 'Gender', 103.

39 Sylvia Harcstark Myers, *The Bluestocking Circle: Women, Friendship, and the Life of the Mind in Eigtheenth-Century England* (Oxford, 1990) 121–50.

40 Gary Kelly, 'General introduction', in Gary Kelly, gen. ed., *Bluestocking Feminism: Writings of the Bluestocking Circle*, 6 vols. (London, 1999) ix–liv, especially xlv–xlviii, and 'Bluestocking feminism', in Eger et al., eds, *Women, Writing and the Public Sphere*, 163–80.

41 Evidence of the discourse of civic humanism in Mary Wollstonecraft's *Vindication of the Rights of Woman* (1792) can be found *passim* in her praise for 'masculine virtue' and her remarks on the effeminacy of professional soldiers and the effects of consumerism. Note also the negative view of commerce in *Letters written during a short residence in Sweden, Norway and Denmark* (1796), and her critique of the capitalist division of labour and the factory system in *An Historical and Moral View of ... the French Revolution* (1794) in *The Works of Mary Wollstonecraft*, eds Janet Todd and Marilyn Butler (London, 1989) VI, 234. See Mary Taylor, *Mary Wollstonecraft and the Feminist Imagination* (Cambridge, 2003) for an excellent survey of her views on commerce; 154–75.

1   Sexual Alchemy in the Coffee-House

1 My account of the early history of the coffee-house is based on Aytoun Ellis, *The Penny Universities: A History of the Coffee-Houses* (London, 1956) 1–9; the quote is from p. 15.
2 William Biddulph's *The Trauels of certaine Englishmen into Africa, Asia &c.*, 1609; cit. Ellis, *Penny Universities*, 8.
3 Full title: *Organum Salutis. An Instrument to cleanse the stomach, as also divers new experiments of tobacco and coffee.*
4 Ellis, *Penny Universities*, 14–15.
5 Richard Kroll 'The Pharmacology of *The Rape of the Lock*', *English Literary History*, 67:1 (Spring 2000) 99–141.
6 Cit. Ellis, *Penny Universities*, 18.
7 Reproduced in Ellis, *Penny Universities*, facing p. 30.
8 Cit. Ellis, *Penny Universities*, 31.
9 See, for instance, the advertisement in the trade newspaper *The Publick Adviser* (1657), reproduced in Ellis, *Penny Universities*, facing p. 62.
10 Ellis, *Penny Universities*, 48–9.
11 For example, *The Character of a Coffee-House* (1665), reproduced in Ellis, *Penny Universities*, 255–63.
12 First stanza of *New from the Coffee House* (1667), reproduced in Ellis, *Penny Universities*, 264–6.
13 See the surveys of political pamphlets in Stephen B. Dobranski, '"Where men of differing judgements croud": Milton and the culture of the coffee houses', *Seventeenth Century*, 9: 1 (Spring 1994) 35–56; Steven Pincus,'"Coffee politicians does create": coffeehouses and Restoration political culture', *The Journal of Modern History*, 67 (December 1995) 807–34. Dobranski has a better grasp of their political nature than Pincus, who refers to them as 'playful' and tends to cite them as straightforward description.
14 Cit. Dobranski, '"Where men of differing judgements croud"', 40; also Pincus, '"Coffee politicians does create"', 814–15.
15 The key passage is: 'As for coffee, tea, and chocolate, I know no good they do; only the places where they are sold are convenient for persons to meet in, sit half the day, and discourse with all companies that come in of State matters, talking of news and broaching of lies, arraigning the judgements and discretion of their governors, censuring all their actions, and insinuating into the ears of the people a prejudice against them; extolling and magnifying their own parts, knowledge and wisdom, and decrying that of their rulers; which if suffered too long, may prove pernicious and destructive ...'; cit. Ellis, *Penny Universities*, 91.

16   Cit. Pincus, 'Coffee Politicians Does Create', 815.
17   Jürgen Habermas, *The Structural Transformation of the Public Sphere: An Inquiry into a Category of Bourgeois Society* (1962), trans. Thomas Burger (London, 1989) 37.
18   Dena Goodman, 'Public sphere and private life: toward a synthesis of current historiographical approaches to the old regime', *History and Theory* 31 (1992) 1–20; Lawrence E. Klein, 'Coffeehouse civility, 1660–1714: an aspect of post-courtly culture in England', *Huntingdon Library Quarterly* 59: 1 (1997) 31–51.
19   Habermas, *Structural Transformation*, 32.
20   Habermas states, 'critical debate ignited by works of literature and art was soon extended to include economic and political disputes, without any guarantee (such as was given in the *salons*) that such discussions would be inconsequential, at least in the immediate context. The fact that only men were admitted to coffee-house society may have had something to do with this, whereas the style of the *salon*, like that of the rococo in general, was essentially shaped by women' (ibid., 33). See Landes, *Women and the Public Sphere* and E.J. Clery, 'Women, publicity and the coffee-house myth', *Women: A Cultural Review*, 2: 2 (1991) 168–77.
21   Dobranski, '"Where men of differing judgements croud"', 37.
22   Ellis, *Penny Universities*, xiv.
23   Leslie Stephen, *English History in the 18th Century* (London, 1903) 47.
24   The following summary is based on Ellis, *Penny Universities*, chapter 9.
25   Issued in answer to an oppositional pamphlet, *The Character of the Coffee House*.
26   Ellis, *Penny Universities*, quotes the pamphlet at length, 56–7.
27   Peter Stallybrass and Allon White, *The Politics and Poetics of Transgression* (London, 1986) 96–7.
28   As both Ellis and Habermas imply; *Penny Universities*, 88; *Structural Transformation of the Public Sphere*, 257 n.11.
29   The full title is *The Mens Answer to the Women's Petition against Coffee: Vindicating Their own Performances, and the Vertues of their Liquor, from the Undeserved Aspersions lately Cast upon them, in their SCANDALOUS PAMPHLET*. See Richard Kroll for an interesting discussion of the exchange in pharmacological context. He suggests they may have been the work of the same author; the second is, however, not so well written or well printed as the first.
30   *Spectator*, No. 155 (Tuesday, 28 August 1711) II, 107. Pincus has proposed that '[t]here is every reason to believe that women frequently attended the newly fashionable coffeehouses' ('"Coffee politicians does create"', 815–16), but all the evidence denies this. The few references he offers to support the claim have been examined and dismissed by Markman Ellis, 'The coffee-women, the *Spectator* and the public sphere in the early eighteenth century', in Eger et al., eds, *Women, Writing and the Public Sphere*, 31 and 47 n.17.
31   See examples of pamphlets and ballads given in Michael S. Kimmel, 'The contemporary "crisis" of masculinity in historical perspective', in *The Making of Masculinities: The New Men's Studies*, ed. Harry Brod (Boston, 1987) 121–53.
32   This slur contradicts Lawrence Klein's suggestion that the Orientalist denigration of coffee 'dropped from view after 1688'; 'Coffeehouse civility', 32 n. See Kroll, 'Pharmacology of *The Rape of the Lock*', for the fullest treatment so far of coffee and exoticism.
33   [Edward Ward] *The Humours of a Coffee-House: A Comedy* (London, 1707) No. 6 (Wednesday, 30 July 1707) 24.
34   Ibid., 27.
35   Pocock, *Virtue, Commerce and History*, 109.
36   To say this is to qualify the idea put forward by Stallybrass and White that the space of the coffee-house was 'de-libidinized'. See Armstrong, *Desire and Domestic*

Fiction for an account of the politicised role of heterosexual desire in narratives of bourgeois ascendancy from Richardson to the Brontës.

37   *Spectator*, II, 107.
38   *Spectator*, I, 313.
39   *Spectator*, No. 87, 9 June 1711, I, 369–72; 371.
40   Horace, *Ars Poetica*, l.451, trans. Roscommon.
41   *Spectator*, IV, 407–8.
42   Tom Brown, 'Amusement VIII', *Amusements Serious and Comical, Calculated for the Meridian of London*, (first published London, 1702), in *The Works of Mr. Thomas Brown*, 4 vols. (1707; 5th edition, London, 1715) III, 71–2; cit. Ellis, 'Coffee-Women', 32.
43   [Edward Ward], *The London-Spy Compleat, in Eighteen Parts*, 2nd edition (London, 1704) Pt II, 25–32; cit. Ellis, 'Coffee-Women', 32. Ward and Brown are the most notable opponents of the coffee-house; it is entirely predictable that the regular targets of their satire are (in no particular order) women, coffee-houses and the Whigs. Both wrote anti-feminist diatribes: Brown, *A Legacy for the Ladies* (1705); Ward, *Female Policy Detected: Or, The Arts of Designing Women Laid Open* (1716).
44   Pocock, *Virtue, Commerce, and History*, 99. See also Ingrassia, *Authorship, Commerce and Gender*.

2   *The Athenian Mercury* and the Pindarick Lady

1   *The Athenian Gazette, or Casuistical Mercury, Resolving all the most Nice and Curious Questions proposed by the Ingenious* first appeared on 17 March 1691 as a weekly, and continued almost without interruption, for the most part twice-weekly on Tuesdays and Saturdays, until 14 June 1697. Briefly in 1692 it appeared three times a week, stimulated by rivalry with Tom Brown's *London Mercury*. There were two brief suspensions: in 1692, by order of the Licenser; and in 1696–97, for business reasons. There was a total of 20 volumes, 580 numbers, with 6,000 questions answered altogether. See Gilbert D. McEwen, *The Oracle of the Coffee House: John Dunton's 'Athenian Mercury'* (San Marino, 1972) 3.
2   He was born in 1659, the son of a clergyman. At 15 he was apprenticed to Presbyterian bookseller, and fulfilled his articles in 1681. The next year he was sufficiently well established with a shop in the Stock Market area of the City of London to marry Elizabeth Annesley, the daughter of Rev. Samuel Annesley; another daughter married Samuel Wesley, later Dunton's associate (and parent of John Wesley). Around the time of the Monmouth Rebellion he spent two years in America and the Netherlands, while his strong-minded wife kept shop. He returned on 15 November 1688, in advance of the arrival of William of Orange and his forces.
3   McEwen, *Oracle*, 4–16.
4   Dunton recruited Richard Sault, Samuel Wesley and a 'Dr. Norris', a physician (probably Dr. Edward Norris, younger brother of Sir Willliam Norris the envoy to India; see n. 20), each with their areas of specialization, to work alongside him as respondents. He drew up a contract offering to pay of ten shillings per issue, and requiring that they engage to write only for the *Athenian Mercury*, and meet every Friday to sift through and distribute the questions.
5   It took the form of a half-folio sheet, printed on both sides in double columns. For eloquent accounts of Dunton's significance as a representative of 'the new', see J. Paul Hunter, 'The Insistent I', *Novel* 13: 1 (Fall 1979) 19–31, and by the

same author, *Before Novels: The Cultural Contexts of Eighteenth-Century English Fiction* (New York and London, 1990) especially 12–18, 99–106.

6 [Charles Gildon] *The History of the Athenian Society, For the Resolving of all Nice and Curious Questions. By a Gentleman, who got Secret Intelligence of their Whole Proceedings. To which are prefixed Several Poems, written by Mr. Tate, Mr. Motteux, Mr. Richardson, and others.* (London, 1692) 15.

7 McEwen, *Oracle*, 46.

8 In No. 4 of the first volume, the questions are posed 'What sort of Government is best?' and 'The strait Line is 6000 foot, and the Hill 6620, *quaere* How many more Pales (each 6 Inches broad) will the Hill require than the strait Line, all set at equal distances?' (Sault was a mathematician, and enjoyed this sort of challenge.) Both are given roughly a paragraph in response, and the mathematical problem dealt with before the other. Sometimes apparently incongruous juxtapositions were suggestive. In the second issue of the first volume the rhetorical question was put, 'What can prompt that Monster of a Man, that calls himself by the name of Protestant, to bring in the French, and restore King James?', prompting the echoing sentiment that God's hand could be seen in William's victory in Ireland and recent safe visit to Holland. Further down the page, appears 'Whether a wife having a sot to her husband, may not (if able) beat him'. The analogy between the divine right of husbands and the divine right of kings was a commonplace of the time, but the revolutionary lesson of 1688 is not extended and the questioner firmly told that authority is vested by God in the male head of the household, however inadequate his character.

9 See McEwen, *Oracle*, 30. There was a temporary shutdown of the *Athenian Mercury* after it strayed into a political minefield over a reply to an apparently innocent question about family ethics, which disguised an attack on the High Church faction; described by McEwen, *Oracle*, 59–66. Even after the lapsing of the Licensing Act in 1695, party politics were generally excluded.

10 In the first number of the later journal, Mr. Spectator announced, 'I never espoused any Party with Violence, and am resolved to observe an exact Neutrality between the Whigs and Tories, unless I shall be forc'd to declare my self by the Hostilities of either side' (I, 5).

11 McEwen, *Oracle*, 17.

12 See Klein, 'Coffeehouse Civility', 46–7; D.W.R. Bahlmann, *The Moral Reformation of 1688* (New Haven, 1957); David Hayton, 'Moral Reform and Country Politics in the Late-Seventeenth-Century House of Commons', *Past and Present*, No. 128 (1990) 48–89; Craig Rose, 'Providence, Protestant Union, and Godly Reformation in the 1690s', *Transactions of the Royal Historical Society*, 6th ser., 3 (1993) 151–69; Tony Claydon, *William III and the Godly Revolution* (Cambridge, 1996).

13 On the tradition of casuistry, 'the resolution of cases of conscience by the application of general rules to particular instances' (OED), see G.A. Starr, *Defoe and Casuistry* (Princeton, 1971); and on Defoe's connection with the *Athenian Mercury*, 12.

14 18 August–17 October 1691.

15 He is still discussing Boccalin and She-Wits in *Athenianism* (1710) 16–17.

16 Cf. the question and answer from a later issue, 'What is Platonick Love?' 'Nothing at all, unless it be Friendship, and of that see a former Answer' – i.e. the answer on male-female friendship quoted here (18: 9).

17 As the present study was being prepared for publication, this previous neglect was remedied by the appearance of Helen Berry's *Gender, Society and Print Culture in Late Stuart Britain: The Cultural World of the Athenian Mercury* (Aldershot and

Burlington, VT, 2003) with its valuable discussion of platonic friendship, 212–25. Berry's volume is a very welcome updating of our picture of the *Athenian Mercury*, with a particular emphasis on the address to women readers, but she dismisses the significance of the involvement of Elizabeth Singer Rowe (55), foregrounded here. Another interesting feminist review is offered in Shawn Lisa Maurer, *Proposing Men: Dialectics of Gender and Class in Eighteenth-Century Periodicals* (Stanford, 1998).

18 See Stephen Orgel and Roy Strong, *Inigo Jones: the Theatre of the Stuart Court*, 2 vols. (London, 1973) I, 55; especially chapter 4, 'Platonic Politics'; and K. Sharpe, *Criticism and Compliment: the Politics of Literature in the England of Charles I* (Cambridge 1987) chapter 5, 'The Caroline Court Masque'.

19 See Jill Kraye, 'The transformation of Platonic love in the Italian Renaissance', in Anna Baldwin and Sarah Hutton, eds, *Platonism and the English Imagination* (Cambridge, 1994) 76–85.

20 See Derek Taylor, 'Clarissa Harlowe, Mary Astell and Elizabeth Carter: John Norris of Bremerton's Female "Descendants"', *Eighteenth-Century Fiction* 12: 1 (October 1999), 19–38; 31 n.28.

21 See Robert Wieder, *Pierre Motteux and les débuts du journalisme en Angleterre au XVIIe siècle: Le Gentleman's Journal (1692–94)* (Paris, 1944).

22 Numbers for April and May 1692.

23 McEwen, *Oracle*, 145–7. This material appears again first in the *Ladies Dictionary* in 1694, and was then published with additions in monthly serial form as the *Night Walker* (1696–97); McEwen, *Oracle*, 213–15; Stephen Parks, *John Dunton and the English Book Trade: A Study of His Career with a Checklist of His Publications* (New York and London, 1976) 317. In his autobiography Dunton confessed that he himself had undertaken the 'Night Rambles' with two young dissenting clergymen, and all had been led into temptation; *The Life and Errors of John Dunton* (London, 1705) 269–77.

24 McEwen, *Oracle*, 34–47.

25 Kathryn Shevelow, *Women and Print Culture: The Construction of Femininity in the Early Periodical* (London and New York, 1989) 74–8.

26 An early example is found in *Spectator* No. 6 (Tuesday, 6 March 1711), where an anecdote contrasting Athenian 'degeneracy' and Lacedemonians 'Virtue' demonstrates 'that the most polite Age is in danger of being the most vicious'.

27 McEwen wrongly identifies Swift and Charles Gildon as the originators of the idea of a learned 'Athenian Society'; *Oracle*, 24. In fact, the idea appears in another question attributed to Elizabeth Singer (V: 1; 17 October 1691) printed months before Swift's Ode: 'Is there ever a Poet among the Athenian Society, and suppose a Question shou'd be sent in Verse, shou'd it be answer'd in the same?' See also Parks, *John Dunton*, 85.

28 McEwen, *Oracle*, 89.

29 For Rowe's biography, see *The Miscellaneous Works in Prose and Verse of Mrs Elizabeth Rowe* (London, 1739) with a memoir by her brother-in-law Theophilus Rowe; and Henry F. Stecher, *Elizabeth Singer Rowe, the Poetess of Frome: A Study of Eighteenth-Century Pietism*, European University Papers vol. 5 (Bern and Frankfurt, 1973).

30 Sarah Prescott provides an extensive discussion of the political and religious affiliations of the poetry Singer published with Dunton in *Women, Authorship and Literary Culture 1690–1740* (Basingstoke, 2003) chapter 5.

31 Both Katherine Phillips and Aphra Behn wrote Pindarick odes.

32 See McEwen, *Oracle*, 103, 104; Parks, *John Dunton*, 104; Bertha-Monica Stearns, 'The first English periodical for women', *Modern Philology*, 28 (1930–31) 45–59.

33 Gertrude E. Noyes, 'John Dunton's *Ladies Dictionary*, 1694', *Philological Quarterly*, 21 (1942) 129–45.
34 The *Athenian Oracle* refers to him as the 'Frome-Spy or Argus', 5, 26, 57.
35 Recounted in *Athenianism* (1710); see Parks, *John Dunton*, 130.
36 See below p. 46.
37 Four poems were printed on 24 December, and another on 28 December. On 21 January three items, two paraphrases of the Bible and an enigmatic exercise in self-reproof, 'The Reflection', were printed.
38 [Elizabeth Singer Rowe]. pseud., Philomela, *Poems on Several Occasions* (London, 1696), vi–vii.
39 *The Song of Songs; Being a Paraphrase Upon the most Excellent Canticles of Solomon. In a Pindarick Poem* (London, 1682), from chapter III, pp. 10–11. The poem continues in the passages parallel to my quotations of Singer:

> CHURCH
> 'Twas dark, the Stars withdrew their light;
> The Sullen Moon obscur'd her head;
> A melancholick, gloomy night;
> The most unhappy relict of a day
> In which the nighted Traveller could stray;
> When over-charg'd with Passions on my Bed,
>   And fraight with fear,
>   I sought my Love, but he was fled;
> I call'd aloud, and knockt, but no one near.
>   Must then (said I) an hapless, poor,
>   Distressed Lover, thus give or'e?
> Are all these breathings spent in vain?
> I'le wander out, and call again;
> Sure he will pity't, since he made the pain.
>   Or else I'le bend my speedy pace
>   Unto that Sacred place
> Whither the Tribes go up to bless
>   The Testament of Holiness.
> How know I what may there be done?
> 'Twas there the *Blessed Virgin* found her *Son*,
>   Perhaps, we once again may meet
>   In some more lucky street,
> Whilst thus he wanders up and down,
> And blesses every corner of the Town;
>   'Tis but to try;
>   Or if withdrawn, I'le trace,
>   His footsteps to some wider place;
>   Or seek him out, if nigh.
>   Ah! so I panting did,
>   But found him not, for he was hid:
> [Hid from the reach of purblind Natures Eye,
> Which takes no Species from the Diety.]
>
> Next to the Wakeful Guardians of the night
> (The Watchmen of the Sacred Tower
> Arm'd with his Sword, and guarded with his power)
>   I took my humble flight;

> Tell me, O can ye tell! said I,
> When he whom I adore pass'd by?
> Can no kind Oracle declare
> How he demeans himself, and where?
> But these were all grown dumb;
> Then sure (thought I) *Messias* must be come.
> Just thus it was; my fanci'd bliss
> Prov'd true; I heard a voice, 'twas his:
> Then straight I caught him in my Arms,
> And held him fast; successful were my Charms;
> Till through the private passages we went,
> And came into my Mothers Tent;
> That Tent in which th'*Almighty* once did give
> That life to her who gave me life to live.

40   On prominent men who read and praised the *Athenian Mercury*, see Parks, *John Dunton*, 89–93.

41   Ruth Perry gives a valuable summary in *The Celebrated Mary Astell: An Early English Feminist* (Chicago and London, 1986), but sees Astell's *Serious Proposal* as the main catalyst.

42   It has been attributed to Mary Astell, but now more often to Judith Drake.

43   Daniel Defoe, *The True-Born Englishman and Other Writings*, eds. P.N. Furbank and W.R. Owens (Harmondsworth, 1997) 225.

44   McEwen, *Oracle*, 226.

45   No. 1 (Tuesday, 12 April 1709), Richard Steele et al., *The Tatler*, ed. D.F. Bond, 3 vols (Oxford, 1987) I, 15. Further references will be given in the main text.

46   Letter XL, 8 February 1712, *Journal to Stella*, ed. Harold Williams, 2 vols. (Oxford, 1948) II, 482.

47   For instance, as an element in the attack on the *Tatler*'s bad faith in the *Female Tatler* (1709–10), a periodical to which Bernard Mandeville, shameless proponent of the monied interest, notably contributed, see M.M. Goldsmith, *Private Vices, Public Benefits: Bernard Mandeville's Social and Political Thought* (Cambridge, 1985) 35–46; and below pp. 63–5.

48   'Richard Steele and the Status of Women', *Studies in Philology* 26 (1929) 325–55.

49   Shevelow, *Women and Print Culture*, 96.

50   On the later career of Elizabeth Rowe, see Prescott, *Women, Authorship and Literary Culture*, chapter 6.

51   McEwen, *Oracle*, 223–7.

52   *Dunton's Recantation; Or, His Reasons for Deserting his Whiggish Principles and Turning Jacobite* (1716) includes complaints of neglect and lack of reward along with a long list of what he would have done for the Whig cause if he had not converted to Jacobitism, but also a promise of a new weekly paper 'Athenian News' to dedicated to 'the Immortal Addison'. *Mr John Dunton's Dying Groans from the Fleet-Prison: or the National Complaint* (1725) continues to bemoan the lack of reward from the miserly Sir Robert Walpole, leading to Dunton's utter ruin. His claims on goodwill of the Whigs are based mainly on the success of the political pamphlet *Neck or Nothing* (he cites praise of it by Swift), but also discovery of Jacobite plots. The *Dying Groans* ends with notice of his legacy in 'Six Hundred *Dying Farewells*', all of them currently 'preparing for the Press', including one entitled 'The Real Pindarick Lady, or a Dying Farewell to that celebrated Poetess Madam *Elizabeth Singer*, Mr Dunton's Correspondent so long as he and

his Athenian Brethren continue to answer to all nice and curious Questions concealing the Querist, which useful Novelty he intitled the Athenian Oracle, and
was himself the first projector and Author of it' (14–15).
53 McEwen, *Oracle*, 237–8.
54 Rawlinson MS, d72/letter 66/fol. 119 Bodleian Library, among John Dunton's
personal papers. John Bowyer Nichols, the nineteenth-century editor of
Dunton's memoirs, speculates that the author is Dr John Woodward on the basis
of the handwriting; *Life and Errors of John Dunton* (London, 1818) xxix–xxx.
Cf. McEwen who attributes it to Isaac Watts, *Oracle*, 107, following Thomas
M. Hatfield, 'The Secret Life of John Dunton', unpublished dissertation, Harvard,
1926, p. 345.
55 Moralizing female writers, like Penelope Aubin, Mary Davys and Elizabeth Rowe
herself, existed in these decades, but they did not figure in the public cultural
debate of the time to anything like the same degree as their more scurrilous
counterparts, and Aubin and Davys made some concessions to the contemporary taste for bawdy.
56 Harrington presided over meetings of the Rota Club at Miles's coffee-house in
New Palace Yard, Westminster, around 1659. John Aubrey wrote an account of
the discussions as 'the most ingeniose, and smart, that I ever heard'; see Ellis,
Penny Universities, 37–41. For an account of the seminal importance of *Oceana*,
see Pocock, *Machiavellian Moment*, especially 383–422.
57 Cit. Peter Murray Hill, *Two Augustan Booksellers: John Dunton and Edmund Curll*
(University of Kansas Publications Library Series No. 3, 1958) 20.
58 *The Miscellaneous Works in Prose and Verse of Mrs Elizabeth Rowe*, 2 vols (London,
1739) I, xvi.
59 See Ellis, 'Coffee-Women', 34–9. And for a fictional equivalent, see Mrs Coupler
in Smollett's *The Adventures of Roderick Random* (1748), ed. Paul-Gabriel Boucé
(Oxford, 1979) 132–3.
60 Ellis, *Penny-Universities*, 223–39.
61 See Elizabeth Kowaleski-Wallace, *Consuming Subjects: Women, Shopping and
Business in the Eighteenth Century* (New York, 1997) 19–36, on the tea-table as a
site of discipline for the female subject, and for the suggestion that this consti-
tutes part of a relatively undefined 'feminizing process' (29).
62 Cit. Jon Klancher, *The Making of English Reading Audiences 1790–1832* (Madison,
1987) 24.
63 For the category of 'polite Whigs', see Pocock, *Virtue, Commerce, and History*,
236–8; also Klein, *Shaftesbury and the Culture of Politeness, passim*.

3   The South Sea Bubble and the Resurgence of Misogyny

1 Ronald Paulson, *Hogarth*, 3 vols (New Brunswick and London, 1991) I, 68.
2 Ibid., I, 67.
3 The best known of these is Bernard Picart's *Monument Dedicated to Posterity in
Commemoration of ye Incredible Folly Transacted in the Year 1720* (1720), which
Paulson sees as a model for Hogarth, *Hogarth*, I, 68; see also Ingrassia, *Authorship,
Commerce and Gender*, 26–7. See Pocock, *Machiavellian Moment*, on the gendered
opposition of virtue and fortune: 'This opposition was frequently expressed [in the
classical tradition] in the image of a sexual relation: a masculine intelligence was
seeking to dominate a feminine passive unpredictability which would submis-
sively reward him for his strength or vindictively betray him for his weakness'; 37.

4   On the link between the stock market and the marriage market at the time of the Bubble, see Shirlene Mason, *Daniel Defoe and the Status of Women* (St. Alban's, Vermont and Montreal, 1978) 87–8.

5   *A Parallel Between the Roman and British Constitution; Comprehending Polibius's Curious Discourse of the Roman Senate* (London, 1747) 43.

6   Pocock, *Virtue, Commerce, and History*, 113.

7   I have myself previously characterized the South Sea Bubble as an irrational proto-'Gothic' phenomenon in *Rise of Supernatural Fiction*, 7–8; see also Sandra Sherman, 'Credit, simulation, and the ideology of contract in the early eighteenth century', *Eighteenth-Century Life* 19 (1995) 86–102; and Ingrassia, *Authorship, Commerce, and Gender*, 5–6.

8   Pocock, *Virtue, Commerce, and History*, 112: 'Specialised, acquisitive and post-civic man ... does not even live in the present, except as constituted by his fantasies concerning the future.' Cf. Ingrassia, *Authorship, Commerce, and Gender*, 18.

9   P.G.M. Dickson, *The Financial Revolution in England. A Study in the Development of Public Credit 1688–1756* (London and New York, 1967) 154. Cf. Larry Neal, who characterizes the Mississippi and South Sea Bubbles as 'rational' using a formula to determine probability, i.e. rational expectation, in *The Rise of Financial Capitalism: International Capital Markets in the Age of Reason* (Cambridge, 1990) 80–8.

10   John Carswell, *The South Sea Bubble* (London, 1960) 136–7.

11   Dickson, *Financial Revolution*, 156.

12   Ronald Paulson, *Hogarth*, 66–7.

13   Carswell, *South Sea Bubble*, 10–11; Ingrassia, *Authorship, Commerce, and Gender*, 30–1. Cf. Perry, *Celebrated Mary Astell*, 305–11 for a notable case history.

14   Virginia Cowles, in a popular account of the Bubble, is unique among historians in emphasizing backstairs female intervention of the most time-honoured kind. The Duchess of Kendal, and another royal favourite, Baroness von Kiemansegge, were each bribed £10,000 for facilitating the passing of the South Sea Bill (whereby Parliament gave approval for the conversion of the national debt) and permission to appoint the King as Governor of the South Sea Company. *The Great Swindle: The Story of the South Sea Bubble* (London, 1960) esp. pp. 41–53, 95–6, 161–4, 174. It is interesting to note that where Cowles, and some contemporary commentators, saw these female courtiers as key players in the affair, they are entirely absent from the 'serious' treatments of Carswell and Dickson.

15   On the innovative or transformative nature of the Bubble and women's agency, see Ingrassia, *Authorship, Commerce, and Gender*, 19–20, 30, 32–8. Ingrassia somewhat ambiguously stresses that female speculators enjoyed new possibilities of participation in public finance and economic autonomy, while she relies for evidence of their cultural centrality on misogynist satires, but she goes on to acknowledge the convergence of unprecedented economic crisis with venerable misogynist strategies of representation, 25–7. For a contemporary view of women's novel participation in speculation, see Anne Finch's 'A Song on the South Sea, 1720'.

16   Nussbaum, *'The Brink of All We Hate'*, 20.

17   Cit. Cowles, *The Great Swindle*, 174; see Ingrassia, *Authorship, Commerce, and Gender*, 26–7, 36–7, for other texts associating the Bubble with prostitution.

18   'Philalethes Britannicus', *A Memorial of the Present State of the British Nation* (London, 1722) 70.

19   Pocock, *Machiavellian Moment*, 465.

20   See Introduction, pp. 10–11.

21 John Dennis, *Vice and Luxury Public Mischiefs: Or, Remarks on the Book Intituled the Fable of the Bees* ... (London, 1724), in J. Martin Stafford, ed., *Private Vices, Publick Benefits? The Contemporary Reception of Bernard Mandeville* (Solihull, 1997) 195.

22 *Machiavellian Moment*, 470.

23 From September 1722 the letters moved to the *British Journal*, due to a change in the *London Journal*'s political loyalties. See Donaldson, *Rapes of Lucretia*, 150–66, for a brief but useful survey of eighteenth-century representations of Cato.

24 For an interesting reading of Addison's *Cato* and remarks on its relation to *Cato's Letters* see Julie Ellison, 'Cato's Tears' in *ELH* 63 (1996) 571–601; republished in Ellison's *Cato's Tears and the Making of Anglo-American Emotion* (Chicago, 1999). For a survey of the importance of 'the Catonic perspective' in English politics of the early eighteenth century, see Reed Browning, *Political and Constitutional Ideas of the Court Whigs* (Baton Rouge and London, 1982) 1–34.

25 John Trenchard and Thomas Gordon, *Cato's Letters, or Essays on Liberty, Civil and Religious, and Other Important Subjects*, ed. Ronald Hamowy, 2 vols. (Indianapolis, 1995) I, 25.

26 *Cato's Letters*, I, 188–94; No. 26, 22 April 1721. Cf. Trenchard's pamphlet *Some Considerations upon the State of our Public Debts in General and of the Civil List in Particular* (London, 1720) 31, cited in Kramnick, *Bolingbroke*, 165.

27 *Cato's Letters*, I, 442–3, No. 64, 3 February 1721. In this passage I have retained the capitalization and spelling of the original. Ideological ambivalence is sustained in this essay: Cato sees the strength of Britain's naval power as dependent on trade, positing a seamless accord of private and public interest; at the same time the merchant navy is envisaged in traditional terms as a patriot militia, with the superiority over a standing army that is a central tenet of civic humanist thought.

28 Pocock, *Machiavellian Moment*, 471.

29 Ronald Hamowy levels this accusation in 'Cato's Letters, John Locke, and the Republican Paradigm', *History of Political Thought* XI: 2 (1990) 272–94; 278 n.21. Hamowy's critique of Kramnick and Pocock includes many quotations that demonstrate Cato's debt to the ideas of natural law and natural rights, but fails to convince overall by neglecting passages used by his opponents.

30 Shelley Burtt, *Virtue Transformed: Political Argument in England 1688–1740* (Cambridge, 1992) 36.

31 *Cato's Letters*, I, 432: No. 62, 20 January 1721.

32 *Some Fables after the Easie and Familiar Manner of Monsieur La Fontaine* (1703) and *AEsop Dress'd or a Collection of Fables Writ in Familiar Verse* (1704).

33 Bernard Mandeville, *The Fable of the Bees: or, Private Vices, Public Benefits*, ed. F.B. Kaye (1924; rpt. Indianapolis, 1988) I, 384, 385; citations hereafter given in the main text. *British Journal* No. 39 (on charity schools) was presented on 3 July; *British Journal* Nos. 26, 35, 36 and 39 and *Fable of the Bees* were presented on 8 July. See W.A. Speck, 'Bernard Mandeville and the Middlesex Grand Jury', *Eighteenth-Century Studies*, XI (1977–78) 362–74. The text of the 'Presentment of the Middlesex Grand Jury' was published in the *Evening Post*, 11 July 1723.

34 The letter was first published in the *London Journal* (now a bastion of government propaganda) on 27 July 1723. Mandeville's response was published in the *London Journal*, August 10, 1723. While the attacks coincided with the disappearance of Cato (John Trenchard died in December 1723), they served to generate the Mandeville phenomenon.

35 On the political contexts of the 1705 and 1714 texts, see Kramnick, *Bolingbroke*, 201–3.

36   Reed Browning traces the initial confusion of the government response to *Cato's Letters* through to the evolution of a more concerted 'Ciceronian' counter-argument, *Court Whigs*, 210–30. On Mandeville's contribution to Court Whig political economy, see Kramnick, *Bolingbroke*, 201–4; and J.A.W. Gunn, *Beyond Liberty and Property: The Process of Self-Recognition in Eighteenth-Century Political Thought* (Kingston and Montreal, 1983) 96–119. On his position as a maverick Whig, see H.T. Dickenson, 'The politics of Bernard Mandeville', in *Mandeville Studies: New Explorations of the Art and Thought of Dr Bernard Mandeville*, ed. Irwin Primer (The Hague, 1975) 80–97; and M.M. Goldsmith, *Private Vices, Public Benefits: Bernard Mandeville's Social and Political Thought* (Cambridge, 1985) 104–7.

37   On Mandeville's combative relationship with the Societies see W.A. Speck, 'Mandeville and the eutopia seated in the brain', in Primer, ed., *Mandeville Studies*, 66–79, and Goldsmith, *Private Vices, Public Benefits*, 21–5.

38   The new *Fable of the Bees*, with its essay on charity schools, was announced as 'just published' in the *Daily Post* for 10 April. A letter from Cato (Trenchard) on charity schools appeared in the *British Journal* for 15 June 1723. The 'Presentment' and the tirade from 'Philo-Britannus' were printed in July. Charity schools were, on the face of it, a curious target for Mandeville and Cato, both in their ways advocates of trade. But their visions of improvement stopped short at improvement of the lot of the workforce. Mandeville with typical bluntness argued that over-educating the lower orders would make them discontented and deprive the national economy of the necessary cheap labour. Cato concurred on the matter of raising false expectations and added less persuasively that charity schools deprived other charities, spread Jacobitism (most were run by dissenters or the Low Church element), and risked the livelihood of shopkeepers' children by raising up the children of labourers. What is even more puzzling is the ardent support for charity schools among their opponents. W.A. Speck's careful exploration of the composition and workings of the Middlesex Grand Jury only uncovers the shadowy motives and shifting allegiances of groupings to which we attempt to pin the labels, 'Court Whig', 'Country Whig' and 'Tory'. His claim that the condemnations were pragmatically motivated by the Tory jurymen's need to show support for the government and keep their distance seems tenuous and fails to address ideological questions, 'Bernard Mandeville and the Middlesex Grand Jury', 361–8. Speck unconvincingly suggests that Societies for the Reformation of Manners and the Country party were united; 'Bernard Mandeville and the Middlesex Grand Jury', 372–3. E.J. Hundert, who disregards the anomalous pairing of Cato and Mandeville and the Grand Jury's religious quarrel, has asserted that their opposition to Mandeville is Old Whig or civic humanist; *The Enlightenment's Fable: Bernard Mandeville and the Discovery of Society* (Cambridge, 1994) 8–10. More likely is the possibility that the detractors were disturbed by Mandeville's systematic disruption of established pieties, with charity schools co-opted among them.

39   See Kaye's Introduction to the *Fable*, Thomas A. Horne, *The Social Thought of Bernard Mandeville: Virtue and Commerce in Early Eighteenth-Century England* (New York and London, 1978) 19–31; and E.D. James, 'Faith, sincerity and morality: Mandeville and Bayle', in Irwin Primer, ed., *Mandeville Studies*, 43–65. James and Horne discuss his related debts to Jansenist fideism, involving opposition to Stoic philosophy and the ideal of rational control.

40   In addition to Kaye's Introduction, see the useful discussion, 'Verbal Disputes', by Stafford in the Introduction to *Private Vices, Public Benefits?*, xiii–xvi and Horne, *Social Thought*, 19–31.

41 Notably John Dennis in his classical republican diatribe *Vice and Luxury Public Mischiefs* (1724) reprinted in Stafford, ed., *Private Vices, Public Benefits?*
42 See Kaye's more limited account of paradox as a dispensable result of rigoristic premise, i.e. once more liberal definitions of vice and virtue are employed, the paradox dissolves; *FB*, I, cxxx. 'An Enquiry, Whether a General Practice of Virtue tends to the Wealth or Poverty of a People' (London, 1725) attributed to George Bluet, was the most determined attempt prior to Hume's 'Essay on Luxury' to reintroduce the division between virtuous prosperity and vicious luxury in reply to Mandeville; reprinted in Stafford, ed., *Private Vices, Public Benefits?*
43 Cf. *FB*, II, 147: 'Luxury and Politeness ever grew up together, and were never enjoy'd asunder'.
44 No. 1 (Friday, 8 July 1709) is reprinted in Fidelis Morgan, ed., *Female Tatler* (London, 1992) 1.
45 Richard Steele, et al., *The Tatler*, ed. D.F. Bond, 3 vols. (Oxford, 1987), I, 15.
46 See chapter 2, p. 44.
47 See Goldsmith, *Private Vices, Public Benefits*, 78 and 35–46, and his Introduction to Bernard Mandeville, *By a Society of Ladies: Essays in the 'Female Tatler'*, ed. M.M. Goldsmith (Bristol, 1999). See also Horne, *Social Thought*, 9–13.
48 Mandeville, *Female Tatler*, No. 52 (Friday, 4 November 1709) in *By a Society of Ladies*, 77; future references in the text.
49 See *Tatler*, Nos. 25, 26, 28, 29, 31, 38 and 39.
50 Cf. further reflections on the need to instil fear with the threat of violence in order to maintain social hierarchy and politeness in *FT*, No. 94; *FB*, I, 219–20; II, 101–2, 267–70.
51 My use of the terms 'feminist' and 'antifeminist' and 'misogynist' and 'anti-misogynist' relates to broadly distinguishable modes of discourse. When using 'feminist' and 'antifeminist' I refer to intellectual arguments for or against the improved social status of women, whereas 'misogynist' representations are in general purely abusive attacks on the nature of woman, and 'anti-misogynist' responses are protests against such representations. There is, however, often overlap in a given text. Indeed, in the present chapter my case is that feminist rhetoric is deployed in the interests of a misogynist agenda, designed to demonstrate the vicious passions manifested by a woman who is left to her own devices. On the question of whether the use of 'feminist' is anachronistic in this period, while acknowledging that the modern feminist tradition begins with Mary Wollstonecraft, I follow Ruth Perry and others in choosing to apply the term 'feminist' to earlier proponents of the improvement of woman's condition; Perry, *Mary Astell*, 17–18.
52 Cf. *FT*, No. 92, 191, which again acknowledges the neglect of learned women but does little to remedy it.
53 The critique of Alexander was a touchstone of Ancients vs. Moderns debate, and often appears in conjunction with progressivist sentiments. See, for instance, *FT*, No. 70, 123–5; and Samuel Richardson, *The History of Sir Charles Grandison*, ed. Jocelyn Harris, 3 vols (London, 1972) III, 197. Pope, by contrast, includes him in *The House of Fame* (c. 1710), though at a lower level than selfless patriots.
54 A translation of *La Gallerie des femmes fortes* (1647).
55 Cf. Bernard Mandeville, *The Virgin Unmask'd: or, Female Dialogues Betwixt an Elderly Maiden Lady and her Niece, On several Diverting Discourses on Love, Marriage, Manners and Morals & C. Of the Times* (2nd edition, London, 1724) 115; and Daniel Defoe, *Roxana*, ed. David Blewett (Harmondsworth, 1982) 288. See also Defoe's chapter 'Of the Tradesman Letting His Wife be Acquainted with His Business', in *The Complete English Tradesman* (1726) (1839; Gloucester, 1987).

56   Mandeville, *The Virgin Unmask'd*, 9; future references in the text. Richard I. Cook has pointed out that Mandeville, like Antonia, defends revealing fashions when they are 'the Custom of the Country' in *Fable of the Bees*, 'Remark C'; *Bernard Mandeville* (New York, 1974) 57.

57   I am largely in agreement with Cook's judgement: 'In a rhetorical tactic analogous to that so often used by his contemporary, Jonathan Swift, Mandeville employs his fictional creation to argue persuasively, logically, and even compellingly on behalf of what is ultimately a crankish absurdity – the renunciation by women not only of their subordinate status, but of marriage and sex itself'; *Bernard Mandeville*, 58; though some of Lucinda's ideas coincide with those Mandeville expressed in other works.

58   Laura Mandell, *Misogynous Economies: The Business of Literature in Eighteenth-Century Britain* (Lexington, 1999) 64–83.

59   *Roxana*, ed. Blewett, 187; future references in the text.

60   On the linking of the dress with slavery, see *Roxana*, 214–15, and Ros Ballaster's valuable discussion, 'Performing *Roxane*: the Oriental woman as the sign of luxury in eighteenth-century fictions', in Berg and Eger, eds, *Luxury in the Eighteenth Century*, 165–77.

61   In the latter case, although Roxana refuses the '*Golden Chain*' of a legally binding financial settlement, she nevertheless grants Lord L— a monopoly of her body and private access to her house at all hours, 225.

62   Bram Dijkstra, *Defoe and Economics: The Fortunes of 'Roxana' in the History of Interpretation* (Basingstoke, 1987).

63   Laura Brown, *Ends of Empire: Women and Ideology in Early Eighteenth-Century English Literature* (Ithaca, 1993) 154.

64   Brown, *Ends of Empire*, 157.

65   See p. 276 for Roxana's flippant remark when she decides to wed the merchant, 'I had left off talking my Platonicks, and of my Independency, and being a *Free Woman, as before*'.

66   David Blewett notes that he is attacked directly in *The Reformation of Manners* (1702) and obliquely in *A Journal of the Plague Year* (1722; Penguin, 1966), *Roxana*, 392–3 n; see also 204, 223.

67   Paula Backscheider, *Daniel Defoe: Ambition and Innovation* (Lexington, 1986) 213–14.

68   Cf. *FB*, II, 123–4.

69   There has been some disagreement over attribution of the *Modest Defence*, but it is generally accepted as the work of Mandeville. *A Modest Defence of Publick Stews*, Augustan Reprint Society No. 162 (1724; reprint Los Angeles: Clark Memorial Library) 41. Note alternatively Part II of the *Fable*, where the distinctive and more refined 'workmanship' of women, inner and outer, is discussed, 172–3.

70   See Mason, *Defoe and the Status of Women*, 79–102, especially 79, 93, 95–6.

71   Cf. the disparagement of 'anything that's *Neutrius Generis*' in *FT*, No. 74 (26 December 1709) 132.

72   See Goldsmith's discussion of this tale, 'Mandeville and the spirit of capitalism', *Journal of British Studies* 17: 1 (Fall, 1977) 63–81.

73   On the implications of this figure in relation to Mandeville's support for capitalism, see Nathan Rosenberg, 'Mandeville and laissez-faire', *Journal of the History of Ideas* 24 (1963) 183–96 and Horne, *Social Thought*, 51–75, arguing for the relevance of mercantilism.

74   This transition is discussed as an inconsistency in Mandeville's argument by J. Martin Stafford, *Private Vices, Public Benefits?*, xvi–xvii. While Kaye and

Goldsmith also remark on the divergence they try to assimilate the idea of the manipulative legislator to the evolutionary theory by identifying the former as a metaphor. The two parts were reissued together in 1734.

4 Elizabeth Carter in Pope's Garden: Literary Women of the 1730s

1 Cit. Isobel Grundy, *Lady Mary Wortley Montagu* (Oxford, 1999) 273.
2 Cit. Montagu Pennington, *Memoirs of the Life of Mrs. Elizabeth Carter, with A New Edition of her Poems; To Which are added, Some Miscellaneous Essays in Prose* (London, 1807) 29. Ironically, Oxendon himself had a scurrilous reputation and was rumoured to have illegitimately fathered Walpole's grandson, the third Earl of Orford; see *DNB* and Grundy, *Montagu*, 243, 319.
3 Hampshire, 221; cit. Myers, *BC*, 48.
4 The first literary version of the fairy-tale 'Beauty and the Beast', by Gabrielle de Villeneuve, was published in 1740; the better-known version by Jeanne-Marie LePrince de Beaumont, in 1757.
5 All four of the poems appear in *GM* 8 (August 1738) 429. James M. Kuist, *The Nichols File of 'The Gentleman's Magazine': Attributions of Authorship and Other Documentations in Editorial Papers at the Folger Library* (Madison, Wisconsin, 1982) throws no light on the identity of 'Alexis', or of 'Sylvius' mentioned below, pp. 85–6.
6 Maynard Mack, *Alexander Pope: A Life* (New Haven and London, 1985) 652 and 914 n.
7 On the continuity of imagery and enduring relevance of the South Sea Bubble in the early 1730s, particularly in connection with the crisis over Walpole's Excise Bill in 1733–34, see Vincent Carretta, 'Pope's *Epistle to Bathurst* and The South Sea Bubble', *Journal of English and Germanic Philology* 77 (1978) 212–31; and Colin Nicholson, *Writing and the Rise of Finance: Capital Satires of the Early Eighteenth Century* (Cambridge, 1994) 141–57.
8 See Robert Halsband, *The Life of Lady Mary Wortley Montagu* (Oxford, 1956) 101–4; Grundy, *Montagu*, 204–7; Mack, *Pope*, 388.
9 Myers, *Bluestocking Circle*, 61.
10 For an indication of the resonance of such a scenario in the imagination of the period, see the apocryphal *Life of Pamela* (1741 or 1742) written in the third person by a hack intent on capitalizing on Richardson's success, which gives the date of Pamela's marriage as 1726 and states that her parents lost their fortune in the South Sea Bubble; T.C. Duncan Eaves, and Ben D. Kimpel, *Samuel Richardson: A Biography* (Oxford, 1971) 140.
11 Montagu Pennington, *Memoirs*, 6.
12 Myers, *Bluestocking Circle*, 47.
13 The clergymen of Kent were a notable class of contributor. See Anthony D. Barker, 'Poetry from the provinces: amateur poets in the *Gentleman's Magazine* in the 1730s and 1740s', in Alvaro Ribeiro and James G. Basker, eds, *Tradition in Transition: Women Writers, Marginal Texts, and the Canon* (Oxford, 1996) 241–56; 251.
14 W.B. Todd gives the sales figures as 9,000 copies per month in 1734 rising to 15,000 in 1744; 'A bibliographical account of *The Gentleman's Magazine*, 1731–1754', *Studies in Bibliography* 18 (1965) 85.
15 Halsband, *Montagu*, 180.

16 See Myers, *Bluestocking Circle*, 52–4.
17 Art XXXI, June 1739, 392; cit. Myers, *Bluestocking Circle*, 53.
18 Letter 27 August 1738; cit. Edward Ruhe, 'Birch, Johnson, and Elizabeth Carter: an episode of 1738–39', *PMLA* 73 (1958) 491–500; 494.
19 See Ruhe, 'Birch, Johnson, and Elizabeth Carter', and Myers, *BC*, 54–9, 105–8.
20 Letter dated 21 September 1738, Hampshire Collection; cit. Myers, *BC*, 105.
21 6 March 1749 (MS private collection, Gwen Hampshire); cit. Myers, *BC*, 110.
22 Myers, *BC*, 47.
23 Nussbaum, *'Brink of All We Hate'*, 20.
24 See Nussbaum, *'Brink of All We Hate'*, 20.
25 Finch's poem was published in *Pope's Own Miscellany* (1717). Williams cites the poem and refers indirectly to Pope's apparent comparison of his own refusal, as a Catholic, to swear an oath of allegiance to the House of Hanover with the Lacedaemonians' refusal 'to do shameful and dishonest things' under the command of their conqueror Antipater, *Pope, Homer and Manliness*, 52. See also Mack, *Pope*, 285–6.
26 Isaac Kramnick has suggested that the influence of the journal was at its height in 1732–33, when by swaying both gentry and City opinion it was instrumental in the dramatic defeat of the Excise Bill; *Bolingbroke and His Circle*, 24.
27 Myra Reynolds supports this on the basis of two contemporary sources, *The Poems of Anne Countess of Winchelsea* (Chicago, 1903) lxiii–lxiv. It has been strongly disputed by Barbara McGovern who maintains that relations between Swift, Pope and Finch were unwaveringly amicable; *Anne Finch and Her Poetry: A Critical Biography* (Athens and London, 1992) 102–7. It was earlier questioned by George Sherburn, 'The Fortunes and Misfortunes of *Three Hours After Marriage*', *Modern Philology* 25 (1926–7) 91–109.
28 John Gay, *Dramatic Works*, ed. John Fuller, 2 vols. (Oxford, 1983) I, 438.
29 See, for instance, *The Female Wits* (1697) and Colley Cibber's *The Refusal* (1721) for the destruction of manuscripts, and Centlivre's *The Basset-Table* (1705) for the smashing of a laboratory. In Charles Johnson's *The Generous Husband: or, The Coffee House Politician* (London, 1713), the successful suitor tries to extract from the female philosopher the promise to 'burn your Books' (48).
30 Cit. Rhoda Zuk, in *BF*, III, 6. Myers references the same letter more fully in *BC*, 213: from the Bedfordshire County Record Office, Lucas Papers, 11 June [1745], L 31/106. Some of Talbot's early poetry had circulated in manuscript while she was living in Bath. In 1741 in the *Gentleman's Magazine* a poem had appeared 'On Miss Talbot's conversing with a Lawyer at Bath', which embarrassingly compared the wisdom of this 'accomplish'd fair' to that of her uncle, the Lord Chancellor. See *BC*, 63.
31 Cf. Carolyn D. Williams, 'Poetry, pudding and Epictetus: the consistency of Elizabeth Carter', in Ribeiro and Basker, eds, *Tradition in Transition*, 3–24. Williams has interestingly dwelt on the opposition as a conflict between mind and quotidian cares in Carter's life and writings, but does not pursue the reference to conventional satire of the learned lady.
32 Montagu Pennington, ed., *A Series of Letters between Mrs. Elizabeth Carter and Miss Catherine Talbot*, 2 vols. (London, 1809), 15 September 1747, I, 218–19; and James Boswell, *Life of Johnson*, ed. George Birkbeck Hill, rev. edition L.F. Powell, 6 vols. (Oxford, 1934) I, 123 n.
33 MO 1000, [?1737], cit. *BC*, 41.
34 Richardson, *Sir Charles Grandison*, I, 215, 179–80, cf. I, 102.
35 Eliza Haywood, Elizabeth Thomas, Susannah Centlivre and Aphra Behn.

36 Ingrassia, *Authorship, Commerce, and Gender*, 49.
37 II, 161–6. Pope comments at greater length on Dacier's response to this passage of Homer in his own translation of *The Iliad*, noting her complaint that 'the Value of Women is not rais'd even in our Days' and ironically attributing the fault to 'a want of Taste in both Ancients and Moderns'; see Williams, *Pope, Homer, and Manliness*, 147–53 and Ingrassia, *Authorship, Commerce, and Gender*, 61.
38 For more on Pope's quarrel with Dacier, see Williams, *Pope, Homer, and Manliness*; and Brean S. Hammond, *Pope and Bolingbroke: A Study of Friendship and Influence* (Columbia, 1984) 33–7.
39 See J.V. Guerinot, *Pamphlet Attacks on Alexander Pope 1711–1744: A Descriptive Bibliography* (London, 1969) 114–16.
40 Bertrand A. Goldgar, *Walpole and the Wits: the Relation of Politics and Literature, 1722–1742* (Lincoln and London, 1976) 127. The Earl of Peterborough had first publicly alluded to her under the name of 'Sappho' ten years earlier, in his poem 'I said to my heart'; see Valerie Rumbold, *Women's Place in Pope's World* (Cambridge, 1989) 158. Cf. Grundy, *Montagu*, 270, for other early references.
41 For a useful chart of Pope's allusions to Montagu, see Rumbold, *Women's Place*, 156–8.
42 *The Correspondence of Alexander Pope*, ed. George Sherburn, 5 vols. (Oxford, 1956) III, 352; cit. Rumbold, *Women's Place*, 158.
43 Richardson, *Grandison*, I, 431.
44 Haywood authored *Memoirs of a Certain Island Adjacent to the Kingdom of Utopia* (1724) libelling Pope's friend Martha Blount and interestingly associating her sexual corruption with the economic corruption of the South Sea Bubble. See Guerinot on attribution of two other pamphlets to Haywood, and to Edmund Curll and Elizabeth Thomas jointly, a fantastical and libellous 'biography' of Pope; *Pamphlet Attacks*, 90–1, 99, 153–6, 217–20.
45 See Grundy, *Montagu*, 338–9.
46 Lady Mary Wortley Montagu, *Essays and Poems and 'Simplicity, A Comedy'*, ed. Robert Halsband and Isobel Grundy (1977; Oxford, 1993) 270, ll. 110–12.
47 Mack, *Pope*, 559.
48 Grundy, *Montagu*, 340. Grundy records James McLaverty's speculation that Pope obtained the *Verses Address'd* in manuscript and published them himself, in order to expose Montagu to publicity.
49 *GM* 3 (April, 1733) 206.
50 I am grateful to Carolyn D. Williams for pointing out the significance of *Peri Bathous*.
51 Alexander Pope, *The Twickenham Edition of the Poems of Alexander Pope*, ed. John Butt et al., 11 vols (London, 1939–69) I, 6.
52 Lawrence Lipking, *Samuel Johnson: The Life of an Author* (Cambridge, Mass. and London, 1998) 54.
53 Bedfordshire County Record Office, Lucas papers, BCRO (L31/106), cit. *BF*, 6.
54 Moira Ferguson, ed., *First Feminists: British Women Writers, 1578–1799* (Bloomington, 1985) 19. Myers cites research showing the rapid obsolescence of the work of Egerton and Astell, *BC*, 122.
55 The writer was John Duick; for identification of pen names, see Albert Pailler, *Edward Cave et le 'Gentleman's Magazine'* (Lille, 1975).
56 Jean E. Hunter, 'The eighteenth-century Englishwoman: according to the *Gentleman's Magazine*', in Paul Fritz and Richard Morton, eds, *Woman in*

the Eighteenth Century and Other Essays (Toronto and Sarasota, 1976) 73–88; Barker, 'Poetry from the Provinces', 253; *BC*, 124–5.

57 Pennington, ed., *Series*, I, 382–3 (5 March 1755).

58 *GM* 5 (September 1735) 553.

59 On gender hybridization, see chapter 3, p. 57. For more on *Epistle to a Lady* and Richardson's response to it, see chapter 5, pp. 105–7. On the ambiguous idealization of Martha Blount, see Nussbaum, *'Brink of All We Hate'*, 154–8.

60 Mary Douglas, *Purity and Danger: An Analysis of the Concepts of Pullution and Taboo* (London, 1984) 35.

61 See Claudia N. Thomas, *Alexander Pope and His Women Readers* (Carbondale and Edwardsville, 1994); and Rumbold, *Woman's Place in Pope's World*, 264–5.

62 Ironically, Rowe had meekly accepted Pope's 'Characters of Women' as 'more mild than I expected; and if well us'd, may reform the sex', *Miscellaneous Works*, II, 240; cit. Thomas, *Alexander Pope*, 93.

63 For instance, 'On the Loss of my eminent and pious Friend Mrs. Rowe', *GM* 8 (April 1738) 210; and 'On the present publication of Mrs. Rowe's Poems after her death', *GM* 9 (March 1739) 152.

64 The first four lines as published in *GM* 9 (March 1739) 152 and in the second edition to Rowe's *Miscellaneous Works* (1749) are a version of the elegiac address to Rowe found in the earlier poem. But the importance to Carter of the lines I have cited is shown by her decision, in *Poems on Several Occasions* (1762), to omit this more conventional starting point and open with the counterattack on the enemies of women's writing.

65 For more on the choice of Elizabeth Rowe as a role model by Carter and Talbot, see Myers, *BC*, 48–9, 59, 153–4. She suggests that Rowe was 'probably too intense and other-worldly a religious poet to be entirely suitable for them' (154). But see also Sarah Prescott's excellent account of Rowe's post-*Athenian* writing career, which indicates many ways in which her discreet example would have appealed to the early Bluestockings, from her staunch provincialism to the adept use of aristocratic connections; *Women, Authorship and Literary Culture*, chapter 6.

66 Claudia Thomas, '"Th' instructive moral, and important thought": Pope, Johnson, and Epictetus', *The Age of Johnson* 4 (1991); 137–69; 151.

67 Montagu, *Essays and Poems*, 279–84.

68 Thomas, '"Th' instructive moral"', 151, 149, 152.

69 Mack, *Pope*, 388.

70 The poem has been read as an anti-capitalist intervention in Nicholson, *Writing and the Rise of Finance*, 167–72. Laura Brown has described its philosophy as hanging 'between a capitalist ethic and traditional Christian morality'; *Alexander Pope* (Oxford, 1985) 79–93. My reading is more in line with those of Douglas White, *Pope and the Context of Controversy: The Manipulation of Ideas in 'An Essay on Man'* (Chicago and London, 1970); and Rebecca Ferguson, *The Unbalanced Mind: Pope and the Rule of Passion* (Brighton, 1986). White in particular draws attention to the borrowings from Mandeville. Louis I. Bredvold refers to the *Essay*'s 'uncommon optimism' when compared with the accustomed Patriot emphasis on decline in 'The gloom of the Tory satirists', in James L. Clifford and Louis A. Landa, eds, *Pope and His Contemporaries* (Oxford, 1949) 1–19; 3.

71 On Pope's 'expertise as a market-analyst' during and after the Bubble see Nicholson, *Writing and the Rise of Finance*, 54, 63–8.

72 Warburton justified these heterogeneous borrowings as a determination to 'reject the Extravagances of every System, and take only what is rational and real'; he asserts that Pope has taken from Shaftesbury the principle that 'Virtue would be worth having tho' itself was its only Reward' and from Mandeville the tenet that 'God makes Evil, against its Nature, productive of Good'; *A Critical and Philosophical Commentary on Mr Pope's 'Essay on Man'* (London, 1742) 18.

73 Cf. Mandeville's opposition to the Stoic ethic of self-sufficiency as 'a pretence to a Chimera, and a Romantick Notion'; *Female Tatler* 109 (24 March 1710) 235.

74 See John Barrell and Harriet Guest, 'The uses of contradiction: Pope's "Epistle to Bathurst"', in J. Barrell, *Poetry, Language and Politics* (Manchester, 1988) 79–99.

75 As illustration of the latter, see *The Nonsense of Commonsense*, No. 2 (Tuesday, 27 December 1737), which combines support for the government's policy of lowering interest rates with sentiments designed to outflank the Opposition' 'What a great Advantage then will [ladies] bring to their Country by the suppression of Luxury when the plainest Dress will be thought the Genteelest!' and 'We have too long mistaken Paper for Money', Montagu, *Essays and Poems*, 112 and 113. A similar tactic is used in No, 8 with its re-examination of the term 'Liberty' and No. 9 with its further dismissal of luxury; 141 and 147. On Lord Hervey and Court Whig ideology, see Browning, *Court Whigs*, 35–66.

76 On Carter's Whig allegiance and disapproval of Bolingbroke, see Thomas, *Alexander Pope*, 86–7. See also John Nichols, *The Rise and Progress of the Gentleman's Magazine* (London, 1821) iv, and on the benefits resulting from Cave's connection with the Post Office, v.

77 *BF*, II, 342–3. See Thomas, '"Th' Instructive Moral"', for comments on the relation of the poem to parts of *Essay on Man*, 145–6.

78 *GM* 7 (November 1737) 692. Carter's rendering can be compared with another that appeared in *GM* 8 (March 1738) 159, which uses a more regular rhyme scheme, with less heartfelt effect.

79 *GM* 8 (March 1738) 159.

80 *BF*, II, 346–7. Satire X, 11. 365–6, from [Thomas Sheridan], *The Satires of Juvenal Translated* (London, 1739) 295. Thomas Sheridan (1687–1738) was a schoolmaster and friend of Swift. Thomas Kaminski has suggested that 'Fortune', and Elizabeth Carter's turn to philosophy at this time, was a consequence of her friendship with Johnson; *The Early Career of Samuel Johnson* (Oxford and New York, 1987) 35–6.

81 See Kaminski, *Johnson*, 76–81. Johnson undertook to translate Crousaz's later and longer, but less influential, *Commentary* on *Essay on Man* for Cave.

82 Goldgar, *Walpole and the Wits*, 176.

83 A.D. Nuttall, *Pope's 'Essay on Man'* (London, 1984).

84 Harry M. Solomon, *The Rape of the Text: Reading and Misreading Pope's 'Essay on Man'* (Tuscaloosa and London, 1993).

85 Pennington, *Memoirs*, 30.

86 Pennington, ed., *Series*, I, 36, 46.

5   *Clarissa* and the 'Total Revolution in Manners'

Full details of editions of the novels and Richardson reference works are given in the Abbreviations section, p. xi above. I have generally included letter numbers as well as page numbers from the Penguin edition of *Clarissa* (based on the first edition) in order to facilitate cross-referencing with other current editions using the guide provided by the editor Angus Ross at *C* 1511.

1 The remark appears in a 'Letter to a Lady', a reply to a correspondent who wrote to ask if the story of Grandison might be continued into parenthood. Richardson rules out the possibility of a sequel; *G*, III, 467–70.

2 The elevation of the novel form did not involve simply the production of 'familiar histories' as models for instruction, as Samuel Johnson put it in *Rambler* 4, but also the bringing of fiction into line with history and philosophy: it would transcend its destiny as ephemeral entertainment to address the central questions of the day. The historical design has been recognized in the work of Fielding, but in the case of Richardson the focus of discussion has been the added weight provided by didacticism. Historicism has been identified only as an incidental or unconscious feature.

3 See Mark Salber Phillips, *Society and Sentiment: Genres of Historical Writing in Britain, 1740–1820* (Princeton, 2000) 147–70, especially 152.

4 Lovelace refers to the South Sea Bubble in Letter 241, 816 dated 'Sat. morn. June 10' and the action therefore occurs after 1720. Letter 11, dated Wednesday, 1 March, is the first to be headed by the day of the week as well as the date of the month, which if it is intended to be taken as accurate would make 1721, 1727 and 1732 possible years (E&K, 239). Angus Ross notes that the reference to 'new streets about Grosvenor Square' makes 1732 the most likely year; *C* 23. However there are literary references, for instance to Pope's *Epistle to a Lady* (1735), that might indicate a later date.

5 Letter to Lady Bradshaigh, 15 December 1748, *SL*, 103.

6 I am here caricaturing one negative view of Richardson; the question of individual salvation was of course a crucial one for some of the most influential thinkers of the age, notably Richardson and Johnson, and informed their view of society and politics.

7 Although Walpole clung to power until 1742, his government was failing. With the death of Queen Caroline in 1737, he lost his main conduit of influence with the King. The political discourse associating luxury with corruption was losing much of its force. Its chief literary proponents – Bolingbroke, Pope, Swift and Gay – were dead or in decline.

8 See Ferguson, *First Feminists*, 19.

9 Letter to Lady Bradshaigh, 15 December 1748, *SL*, 117.

10 Lois E. Bueler has also identified a link between Richardson and the *Athenian Mercury* in the common concern with applied ethics explored through casuistry, and believes Richardson must have come across *Athenian* publications in his youth; *Clarissa's Plots* (Newark; and London and Toronto, 1994) 16–18.

11 These figures are derived from *Eighteenth-Century Fiction: A Full-Text Database of English Prose Fiction from 1700–1780* (Cambridge, 1996), a selective but substantial collection. Among the 88 texts including the term 'sex', those with the greatest number of appearances after Richardson are *The History of Emily Montague* (1769) by Frances Brooke with 80 and *The History of Betsy Thoughtless* (1751) and *Jemmy and Jenney Jessamy* (1753) both by Eliza Haywood, with 70 and 49, respectively. Both authors were strongly influenced by Richardson.

12 Letter to George Cheyne, 31 August 1741, *SL*, 49.
13 Laqueur, *Making Sex*, 8. Cf. Lois A. Chaber, '"This affecting subject": an "interested" reading of childbearing in two novels by Samuel Richardson', *Eighteenth-Century Fiction* 8: 2 (January 1996) 193–250; especially 243–45, which finds elements of the one-sex theory of reproduction still informing scenes from *The History of Sir Charles Grandison* but also identifies a transformation towards 'the two-sex theory of opposite and incommensurable sexes' (245).
14 There were, however, attempts to argue that the greater refinement of women's bodily organs might account for superiority of intellect or soul; Mandeville, *FB*, II, 172–3; 'Sophia', *Woman Not Inferior to Man: Or, A Short and Modest Vindication of the Natural Right of the Fair-Sex to a Perfect Equality of Power, Dignity, and Esteem* (London, 1739) 23–4; Richardson's closest approach to this argument comes in *G*, III, 250, when Sir Charles uses it to justify women's social inequality, and is challenged by his female interlocutors. See below p. 161.
15 Originally by Edward Young, who spoke of *Clarissa* as '*The Whole Duty of WOMAN*' by analogy with *The Whole Duty of Man* (1674 and many later editions) by Richard Allestree (cit. E&K, 286). See Rita Goldberg, *Sex and Enlightenment: Women in Richardson and Diderot* (Cambridge, 1984) chapter 1, '*Clarissa* and the Puritan conduct books'. Cf. Armstrong, *Desire and Domestic Fiction*, who identifies a dematerialization of the female body in conduct books, comparable to the one I am describing; 88, 95. While both the conduct book ideal and the Richardsonian heroine are implicated in the emergence of the two-sex model, what the conduct books appear to lack is the polemical spirit of Richardson's works, and the explicit recognition of an alternative model.
16 Letter to Frances Grainger, 22 January 1749/50, *SL*, 141–2.
17 See Rosemary Bechler, '"Triall by what is contrary": Samuel Richardson and Christian dialectic', in Valerie Grosvenor Myer, ed., *Samuel Richardson: Passion and Prudence* (London and Totowa, NJ, 1986) 93–113; and Taylor, 'Clarissa Harlowe', 19–38. See Taylor for further references.
18 See above pp. 30–1.
19 Cf. letters to Lady Bradshaigh, 15 December 1748 p. 112, and Hester Mulso, 30 September 1751; also *G*, III, 47.
20 *Rise of the Novel*, 162
21 Other examples can be found at L 55, 236; L57, 241; L76, 298; L78, 309; L85, 345; L132, 477, L262, 898; L366, 1070.
22 For other examples see L19, 105; L64, 270; L63, 264; L46, 209; L217, 696; L228, 736; L238, 809; L242, 819; L273, 927; L442, 1280.
23 See, for instance, L339, 1078 also 1342.
24 See the first letter of the novel from Anna Howe to Clarissa, 'You see what you draw upon yourself by excelling all your sex. Every individual of it who knows you, or has heard of you, seems to think you answerable to *her* for your conduct in points so very delicate and concerning' (L1, 40; cf. L296, 975 – 'The whole sex is indeed wounded by you').
25 'Sophia', *Woman Not Inferior to Man*, 51. It is part of Richardson's revisionism that he generally avoids the derogatory use of the term 'effeminacy'. An exception to this rule comes when Clarissa is asked by Anna early in the novel to examine the nature of her feelings for Lovelace, and says that she finds his own consciousness of his attractiveness to women a cause for suspicion, 'for a man to be vain of his person, how effeminate?' (L140, 186).
26 Cf. L261, 894; L274, 929; L314, 1011.

27 Tassie Gwilliam finds this overlap between feminist and anti-feminist rhetoric a 'mystification' of the categories of gender; I am arguing that there is a distinctive logic in each case; *Samuel Richardson's Fictions of Gender* (Stanford, 1993) 86–8.

28 See for instance L8, 64; L10, 68; L17, 96; L20, 110; L29, 138–9; L32, 154–5, L47, 212–13; L50, 219; L52, 223; L78, 306–7, 309.

29 In the miniature pen-portrait of Lovelace by a bailiff dismissed from his uncle's service, we learn that he 'was never known to be disguised by liquor' but 'was a sad gentleman ... as to women' and 'lived a wild life in town' with a constant series of sexual adventures (L4, 50). See also the comical list of his 'negative virtues': 'no gamester; no horse-racer; no fox-hunter; no drinker' (L40, 181), and Richardson's insistence on his decency of language in the Preface to the first edition and in the pamphlet defending the fire scene, *SRPCC*, I, 130.

30 Cf. Carol Houlihan Flynn, *Samuel Richardson: A Man of Letters* (Princeton, 1982); Tom Keymer, *Richardson's 'Clarissa' and the Eighteenth-Century Reader* (Cambridge, 1992) 157–76; James Grantham Turner, 'Lovelace and the paradoxes of libertinism', in Margaret Anne Doody and Peter Sabor, eds, *Samuel Richardson: Tercentenary Essays* (Cambridge, 1989) 70–88, all argue for a broad conception of Lovelace's libertinism in order to account for his disruptive effect, Richardson's animadversions notwithstanding. My suggestion would be that Lovelace's sceptical thinking, however wide-ranging in its implications, is always filtered through the crucial trial of the female sex.

31 Margaret Anne Doody, *A Natural Passion: A Study of the Novels of Samuel Richardson* (Oxford, 1974) 108–13.

32 When Pope says, in lines 269–70, 'believe me, good as well as ill, / Woman's a Contradiction still', he does not mean that women display contradictions in their nature, but that the supposed existence of a separate female sex is an ontological contradiction. Women have no characters, because all of their characters are taken from men; the only distinction is the bizarre pattern of these translated features, displayed in the series of portraits that make up the greater part of the poem. Pope compares the ladies in the portrait gallery to variegated tulips and this image perfectly makes the point (ll. 41–4). He observes that the most spectacular tulips, 'fine by defect', owe their charms to a defect in the bulb, the organ of generation. The spectacular follies of ladies have precisely the same source.

33 For further references to Lovelace's creed on this score, see L219, 703; L236, 801–2; L237, 803; L336, 1069.

34 Around the same time he printed several of Archibald Hutcheson's treatises 'on the Publick Debts and South Sea Stock'. Hutcheson was a Tory MP who criticized the government in the *Freeholder's Journal*.

35 Payne was sentenced to a fine and a year's imprisonment.

36 My account is based on chapter II of E&K, 19–36. For an interesting discussion of the possible political resonances of *Clarissa* in the context of the Jacobite threat in the 1740s, see Keymer, *Richardson's 'Clarissa'*, 168–76.

37 See Doody, *A Natural Passion*, 224–5.

38 Remarkably, Mary Wortley Montagu seems to have anticipated Lovelace with a plan for renewable marriages lasting a term of seven years. Joseph Spence reported that she had written a treatise on the subject; Grundy, *Montagu*, 430.

39 Keymer, *Richardson's 'Clarissa'*, 171.

40 E&K, 193–6; for another useful summary of the relationship, see Tom Keymer's headnote to the Warburton preface to *Clarissa* in *SRPCC* I: 23–32.

41 Samuel Richardson, *Pamela, or Virtue Rewarded*, 4 vols (Oxford, 1929), IV, 367.

42 Letter to Lady Bradshaigh, 23 February 1752, *SL*, 198.
43 *SL*, 56–60.
44 Letter to Thomas Edwards, *SL*, 227.
45 Keymer suggests the offending passage may have been Anna Howe's remark, 'Have we not, in the case of a celebrated bard, observed, that those who aim at more than their due will be refused the honours that they may justly claim?' (L47, 212); see *SRPCC* I: 29. The regular allocation of Pope's ideas to Lovelace may also have created unease.
46 Letter to Young, 29 May 1759, Edward Young, *Correspondence*, ed. Henry Pettit (Oxford, 1971) 502; *SRPCC* I: 32 n.22.
47 See E&K, 433–6, on Richardson's considerable involvement in revising and expanding the eulogy to Addison and criticism of Pope.
48 Eve Tavor, *Scepticism, Society and the Eighteenth-Century Novel* (Basingstoke, 1987) 54–77. Tavor forcefully demonstrates the way sceptical theories of motivation are not only thematized in the novel, but transmuted into dramatic conflict (though one should not assume, as she seems to do, that Richardson had a detailed knowledge of Mandeville's works). Tavor's misreading of the one direct reference, quoted in my discussion on p. 112, is however indicative of a general problem in her interpretation. The *'private vices'* belong to Lovelace, not Clarissa, and Tavor's Lovelacian reading of the action pillories Clarissa for moral hypocrisy and ignores her active struggle against injustice.
49 Tavor, *Scepticism*, 61, 67, 72.
50 It is possible that fellow-rake Mowbray's mockery of the self-important 'Middlesex Justice' is also a Mandevillian reference: to the attempt by the Grand Jury of Middlesex to suppress *The Fable of the Bees* (L292, 963); see chapter 3, p. 60.
51 Letter to Frances Grainger, 22 January 1749/50, *SL*, 142.
52 *FB*, I, 42–4; see also the discussion in chapter 3 above, p. 62.
53 No. 97 (19 Febrary 1751), *The Rambler*, ed. W.J. Bate and Albrecht B. Strauss, *The Yale Edition of the Works of Samuel Johnson*, vol. 6 (New Haven, 1969) IV, 153.
54 If indeed Richardson is working on women through their pride, then he partly concurs with the prevailing view of women's faulty nature. Clarissa rejects flattery, and transcends the trial set up by Lovelace to test the very moral weakness that Richardson may have been playing on in his appeal to a female readership.
55 It was only when my work on this book was nearing completion that Lois Chaber drew my attention to the close relevance of Lois E. Bueler's *Clarissa's Plots* to my argument in this chapter. She has discovered a wealth of antecedents in Renaissance literature for what she terms 'the Tested Woman Plot', and I wholly concur with the central place she gives this plot in her reading of *Clarisssa*. My aim here is to explore the distinctive urgency and topicality of the plot as Richardson employs it, with the difference from earlier examples that here there is a real alternative to 'woman' as traditionally defined, in a way that only becomes possible with the erosion of the one-sex paradigm.
56 For Clarissa's early and justifiable scepticism regarding his bashfulness, see L2, 42–3.
57 Laqueur, *Making Sex*, 44; Ovid, *Metamorphoses*, trans. Mary M. Innes (Harmondsworth, 1955) 82–3. See also Gwilliam, *Samuel Richardson's Fictions of Gender*, 50–1, 59–62 and 179 n.2 for further references.
58 Elsewhere, interestingly, he acknowledges that 'in every friendship, whether male or female, there must be a man and a woman spirit (that is to say, one of them a

forebearing one) to make it permanent)' (L252, 864), that is to say, it depends on a division of function between friends, conceptualized in gendered terms.

59   Clarissa calls it a '*libertine* presumption to imagine that there was no difference in *heart*, nor any but what proceeded from *education* and *custom*, between the pure and the impure – And yet custom *alone*, as she observed, would make a second nature, as well in good as in bad habits' (L219, 702).

60   See Judith Wilt, 'He could go no farther: a modest proposal about Lovelace and Clarissa', *PMLA* 92 (1977) 19–32, for a stimulating and splendidly immodest rectification of previous critical neglect of the fallen women: at the expense of Clarissa herself who almost disappears from view, and without considering Lovelace's characterization as rake. See also Gwilliam, *Samuel Richardson's Fictions of Gender*, 88–94.

61   Wilt, 'He could go no farther', 26.

62   Lovelace clams 'the man, however a Tarquin, as some may think me in this action, is not a Tarquin in power, so that no *national point* can be made of it', but like the comparison of his bribery of the landlady Mrs Moore with the South Sea Bubble, a 'scheme big with national ruin' (816), it invites the opposite perception that Clarissa's downfall is of public consequence. See Introduction, n. 15.

63   The full title is *A Collection of the Moral and Instructive Sentiments, Maxims, Cautions, Reflections, Contained in the Histories of Pamela, Clarissa, Sir Charles Grandison* (1755), SRPCC, III, 189.

64   'Answer to the Letter of a Very Reverend and Worthy Gentleman, Objecting to the Warmth of a particular Scene in the History of CLARISSA', SRPCC, I, 130.

65   For a contrary interpretation, which sees Clarissa's isolation as necessary penance for her initial act of rebellion, see Lois A. Chaber, 'Christian form and anti-feminism in *Clarissa*', *Eighteenth-Century Fiction*, 15:3 (2003) 507–37; 531–2. Although the heroine frequently indulges in self-blame, I believe this is to be taken as a sign of her overactive conscience, rather than confirmation of genuine guilt.

66   Letter from Aaron Hill to Richardson, 29 November 1748, FM XIII, 3.f.146; cit. Keymer, SRPCC, I, 54.

67   Letter from Collier to Richardson, 9 July 1749, FM XV, 2, ff. 8–9; cit. Tom Keymer, SRPCC, I, 126; see Keymer's essay 'Jane Collier, reader of Richardson, and the fire-scene in *Clarissa*', in Albert Rivero, ed., *New Essays on Samuel Richardson* (New York, 1996) 141–61.

68   Cf. L512, 1431 for the revival and renewed usurpation of conscience.

69   *The English Novel: Form and Function* (New York, 1953) 47.

70   See Wilt, 'He could go no farther', 19, Eagleton, *Rape of Clarissa*, 64–5; Siobhan Kilfeather, 'The rise of Richardson criticism', in Doody and Sabor, eds, *Samuel Richardson*, 251–66, especially 257–8.

71   Lois Bueler helpfully identifies this element of suspense as a delusion created by the common misreading of *Clarissa* as a courtship or love story; *Clarissa's Plots*, 11–12.

72   *Reading Clarissa: The Struggles of Interpretation* (New Haven, 1979).

73   Hester Mulso Chapone, 'Letters on filial obedience', in BF, III, 206, 223–5, 245–7; L148, 510–12. But see Brian McCrea's argument that it is in part Clarissa's acceptance of the efficacy of the curse that sustains her resistance to Lovelace, 'Clarissa's pregnancy and the fate of patriarchal power', *Eighteenth-Century Fiction* 9: 2 (January 1997) 124–48; 138–89, and Chaber, 'Christian form', 526, for the suggestion that the novel is structured around the curse.

74 Her superstition does not extend to the ghostly; though as Anna Howe points out, the astonishing facility of Lovelace's schemes might lead one to attribute to him supernatural powers and to credit his creatures Mr Tomlinson and Mrs Sinclair with being familiars; L316, 1014.

75 Richard Burn, *Justice of the Peace* (London, 1756) 598; cit. Laqueur, *Making Sex*, 161–2.

76 L402 and L406, 1192 and 1195 cf. 1156; L424, 1239; L139 and L140, 494, 495.

77 Cf. Peggy Thompson, 'Abuse and atonement: the passion of Clarissa Harlowe', *Eighteenth-Century Fiction* 11 (1999) 255–70.

78 Cf. Clarissa's response to Anna Howe when the latter tells her that adversity is her 'SHINING TIME'; affliction will give Anna, too, an opportunity to 'exert those qualities, which not only ennoble our sex, but dignify human nature' (L178, 579).

79 Letter from Hill to Richardson, 5 May 1748; cit. E&K, 217.

80 Lovelace discusses a distinctive feminine lexicon, including '*figaries* (a good female word, Jack!)' and '*tostications*' (L242, 818). He derides women's characteristic use of the word 'choose' 'as if they were always to have their own wills!' (L248, 854) and refers to talk of Clarissa's broken heart as 'the true women's language' (L341, 1084).

81 Cf. Mary Wollstonecraft's call for 'a revolution in female manners', *Vindication*, 117.

82 Spadafora, *Idea of Progress*, 101; he takes the term from James West Davidson, *The Logic of Millenial Thought: Eighteenth-Century New England* (New Haven, 1977) 129–41.

83 Goldberg, *Sex and Enlightenment*, 41; she notes that in conduct books 'the imagery is often mercantile or political, and the virtues extolled are those of the merchant: frugality, temperance, sobriety' (29).

84 It is no accident that imprisonment for debt brings about the steep decline in her health.

85 Margaret Anne Doody, 'The man-made world of Clarissa Harlowe and Robert Lovelace', in Myer, ed., *Samuel Richardson*, 52–77; 54.

86 See note 86.

87 I refer to Hogarth's famous series of engravings *A Rake's Progress* (1733/4) and Mary Davys' novel *The Accomplish'd Rake* (1727). The connection between the two is discussed in Paulson, *Hogarth*, II, 20.

88 The superiority of Doody's analysis derives from unsurpassed knowledge of the text and her sensitivity to Richardson's own rhetorical emphasis. In this it differs from the well-known Marxist readings by Christopher Hill ('*Clarissa* and Her Times', 1955), Ian Watt (*The Rise of the Novel*, 1957), and Terry Eagleton (*The Rape of Clarissa*, 1982), which, though bracingly irreverent, sacrifice accuracy to doctrinaire generalizations. Daniel P. Gunn valuably identifies the distortions and self-contradictions involved in the assertion that *Clarissa* represents a bourgeois revolt again the values of the ruling aristocracy, but unfortunately his alternative sketch of the ideological work of the novel falls into the same trap by abstracting the struggle between the sexes that is at the heart of the narrative as a mystification of the 'real' issue: the renewal of hegemony over the dispossessed; 'Is *Clarissa* bourgeois art?', *EF* 10: 1 (October 1997) 1–14. See also April London's trenchant remarks on *Clarissa* and the Georgic mode; *Women and Property in the Eighteenth-Century English Novel* (Cambridge, 1999).

89   It seems to be Mrs Townshend's sex and the femino-centric nature of her trade that sets her apart from the other, punishable smuggler 'Captain Tomlinson', Lovelace's agent (L514, 1434).
90   Lovelace, having intercepted her letter, denounces the hope in patrician terms ('Who can bear this porterly threatening! – Broken bones, Jack! – Damn the little vulgar'), and threatens to inflict on Anna and Clarissa breakages of a different kind (L252, 865).
91   See Ellis, 'Coffee-women', 35–7; Moll King's biography is referred to above, chapter 2, p. 50.
92   Cf. L334, 1068.
93   Doody, 'Man-made World', 75.

6   Out of the Closet: Richardson and the Cult of Literary Women

1   Critics who have explored the relevance of Habermas's definitions to the work of Richardson include Elizabeth Heckendorn Cook, *Epistolary Bodies: Gender and Genre in the Eighteenth-Century Republic of Letters* (Stanford, 1996); Rachel K. Carnell, '*Clarissa*'s treasonable correspondence: gender, epistolary politics, and the public sphere', *Eighteenth-Century Fiction* 10: 3 (April 1998) 269–86; and Miranda Burgess, *British Fiction and the Production of Social Order 1740–1830* (Cambridge, 2000). Habermas himself refers to Richardson and the epistolary form in discussing 'the bourgeois family and the institutionalization of a privateness oriented to an audience', *Structural Transformation*, 43, 48–51. Since, unlike Habermas, I am not describing the bourgeois public sphere as a 'normative ideal' I do not distinguish the work of the closet from the ideological legitimation of commercial expansion. For the description 'normative ideal' and a review of eighteenth-century notions of the 'public', see Keith Michael Baker, 'Defining the public sphere in eighteenth-century France: variations on a theme by Habermas', in Craig Calhoun, ed., *Habermas and the Public Sphere* (Cambridge, Mass, 1992) 181–211.
2   Cf. Habermas, *Structural Transformation*, 160: 'The rational-critical debate of private people in the *salons*, clubs, and reading societies was not directly subject to the cycle of production and consumption, that is, to the dictates of life's necessities.'
3   In the postscript Conclusion of *Clarissa*, the heroine's profitable use of excess time in the closet is implicitly contrasted with the faulty formation of the prostitutes Sally and Polly, whose parents were 'in great measure answerable for their miscarriages, by indulging them in the fashionable follies and luxury of an age given up to those amusements and pleasures which are so apt to set people of but *middle fortunes* above all the useful employments of life; and to make young women an easy prey to rakes and libertines' (1491). For an attempt, in my view perverse and unconvincing, to demonstrate that the Richardson heroine can share the economic passions of a speculative society, see the Shamela-esque reading of *Pamela* by Catherine Ingrassia, '"I am become a mere usurer": *Pamela* and domestic stock-jobbing', *Studies in the Novel* 30: 3 (Fall 1998) 303–23.
4   Doody, *A Natural Passion*, 150.
5   Eliza Haywood, *Idalia, or The Unfortunate Mistress* (London, 1723) 21–2.
6   See William B. Warner, *Licensing Entertainment: The Elevation of Novel Reading in Britain, 1684–1750* (Berkeley, 1998) especially 193–95, on the elevation of the

mid-century novels of Richardson and Fielding through their 'overwriting' ('writing above and beyond ... toward higher cultural purposes') of amatory fiction. My argument endorses his view, though with more emphasis on the transformation of values forwarded by the strategy, rather than jockeying for position in the market for print.

7 See J.W. Fisher, '"Closet-work": the relationship between physical and psychological spaces in *Pamela*', in Myer, ed., *Samuel Richardson*, 21–37; 22–23.

8 Henry Fielding, *The History of the Adventures of Joseph Andrews*, ed. Judith Hawley (Harmondsworth, 1999) 87.

9 Henry Fielding, *The History of Tom Jones*, ed. R.P.C. Mutter (Harmondsworth, 1966) 265.

10 See Kathryn M. Rogers, 'Sensitive feminism vs. conventional sympathy: Richardson and Fielding on women', *Novel* 9 (1975) 256–70, for a persuasive but rather partisan argument in favour of the former's 'sensitive feminism'; his punitive representation of prostitutes is not addressed. For defences of Fielding, see Angela Smallwood, *Fielding and the Woman Question: The Novels of Henry Fielding and Feminist Debate 1700–1750* (Brighton, 1989); and Avril London, 'Controlling the text: women in *Tom Jones*', *Studies in the Novel* 19 (1987) 323–33, who argue respectively for his engagement with the 'Woman Question' or the 'feminization of discourse', but without addressing the question of form.

11 Watt, *Rise of the Novel*, 195.

12 Ibid.

13 See Nussbaum, *'Brink of All We Hate'*, 94–116; Ellen Pollack, *Poetics of Sexual Myth*; Brenda Bean, 'Sight and self-disclosure: Richardson's revision of Swift's "The Lady's Dressing Room"', *Eighteenth-Century Life* 14 (February 1990) 1–23.

14 Nussbaum, *'Brink of All We Hate'*, 105.

15 Nussbaum, Bean and Pollack, all take this line; see also Margaret Anne Doody in 'Swift among the Women', *Yearbook of English Studies* 18 (1988) 68–92. For a useful overview, see Donald C. Mell, Introduction, *Pope, Swift, and Women Writers*.

16 'The Gentleman's Study, In Answer to the Lady's Dressing Room' by Miss W——, Roger Lonsdale, ed., *Women Poets of the Eighteenth Century*; 'The Reasons that Induc'd Dr S[wift] to write a Poem call'd the Lady's Dressing-Room', *Essays and Poems*, 273; Lord Orrery, *Remarks on the Life and Writing of Dr Jonathan Swift* (1752) 121–4.

17 Clarissa comments of the books that she will 'think the better of the people of the house for their sakes', 525.

18 See, for instance, *C*: 1037; *G*: I, 13; I, 19; II, 206; II, 630; III, 457.

19 MO 1000 [?1737]; cit. Myers, *BC*, 41. Cf the reader's letter in *Spectator* 53 (Tuesday, 1 May 1711), which interestingly, in view of Carter's studies, quotes the Stoic philosopher Epictetus in support of an attack on 'that *Mahometan* Custom ... of treating Women as if they had no Souls', I, 224.

20 Robert Dodsley, ed., *A Collection of Poems by Various Hands* (London, 1748) II, 296–308.

21 For more on the iconographic tradition of St Cecilia in relation to this scene, see Doody, *A Natural Passion*, 232–4.

22 *SL*, 68. Carroll gives her name as 'Sophia Westcomb', and E&K as 'Sarah Wescomb'.

23 *The Correspondence of Samuel Richardson*, ed. Anna Laetitia Barbauld, 6 vols. (London, 1804) II, 208.

24 *SL*, 67–8.
25 'Sophia', *Woman not Inferior*, 47; for Carter's response see Myers, *BC*, 57, 125–6.
26 See above p. 78.
27 On Talbot's early life, see Myers, *BC*, 61–75; and Zuk, 'Talbot: Introduction', *BF*, III, 4–6.
28 From 1735 to 1739, when Secker became Rector of St James's in London, she became friendly with Lady Mary Grey and Jemima Campbell, the daughter and granddaughter of the Duke of Kent, both close in age, who lived part of the year in the Duke's residence in St James's Square. They read together, exchanged views on books in letters that have been preserved, and shared dreams of a life of writing and scholarship. One fantasy written by Jemima describes how 'Lady C. T-l-t took her Degree' at Oxford and 'held a Publicke Disputation in the Divinitie Schoole'. MS Bedfordshire County Record Office, Lucas Papers 30/21/3/12; cit. Zuk, 'Talbot: Introduction', *BF*, III, 16 n.22.
29 See 'Philip Yorke, 2nd Earl of Hardwicke', *DNB*.
30 But the volume was reissued and went through a vogue long after Talbot's death, with five English editions and two French editions between 1781 and 1810. The 1798 edition provided an authors' key. See Zuk, *BF*, III, 25, 381 n.1, and 'Philip Yorke, 2nd Earl of Hardwicke', *DNB*.
31 Pennington, ed., *Series*, I, 11. 13, 16, 49, 58, 76–9, 113, 114, 126, 128.
32 Pennington, ed., *Series*, I, 160.
33 The poem was printed in the December issue of the *Gentleman's Magazine* (vol. XVII), after Richardson wrote to apologize to Carter, and the introduction complains only mildly about the appropriation. My account of the exchanges with Cave and Richardson is based on E&K, 215–16. The letters were printed in 'Original Letters of Mrs E. Carter and Mr Samuel Richardson', *Monthly Magazine* 33 (1812) 533–43.
34 Guest, *Small Change*, 147–50.
35 Pennington, ed., *Series*, I, 161.
36 See Isobel Grundy, 'Samuel Johnson as patron of women', *Age of Johnson*, 1 (1987) 59–77; James Basker, 'Johnson, gender, and the misogyny question', *Age of Johnson* 8 (1997) 175–87; and Norma Clarke, *Dr Johnson's Women* (London and New York, 2000). But Johnson remained an ambivalent member of the feminizing camp, as a remark resurrecting the Augustan bogey of the literary Amazon indicates: 'a generation of Amazons of the pen, who with the spirit of their predecessors have set masculine tyranny at defiance, asserted their claim to the regions of science, and seem resolved to contest the usurpations of virility', *Adventurer*, No. 115, Tuesday 11 December 1753, The Adventurer, ed., W.J. Bate, John M. Bullitt and L.F. Powell, *The Yale Edition of the Works of Samuel Johnson*, II (New Haven, 1963) 458.
37 Carter, 'Original Letters', 534–5.
38 It was also unfortunate that a Mrs Carter is introduced into *Clarissa* as the sister of Mrs Sinclair 'who keeps the bagnio near Bloomsbury' (1387).
39 Pennington, ed., *Series*, I, 207–8.
40 Talbot to Carter, 15 February 1748, Pennington, ed., *Series*, I, 166.
41 See letters December 1749 to October 1750, Pennington, ed., *Series*, I, 211–40. Cf. Carter's earlier letters on reverting to savagery, 24 May [1744] and 29 October 1747, I, 38, 150.
42 *BF*, II, 414 and Johnson, *Rambler*, III, 242.
43 Pennington, ed., *Series*, I, 244, 246–7.
44 *BF*, II, 416, 417, 415 and Johnson, *Rambler*, IV, 171, 173, 169. The essay was published as No. 100, Saturday, 2 March 1751.

45 Pennington, ed., *Series*, I, 247, 248, 249, 250.
46 Pennington, ed., *Series*, I, 251.
47 Pennington, ed., *Series*, I, 254.
48 See Jean-Jacques Rousseau, *Emile; or, On Education* (1762) Part V 'Sophie, or The Woman', and Mary Wollstonecraft, *A Vindication of the Rights of Woman*, ed. Sylvana Tomaselli (1792; Cambridge, 1995) e.g. 87 and 110–11, employing the Mahometan slur, 156–73 where Rousseau is quoted and denounced at length, and the comparable criticisms of Dr Gregory, author of *A Father's Legacy to His Daughters* (1774) especially 97–108 and 178–82.
49 See *C* 704, and 1037. In the first of these references Lovelace's assertion 'I am a very Jew in this point' was changed in the third edition to 'I am a very Turk'.
50 Pennington, ed., *Series*, I, 256–7.
51 Pennington, ed., *Series*, I, 258.
52 To Sarah Chapone, 6 December 1751; cit. *SL*, 173 n.68.
53 The novel was advertised on 23 January 1751, published 25 February; see James L.Clifford, Introduction, *The Adventures of Peregrine Pickle in which are included Memoirs of a Lady of Quality* by Tobias Smollett, ed. James L. Clifford, rev. by Paul-Gabriel Boucé (Oxford, 1983) xvi.
54 Cit. Nussbaum, *'The Brink of All We Hate'*, 149.
55 'Oxford Scholar', *The Parallel; or, Pilkington and Phillips Compared. Being Remarks upon the Memoirs of those two celebrated Writers* (London, 1748) 62.
56 Cit. *SL*, 173 n.68
57 The description is by Eaves and Kimpel, see E&K, 343.
58 E&K, 351.
59 6 December 1750, cit. *SL*, 173 n.68.
60 Richardson to Mrs Chapone, 11 January 1751, *SL*, 173.
61 E&K, 352. The correspondence continues Mrs C to R 15 December 1750, Mrs C to R 25 February 1751, 20 March 1751, R to Mrs C 25 March 1751.
62 Smollett, *Peregrine Pickle*, 793n. and *DNB*, 'Frances Anne, Viscountess Vane'. If her claim that she was 15 at the time of her marriage to Lord William Douglas in 1732 is accepted, then she was born *c*. 1717.
63 Smollett, *Peregrine Pickle*, 452 cf. 487; 452.
64 Ibid., 532.
65 'Teresia Constantia Phillips', *DNB*.
66 Whitehead went on to serve as secretary and steward of the Hellfire Club, and was rewarded, on Sir Francis Dashwood's accession to the post of Chancellor of the Exchequer in Bute's government (1762–3), with a sinecure worth £800 p.a.; 'Paul Whitehead', *DNB*.
67 Horace Walpole: 'Her adventures are worthy to be bound up with those of my good sister-in-law, the German princess [Mary Moders], and Moll Flanders', *The Yale Edition of Horace Walpole's Correspdence*, ed. W.S. Lewis, 48 vols. (New Haven, 1937–83) 17: 459. Montagu had remarked at the time of Vane's liaison with Lord Berkeley 'I am told that though she does not pique herself upon fidelity to any one man (which is but a narrow way of thinking), she boasts that she has always been true to her nation, and, notwithstanding foreign attacks, has always reserved her charms for the use of her own countrymen', *The Complete Letters of Lady Mary Wortley Montagu*, ed. Robert Halsband, 3 vols. (Oxford, 1965) II, 133–4.
68 Myers cites letters by Elizabeth Montagu and Elizabeth Carter deprecating the way her outstanding talents were unredeemed by virtue or delicacy; *BC*, 154–5.
69 'Her style is clear and concise with some Strokkes of Humour which appear to me so much above her, I can't help being of opinion the whole has been

modell'd by the Author of the Book in which it is inserted who is some subaltern admirer of hers.' *Complete Letters,* III, 1, 2–3, 5–6, 7.
70 To Lady Bute, 22 September [1755], *Complete Letters,* III, 90.
71 Cit. Clifford, Intro, xvii.
72 My account is based on *The Letters of Mrs. Elizabeth Montagu, with some of the Letters of her Correspondents,* ed. Matthew Montagu, 3 vols. (third edition, London, 1810); and Myers, *BC,* 21–44.
73 The relations were her maternal grandmother and her second husband, Dr Conyers Middleton, a controversial theologian.
74 *BC,* 30–1.
75 On the sermons, see Myers, *BC,* 37, on the evening readings, 40; the letter is to Anne Donnellan, 17 October 1740, BL, Portland Loan 29/325, p. 13; cit. *BC,* 36.
76 To Sarah Robinson, MO 5556; cit. *BC,* 36.
77 Myers, *BC,* 41–2.
78 See *BF,* III, 203–47; E&K, 345; *BC,* 141–6. Myers interprets the exchange as a serious disagreement and evidence of Richardson's conservatism, a view largely shared by Caroline Gonda, *Reading Daughter's Fictions 1709–1834* (Cambridge, 1996) 82–93.
79 John Mulso, *Letters to Gilbert White,* 45 (13 December 1750); cit. Gonda, *Reading Daughter's Fictions,* 83.
80 *The Works of Hester Chapone,* 4 vols. (London and Edinburgh, 1807) I, 26–8.
81 See Shirley Van Marter, 'Richardson's debt to Hester Mulso concerning the curse in *Clarissa', Papers in Language and Literature* 14 (1978) 22–31.
82 To Lady Bradshaigh [1751], *SL,* 184.
83 Cit. *SL,* 183.
84 *SL,* 184.
85 Ibid.
86 In a letter to Elizabeth Carter on the subject of the recently passed Marriage Act which clamped down on runaway matches, he joked that the force of Mulso's arguments against parental authority must have provoked this legislative backlash, adding more earnestly: 'Things done in private have sometimes, and, when least thought of, been proclaimed on the house-top'; 17 August 1753, Carter, *Original Letters,* 540.
87 Cit. *BF,* III, 203.
88 Several recent critics have attended to the creation of the character of Grandison as an object of female desire, notably John Mullan, *Sentiment and Sociability: The Language of Feeling in the Eighteenth Century* (Oxford, 1988) 83; and Betty A. Schellenberg, 'Using "femalities" to "make fine men": Richardson's *Sir Charles Grandison* and the feminization of narrative', *Studies in English Literature* 34 (1994) 599–616. None, I think, have ventured as far as I do in this brief discussion to suggest that the novel is the culmination of Richardson's feminizing agenda, rather than a patriarchal recuperation of it (as Eagleton describes it in *Rape of Clarissa,* 94).
89 *SL,* 164.
90 To Lady Bradshaigh, [1750?], *SL,* 171.
91 See above pp. 145–6.
92 3 December 1751, 'Journals', MS London, British Library; cit. E&K, 359.
93 Doody, *A Natural Passion,* 273.
94 Ibid., 275. Lois A. Chaber's article '"Sufficient to the day": anxiety in *Sir Charles Grandison'* is the most convincing counter-argument to the optimistic reading of the novel, with its attention to theology and linguistic form, but I would

maintain that the more troubled elements only set in relief the overpowering momentum towards resolution; *Eighteenth-Century Fiction* I: 4 (1789) 281–304.

95 *G*, II, 124. Grandison is making his first visit to Italy and to the della Porretta's when news arrives of the Young Pretender's invasion. Some time soon after this he learns that his father is dangerously ill and travels to France. He is recalled home after his death and the action of the novel begins.

96 See Doody's valuable examination of the basis of this ethos in latitudinarian theology, *A Natural Passion*, 265–71.

97 Rae Blanchard has noted Steele's campaign against the double standard in male and female morals in *Tatler*, nos. 33, 58 and 201, and *Guardian*, No. 45, including a call for male chastity, 'Richard Steele', p. 349. Cf. Lovelace's suspicion that Hickman is a *'male-virgin'* (L237, 802).

98 See Barker-Benfield, *The Culture of Sensibility*, 80–1.

99 See above p. 64.

100 To Hester Mulso, 11 July 1751, *SL*, 186. By invoking pride as Sir Charles's ruling passion, Richardson engages with Mandeville's view that morality and politeness are ultimately derived from pride. See Mandeville's two sketches of the ideal gentleman uncannily like Richardson's hero, in *Virgin Unmask'd*, 161–9 (an allegory of Louis XIV), and *FB*, Part II, 67–83. Doody comments on the troubling link with Mandeville's analysis of pride and hypocrisy, *A Natural Passion*, 266–7.

101 See *G*, III, 476n, referring to her letter to Richardson of 11 December 1753, Forster Collection, Victoria and Albert Museum, XI.54–7.

102 Guest, *Small Change*, 109.

103 Another interesting point of comparison would be with the conversation at the menacing occasion of Clarissa's dinner with Lovelace and his fellow-rakes, L222.

104 Compare Sir Charles's approval of Addison as 'an ingenious man, to whose works your sex, and if *yours*, *ours*, are more obliged, than to those of any single man in the British world', II, 103.

105 Cit. Grundy, *Montagu*, 544.

106 Elsewhere, as has been noted in E&K, 566, Richardson espoused the idea that the knowledge of women could be derived from studying men, and vice versa, and reeiterated Carter's idea that 'they are too much considered as a species apart'. Letter to Lady Bradshaigh, 14 February 1754, and letter to Johannes Stinstra, 20 March 1754, *SL*, 292 and 297.

107 On these grounds I would dispute Betty Schellenberg's conclusion that 'the consequence of making a fine man is submission to the authority of the finished product' ('Using "femalities"', 613), in spite of the fact that Richardson identified Grandison's view with his own in a letter to Mrs. Watts, 27 Sept. 1754, cit. E&K, 564.

108 To Lady Bradshaigh [1751], *SL*, 184.

109 The issue of Charlotte's uppitiness and its domestication in motherhood is beyond the scope of this discussion; on comparisons of her 'genius' with that of her brother, see I, 193, and of her understanding with her suitors', I, 230, II, 506.

110 Pennington, ed., *Series*, I, 362–3.

111 Carter, 'Original Letters', 533–43.

112 My account is based on Sylvia Myers, *BC*, 129–34; Ada Wallas, *Before the Bluestockings* (London, 1929) 155–85; and the *DNB* article on Ballard. See Guest, *Small Change*, chapter 2 'The female worthies: memorializing women' for an

interesting and detailed discussion of Ballard, also referring to Amory and
Duncombe, which is very much in accord with the present argument. Guest
explores the genre of biography as the context for these efforts to demonstrate
'that the spread of education among women is a sign of cultural progress' (57),
rather than, as here, the connection with Richardson's novels.

113   George Ballard, *Memoirs of Several Ladies of Great Britain* (Oxford, 1752) vi.
114   Myers notes that as a young woman Elizabeth Montagu sat up until late into
the night to write secretly a letter to a friend 'which included gossip about
the scandal involving Theophilus Cibber and his wife'; reference to MO 273,
17 December [1738], Mount Morris, *BC*, 31.
115   Account based on *DNB*.
116   [Theophilus] Cibber, *The Lives of the Poets of Great Britain and Ireland to the Time
of Dean Swift*, 5 vols. (London, 1753) II, 151.
117   Cibber, *Lives*, III, 26.
118   [George Colman and Bonnell Thornton], *Poems by Eminent Ladies*, 2 vols.
(London, 1755).
119   Thomas Amory, *Memoirs of Several Ladies of Great Britain. Interspersed with Literary
Reflexions and Accounts of Antiquities and Curious Things* (London, 1755) xxx.
120   Amory, *Memoirs*, xiv, xxiv.
121   See Myers, *BC*, 117, cf. 120 and Jocelyn Harris, Introduction, *The Feminiad*
(1754), Augustan Reprints No. 207 (Los Angeles, 1981).
122   John Nichols, *Literary Anecdotes of the Eighteenth Century* (London, 1812–15)
VIII, 277.
123   Harris, Intro., *Feminiad*, v.
124   Pennington, *Memoirs*, 141.
125   See notably *Monthly Review* 18 (1758) 588–96 and *Critical Review* 6 (1758)
149–58.
126   *Critical Review* 13 (1762) 180–[5]. Vivien Jones, ed., *Women in the Eighteenth
Century: Construction of Femininity* (London and New York, 1990) includes
extracts of the review of *Epictetus* from *MR* and of *Poems* from *CR*.
127   The scandal attached to her second marriage at the age of 47 to a man of low
birth 14 years her junior was fatal to her reception as an exemplar of morality
and learning. The final three volumes of the *History*, published 1781–83, were
relatively neglected.
128   The ambivalence of her position was increased by the fact that the family
fortune was established by her grandfather Jacob Sawbridge, who had been one
of the directors of the South Sea Company, but had managed to emerge from
the crash with most of his assets intact, confirming public suspicions of official
corruption. See Bridget Hill, *The Republican Virago: The Life and Times of
Catharine Macaulay, Historian* (Oxford, 1992) 4–5.
129   On Macaulay's lack of interest in a progressive 'history of women', see
Tomaselli, *Enlightenment Debate*, 107.
130   For examples of these views along with the gender valence, from Carter's translation, see *BF* II, 135, 139, 164–68, and from the *Enchiridion*, 296 (XXXIII), and
299 (XXXIX).
131   See Lawrence E. Klein's interesting discussion of Shaftesbury's interest in
Stoicism, which is of considerable relevance to Carter. In particular, the
concern with the dangers of *'epideixis'*, 'making a show of oneself'; *Shaftesbury
and the Culture of Politeness: Moral Discourse and Cultural Politics in Early
Eighteenth-Century England* (Cambridge, 1994) 74–5.

132 *Complete Letters*, I, 44–5.
133 Pennington, *Memoirs*, 165.
134 In this paragraph, Pennington, *Memoirs*, 165. 188, 196, and in brackets, 196.
135 *BF* II, 13.
136 See Roland Barthes' famous analysis of myth as a 'semiological system', *Mythologies*, trans. Annette Lavers (London, 1973) 114–15.
137 This conclusion is borne out by the reviews in the *Monthly Review* and the *Critical Review* (see notes 125 and 126 for references), both of which begin by quoting at length from the discussion of religion in the Introduction and then select relevant passages from the translation; see also the quaintly titled 'An Ejaculation made upon reading over the learned Miss Carter's Translation of *Epictetus*', *GM* 28 (1758) 596, a short piece of religious fervour. For detailed readings of Carter's translation that tend to find more continuity with her previous work, see Thomas, '"Th' Instructive Moral"', 161–6 and Williams, 'Poetry, Puddings and Epictetus', 17–24. Kelly reaches a conclusion similar to that presented here, 'Bluestocking feminism', 175, as does Guest, *Small Change*, 150.
138 On these arrangements, see Pennington, *Memoirs*, 241–4.
139 Listed in *BF*, II, xxxi.
140 The South Sea Company continued to exist after the Bubble and was not wound up until 1854. But by the 1750s 'its only function was to distribute in dividends the annuity it received from the government as interest on a diminishing portion of the National Debt'; Carswell, *South Sea Bubble*, 268.

Coda: From Discourse to a Theory of Feminization in the *Essays* of David Hume

1 *MR* 18 (1758) 588; Pennington, *Memoirs*, 212–13.
2 [John Brown], *An Estimate of the Manners and Principles of the Times*, (fifth edition, London, 1757) 51.
3 *MR* 18 (1758) 608.
4 Cit. F.T.H. Fletcher, *Montesquieu and English Politics (1750–1800)* (1939; Philadelphia, 1980) 162, 165. Ralph is quoted from *The Case of Authors by Profession or Trade* (1758), Cowper from *Table Talk* (1782). But Fletcher also cites more enthusiastic judgements from Voltaire, who believed Brown was responsible for reviving the fighting spirit of England, and from Burke, 165.
5 The exceptions are Jerome Christensen, *Practicing Enlightenment: Hume and the Formation of a Literary Career* (Madison, 1987); and Barker-Benfield, *Culture of Sensibility*, 133–6. More recently, commentators on the bluestockings have pointed out the relevance of the *Essays*: see Guest, *Small Change*, 87–9, 238; and remarks by Grant, Eger and Kelly, in Eger et al., eds, *Women, Writing and the Public Sphere*, 85–6, 114, 165–6. Critics who have explored parallels between the philosophy of Hume and Richardson's novels include Carol Kay, *Political Constructions: Defoe, Richardson, and Sterne in Relation to Hobbes, Hume, and Burke* (Ithaca and London, 1988); and Burgess, *British Fiction*, 59–64, but they focus on the *Treatise* and do not engage with issues raised by the *Essays* or relating to gender difference. In the 1741–2 volumes, other essays discussing women and their influence are 'Of the Study of History', 'Of Moral Prejudices', 'the Epicurean', in addition to 'Of Love and Marriage' and 'Of Polygamy and Divorce'.

6 As Ernest Mossner suggests; *The Life of David Hume* (second edition, Oxford, 1980) 139.
7 The significance of the *Tatler* and the *Spectator* for Hume and for the Scottish literati in general has been described by Nicholas Phillipson in *Hume* (London, 1989) 26–9 and in the same author's classic essay 'Culture and society in the 18th-century province: the case of Edinburgh and the Scottish Enlightenment', in *The University in Society*, 2 vols. (Princeton and London, 1975) II, 407–48; see 429–30 and 434.
8 *The Letters of David Hume*, ed., J.Y.T. Grieg, 2 vols. (Oxford, 1932) I, pp. 20, 22.
9 David Hume, *Essays Moral, Political, and Literary*, ed. Eugene F. Miller (revised edition, Indianapolis, 1985) 536. Page references will henceforth be given in brackets after quotes.
10 Goodman, *Republic of Letters*, 6.
11 Cit. ibid.
12 Hammond, *Pope and Bolingbroke*, 51–4.
13 He adds that although 'modern politeness' may run into 'affectation and foppery [a reference to the charge of effeminacy] ... ancient simplicity ... often degenerates into rusticity and abuse, scurrility and obscenity', i.e. including misogynist satire, 130–1.
14 Cit. Mossner, *Hume*, 449.
15 See J.A.W. Gunn, 'Mandeville: poverty, luxury, and the Whig theory of government', in *Beyond Liberty and Property: The Process of Self-Recognition in Eighteenth-Century Political Thought* (Kingston and Montreal, 1983) 96–119, especially 99–101 and 110–11. Gunn comments on the strangeness of continuing influence of the Machiavellian connection 'between political libery and poverty' (99).
16 Antoine-Leonard Thomas, *L'Esprit des Femmes* (1772) translated and revised as *Essay on the Character, Manners, and Genius of Women in Different Ages* (1773) by William Russell; William Alexander, *History of Women from the Earliest Antiquity to the Present Time* (1779).
17 See Paul Bowles, 'John Millar, the four-stages theory, and women's position in society', *History of Political Economy* 16: 4 (1984) 619–38.
18 Franz Neumann, Introduction, *The Spirit of the Laws* by Charles Louis de Secondat de Montesquieu, trans. Thomas Nugent (New York, 1949) xiii.
19 Mossner, *Hume*, 229.
20 Christensen, *Practicing Enlightenment*, 100.
21 Charles Louis de Secondat de Montesquieu, *Persian Letters*, trans. C.J. Betts (Harmondsworth, 1973) 194.
22 Horne, *Social Thought of Bernard Mandeville*, 33: 'It was because [Mandeville] posed the conflict between virtue and commerce so starkly that he also had such great influence upon the most important moral philosophers of the late part of the century – Hutcheson, Hume, and Smith – all of whom had to rejoin what Mandeville had torn asunder'; i.e. the opposition between altruistic virtue and worldly properity. Cf. F.A. Hayek's remark that Mandeville 'made Hume possible'; *Dr Bernard Mandeville (Lecture on a Master Mind), Proceedings of the British Academy*, LII, 139.

Bibliography

Periodicals: primary

Athenian Mercury
Female Tatler
Gentleman's Journal
Gentleman's Magazine
London Mercury (later *Lacedemonian Mercury*)

Digital publications

Eighteenth-Century Fiction: A Full-Text Database of English Prose Fiction from 1700–1780 (Cambridge: Chadwyck-Healey, 1996).

Books

Addison, Joseph, and Richard Steele et al., *The Spectator*, ed. D.F. Bond, 5 vols. (Oxford: Clarendon Press, 1965).

Alexander, William, *The History of Women, From the Earliest Antiquity to the Present Time* (London, 1779).

Amory, Thomas, *Memoirs of Several Ladies of Great Britain. Interspersed with Literary Reflexions and Accounts of Antiquities and Curious Things* (London, 1755).

Anonymous, *An Essay in Defence of the Female Sex* (1696).

— *The Mens Answer to the Womens Petition against Coffee: Vindicating Their own Performances, and the Vertues of their Liquor, from the Undeserved Aspersions lately Cast upon them, in their SCANDALOUS PAMPHLET* (London, 1674).

— *A Parallel Between the Roman and British Constitution; Comprehending Polibius's Curious Discourse of the Roman Senate* (London, 1747).

— *The Women's Petition against Coffee. Representing to The Publick Consideration the Grand Inconveniences accruing to their Sex from the Excessive Use of that Drying, Enfeebling Liquor. Presented to the Right Honorable the Keeper of the Liberty of Venus* (London, 1674).

Armstrong, Nancy, *Desire and Domestic Fiction: A Political History of the Novel* (New York and Oxford: Oxford University Press, 1987).

Backscheider, Paula R., *Daniel Defoe: Ambition and Innovation* (Lexington: University Press of Kentucky, 1986).

— and Timothy Dykstal, eds, *The Intersections of the Public and Private Spheres in Early Modern England* (London: Frank Cass, 1996).

Bahlmann, D.W.R., *The Moral Revolution of 1688* (New Haven, Conn: Yale University Press, 1957).

Baker, Keith Michael, 'Defining the public sphere in eighteenth-century France: variations on a theme by Habermas', in *Habermas and the Public Sphere*, ed. Craig Calhoun (Cambridge, Mass: MIT Press, 1992) 181–211.

Ballard, George, *Memoirs of Several Ladies of Great Britain* (Oxford, 1752).

Ballaster, Ros, 'Performing *Roxane*: the Oriental woman as the sign of luxury in eighteenth-century fictions', in *Luxury in the Eighteenth Century*, ed. Berg and Eger.

Barker, Anthony D., 'Poetry from the provinces: amateur poets in the *Gentleman's Magazine* in the 1730s and 1740s', in *Tradition in Transition: Women Writers, Marginal Texts, and the Canon*, ed. Alvaro Ribeiro and James G. Basker, 241–56.

Barker, Hannah and Elaine Chalus, eds, *Gender in Eighteenth-Century England: Roles Representations and Responsibilities* (London and New York: Longman, 1997).

Barker-Benfield, G.J., *The Culture of Sensibility: Sex and Society in Eighteenth-Century Britain* (Chicago and London: University of Chicago Press, 1992).

Barrell, John, *The Political Theory of Painting from Reynolds to Hazlitt* (New Haven and London: Yale University Press, 1986).

— and Harriet Guest, 'The uses of contradiction: Pope's "Epistle to Bathurst"', in J. Barrell, *Poetry, Language and Politics* (Manchester: Manchester University Press, 1988).

Barthes, Roland, *Mythologies*, trans. Annette Lavers (London: Granada, 1973).

Basker, James, 'Johnson, gender, and the misogyny question', *Age of Johnson* 8 (1997), 175–87.

Bean, Brenda, 'Sight and self-disclosure: Richardson's revision of Swift's "The Lady's Dressing Room"', *Eighteenth-Century Life* 14 (1990), 1–23.

Bechler, Rosemary, '"Triall by what is contrary": Samuel Richardson and Christian dialectic', in *Samuel Richardson: Passion and Prudence*, ed. Myer, 93–113.

Berg, Maxine and Elizabeth Eger, eds, *Luxury in the Eighteenth Century: Debates, Desires and Delectable Goods* (Basingstoke: Palgrave Macmillan, 2003).

Berry, Christopher J., *The Idea of Luxury: A Conceptual and Historical Investigation* (Cambridge: Cambridge University Press, 1994).

Berry, Helen, *Gender, Society and Print Culture in Late Stuart Britain: The Cultural World of the Athenian Mercury* (Aldershot and Burlington, VT: Ashgate, 2003).

Blanchard, Rae, 'Richard Steele and the status of women', *Studies in Philology* 26 (1929) 325–55.

Boswell, James, *Life of Johnson*, ed. George Birkbeck Hill, revised edition, L.F. Powell, 6 vols. (Oxford: Clarendon Press, 1934).

Bowles, Paul, 'John Millar, the four-stages theory, and women's position in society', *History of Political Economy* 16: 4 (1984).

Bredvold, Louis I., 'The gloom of the Tory satirists', in James L. Clifford and Louis A. Landa, eds, *Pope and His Contemporaries* (Oxford: Clarendon Press, 1949) 1–19.

Brown, Laura, *Alexander Pope* (Oxford: Basil Blackwell, 1985).

— *Ends of Empire: Women and Ideology in Early Eighteenth-Century English Literature* (Ithaca, NY: Cornell University Press, 1993).

[Brown, John], *An Estimate of the Manners and Principles of the Times*, (5th edition, London, 1757).

Browing, Reed, *Political and Constitutional Ideas of the Court Whigs* (Baton Rouge and Lodon: Louisiana State University Press, 1982).

Bueler, Lois E., *Clarissa's Plots* (Newark: University of Delaware Press; London and Toronto: Association of University Presses, 1994).

Burgess, Miranda, *British Fiction and the Production of Social Order 1740–1830* (Cambridge: Cambridge University Press, 2000).

Burtt, Shelley, *Virtue Transformed: Political Argument in England 1688–1740* (Cambridge: Cambridge University Press, 1992).

Carnell, Rachel K., *Clarissa*'s treasonable correspondence: gender, epistolary politics, and the public sphere', *Eighteenth-Century Fiction* 10: 3 (April 1998) 269–86.

Carretta, Vincent, 'Pope's *Epistle to Bathurst* and The South Sea Bubble', *Journal of English and Germanic Philology* 77 (1978) 212–31.

Carswell, John, *The South Sea Bubble* (London: Cresset Press, 1960).

Carter, Elizabeth, 'Original letters of Miss E. Carter and Mr Samuel Richardson', *Monthly Magazine* 33 (1812) 533–43.

Carter, Philip, 'An effeminate or efficient nation? Masculinity and 18th-century social commentary', *Textual Practice*, 11:3 (1997) 429–44.

— 'Men about town: representations of foppery and masculinity in early eighteenth-century urban society', in Barker and Chalus, eds, *Gender in Eighteenth-Century England*, 31–57.

— *Men and the Emergence of Polite Society, Britain 1660–1800* (Harlow: Longman, 2001).

Castiglione, Dario and Lesley Sharpe, eds, *Shifting the Boundaries: Transformation of the Languages of Public and Private in the Eighteenth Century* (Exeter: University of Exeter Press, 1995).

Chaber, Lois A., 'Christian form and anti-feminism in *Clarissa*', *Eighteenth-Century Fiction*, 15: 3 (2003) 507–37.

— '"Sufficient to the day": anxiety in *Sir Charles Grandison*', *Eighteenth-Century Fiction* I: 4 (1789) 281–304.

— '"This affecting subject": an "interested" reading of childbearing in two novels by Samuel Richardson', *Eighteenth-Century Fiction* 8: 2 (January 1996) 193–50.

Chapone, Hester, *The Works of Hester Chapone*, 4 vols. (London and Edinburgh, 1807).

Cibber, [Theophilus], *The Lives of the Poets of Great Britain and Ireland to the Time of Dean Swift*, 5 vols. (London, 1753).

Christensen, Jerome, *Practicing Enlightenment: Hume and the Formation of a Literary Career* (Madison: University of Wisconsin Press, 1987).

Clarke, Norma, *Dr Johnson's Women* (London and New York: Hambledon and London Press, 2000).

Claydon, Tony, *William III and the Godly Revolution* (Cambridge: Cambridge University Press, 1996).

Clery, E.J., *The Rise of Supernatural Fiction 1762–1800* (Cambridge: Cambridge University Press, 1995).

— 'Women, publicity and the coffee-house myth', *Women: a Cultural Review*, 2: 2 (1991) 168–77.

Clinton, Katherine B., 'Femme et philosophe: enlightenment origins of feminism', *Eighteenth-Century Studies* 8: 3 (Spring, 1975) 283–99.

Cohen, Michèle, *Fashioning Masculinity: National Identity and Language in the Eighteenth Century* (London and New York: Routledge, 1996).

[Colman, George, and Bonnell Thornton], *Poems by Eminent Ladies*, 2 vols (London, 1755).

Cook, Elizabeth Heckendorn, *Epistolary Bodies: Gender and Genre in the Eighteenth-Century Republic of Letters* (Stanford: Stanford University Press, 1996).

Cook Richard I., *Bernard Mandeville* (New York: Twayne Publishers, 1974).

Copley, Stephen, *Literature and the Social Order in Eighteenth-Century England* (London: Croom Helm, 1984).

Cowles, Virginia, *The Great Swindle: The Story of the South Sea Bubble* (London: Collins, 1960).

Defoe, Daniel, *The Complete English Tradesman* (1839; Gloucester: Alan Sutton, 1987).

— *Roxana*, ed. David Blewett (Harmondsworth: Penguin, 1982).

— *The True-Born Englishman and Other Writings*, ed. P.N. Furbank and W.R. Owens (Harmondsworth: Penguin, 1997).

Dickenson, H.T., 'The politics of Bernard Mandeville', *Mandeville Studies*, ed. Primer, 80–97.

Dickson, P.G.M., *The Financial Revolution in England. A Study in the Development of Public Credit 1688–1756* (London: Macmillan; New York: St. Martin's Press, 1967).

Dijkstra, Bram, *Defoe and Economics: The Fortunes of 'Roxana' in the History of Interpretation* (Basingstoke: Macmillan, 1987).

Dobranski, Stephen B., '"Where men of differing judgements croud": Milton and the culture of the coffee houses', *Seventeenth Century*, 9: 1 (Spring 1994) 35–56.

Dodsley, Robert, ed., *A Collection of Poems by Various Hands* (London, 1748).

Donaldson, Ian, *The Rape of Lucretia: A Myth and its Transformations* (Oxford: Clrendon Press, 1982).

Doody, Margaret Anne, *A Natural Passion: A Study of the Novels of Samuel Richardson* (Oxford: Clarendon Press, 1974).

— and Peter Sabor, ed., *Samuel Richardson: Tercentenary Essays* (Cambridge: Cambridge University Press, 1989).

— 'Swift among the women', *Yearbook of English Studies* 18 (1988) 68–92.

Douglas, Mary, *Purity and Danger: An Analysis of the Concepts of Pollution and Taboo* (London: Ark Press, 1984).

Duncombe, John, *The Feminiad* (1754), intr. Jocelyn Harris, Augustan Reprints No. 207 (Los Angeles: William Andrews Clark Memorial Library, University of California, 1981).

Dunton, John, *Athenianism* (London, 1710).

— *Dunton's Recantation; Or, His Reasons for Deserting his Whiggish Principles and Turning Jacobite* (London, 1716)

[—] pseud. Philaret, *The Challenge, Sent by a Young Lady to Sir Thomas – &c. Or, The Female War* (London, 1697).

— *The Life and Errors of John Dunton* (London, 1705).

— *Mr John Dunton's Dying Groans from the Fleet-Prison: or the National Complaint* (1725).

— *Life and Errors of John Dunton*, ed. John Bowyer Nichols (London, 1818).

Eagleton, Terry, *The Rape of Clarissa: Writing, Sexuality, and Class Struggle in Samuel Richardson* (Oxford: Basil Blackwell, 1982).

Eaves, T.C. Duncan and Ben. D. Kimpel, *Samuel Richardson: A Biography* (Oxford: Clarendon Press, 1971).

Eger, Elizabeth, Charlotte Grant, Clíona Ó Gallchoir and Penny Warburton, *Women, Writing and the Public Sphere, 1700–1830* (Cambridge: Cambridge University Press, 2001).

Ellis, Aytoun, *The Penny Universities: A History of the Coffee-Houses* (London: Secker & Warburg, 1956).

Ellis, Markman, 'The coffee-women, the *Spectator* and the public sphere in the early eighteenth century', in *Women, Writing and the Public Sphere, 1700–1830*, ed. Eger et al., 27–52.

Ellison, Julie, 'Cato's tears', *English Literary History* 63 (1996), 571–601.

— *Cato's Tears and the Making of Anglo-American Emotion* (Chicago: University of Chicago Press, 1999).

Ferguson, Moira, ed., *First Feminists: British Women Writers, 1578–1799* (Bloomington: Indiana University Press, 1985).

Ferguson, Rebecca, *The Unbalanced Mind: Pope and the Rule of Passion* (Brighton: Harvester Press, 1986).

Fielding, Henry, *The History of the Adventures of Joseph Andrews*, ed. Judith Hawley (Harmondsworth: Penguin, 1999).
— *The History of Tom Jones*, ed. R.P.C. Mutter (Harmondsworth: Penguin, 1966).
Fisher, J.W., '"Closet-work": the relationship between physical and psychological spaces in *Pamela*', in Myer, ed., *Samuel Richardson*, 21–37.
Fletcher, Anthony, *Gender, Sex and Subordination in England 1500–1800* (New Haven and London: Yale University Press, 1995).
Fletcher, F.T.H., *Montesquieu and English Politics (1750–1800)* (1939; Philadelphia: Porcupine Press, 1980).
Flynn, Carol Houlihan, *Samuel Richardson: A Man of Letters* (Princeton: Princeton University Press, 1982).
Gay, John, *Dramatic Works*, ed. John Fuller, 2 vols. (Oxford: Clarendon Press, 1983).
Ghent, Dorothy van, *The English Novel: Form and Function* (New York: Rinehart, 1953).
[Gildon, Charles], *The History of the Athenian Society, For the Resolving of all Nice and Curious Questions. By a Gentleman, who got Secret Intelligence of their Whole Proceedings. To which are prefixed Several Poems, written by Mr. Tate, Mr. Motteux, Mr. Richardson, and others* (London, 1692).
Goldberg, Rita, *Sex and Enlightenment: Women in Richardson and Diderot* (Cambridge: Cambridge University Press, 1984).
Goldgar, Bertrand A., *Walpole and the Wits: the Relation of Politics and Literature, 1722–1742* (Lincoln and London: University of Nebraska Press, 1976).
Goldsmith, M.M., 'Mandeville and the spirit of capitalism', *Journal of British Studies* 17: 1 (Fall 1977) 63–81.
— *Private Vices, Public Benefits: Bernard Mandeville's Social and Political Thought* (Cambridge: Cambridge University Press, 1985).
Gonda, Caroline, *Reading Daughter's Fictions 1709–1834* (Cambridge: Cambridge University Press, 1996).
Goodman, Dena, 'Public sphere and private life: toward a synthesis of current historiographical approaches to the old regime', *History and Theory*, 31 (1992) 1–20.
— *The Republic of Letters: A Cultural History of the French Enlightenment* (Ithaca and London: Cornell University Press, 1994).
Grundy, Isobel, *Lady Mary Wortley Montagu* (Oxford: Oxford University Press, 1999).
— 'Samuel Johnson as Patron of Women', *Age of Johnson* 1 (1987), 59–77.
Guest, Harriet, *Small Change: Women, Learning, Patriotism, 1750–1810* (Chicago and London: University of Chicago Press, 2000).
Gunn, Daniel P., 'Is *Clarissa* bourgeois art?', *Eighteenth-Century Fiction* 10: 1 (October 1997), 1–14.
Gunn, J.A.W., *Beyond Liberty and Property: The Process of Self-Recognition in Eighteenth-Century Political Thought* (Kingston and Montreal: McGill-Queen's University Press, 1983).
Gutwirth, Madelyn, *The Twilight of the Goddesses: Women and Representation in the French Revolutionary Era* (New Brunswick, NJ: Rutgers University Press, 1992).
Gwilliam, Tassie, *Samuel Richardson's Fictions of Gender* (Stanford: Stanford University Press, 1993).
Habermas, Jürgen, *The Structural Transformation of the Public Sphere: An Inquiry into a Category of Bourgeois Society* (1962), trans. Thomas Burger (London: Polity Press, 1989).
Halsband, Robert, *The Life of Lady Mary Wortley Montagu* (Oxford: Clarendon Press, 1956).
Hammond, Brean S., *Pope and Bolingbroke: A Study of Friendship and Influence* (Columbia: University of Missouri Press, 1984).

Hamowy, Ronald, 'Cato's letters, John Locke, and the republican paradigm', *History of Political Thought* XI: 2 (1990) 272–94.

Hayek, F.A., *Dr Bernard Mandeville (Lecture on a Master Mind)*, *Proceedings of the British Academy*, 52 (1966) 125–41.

Hayton, David, 'Moral reform and country politics in the late seventeenth-century House of Commons', *Past and Present* 128 (1990), 48–89.

Hill, Bridget, *The Republican Virago: The Life and Times of Catharine Macaulay, Historian* (Oxford: Clarendon Press, 1992).

Hill, Christopher, '*Clarissa* and her times', *Essays in Criticism* 5 (1955), reprinted in *Samuel Richardson: A Collection of Essays*, ed. John Carroll (Englewood Cliffs, NJ: Prentice-Hall, 1969) 102–23.

Hill, Peter Murray, *Two Augustan Booksellers: John Dunton and Edmund Curll* (University of Kansas Publications Library Series No. 3, 1958).

Hirschman, Albert O., *The Passions and the Interests: Political Arguments for Capitalism before Its Triumph* (1977; Princeton, NJ: Princeton University Press, 1984).

Hont, Istvan and Michael Ignatieff, eds, *Wealth and Virtue: The Shaping of Political Economy in the Scottish Enlightenment* (Cambridge: Cambridge University Press, 1983).

Horne, Thomas A., *The Social Thought of Bernard Mandeville: Virtue and Commerce in Early Eighteenth-Century England* (New York and London: Macmillan, 1978).

Hume, David, *Essays Moral, Political, and Literary*, ed. Eugene F. Miller (revised edition., Indianapolis: Liberty Fund, 1985).

— *The Letters of David Hume*, ed. J.Y.T. Grieg, 2 vols. (Oxford: Clarendon Press, 1932).

Hundert, E.J., *The Enlightenment's Fable: Bernard Mandeville and the Discovery of Society* (Cambridge: Cambridge University Press, 1994).

Hunter, J. Paul, 'The Insistent I', *Novel* 13:1 (Fall 1979) 19–31.

— *Before Novels: The Cultural Contexts of Eighteenth-Century English Fiction* (New York and London: W.W. Norton, 1990).

Hunter, Jean E., 'The eighteenth-century Englishwoman: according to the *Gentleman's Magazine*', in Paul Fritz and Richard Morton, eds, *Woman in the Eighteenth Century and Other Essays* (Toronto and Sarasota: Samuel Steverns, Hakkert, 1976).

Ingrassia, Catherine, *Authorship, Commerce and Gender in Early Eighteenth-Century England* (Cambridge: Cambridge University Press, 1998).

— '"I am become a mere usurer": *Pamela* and domestic stock-jobbing', *Studies in the Novel* 30: 3 (Fall 1998) 303–23.

Johnson, Samuel, *Adventurer*, ed. W.J. Bate, John M. Bullitt and L.F. Powell, *The Yale Edition of the Works of Samuel Johnson*, II (New Haven: Yale University Press, 1987).

— *The Rambler*, ed. W.J. Bate and Albrecht B. Strauss, *The Yale Edition of the Works of Samuel Johnson*, vols. III–V (New Haven: Yale University Press, 1969).

Jones, Vivien, ed., *Women in the Eighteenth Century: Construction of Femininity* (London and New York: Routledge, 1990).

Kaminski, Thomas, *The Early Career of Samuel Johnson* (Oxford and New York: Oxford University Press, 1987).

Kay, Carol, *Political Constructions: Defoe, Richardson, and Sterne in Relation to Hobbes, Hume, and Burke* (Ithaca and London: Cornell University Press, 1988).

Kelly, Gary, gen. ed., *Bluestocking Feminism: Writings of the Bluestocking Circle*, 6 vols. (London: Pickering and Chatto, 1999).

— *Women, Writing, and Revolution* (Oxford: Clarendon Press, 1993).

Keymer, Tom, 'Jane Collier, reader of Richardson, and the fire-scene in *Clarissa*', in Albert Rivero, ed., *New Essays on Samuel Richardson* (New York: St. Martin's Press, 1996).
— *Richardson's 'Clarissa' and the Eighteenth-Century Reader* (Cambridge: Cambridge University Press, 1992).
Kilfeather, Siobhan, 'The rise of Richardson criticism', in *Samuel Richardson*, eds. Doody and Sabor, 251–66.
Kimmel, Michael S., 'The contemporary "crisis" of masculinity in historical perspective', in Harry Brod, ed., *The Making of Masculinities: The New Men's Studies* (Boston: Allen & Unwin, 1987) 121–53.
Klancher, Jon, *The Making of English Reading Audiences 1790–1832* (Madison, Wisconsin: University of Wisconsin Press, 1987).
Klein, Lawrence E., 'Coffeehouse civility, 1660–1714: an aspect of post-courtly culture in England', *Huntingdon Library Quarterly* 59: 1 (1997) 31–51.
— 'Gender and the public/private distinction in the eighteenth century: some questions about evidence and analytical procedure', *Eighteenth-Century Studies* 29: 1 (1995) 97–109.
— 'Gender, conversation and the public sphere in the early eighteenth-century England', in Judith Still and Michael Worton, eds, *Textuality and Sexuality: Reading theories and practices* (Manchester and New York: Manchester University Press, 1993) 100–15.
— *Shaftesbury and the Culture of Politeness: Moral Discourse and Cultural Politics in Early Eighteenth-Century England* (Cambridge: Cambridge University Press, 1994).
Kowaleski-Wallace, Elizabeth, *Consuming Subjects: Women, Shopping and Business in the Eighteenth Century* (New York: Columbia University Press, 1997).
Kraye, Jill, 'The transformation of Platonic love in the Italian Renaissance', in Anna Baldwin and Sarah Hutton, eds, *Platonism and the English Imagination* (Cambridge: Cambridge University Press, 1994) 76–85.
Kroll, Richard, 'The pharmacology of *The Rape of the Lock*', *English Literary History* 67:1 (Spring 2000) 99–141.
Kuist, James M., *The Nichols File of 'The Gentleman's Magazine': Attributions of Authorship and Other Documentation in Editorial Papers at the Folger Library* (Madison, WI: University of Wisconsin Press, 1982).
Landes, Joan B., *Women and the Public Sphere in the Age of the French Revolution* (Ithaca and London: Cornell University Press, 1988).
Langford, Paul, *A Polite and Commercial People: England 1727–1783* (Oxford: Clarendon Press, 1989).
Laqueur, Thomas, *Making Sex: Body and Gender from the Greeks to Freud* (Cambridge, Mass. and London: Harvard University Press, 1990).
Lipking, Lawrence, *Samuel Johnson: The Life of an Author* (Cambridge, Mass. and London, Harvard University Press, 1998).
Lloyd, John, *The Song of Songs; Being a Paraphrase Upon the most Excellent Canticles of Solomon. In a Pindarick Poem* (London, 1682).
London, April, 'Controlling the text: women in *Tom Jones*', *Studies in the Novel* 19 (1987) 323–33.
— , *Women and Property in the Eighteenth-Century English Novel* (Cambridge: Cambridge University Press, 1999).
Lougee, Carolyn C., *Le Paradis des Femmes: Women, Salons, and Social Stratification in Seventeenth-Century France* (Princeton, NJ: Princeton University Press, 1976).
McCrea, Brian, 'Clarissa's pregnancy and the fate of patriarchal power', *Eighteenth-Century Fiction* 9: 2 (January 1997) 124–48.

McEwen, Gilbert D., *The Oracle of the Coffee House: John Dunton's 'Athenian Mercury'* (San Marino, Calif: The Huntingdon Library, 1972).

McGovern, Barbara, *Anne Finch and Her Poetry: A Critical Biography* (Athens and London: University of Georgia Press, 1992).

Mack, Maynard, *Alexander Pope: A Life* (New Haven and London: Yale University Press, 1985).

McKeon, Michael, 'Historicizing patriarchy: the emergence of gender difference in England, 1660–1760', *Eighteenth-Century Studies*, 28: 3 (1995) 295–322.

Mackie, Erin, *Market à la Mode: Fashion, Commodity, and Gender in 'The Tatler' and 'The Spectator'* (Baltimore and London: The Johns Hopkins University Press, 1997).

MacLean, Ian, *Woman Triumphant: Feminism in French Literature 1610–1652* (Oxford: Clarendon Press, 1977).

Mandell, Laura, *Misogynous Economies: The Business of Literature in Eighteenth-Century Britain* (Lexington: University Press of Kentucky, 1999).

Mandeville, Bernard, *By a Society of Ladies: Essays in the 'Female Tatler'*, ed. M.M. Goldsmith (Bristol: Thoemmes Press, 1999).

— *The Fable of the Bees: or, Private Vices, Public Benefits*, ed. F.B. Kaye (1924; rpt. Indianapolis: Liberty Fund, 1988).

— *A Modest Defence of Publick Stews*, Augustan Reprint Society No. 162 (1724; reprint, Los Angeles: Clark Memorial Library, 1973).

— *The Virgin Unmask'd: or, Female Dialogues Betwixt an Elderly Maiden Lady and her Neice, On several Diverting Discourses on Love, Marriage, Manners and Morals & C. Of the Times* (2nd edition, London, 1724).

Mason, Shirlene, *Daniel Defoe and the Status of Women* (St. Alban's, Vermont and Montreal: Eden Press Women's Publications, 1978).

Maurer, Shawn Lisa, *Proposing Men: Dialectics of Gender and Class in Eighteenth-Century Periodicals* (Stanford: Stanford University Press, 1998).

Mell, Donald C., ed., *Pope, Swift, and Women Writers* (Neward: University of Delaware Press; London: Association of University Presses, 1996).

Mellor, Anne K., *Mothers of the Novel: Women's Political Writing in England, 1780–1830* (Bloomington and Indianapolis: Indiana University Press, 2000).

Montagu, Elizabeth, *The Letters of Mrs. Elizabeth Montagu, with some of the Letters of her Correspondents*, ed. Matthew Montagu, 3 vols. (third edition, London: 1810).

Montagu, Lady Mary Wortley, *The Complete Letters of Lady Mary Wortley Montagu*, ed. Robert Halsband, 3 vols. (Oxford: Clarendon Press, 1965).

— *Essays and Poems and 'Simplicity, A Comedy'*, ed. Robert Halsband and Isobel Grundy (1977; Oxford: Clarendon Press, 1993).

Montesquieu, Charles Louis de Secondat de, *Persian Letters*, trans. C.J. Betts (Harmondsworth: Penguin, 1973).

— *The Spirit of the Laws*, trans. Thomas Nugent, intr. Franz Neumann (New York: Hafner Press, 1949).

Morgan, Fidelis, ed., *Female Tatler* (London: J.M. Dent & Sons, 1992).

Mossner, Ernest, *The Life of David Hume* (second edition, Oxford: Clarendon Press, 1980).

Mullan, John, *Sentiment and Sociability: The Language of Feeling in the Eighteenth Century* (Oxford: Clarendon Press, 1988).

Myer, Valerie Grosvenor, ed., *Samuel Richardson: Passion and Prudence* (London: Vision Press and Totowa, NJ: Barnes & Noble, 1986).

Myers, Sylvia Harcstark, *The Bluestocking Circle: Women, Friendship, and the Life of the Mind in Eighteenth-Century England* (Oxford: Clarendon Press, 1990).

Neal, Larry, *The Rise of Financial Capitalism: International Capital Markets in the Age of Reason* (Cambridge: Cambridge University Press, 1990).

Nichols, John, *Literary Anecdotes of the Eighteenth Century* (London, 1812–15).
— *The Rise and Progress of the Gentleman's Magazine* (London, 1821).
Nicholson, Colin, *Writing and the Rise of Finance: Capital Satires of the Early Eighteenth Century* (Cambridge: Cambridge University Press, 1994).
Noyes, Gertrude E., 'John Dunton's *Ladies Dictionary*, 1694', *Philological Quarterly*, 21 (1942) 129–45.
Nuttall, A.D., *Pope's 'Essay on Man'* (London: George Allen & Unwin, 1984).
Orgel, Stephen and Roy Strong, *Inigo Jones: the Theatre of the Stuart Court*, 2 vols. (London: Southeby, Parker, Barnet; Berkeley and Los Angeles: Yale University Press, 1973).
Ovid, *Metamorphoses*, trans. Mary M. Innes (Harmondsworth: Penguin, 1955).
'Oxford Scholar', *The Parallel; or, Pilkington and Phillips Compared. Being Remarks upon the Memoirs of those two celebrated Writers* (London, 1748).
Pailler, Albert, *Edward Cave et le 'Gentleman's Magazine'*, 2 vols (Lille: Atelier Reproduction de Thèses, 1975).
Parks, Stephen, *John Dunton and the English Book Trade: A Study of His Career with a Checklist of His Publications* (New York and London: Garland, 1976).
Paulson, Ronald, *Hogarth*, 3 vols. (New Brunswick and London: Rutgers University Press, 1991).
Peace, Mary, and Vincent Quinn, ed., *Luxurious Sexualities*, *Textual Practice* 11: 3 (1997).
Pennington, Montagu, *Memoirs of the Life of Elizabeth Carter, with A New Edition of her Poems; To Which are added, Some Miscellaneous Essays in Prose ...* (London: F.C. and J. Rivington, 1807).
— ed., *A Series of Letters between Mrs. Elizabeth Carter and Miss Catherine Talbot*, 2 vols. (London: Rivington, 1808).
Perry, Ruth, *The Celebrated Mary Astell: An Early English Feminist* (Chicago and London: University of Chicago Press, 1986).
'Philalethes Britannicus', *A Memorial of the Present State of the British Nation* (London, 1722).
Phillips, Mark Salber, *Society and Sentiment: Genres of Historical Writing in Britain, 1740–1820* (Princeton, NJ: Princeton University Press, 2000).
Phillipson, Nicholas, 'Culture and society in the 18th-century province: the case of Edinburgh and the Scottish enlightenment', in *The University in Society*, 2 vols. (Princeton, NJ: Princeton University Press, and London: Oxford University Press, 1975) II, 407–48.
— *Hume* (London: George Weidenfeld & Nicolson, 1989).
Pincus, Steven, '"Coffee politicians does create": coffeehouses and restoration political culture', *The Journal of Modern History*, 67 (December 1995) 807–34.
Pocock, J.G.A., *The Machiavellian Moment: Florentine Political Thought and the Atlantic Republican Tradition* (Princeton, NJ: Princeton University Press, 1975).
— *Virtue, Commerce, and History: Essays on Political Thought and History, Chiefly in the Eighteenth Century* (Cambridge: Cambridge University Press, 1985).
Pollack, Ellen, *The Poetics of Sexual Myth: Gender and Ideology in the Verse of Swift and Pope* (Chicago and London: University of Chicago Press, 1985).
Pope, Alexander, *The Twickenham Edition of the Poems of Alexander Pope*, ed John Butt et al., 11 vols (London: Methuen, 1939–69).
Prescott, Sarah, *Women, Authorship and Literary Culture 1690–1740* (Basingstoke: Palgrave, 2003).
Primer, Irwin, ed., *Mandeville Studies: New Explorations of the Art and Thought of Dr Bernard Mandeville* (The Hague: Martinus Nijhoff, 1975).

Reynolds, Myra, *The Poems of Anne Countess of Winchelsea* (Chicago: University of Chicago Press, 1903).

Ribeiro, Alvaro and James G. Basker, eds., *Tradition in Transition: Women Writers, Marginal Texts, and the Eighteenth-Century Canon* (Oxford: Clarendon Press, 1996).

Richardson, Samuel,

— *Clarissa; or, The History of a Young Lady*, ed. Angus Ross (Harmondsworth: Penguin, 1985).

— *The Correspondence of Samuel Richardson*, ed. Anna Laetitia Barbauld, 6 vols. (London, 1804).

— *The History of Sir Charles Grandison*, ed. Jocelyn Harris, 3 vols. (London: Oxford University Press, 1972).

— *Pamela; or, Virtue Rewarded*, ed. Thomas Keymer (Oxford: Oxford University Press, 2001).

— *Pamela, or Virtue Rewarded*, 4 vols (Oxford: Shakespeare Head, 1929).

— *Samuel Richardson's Published Commentary on 'Clarissa' 1747–65*, gen. ed. Florian Stuber, 3 vols. (London: Pickering and Chatto, 1998).

— *Selected Letters of Samuel Richardson*, ed. John Carroll (Oxford: Clarendon Press, 1964).

Rogers, Kathryn M., 'Sensitive feminism vs. conventional sympathy: Richardson and Fielding on women', *Novel* 9 (1975) 256–70.

Rose, Craig, 'Providence, Protestant union, and godly reformation in the 1690s', *Transactions of the Royal Historical Society*, 6th ser., 3 (1993), 151–69.

Rosenberg, Nathan, 'Mandeville and laissez-faire', *Journal of the History of Ideas* 24 (1963) 183–96.

Rowe, Elizabeth Singer, *The Miscellaneous Works in Prose and Verse of Mrs Elizabeth Rowe* (London, 1739).

[—], pseud. Philomela, *Poems on Several Occasions* (London, 1696).

Ruhe, Edward, 'Birch, Johnson, and Elizabeth Carter: an episode of 1738–39', *PMLA* 73 (1958) 491–500.

Rumbold, Valerie, *Women's Place in Pope's World* (Cambridge: Cambridge University Press, 1989).

Schellenberg, Betty A., 'Using "femalities" to "make fine men": Richardson's *Sir Charles Grandison* and the feminization of narrative', *Studies in English Literature* 34 (1994) 599–616.

Sekora, John, *Luxury: The Concept in Western Thought, Eden to Smollet* (Baltimore and London: Johns Hopkins University Press, 1977).

Sharpe, Kevin, *Criticism and Compliment: the Politics of Literature in the England of Charles I* (Cambridge: Cambridge University Press, 1987).

Sherburn, George, 'The Fortunes and Misfortunes of *Three Hours After Marriage*', *Modern Philology* 24 (1926–7) 91–109.

[Sheridan, Thomas], *The Satires of Juvenal Translated* (London, 1739).

Sherman, Sandra, 'Credit, simulation, and the ideology of contract in the early eighteenth century', *Eighteenth-Century Life* 19 (1995) 86–102.

Shevelow, Kathryn, *Women and Print Culture: The Construction of Femininity in the Early Periodical* (London and New York: Routledge, 1989).

Smallwood, Angela, *Fielding and the Woman Question: The Novels of Henry Fielding and Feminist Debate 1700–1750* (Brighton: Harvester Wheatsheaf, 1989).

Smollett, Tobias, *The Adventures of Peregrine Pickle in which are included Memoirs of a Lady of Quality*, ed. James L. Clifford, rev. by Paul-Gabriel Boucé (Oxford, 1983).

— *The Adventures of Roderick Random* (1748), ed. Paul-Gabriel Boucé (Oxford: Oxford University Press, 1979).

Solomon, Harry M., *The Rape of the Text: Reading and Misreading Pope's 'Essay on Man'* (Tuscaloosa and London: University of Alabama Press, 1993).

'Sophia', *Woman Not Inferior to Man: Or, A Short and Modest Vindication of the Natural Right of the Fair-Sex to a Perfect Equality of Power, Dignity, and Esteem* (London, 1739).

Speck, W.A., 'Bernard Mandeville and the Middlesex Grand Jury', *Eighteenth-Century Studies*, XI (1977–78) 362–74.

— 'Mandeville and the Eutopia seated in the brain', in *Mandeville Studies*, ed. Primer, 66–79.

Stafford, J. Martin, ed., *Private Vices, Publick Benefits? The Contemporary Reception of Bernard Mandeville* (Solihull: Ismeron, 1997).

Stallybrass, Peter and Allon White, *The Politics and Poetics of Transgression* (London: Methuen, 1986).

Starr, G.A., *Defoe and Casuistry* (Princeton, NJ: Princeton University Press, 1971).

Stearns, Bertha-Monica, 'The first English periodical for women', *Modern Philology*, 28 (1930–31), 45–59.

Stecher, Henry F., *Elizabeth Singer Rowe, the Poetess of Frome: A Study of Eighteenth-Century Pietism*, European University Papers vol. 5 (Bern: Herbert Lang; and Frankfurt: Peter Lang, 1973).

Steele, Richard, et al., *The Tatler*, ed. D.F. Bond, 3 vols. (Oxford: Clarendon Press, 1987).

Stephen, Leslie, *English History in the 18th Century* (London, 1903).

Swift, Jonathan, *Journal to Stella*, ed. Harold Williams, 2 vols. (Oxford, Clarendon Press, 1948).

Tavor, Eve, *Scepticism, Society and the Eighteenth-Century Novel* (Basingstoke: Macmillan, 1987).

Taylor, Barbara, *Mary Wollstonecraft and the Feminist Imagination* (Cambridge: Cambridge University Press, 2003).

Taylor, Derek, 'Clarissa Harlowe, Mary Astell and Elizabeth Carter: John Norris of Bemerton's female "descendants"', *Eighteenth-Century Fiction* 12:1 (Oct., 1999) 19–38.

Thomas, Claudia N., *Alexander Pope and His Eighteenth-Century Women Readers* (Carbondale and Edwardsville: Southern Illinois University Press, 1994).

— 'Th' instructive moral, and important thought: Pope, Johnson, and Epictetus', *The Age of Johnson* 4 (1991) 137–69.

Thompson, Peggy, 'Abuse and atonement: the passion of Clarissa Harlowe', *Eighteenth-Century Fiction* 11 (1999) 255–70.

Todd, Janet, *Women's Friendship in Literature* (New York: Columbia University Press, 1980).

Todd, W.B., 'A bibliographical account of *The Gentleman's Magazine*, 1731–1754', *Studies in Bibliography* 18 (1965) 00–0.

Tomaselli, Sylvana, 'The enlightenment debate on women', *History Workshop Journal*, 20 (1985), 101–24.

— 'The most public sphere of all: the family', in *Women, Writing and the Public Sphere*, ed. Elizabeth Eger et al., 239–56.

Trenchard, John and Thomas Gordon, *Cato's Letters, or Essays on Liberty, Civil and Religious, and Other Important Subjects*, ed. Ronald Hamowy, 2 vols. (Indianapolis: Liberty Fund, 1995).

Turner, James Grantham, 'Lovelace and the paradoxes of libertinism', in *Samuel Richardson: Tercentenary Essays*, eds. Doody and Sabor, 70–88.

Trumbach, Ronald, *Sex and the Gender Revolution*, Vol. 1, *Heterosexuality and the Third Gender in Enlightenment London* (Chicago and London: University of Chicago Press, 1998).

Van Marter, Shirley, 'Richardson's debt to Hester Mulso concerning the curse in *Clarissa*', *Papers in Language and Literature* 14 (1978) 22–31.

Vickery, Amanda, 'Golden age to separate spheres? A review of the categories and chronology of English women's history', *The Historical Journal* 36: 2 (1993) 383–414.

Wallas, Ada, *Before the Bluestockings* (London: George Allen & Unwin, 1929).

Walpole, Horace, *The Yale Edition of Horace Walpole's Correspdence*, ed. W.S. Lewis, 48 vols. (New Haven: Yale University Press, 1937–83).

Warburton, William, *A Critical and Philosphical Commentary on Mr Pope's 'Essay on Man'* (London, 1742).

[Ward, Edward], *Female Policy Detected: Or, The Arts of a Designing Woman Laid Open* (London, 1716).

— *The Humours of a Coffee House* (London, 1707).

Warner, William B., *Licensing Entertainment: The Elevation of Novel Reading in Britain, 1684–1750* (Berkeley: University of California Press, 1998).

— *Reading Clarissa: The Struggles of Interpretation* (New Haven: Yale University Press, 1979).

Watt, Ian, *The Rise of the Novel: Studies in Defoe, Richardson and Fielding* (London: Chatto & Windus, 1957).

White, Douglas, *Pope and the Context of Controversy: The Manipulation of Ideas in 'An Essay on Man'* (Chicago and London: University of Chicago Press, 1970).

Wieder, Robert, *Pierre Motteux et les Debuts du Journalisme en Angleterre au XVIIe siècle: Le Gentleman's Journal (1692–94)* (Paris: Didier, 1944).

Williams, Carolyn D., 'Poetry, pudding and Epictetus: the consistency of Elizabeth Carter', in *Tradition in Transition*, ed. Ribeiro and Basker, 3–24.

— *Pope, Homer, and Manliness: Some Aspects of Eighteenth-Century Classical Learning* (London and New York: Routledge, 1993).

Wilt, Judith, 'He could go no farther: a modest proposal about Lovelace and Clarissa', *PMLA* 92 (1977) 19–32.

Wollstonecraft, Mary, *A Vindication of the Rights of Woman*, ed. Sylvana Tomaselli (1792; Cambridge: Cambridge University Press, 1995).

— *The Works of Mary Wollstonecraft*, eds. Janet Todd and Marilyn Butler, 7 vols (London: Pickering & Chatto, 1989).

Index

Addison, Joseph, 5, 23, 24, 43–6, 58, 59, 74, 95, 110, 111, 159, 173, 191n24, 203n47, 211n104
Alexander the Great, 65, 193n53
Alexander, William, 3, 177
Algarotti, Francesco, 77, 78, 139
amatory fiction, 49, 87, 115, 118, 133, 135, 206n6
Ames, Richard, 135
Amory, Thomas, 164–5, 167, 212n112
Anacreon, 86
Anne, Queen, 20, 50, 58, 96
Arbuthnot, John, 49, 80–81
Armstrong, Nancy, 2, 11, 183n36, 201n15
Astell, Mary, 42–3, 45, 47, 64, 66, 85, 136, 163
Athenian Mercury, The, 5, 6, 26–44 *passim*, 88, 98, 184–8n *passim*, 200n10 and coffee-house culture, 27–9, 36, 42, 48, 50, 133, and women, 28–32, 34–6, 38, 42–6, 50, 85, 96, 136, 186n17
Athens, 32, 186n26
Atterbury, Francis, 108
Aubin, Penelope, 189n55
Augustine, Saint, 66
Austen, Jane, 162

Ballard, George, 162–3, 164, 165, 211–2n112
Barbauld, Anna Laetitia, 12, 160
Barrell, John, 5
Barthes, Roland, 213n137
Bath, William Pulteney, Earl of, 170
Bayle, Pierre, 62, 78
Bedford, John Russell, 4th Duke of, 151
Behn, Aphra, 39, 42, 83, 149, 163, 164
Benlow, Marinda, 165
Berry, Helen, 185–6n17
Bible, The, 40–1, 122, *see also* The Song of Solomon
Birch, Thomas, 77, 78, 93, 139
Blackstone, William, 163
Bloom, Harold, 89

Blount, Martha, 86, 197n44, 198n59
Bluestockings, the, 12, 86, 92, 145, 151, 152, 159, 163, 167, 198n65, 213n5
Boccalin, Trajan, 30, 38
Bolingbroke, Henry St John, Viscount, 56, 80, 89, 90, 91, 93, 96, 200n7
Bradshaigh, Lady (*née* Dorothy Bellingham), 111, 116, 143, 153, 155, 159
British East India Company, 50
Brooke, Frances, 12, 200n11
Brown, John, 171–2, 213n4
Brown, Laura, 70, 179n4
Brown, Tom, 24, 31–2, 184n43, 184n1
Bueler, Lois E., 200n10, 203n55
Burnet, Bishop Gilbert, 159, 168
Burney, Frances, 12
Burtt, Shelley, 60
Byron, George Gordon, 175

Campbell, Jemima, 139, 208n28
capitalism, 1, 2, 11, 12, 16–17, 70, 80, 126, 177, 182n41, 198n70, *see also* commerce
Carter, Elizabeth, 1, 4, 11–12, 74–9, 81–2, 84, 85–6, 87–90, 92–4, 138–48, 151, 152, 153, 155, 160, 162, 165, 166, 167, 168–70, 196n31, 198–9n *passim*, 207n19, 209n68, 210n86, 'Ode to Wisdom', 141–3, 161, 208n33, *Poems on Particular Occasions*, 75, 92, 167, *Poems on Several Occasions*, 92, 167, 198n64, *The Works of Epictetus*, 78, 140, 143, 167, 168–70, 171, 212n131, 213n138
Carter, Nicholas, 76–7, 78–9, 84, 92, 93, 94, 165, 170
Castiglione, Baldissare, 30
Cato Uticensis, 6, 58, 98, 110, 180n15, 191n23
Cato's Letters, 1, 55, 58–61, 80, 90, 191–2n *passim*
Cave, Edward, 75, 77, 86, 93, 139, 141, 146, 208n33

Centlivre, Susannah, 81, 83, 196n29
Chaber, Lois A., 201n13, 204n65, 210n88
Chapone, Henry, 163
Chapone, Hester, 12, 120, 143, 146, 152–4, 155, 158, 161, 163, 210n86
Chapone, Sarah, 149–50, 171
Charles I, 30
Charles II, 34
Châtelet, Emilie de, 77
Chesterfield, Philip Dormer Stanhope, 4th Earl of, 148, 150–51, 156
Cheyne, Dr George, 99, 111
Christensen, Jerome, 177
Chudleigh, Mary, Lady, 163
Cibber, Colley, 141, 148, 164, 196n29
Cibber, Susannah, 164, 212n114
Cibber, Theophilus, 164, 212n114
Circe, 6, 24–5, 39–40, 59, 123
civic humanism, 5–9, 12, 32, 49, 54, 56, 59–60, 63, 64, 90, 97, 109, 110, 111, 113, 142, 168, 169, 171–2, 176–7, 178, 182n41, 191n27, 192n38, 193n41
civility, 63, 96, 144, 158, *see also* refinement
class, 6, 15–16, 17–18, 96, 97–8, 126–7, 128, 131, 143, 151, 205n88, 206n90
classical republicanism, *see* civic humanism
Cleomenes, 72
Clinton, Katherine, 4
Clayton, Sir Robert, 70
Cleland, John, 148
Cockburn, Catharine (*née* Trotter), 145
coffee, 13–14, 183n29, 183n32, and masculinity, 14, 17, 18–20
coffee-houses, 5, 13–25 *passim*, 50, 128–9, 184n43, and female workers, 21–25, 35, 50, 133, and the circulation of news, 13, 14–16, 50, and commerce, 16–17, and male clientele, 5, 16, 19–25, 30, 38, 40, 42, 43, 50, 183n20, and political culture, 14–15, 35, 43, 182n13, 182n15, and the public sphere, 15–16, 20–21, 35, 49, 50, 132–3, and women, 16, 18–19, 29, 30, 35, 43–44, 50, 183n36; *see also*, *Athenian Mercury, The*
Collier, Jane, 118, 143
Colman, George, 164

commerce, 1, 2, 5–6, 7, 12, 20–21, 57, 60, 61, 66, 70–71, 72–3, 87, 90–91, 92, 97, 98, 126–31, 132–3, 160, 169–70, 172, 177–8, 206n1, *see also* capitalism, trade, and women and commerce
Commonsense, 92
conduct books, 2, 44, 100, 147, 201n15
consumerism, 1, 97, *see also* luxury
Cook, Richard I., 194n57
corruption, 6, 7, 49, 60, 87, 97, 109, 127, 150–51, 168, 171, 174, 176 *see also* decline, national
Cowley, Abraham, 30–1, 36, 39, 40
Cowper, William, 172
Craggs, James, 55
Craftsman, The, 80, 173, 174
credit, 7–8, 9, 24–5, 54, 57, 59
Crousaz, Jean Paul de, 77, 93–4
Cudworth, Ralph, 43
Curll, Edmund, 49, 93, 197n44

Dacier, Anne, 78, 82, 153, 171, 197n37
Davys, Mary, 127, 189n55
decline, national, 1, 6, 7, 51, 80, 91, 171–2
Defoe, Daniel, 1, 5, 6, 24, 43, 48, 58, 66, 97, 98, 185n13, *Moll Flanders*, 72, *Roxana*, 68–72, 99, 122–3, *Some Considerations upon Street-Walkers*, 72
Delany, Dr Patrick, 148
Delany, Mary, 143, 152, 163
Dennis, John, 57, 81, 193n41
Dickson, P.G.M., 55
Dictionary of National Biography, 165
Diderot, Denis, 4
Dodsley, Robert, 166
Donaldson, Ian, 180n15
Donellan, Anne, 152, 154
Doody, Margaret Anne, 126, 127, 131, 155, 156, 205n88, 211n100
Drake, James, 42
Dryden, John, 39, 83, 115
Duck, Stephen, 74
duelling, 64, 157–8
Duncombe, John, 165–7, 212n112
Dunton, John, 6, 26–7, 29–31, 33, 35–9, 41, 43–9 *passim*, 86, 134, 165, 184–6n *passim*, *The Female War*, 36–7

Eagleton, Terry, 2, 205n88, 210n88
effeminacy, 6, 19–21, 30, 42, 62–3, 79,
    97, 168, 171–2, 173, 176, 178,
    182n41, 214n13, definition of,
    8–10, 103, 180n24, 181n26,
    201n25, *see also* corruption, decline,
    and luxury
Egerton, Elizabeth Fyge Field, 84–5
Eliot, George, 162
Ellis, Aytoun, 16, 18
Elstob, Elizabeth, 49, 96, 163
Enlightenment, the, 4, 5, 10, 166–7,
    174, *see also* feminization,
    enlightenment theory of
Epictetus, 78, 140, 167, 168–70, 171,
    207n19
eschatology, 53, 58
eunuchs, 72

Fancourt, Samuel, 140
Female Tatler, The, 5, 63–7, 188n47
Female War, The, 36–7, 38–9
feminine ideal, 11–12, 21–4, 45–6, 48–9,
    50, 58, 64, 73, 86, 92, 95–103, 110,
    111, 114–25 *passim*, 126, 130, 131,
    132–8, 144, 147, 148–9, 152–4,
    158–9, 160, 163, 165–8, 176, 177,
    178, 201n24, 202n32
femininity, 11, 44–5, 49, 71–2, 100,
    201n14, 203n54, *see also* sexual
    difference
feminism, 11–12, 16, 42, 44, 86, 97,
    100–101, 119, 167, 207n10, and
    anti-feminism, 49, 66–71, 85, 93,
    114, 153, 184n43, 193n51, 202n27,
feminization, definition of, 1, 2, 9–10,
    96, 179n4, 189n61, 207n10,
    discourse of, 3, 6, 11, 151, 160, 168,
    173, 176, 178, and effeminization,
    10, 63, 79, 171–2, 173, 178, 179n4,
    in England, 5, 161–2, 172, 176
    enlightenment theory of, 3–5,
    176–8, first and second waves,
    49–50, 73, 95–6, 97, and feminism,
    11–12, 42–3, 44, 97, 100–101, in
    France, 4–5, 11, 174, 176, 178, and
    heterosexuality, 9–10, 21–5, 30–2,
    34, 37, 39–41, 44–6, 95–6, 119,
    119–20, 154–5, 157, 175–6, 210n88,
    and men, 1, 3, 9–10, 20–1, 23, 30,
    42, 44, 63, 96–7, 113, 122–5, 137,

138, 154–62, 172, 178, and
    nationalism, 33–5, 163–7, and
    women (*see also* feminine ideal),
    1–2, 3–5, 6, 11–12, 21–5, 31–2, 37,
    42, 44–8, 49–50, 63–4, 80, 97,
    132–8, 173–8
Fénelon, François de Salignac de La
    Mothe, 135
Ferguson, Moira, 84–5
financial revolution, the, 55
Fielding, Henry, 1, 98, 99, 111, 140,
    144, 156, 200n2, 206n6, 207n10
Fielding, Sarah, 12, 143, 168
Finch, Anne, Countess of Winchelsea,
    80–1, 96, 190n15, 196n25, 196n27
fortune, 7, 9, 53, 70, 90, 92–3, 109, 168,
    189n3
Friend, William, 136

gallantry, 24, 31, 35, 40, 41, 42, 44, 59,
    76, 85, 103, 161, 175–6, 178
Gay, John, 80–1, 200n7
gender, 1, 2, 5–6, 7–11, 19, 21, 58, 73,
    76, 79–80, 82, 84, 97, 100, 103, 133,
    171, 172, 174, 175, 176, 178,
    202n27, 213n4, *see also* sexual
    difference
Gentleman's Journal, The, 5, 31
Gentleman's Magazine, 74–7, 84, 85–8,
    92, 139, 141, 165, 166, 168, 195–6n
    passim, 208n33
George I, 54, 55, 56
George II, 200n7
George, Prince of Wales (later George
    IV), 167
Gibbon, Edward, 163
Gildon, Charles, 31
Glorious Revolution, the, 5, 25, 26,
    184n2, 185n8
Goodman, Dena, 5, 174
Gordon, Thomas, 58–9
Gould, Robert, 135
Grainger, Frances, 100, 112, 149
Graves, Richard, 149
Great Fire of London, the, 51
Grierson, Constantia, 163, 165
Grundy, Isobel, 84
Guest, Harriet, 4, 12, 142, 212n112
Guez de Balzac, Jean-Louis, 153
Gunn, Daniel P., 205n88
Guy, Thomas, 55

Habermas, Jürgen, 15–16, 17, 19, 50, 132–3, 183n20, 206n1
Hamowy, Ronald, 59, 191n29
Hardwicke, Philip Yorke, 1st Earl of, 139
Harrington, James, 5, 49, 189n56
Harvey, Dr William, 13
Haywood, Eliza, 49, 82, 83, 84, 88, 133, 149, 197n44, 200n11
Henrietta Maria, Queen, 30
Hercules, 6
Hervey, John, Lord, 64–5, 92
heterosexuality, 9, 21, 29, 35, 67, 71, 72, 85, 147, *see also* feminization and platonic love
Highmore, Joseph, 152, 165
Highmore, Susanna, 137, 152, 165
Highmore, Susanna Hiller (Mrs. Joseph), 165
Hill, Aaron, 95, 111, 116
Hill, Christopher, 205n88
Hirschman, Albert, 1
historicism, 2–3, 6, 7, 95, 131, 149, 156, 169, 200n2
Hogarth, William, 1, 127, *Morning*, 128–30, *The South Sea Scheme*, 51–4, 108, 128, 189n3
Hobbes, Thomas, 91, 124
Homer, 79, 82, 100, 141, 166, 197n37
homosexuality, 8–9, 20
honour, 64, 66, 71, 157
Horace, 75, 83, 92, 167
Horne, Thomas A., 214n22
Hume, David, 1, 4, 95, 172–8, 193n42, 213–14n *passim*
Hutcheson, Frances, 214n22

improvement, 59, 63, 156–7, 166, 192n38, see also progress, idea of,
Ingrassia, Catherine, 8, 190n15, 206n3
Irwin, Anne, Viscountess, 87, 166

Jacobitism, 51, 60, 128, 140–1, 156, 188n52, 192n38, 202n36, 211n95
Johnson, Charles, 43, 81, 196n29
Johnson, Elizabeth, 39
Johnson, Samuel, 74–5, 77, 82, 93, 113, 143, 144, 145, 163, 200n2, 208n36, *see also*, *The Rambler*
Jones, Inigo, 128
Julian of Norwich, 163
Juvenal, 66, 67, 75, 86, 92–3, 135

Kames, Henry Home, Lord, 3, 166
Kelly, Gary, 12, 179n4
Kendal, Ehrengard Melusine von der Schulenburg, Duchess of, 56, 190n14
Kiemansegge, Sophia Charlotte, Baroness von, 56, 190n14
King, Moll, 50, 128, 206n91
Klancher, Jon, 50
Klein, Lawrence, 11, 181n38, 212n132
Kroll, Richard, 183n29

La Rochefoucauld, François, duc de, 62, 91
Lambert, Anne Thérèse, marquise de, 153
Langford, Paul, 7
Laqueur, Thomas, 9, 10–11
Law, John, 54, 109
Le Moyne, Pierre, 66
Leibniz, Gottfried, 94
Lennox, Charlotte, 143, 145
Lillo, George, 68
Lipking, Lawrence, 84
Lloyd, John, 41
Locke, John, 2, 4, 86–7, 159
London, 51
Louis XIV, 67
Lucretia, 6, 116, 133, 180n15
luxury, 2, 6, 9, 10, 32, 57, 58, 59, 60, 61, 62–3, 64, 72–3, 80, 92, 97, 98, 127–8, 130–31, 132–3, 168, 170, 171–2, 175–8, 206n3, 214n15, definition of, 7, 62, 175–6, 177–8, 193n42
Lycurgus, 6, 56, 109, 172, 180n15
Lyttelton, Sir George, 163, 168, 171

Macaulay, Catharine, 11–12, 168, 170, 212n128–30
Machiavelli, Niccolò, 5, 56, 59, 61, 72, 91, 214n15
Mack, Maynard, 84
McKeon, Michael, 8
Mackie, Erin, 8
Mandell, Laura, 70,
Mandeville, Bernard, 1, 5, 6, 58, 60–8, 90, 91, 92, 96, 97, 98, 111–13, 118, 119, 124, 130, 157, 172, 178, 188n47, 191–5n *passim*, 198n70, 199n, 203n48, 211n100, 214n22,

214n22, *The Fable of the Bees*, 60–3, 67, 68, 72–3, 91, 113, 178, *A Modest Defence of Public Stews*, 68, 105, 112, *The Virgin Unmask'd*, 67–8, 71, 194n57, see also *The Female Tatler*
Manley, Delarivière, 83, 84, 88, 149, 163, 164
Marlborough, Sarah, Duchess of, 56
masculine ideal, 10, 30, 31, 44, 63, 154–62, 182n41, 210n88, 211n100
masculinity, 8–10, 13, 71, 79–80, 100, 101–2, 157–8, 178, *see also* effeminacy
Masham, Lady Damaris, 43
Millar, John, 3, 166, 177
Milton, John, 35, 38, 137, 159
misogyny, 2, 6, 10, 12, 30, 32, 38, 47, 65–6, 70, 71, 96, 103, 104–8, 117, 125, 127, 139, 148–9, 150, 166, 170, 174, 176, 178, 193n51, 202n32, and satire, 56, 79, 82, 86, 88, 92, 98, 135, 159–60, 173, 190n15, 214n13, *see also* feminism and anti-feminism, and South Sea Bubble
modernity, 2, 5, 12, 51, 56, 61, 79–80, 87, 88, 92, 98, 115, 128, 131, 133, 148, 149, 158, 159, 161, 169, 172, 175, 176, 178, modernization, 49, 58, 166, 173, *see also* progress, idea of, and refinement
Molière (Jean Baptiste Poquelin), 81, 134
monied interest, the, 5, 18, 24, 188n47
Montagu, Edward, 152
Montagu, Elizabeth, 12, 82, 136, 152, 163, 167–8, 170, 171, 209n68, 212n114
Montagu, Lady Mary Wortley, 56, 74, 77, 82–4, 86–7, 89, 151–2, 159–60, 164, 168, 197n, 202n38, 209n67–9
Montesquieu, Charles Louis de Secondat de, 4, 139–40, 172, 177, 178
More, Hannah, 12
Motteux, Pierre, 5, 31
Mulso, Hester, *see* Chapone
Mulso, John, 153
Myers, Sylvia Harcstark, 12, 76, 163

Newcastle, Margaret Cavendish, Duchess of, 34
Newcastle, Thomas Pelham-Holles, Duke of, 156, 171

Norris, John, 31, 42–3, 47
Nussbaum, Felicity, 56
Nuttall, A.D., 93

Onslow, Arthur, 153
Orrery, John Boyle, 5th Earl of, 135
Ovid, 35, 114, 135
Oxenden, Sir George, 74, 92, 93, 195n2

passions, the, 19, 51, 57–63, 64, 67, 69, 70, 72, 86, 87, 90, 91, 92, 96, 97, 98, 99–100, 106, 111–3, 115–6, 133, 158, 168, 169, 193n51, 206n3, 211n100, *see also* Stoicism
patriarchy, 103, 161
Paulson, Ronald, 51
Payne, Thomas, 108
Pelham, Henry, 156, 171
Pennington, Montagu, 76, 93, 94
Philips, Katherine, 34, 35, 39, 42, 163, 164
Phillips, Teresia Constantia, 148–50, 165
Pilkington, Laetitia, 148–9, 164, 165
Pindar, 36
Piozzi, Hester Lynch, 12
Pitt, William, 171
Plato, 30, 40, 46
platonic love, 30–2, 35, 37, 45, 46, 47, 100–1, 152, 185n16
Plutarch, 46
Pocock, J.G.A., 5, 7–8, 9, 20, 54, 55, 57, 59, 189n3, 190n8, 191n29
Pococke, Edward, 13
politeness, 6, 10, 21, 42, 62, 103, 104, 119, 124, 146, 173–5, 186n26, 193n43, 211n100, 214n13
Polybian cycle, 54, 56
Pope, Alexander, 1, 9, 48, 74–6, 79–94 *passim*, 96, 110, 150, 152, 166, 203n45, *The Dunciad*, 47, 49, 56, 82, 83, 87, 174, 193n53, 195–9n *passim*, 200n7 *Epistle to Arbuthnot*, 64–5, 89, *Epistle to Bathurst*, 127, *Epistle to a Lady*, 57, 85, 86–7, 96, 105–7, 124, 174, 198n62, 200n4, 202n32, *Essay on Man*, 79, 89–94, *The Rape of the Lock*, 79, 87, 198n70, *Three Hours After Marriage*, 80–82
Portland, Margaret, Duchess of, 152, 163

Poulain de la Barre, François, 31, 97
Prior, Matthew, 152
progress, idea of, 5, 6, 51–7, 61–2, 66, 90, 113, 125–31, 132, 136, 157, 166–8, 174–8
print culture, 12, 14–16, 19, 42, 50, 76, 84, 91, 138–9, 140, 163, 170, 207n6
prostitution, 31, 41, 51, 56–7, 65, 68, 69, 70, 71–2, 102, 103, 115, 117, 118–9, 120–1, 130, 135, 144, 148, 186n23, 190n17, 204n60, 206n3, 207n10
public spirit, 5, 6, 8, 49, 50, 64, 87, 110, 142, 168
public sphere, bourgeois, 15, 17–18, 20–21, 49, 50, 132, 206n1, literary, 3, 11, 13, 16, 28, 98, 133, 145, 146, 166–8, political, 15–16, 35, 110, and private sphere, 2, 4, 18, 19, 44, 98, 110, 111, 132–3, 138, 142–3, 153–4, 154, 162, 166, 169, 204n62, *see also* coffee-houses
public virtue, *see* public spirit, public welfare and virtue
public welfare ('good' or 'benefits'), 14, 54, 60, 62, 72, 109, 112, 113, 178
Pufendorf, Samuel, 4

rake, the, 96. 104–7, 112, 115, 116, 118, 122–4, 125, 130, 147, 151, 154–5, 157–9, 160, 161, 202n30, 204n60, 206n3
Ralph, James, 172
Rambler, The, 113, 140, 144, 145–8
Reeve, Clara, 12
refinement, 1, 3, 12, 34, 38, 42, 96, 176–8
reformation of manners, the, 1–2, 21–4, 26, 32–3, 35, 42, 50, 95–9, 117, 122–5, 131, 137, 138, 143, 154–5, 159, 176, Societies for, 6, 28, 61, 157, 192n37
religion, 51, 53, 55, 58, 60, 89, 93–4, 98, 100, 112, 122, 125–6, 136, 137, 142, 145, 157, 168, 169, 213n138
Rendall, Jane, 4
Resnel, Jean-François, 93
Richardson, Samuel, 1, 2, 6–7, 11, 50, 73, 95–131 *passim*, 137, 138, 141–51 *passim*, 152–4, 154–62 *passim*, 163, 165, 166, 167, 168, 172, 173, 175,

176, 178, 200–7n *passim*, 213n5, *Clarissa*, 2, 11, 95, 96, 98, 99–131 *passim*, 132, 134, 135, 136–7, 138, 141–3, 144, 145, 147, 148, 150, 151, 153, 154–7, 159, 160, 161, 173, 180n15, 200–206n *passim*, 208n33, *The History of Sir Charles Grandison*, 2, 82, 83, 95, 96–7, 98, 99, 104, 111, 136, 145–6, 151, 154–62, 168, 173, 193n53, 200n1, 210–11n *passim*, *Pamela*, 2, 95–6, 97–8, 99, 104, 110–111, 132–4, 138, 140, 143, 144, 152, 156, 173, 195n10
Rochford, Anne, 50
Rosée, Pasqua, 14
Rousseau, Jean-Jacques, 4, 147, 158, 172, 177, 209n48
Rowe, Elizabeth Singer, 1, 11, 32–41 *passim*, 42, 45–8, 49, 85, 87–9, 96, 166, 186–9n *passim*, 198n, *Poems on Several Occasions*, 36, 37, 38–41, 49
Rowe, Nicholas, 110, 115, 125
Rowe, Theophilus, 49
Rowe, Thomas, 46
Rumsey, Walter, 13

salon culture, 4–5, 11, 15, 38, 174, 176, 178, 181n38, 183n20
Sappho, 39, 139, 197n40
Samuel, Richard, 86
Sault, Richard, 184n4, 185n8
Scott, Sarah, 12, 152, 168
Scottish historical school, 3, 172, 214n7
Secker, Catherine, 139, 169
Secker, Thomas, 77, 139, 153, 155, 163, 169, 208n28
Sekora, John, 7,
Sevigné, Marie de Rabutin-Chantal, marquise de, 153
sex, of souls, 29–30, 97, 100, 102–103, 136, 153, 161
sexes, war of the, 18–19, 36–7, 101–103, 104–105, 159–62
sexual difference, 9–11, 19, 21, 53, 57, 71–3, 86, 96, 99–103, 105, 107–8, 114–16, 121, 122, 134–5, 159–62, 172, 201n13, 202n32, 203n55, 205n80, 211n106
sexuality, 64–5, 71, *see also* heterosexuality and homosexuality
Seward, Anna, 12, 136

Seward, Thomas, 136, 166
Shaftesbury, Anthony Ashley Cooper, 1st Earl of, 5
Shaftesbury, Anthony Ashley Cooper, 3rd Earl of, 8, 72, 91, 168, 169, 199n72, 212n132
Shakespeare, William, 135, *Macbeth*, 118–19
Shebbeare, John, 151
Sheridan, Frances, 143, 168
Sheridan, Richard Brinsley, 12
Sheridan, Thomas, 199n80
Shevelow, Kathryn, 44–5
Shiels, Robert, 163
Sidney, Algernon, 59
Skerrett, Maria, 80, 151
Sloper, William, 164
Smith, Adam, 3, 4, 92, 178, 214n22
Smollett, Tobias, 1, 99, 144, 148, 150, 151, 152
Solomon, Harry M., 93
Song of Solomon, 30, 40–1, 49, 187–8n39
'Sophia' (author of *Women Not Inferior to Man*), 97, 103, 139
South Sea Bubble, 3, 5, 49, 51–8 *passim*, 60–1, 70, 75–6, 90, 108–9, 128, 150, 168, 170, 189–90n *passim*, 195n7, 195n10, 200n4, 202n34, 204n62, 212n129, 213n141, and misogynist backlash, 56–8, 69, 79, 190n14, 190n15, 197n44
Sparta, 32, 56, 58, 72, 80, 87, 109, 172, 186n26, 195n25
Spectator, The, 1, 23–4, 28, 43–6, 47, 48, 50, 59, 64, 95, 133, 147, 173, 174, 185n16, 186n26, 214n7
Spinoza, Baruch, 94
Stallybrass, Peter, 17, 183n36
Steele, Richard, 5, 23–4, 43–6, 62, 64, 95–6, 113, 173, 211n97
stock-jobbing, 17, 20, 54–5, 56, 58, 108, 189n4
Stoicism, 78, 90, 91, 92–3, 140, 168–70, 192n39, 199n73, 207n19, 212n132
Sutton, Isabella, 154–5
Swift, Jonathan, 42, 44, 48, 71, 85, 86, 110–11, 148, 152, 159, 163, 186n27, 188n52, 194n57, 199n80, 200n7 *The Lady's Dressing Room*, 111, 135

Tatler, The, 43–6, 63–5, 95, 188n47, 214n7
Talbot, Catherine, 12, 75, 76, 77–8, 81–2, 84, 94, 138–48, 151, 152, 162, 163, 167, 169, 196n30, 198n65, 208n28
Talbot, Edward, 139
tea, 50
Tavor, Eve, 111–12
Temple, Sir William, 42
Thomas, Claudia, 89
Thomas, Elizabeth, 49, 83, 197n44
Thomas, Antoine-Leonard, 177
Thornton, Bonnell, 163, 164
Tillotson, John, 135
Tomaselli, Sylvana, 4
Tories, the, 56, 91, 108, 185n10, 192n38
Townshend, Charles, Viscount, 128
Trenchard, John, 58–9, 190n34, 192n38, *see also Cato's Letters*
trade, 53, 58, 59, 60, 130–1, 133, 156, 172, 190n27, 192n38, *see also* commerce
True Briton, The, 108
Trumbach, Ronald, 8–9, 180n24

van Ghent, Dorothy, 118–19
van Schurman, Anna Maria, 34, 39, 78, 139
Vane, Frances Ann, Lady, 148–52, 165, 209n67
virtue, 6, 7, 32–3, 49, 50, 64, 71, 91, 95, 97–9, 101, 103, 110, 114, 116, 117, 123–4, 133–4, 142, 145, 152, 154, 155, 156, 158, 165, 168, 170, 176–8, 189n3, 199n72, female virtue, *see* feminine ideal, masculine virtue, *see* masculine ideal; public virtue, *see* public spirit and public welfare
Voltaire, François-Marie Arouet de, 77, 174, 213n4

Waller, Edmund, 39
Walpole, Horace, 151, 209n67
Walpole, Robert, 5, 49, 55–6, 79, 80, 92, 97, 108, 109, 111, 128, 151, 156, 174, 188n52, 195n2, 195n7, 200n7
Warburton, William, 78, 93, 110, 111, 199n72
Ward, Ned, 20, 24, 184n43
Warner, William B., 120, 206n6
Watt, Ian, 101, 135, 136

Watts, Isaac, 46
Wescomb, Sarah, 137
Wesley, Samuel, 30–31, 33, 184n2,
    184n4
Whigs, the, 47, 50, 54, 61, 92, 156, 173,
    184n43, 185n10, 188n52, 189n63,
    192n36, 192n38, Patriot opposition
    to, 87, 91, 92, 97, 108, 109, 171,
    173, 174, 199n70, 200n7
White, Allon, 17, 183n36
Whitehead, Paul, 150–51, 209n66
Wild, Robert, 27
William III, 20, 26, 28, 30, 32–4, 35, 40,
    185n8
Williams, Carolyn, 8, 9, 196n25,
    196n31
Wilt, Judith, 115
Wren, Christopher, 51
Wollstonecraft, Mary, 4, 12, 87, 147,
    182n41, 193n51, 205n81
women, in antiquity, 38, 58, 65–6, 78,
    82, 83, 87, 110, 114, and classical
    culture, 30, 35–6, 66, 75, 76, 78, 80,
    82, 83–4, 86, 92–3, 100, 110,
    139–40, 141, 142, 152, 159, 161–2,
    and commerce, 66, 70–71, 97, 126,
    127–8, 130–31, 160–61, 189n4,
    205n89, domestic, 2, 11, 46, 64,
    132, 142–3, 166, learned, 66, 77,
    79–80, 86–7, 136, 138, 143, 152,
    159, 161–2, 164, 168, 193n52,
    196n29, 196n31, literary, 1, 2, 4, 5,
    6, 11–12, 34, 38–9, 42, 48–9, 50,
    74–94 *passim*, 132–70 *passim*,
    208n36, 'Mahometan' view of, 82,
    136, 147, 207n19, 209n48, man-
    like, 71, 102–103, 159–60, Table of
    Fame for, 65, 66, 71, unmarried,
    64–5, 67, 68–9, 71–2, 86, 102,
    121–2, 130, *see also* femininity and
    feminization
Wright, Thomas, 77

Yorke, Charles, 139
Yorke, Philip, 139
Young, Edward, 111, 140, 152, 203n47